Promiseland

Promiseland

By
Dawn Miller

INTEGRITY®
PUBLISHERS
Nashville

PROMISELAND

Published by Integrity Publishers, a division of Integrity Media, Inc., 5250 Virginia Way, Suite 110, Brentwood, TN 37027.

HELPING PEOPLE WORLDWIDE EXPERIENCE *the* MANIFEST PRESENCE *of* GOD.

Published in association with Alive Communications, 7680 Goddard Street, Suite 200, Colorado Springs, Colorado 80920.

ISBN 0-7394-3488-8

This book is dedicated to You, Lord,
for lighting my way home . . .

PART ONE

Going to the Promiseland

Mama,

Pa and me bot this jernal for you in Virgenya Sity so you culd rite in it. Uncl Jack says we are goin to our promisland. Pa red me the story about Moses so I wrote on the next page to and Pa said that is good enuff.

Love,

Rose

Then Moses liftd his arm and God said,
"Go forth and dont be scairt, IM with
the to make sur you git there."

By Rose McGregor
age 9
Mountana Teritery, 1869

My mama used to say life ain't measured by the breaths we take but by the times that take our breath away . . . This land, this bold stretch of mountain valley Jack calls our "promiseland," takes my breath away. Only I'm not sure if that's good or bad or if I'll ever be able to catch my breath again . . .

We are a day yet from the new homestead, and so many thoughts and feelings flood my mind . . . so many memories. I guess if ever there was a good time for memories, this would be it. When I look out across camp at the other wagons, hearing the bawl of cattle, the snap and pop of a dying fire mingling with the sighs of my Rose and Patrick as they sleep, it's hard not to think of memories of another time . . . of family, of where we've come from or where we're going. And to hope that maybe we're almost through the wilderness that's been our lives.

Drifters—that's what our old preacher back home would call us. *"If you kids don't learn to sit still now,"* he'd say, *"you'll turn to drifters later, mark my words . . ."*

Seeing the tired, dust-smudged faces of my brother, Jack, and his new wife, Lillie, . . . of our old friend Stem and his Jessie . . . of Coy Harper, . . . even my Quinn tonight, I can't help thinking how we *have* all been a bit like drifters, scattered to the wind, not sure where we'd land next—or if we would. But we have a hope now in us, too.

And hope, like the Good Book says, is the anchor of the soul.

If ever there was a family that needed an anchor, it's us.

I can't seem to find the right words to describe how it feels for us all to be a family again, to have Jack back with us. Maybe because I feared so long that I wouldn't—see Jack alive again, I mean. Mama always believed he'd make it, though.

I was half-listening to the men talking at dinner tonight when a memory came to me of when I was just a girl, standing with Mama on the front porch of our farm back in Missouri as we looked together across the field Pa had just plowed for Jack. I remember being mad at Jack for running out on the chores, and I had mumbled that he'd probably lit out for good with the card-sharps he'd been running with. Mama had just looked at me then with a look that wasn't angry—just kind of sad—like I hadn't caught on to what was important.

"Jack's got good in him, Callie," she'd said. "He just doesn't believe it yet. That's what the good Lord puts families together for, to believe in each other when we can't believe in ourselves." Then she just smiled easy and said, "Your brother will be back. Our hearts always lead us home . . ."

Like most everything else she told me, she was right about Jack—he came back—and watching him from across the camp-fire this evening, smiling with Lillie as he held his little boy on his knee, I saw the man he was becoming.

"You just mark my words down in that little journal of yours, Callie," he said to me. "We're gonna be cattle pioneers, sure enough."

"We'll see," I said, grinning in spite of trying not to.

"You just wait," Jack chuckled. "Come next spring you'll be eating crow."

Everyone laughed at that. Crow has always been a tough bird for me to chew—especially when Jack's the one serving it.

"Almost like old times, wouldn't ya say, lass?" Quinn said, smiling, his blue eyes crinkling at the corners. I couldn't help thinking if it weren't for those crinkles, it *could've* been old times. Could have been all of us as we once were, when we'd all started out to find our home in the West.

Stem's here, just like he was that first day, as our scout: a thin, wiry old mulatto dressed in buckskins who took my hand

and told us he'd be leading us west . . . and I remembered my sister saying how he looked like her Bible pictures of Moses, "'*cept for that wooden leg of his,*" she'd added with relish, like Moses should've had a wooden leg, too.

Stem leaned over then and whispered something in Jessie's ear, and as I watched her laugh, her dark face wreathed in a smile, I remembered the day she'd tromped past our wagon train. Folks had whispered she was a *runaway slave.* Stem liked to say he and Jessie had been "weathered" by life. I can't help thinking we've all been weathered by life since that first day . . .

Quinn wasn't my husband yet, but he stood by me, always willing to carry my burden as we buried my pa and sister along the trail . . . and again, when Jack had rode away from us, so heartbroken. And Jack hadn't yet married a Blackfoot woman— Raven was her name, and they had a child together—only to see her murdered before his and their son John-Charles's eyes— hadn't yet met Lillie, who'd become his wife and mama to John-Charles. And Coy, the mighty black oak that refused to topple even after traveling mile after mile to find his pa, only to learn he had been killed trying to save Jack . . .

Sometimes it doesn't seem possible to me that we all made it through alive—or "alive and kickin' back," as Stem likes to say. Seems downright *impossible.* But we're alive and together again—an answer to the months and months of prayers I wouldn't quit. Or maybe couldn't . . .

"You always believed," Quinn whispered to me last night as we lay in the wagon together . . . Sometimes I wonder if he knows how those prayers kept me alive as much as they did Jack. How I clung to them like a lifeline, searching for some sign of land, for somewhere we could all call home together.

Nothing's impossible for the good Lord, child. I hear Mama's voice whisper to me from the past, and as I look up to this never-ending sky that rolls with the land past forever, I feel like that whisper has waited for just this moment . . . waiting for just the right time for me to open the gift. And maybe waiting for just the right people to see it opened.

And like this journal, I feel like this is only the beginning . . .

Thank You, Lord, for giving all of us this new chance, for making me think that maybe crow might not be so hard to swallow after all, if everything works out.

. . . Of course, I'm not planning on telling *Jack* that just yet.

August 31, 1869 . . .

I just told Jack he shouldn't plan on serving that bird up yet.

We reached the valley only a short time ago, halting the wagons at the rise that would lead us to our new home. As we stepped out, the beauty of the land before us near took our breath away . . . almost too pretty to put to words.

Everywhere we looked there was color—wildflowers blanketing the valley clear up to the slopes of the immense mountains in the Absaroka Range with a patchwork of lupine and fairy slipper and ones Lillie calls shooting stars. Three little cabins stood in the distance, barely visible in the heart of the valley, and I could see, just beyond them, a wide spring flowing, necklaced by cottonwoods. Our collies, Jasper and Honey, took off for the spring, barking. Then the cattle and horses saw it, too, taking off in a tired trot for the water. We all grinned at each other, then laughed as Rose quickly led the boys down the slope. So knee-deep was the grass it almost covered their heads. Patrick and John-Charles were stumbling like drunks on their little legs, trying to keep up, and suddenly Lillie, Jessie, and me were running, too, hitching up our skirts, laughing as we headed down the hill and came to a stop in front of the cabins that are to be our homes. And that's when I felt the poetry of the moment die inside of me.

Standing before us was three of the shabbiest log cabins I'd ever seen, the doors hanging sideways like loose teeth to show dirt floors inside. The roofs were dirt, too, with weeds and wild-flowers springing every which way in an almost comical fash-ion—like a Sunday-go-to-meeting hat that had seen better times. The front yard of the main cabin was bare and . . . imag-ine . . . *dirt*, too, trampled down by horses and men too busy to worry for looks.

Jessie, Lillie, and I stepped through the door of the first cabin we came to and found . . . dirt. Jasper and Honey, who were belly-wet from the spring, came trotting in, looked up at me like it had to be a mistake, then went and lay down outside the door.

I admit, there was a part of me that wanted to give in and have a good cry.

I felt like I'd stepped back eight years in time and was stand-ing in the shack of the little mining camp that was Quinn's and my first home, feeling the horror again. Then I thought of all the miles, of what we'd gave up, all of us living in cramped quar-ters for over two years in Virginia City, scrimping and scraping, for *this*. When I looked over at Lillie and saw the tumble of emotions crossing her pretty face, for some reason I thought of Mrs. Murphy standing next to me and the words she'd spoke that day in California.

"Don't look too close at first, honey," she'd said. *"Not till you're more settled. I remember coming to this very shack and thinking, I've come through dust, dirt, mud, and more dirt for this? If I'd had a gun, I think I would've shot my husband on the spot."* I heard myself telling the story, and as I did, I felt myself begin to smile, for I remembered the after of it, too, the way that little shack had become a home once I'd set my mind that it would.

Lillie looked down at the small swell of her belly, and I knew she was wondering what would come of her having a baby here, but then she smiled a kind of wry smile that caused a dim-ple to appear on her cheek.

"Well, I guess it's a good thing we don't have guns," she said, starting to chuckle, and Jessie and I did, too, in spite of it all.

"Lord, have mercy on the husbands of this group, is all I'm gonna say," Jessie said as she inspected the dull light shining through the slits in the logs. "'Cause they sure gonna need it."

It was along about then I noticed a darkening at the door, and we turned to see Stem standing with Rose. Stem took one look at our faces then turned to his constant shadow.

"Light quick t' yer wagon, sis, and git yer ma's Good Book," he told Rose. "We'll hold it in front of us. It'll be the only way t' turn the tide, I'm thinkin'." Rose grinned and took off in a dead run, relishing being a part of Stem's mission.

"He's a sharp one to smell trouble brewin' now, ain't he?" Jessie said, wrapping her arms across her chest to give him a stern look.

"It's a potent brew, Jess," Stem said amiably—but he kept his distance from us just the same.

"Ye call this our promiseland?" Jessie said, waving her arm around the room. Stem winced.

"Well, if ye squint yer eyes jes right . . . ," he started, and Jessie said, "Hmm," as he backed on out the door. I watched her look around, and I knew what she was thinking, because I was thinking it, too. We'd spent everything we had to get here, so there was nothing else to do but dig in and make it different. Jessie turned to us and pushed up the sleeves of her dress then, like she had almost read my mind. "Some fern and mud ought to do the trick on them cracks, don't ye think?"

It was only moments until we had started coming up with a plan on how to spruce up the cabins—but it was at least an hour before the men showed their faces again, bunches of wildflowers stretched out in each of their hands as a peace offering.

"It was my idea," Rose announced from somewhere behind Stem, and the men looked so sheepish we all couldn't help but laugh.

After the laughter died down, we decided on cabins. Quinn and I are to take the center cabin, being that it has a loft we can make over for Rose and Patrick's room. Jack and Lillie will have the cabin on the right, closer to the spring, and Stem and Jessie will take the one to the left of us. Coy's taking over the bunkhouse, being our "bachelor" of the bunch.

So *much* work to be done . . . I best get to it if we have any hopes of sleeping "indoors" by nightfall. Rose, who wants to be *outdoors* with the men, is grumbling under her breath as I quickly pen this, saying she never heard of sweeping a floor that was dirt anyhow.

Later—Such a good night in spite of our rough start.

Lillie, Jessie, and I were getting dinner set out on the makeshift table we'd set up in front of the main cabin just as evening was coming on us when I saw Lillie smile softly, looking up from time to time as she worked. Finally I stopped what I was doing and followed her gaze to the distance. The sun was just beginning to set, lighting up the tops of the mountains with a ridge of goldlike fire, and I was awed seeing it happen like that right before my eyes. Like seeing God put the finish to a great painting.

"This view makes up for a lot, doesn't it?" Lillie said then, and I nodded. "It reminds me of Jack," she added, and Jessie and me must've looked shocked for she laughed softly.

"When I first saw your brother, Callie, right off I thought, *Oh, he's too good-looking to trust*," Lillie explained. "Then I fell in love with him and his charm shortly after that."

We chuckled, and Lillie smiled, turning back to the mountains. "Odd thing is, I have the same feeling about this land . . ."

I think we all feel that way, like we've started to fall in love with the land in spite of the work before us. As we sat around the dinner table tonight, speckled with lanterns, I could hear it in all the voices. "Look at those mountains, will you?" one would say. "How 'bout that spring—I ain't ever tasted water so cold in summer," another would say, and I realized it wasn't a flashy kind of love but a hopeful one, the kind that wished for more than just a night to rest their heads, but for a lifetime . . . a place to finally call home.

It was then I felt right to open and read from our family Bible, and I was surprised when the book opened to a page with a tiny faded flower tucked in the crease. "Rooster fights," Mama called them, with their purple edges and little yellow faces. I looked at the scripture my mama must have under-lined years ago: "They that sow in tears shall reap in joy," it said.

As I read the scripture out loud, I felt a lump in my throat, remembering Mama. I saw the unshed tears shining in Jack's eyes, too, saw him looking down as he worried the brim of his hat. Jack, even in his wildest, reckless days, would turn to butter over Mama. "Sow in tears . . . ," he said, not looking up, and Rose picked that time to pipe in.

"Mama," she said, looking thoughtful. "If Jesus helped Grandma Wade reap joy, He'll help us, too. He's not suspicious. Pa said He's not a *suspector* of persons." There was such an earnestness to her face we all grinned and nodded—trying our best not to laugh—and I asked Stem to lead us in saying grace. He looked at me in surprise—then to Jessie who was fairly beaming at him.

"Age before beauty, isn't that what ye like to say, old man?" Coy said, grinning.

"If'n *yer* beauty, we're all in trouble," Stem countered, and we all laughed, joining hands around the table. I felt we were joined together at that moment by more than hands—but hearts, too. And as Stem began, his dry old voice humbled in thanks, I had the oddest feeling, as if Jesus Himself had sat down at that dingy, makeshift table, smiling as He joined hands with our weary but happy little group of travelers.

September 1, 1869 . . .

I felt like rubbing my eyes this morning to check if I were dreaming or not when I woke to find myself lying on the bedding I'd laid out across the fresh-swept dirt floor last night. Jasper and Honey crept over and peered down at me as if to see whether I'd come to my senses yet, and I couldn't help but smile. Like everyone else we love, the two pups had drifted into our lives one day, taken pity on us, and decided to stay. Now Jasper looked like he was wondering if the decision had been a good one, but Honey's great brown eyes were filled with compassion. I got up and let them out and stood watching them for a moment as they bounded through the tall grass. The sun was already burning a hole through the night sky, peeking fingers of light through the slits in the mountains, and I watched as only moments later the valley came to life, splashed with vivid blues, greens, and yellows, and I felt my heart lift at the beauty of it. Jasper and Honey barked merrily, forgetting the little cowards they'd been last night, begging and scratching at the door until Quinn let them in, only to become fierce guards, growling once they were inside the door.

I can't blame them too much. Sitting out here, even I can't help but think how everything looks better with the sun shining . . .

I best close for now. The natives will soon be stirring, and I haven't yet got the coffee made.

We have all worked so hard today, the men pounding, pounding, pounding with their hammers, trying to make our little cabins livable. Jessie, Lillie, and me set to unpacking our wagons and cleaning everything in sight. Quinn made us some shelves and a little counter for our "kitchen" from our packing boxes, and I filled the logs with "chinking" Jessie made up for each of us, then stretched and tacked burlap over the dirt floor before laying our rugs down. We brought the beds in next, Rose and Patrick's going to the loft, Quinn's and mine in the little curtained-off room. Then I dressed them fine with quilts. Next was Mama's old rocker. I sat it by the fireplace with another rag rug I'd made put at its feet.

Then Quinn brought our cookstove in, and I no sooner had a little fire stoked in it to start dinner when Patrick brought me in a baby squirrel. "A friend for Homey," as he calls Honey. Rose looked up at me so innocent with those pale blue eyes like her pa's, red hair all askew, declaring solemnly she had had nothing to do with it. John-Charles's eyes danced with laughter, reminding me so much of Jack, but he remained quiet as a church mouse, too, as if weighing his odds, his coppery face turning to study us all intently. "Just fell right into his lap," Rose added, then had the good sense to look injured as I shooed them all out.

"If you'd puckered your lip like I told you, she might've let us keep it," I heard her say to Patrick.

Stem, who had happened past our cabin just then, shook his head at me and grinned. "She's somethin' else, ain't she, Callie?" he said, shaking his head in wonder. There was something in the way he watched after Rose, cocking his old white head to one side with a thoughtful look, that touched my heart. Rose has had him wrapped around her little finger since she took her first breath—something they both knew but enjoyed knowing, too.

I tried not to smile, warning him about egging her on, but he just chuckled. "Yes ma'am," he said. Then, with a glint to his eyes, he added, "But there *ain't* no telling what she might do."

Later—I woke with a start this evening in my rocker, feeling something cold and clammy sliding over my face. As my eyes flew open, I saw three very impatient sets of eyes staring back at me.

It appears I had drifted off right in the middle of Daniel being sent to the lions' den. Rose had decided slopping a wet rag across my face might do the trick to wake me.

"Sorry, Mama," she said, solemn as a judge, "but we just *couldn't* go to bed without knowing the end." She sat back down at my feet. Patrick hooked a dirty bare foot over his knee, clapping as I started to read again, and John-Charles, always the stoic little Indian, crossed his short legs, too, and listened intently.

Stem was right. There isn't any telling what Rose might do.

September 2, 1869 . . .

My arms are so sore. Sent Rose to milk the cow this morning while Patrick went for kindling for me. I got the "kitchen" cleared only to turn around and set to baking four loaves of bread—hope it will be enough for our crew. Lillie is making a stew, and Jessie is taking care of dessert. We've decided we like dining "out" and will keep it up as long as the weather holds. The cabins are a bit warm for dining in. It got so warm in the kitchen I came out here to write this. Beautiful scenery—the valley, the mountains, and the sky . . . so much sky. I don't think I'll ever get tired of looking.

Quinn just came trotting by with the pretty filly Rose calls Midnight, saying how I looked like a pretty girl with my red hair "like that." I put a hand to my head and was startled to find in my rush this morning that I'd forgot to pull my hair up.

I told Lillie and Jessie as we struck out to pick berries, if I wasn't careful, I'd end up looking as wild as this land. They looked at each other then back to me, and we couldn't help but laugh. We *all* looked pretty "wild" compared to when we first got here, our "primping" going by the wayside with all the work. But our laughter seemed to say it wasn't such a bad "trade" to finally have a place to call home again.

"Besides," Lillie said, "wild can be pretty, too."

"If ye squint yer eyes jes right," Jessie said wryly.

September 3, 1869 . . .

More work today. I kept Rose indoors with me to help finish unpacking the rest of our things—which was work itself as she proceeded to tell me how being inside "purely takes all the fun out of living." It wasn't until she came across the little box that held all of my journals and asked if she could look at them that I sensed a change in her.

"It's like you still have all those people here with you," Rose said softly as she gingerly turned the pages of one of my journals. "Is that why you like keepin' a journal, Mama?" she asked, and I admit, her words took me back for a moment as I sat down on my bed next to her, looking at the soft honey-red hair that fell across her face as she studied the pages. I have always told Quinn that Rose is an odd mixture of us all: one minute daring as she takes off on one of the horses bareback, the next comical, the next thoughtful and so soft-hearted . . .

"This one's the day I was born," she said, smiling as she looked up at me.

"One of the best days of my life," I said, hugging her to me. Rose, being Rose, squirmed after a bit and asked to go help with the horses. As I watched her run out the door, I found myself drawn again to the box of journals, too. There, lying on top, was the first journal I'd ever wrote in, telling of our journey from Missouri to California. As I opened to the beginning, I found myself thinking how odd it was seeing all of our lives changing with just the turn of a page . . . Turn a page back, and my sister Rose is still alive, another few pages and Pa is there, too. I couldn't help thinking it would be something if life could really be fixed that easy.

I told Quinn about my thoughts when we had the chance to take a walk together after dinner, following the little trail past the new half-built corral to the spring.

Quinn dipped the pail in the water then looked off toward the sun setting behind the mountains in the distance. "'Twould be something, lass," he said softly, then he looked down at me with a look we had shared through our years of marriage. A look that spoke of memories, of loss and endurance and love . . . Then he cocked his head to one side, thoughtful, and I knew he was listening to the sounds of our family talking around the little bonfire Jack had made after dinner. We heard Coy and Stem bantering, then the children all laughed at something, and I saw Quinn smile softlike.

"But then, wouldn't we be missin' out on what's to come if we were always to turn back?" he said, taking my hand as we walked back up the trail. I smiled up at him, feeling such love in my heart.

"I think God must shake His head a lot over my wonderings," I admitted then, and Quinn chuckled.

"'Tis my belief the good Lord favors honest hearts, lass, over the false ones. Perfect is in heaven. It's the tryin' that counts, I'm thinkin' . . ."

I looked at Quinn, really looked at him, and I thought of all we'd been through together, of how his words to me, entwined with our faith, always seem to make life better . . .

"Do you ever wonder what's next?" I asked him then, hooking my arm in his as he grinned down at me.

"With a family like ours?" he said, opening the door of our cabin for me. "All the time, lass, all the time."

Now, as I sit writing this, I can't help but wonder what's next, too. But I must leave my wondering for another day. I am *so* tired . . .

But it is a good tired.

September 4, 1869 . . .

Quinn and I both came down with a stomachache this evening. Coy, who was voted "doctor," came in, tipped his hat back, and announced we had "huckleberry overdose," a wide grin spreading across his dark face. But he did make us a drink of mint jelly diluted in cold water to settle our stomachs. The rest of the group came and went. We should've been embarrassed, but it seemed to take too much effort. We were so tired besides, from working all day, that all we could do was groan, lying next to each other in our curtained-off little room or dashing off to the bushes while Rose looked after Patrick.

After everyone left we were silent for a bit, then Quinn groaned again as he turned over to face me. I turned, too, and it seemed like we met each other with the exact expressions of misery on our faces at the same time. Quinn grinned in spite of his suffering and said, "I fear the honeymoon may be over."

"Already?" I said, and we both laughed in spite of ourselves.

Later—I'm feeling a bit better, although Quinn is still sleeping on and off. Rose and Patrick were having a time earlier, running and playing with Jasper and Honey, when I called out and asked Rose how her sampler was coming. There was a silence, then she said, "Fine, Mama," in the tone of a prisoner going to the gallows. I heard her drag her feet in a slow shuffle to the loft to fetch her sampler. I heard Patrick say then, loftily, "I'm glad I ain't a girl."

"I guess you won't mind fetching the wood, then, will you?" I said and heard silence for the second time, then, "No ma'am," as the door opened and shut and Patrick headed outside.

Sometimes it's hard to be a parent—especially when you want to laugh.

September 5, 1869 . . .

Quinn and I are feeling much better.

Warm, pretty day—not too many left like it, Jack says—which is why we all agreed to ride out for a tour of the country-side. Rose, Patrick, and John-Charles hooted with joy when they found out, as they were prepared to endure the Sabbath indoors. I admit I was feeling a bit guilty when we first headed out so quick after prayer. But as our horses began to work their way slowly through the valley, past our cattle getting fat on the wild hay in the meadows, up toward our "guards of the valley," the mountains, I began to feel God's presence all around us in all the unexpected beauty and grandeur. Everything looked so clean and pure—the view was like nothing I've ever wit-nessed. . . . *"On the seventh day He rested"* came to me, and I thought if ever there were a spot on earth *He* would choose to rest on, this would be it.

Jack must have sensed what I was feeling because he looked over his shoulder at me and grinned then, pulling his horse back to wait for me.

"Ain't no better church than this, is there, sis?" he said with that big, easy grin of his as he sidled up next to me. I told him I couldn't imagine one, and I felt my heart swell as I looked into my brother's green eyes. The haunting, the always searching look that had been there since we were kids, had been eased since, as Jack liked to say, he'd made his peace with God . . . , and I couldn't help wishing our mama had lived long enough to see that.

I stayed back as Jack finally rode off to catch up with the rest of them and just watched as they trailed on, Stem and Jessie in the lead, so deep in gazing at the mountains that Jessie forgot to be scared on her horse . . . Lillie and Jack grinning at each other like kids, then turning to look upward, too . . . Coy cocking his head to one side as he gazed at an eagle soaring down over the valley, and Rose pulling back on Midnight and watching the eagle, too. Then I saw Quinn catch up to John-Charles and Patrick on their ponies, pointing something out to them in the distance. Quinn looked back at me once and smiled and waved, and in his smile, I saw he was as struck by the beauty of it all as I was.

As we all were. It was as if we'd found our sermon in God's creation, speaking to us through the mountains, the trees, and sky . . .

"Is this our promiseland?" I whispered, so full of hope, sitting on my horse in the stillness, but all I heard was the echo of my own voice asking *me*.

I wonder what my answer will be . . .

September 6, 1869 . . .

Sunny today—but a bit cooler. I was hanging wash out when I was caught by the sight of Jack and Coy down at the corrals, breaking a horse. There was something about the sight of Jack on that horse with the morning sun glowing orange behind them that drew me to watch; I saw the horse rear up again as I came to stand next to Coy, its eyes looking wild as it tried to buck Jack from its back. But Jack hung on—not by just strength, it seemed—but by sensing what the horse felt.

After what seemed an eternity, the horse finally gave in to Jack, and I saw him motion to Coy to let them out of the corral. We watched as Jack took off across the valley in a full run, and Coy looked over at me and smiled, soft. "That brother of your'n is *good*," he told me. "I ain't quite figured out how he does it, but it's like they trust his ways."

As I watched Jack push the horse faster I couldn't help thinking how they both seemed to be enjoying it, and it hit me what it was that horse sensed in Jack. My brother, who had loved and lost and learned to love again, understood more than most that sometimes you have to give up your freedom to get it.

Quinn came in from cutting hay tonight to tell us that we will be going to town first thing in the morning for supplies. How strange that sounds—*town*. Even Virginia City seems less than a memory now and more like something I might have made up.

It will be interesting to find out what this place has to offer . . .

September 7, 1869 . . .

They say the test of good manners is to be patient with bad ones . . . I admit I've failed the test today. *I truly want to be good, Lord. But sometimes it's just plain hard.*

Our trip to "town" took us through some of the roughest yet wildly beautiful countryside, through the valley, then up once more along narrow passes that wound around the mountains like a disjointed snake. I kept craning my neck to spot anything that might pass as a town and found nothing but wilderness until an hour or so later. Then it appeared quick, as if it had sprung up from the dirt before our very eyes. There was a big sign as we entered town, all flourishes and curlicues, telling us we'd come to "Audrey," but it almost seemed a joke as I looked around. There was a blacksmith, a few crude log huts, and then, on the other side of the thoroughfare, a mercantile that seemed to be the best-looking building of the bunch. Patrick asked, "Is this the *United of States*, Mama?" which brought a good round of laughter from us all.

Then it was: "There's the hens, girls," Stem declared, grinning, "best get to peckin'." The other men chuckled as we turned to see three women standing in front of the mercantile like they were expecting us. The one in the middle was fair, but angry-looking. She appeared to lead the little group, for she turned and said something to the other ladies, who quickly took their leave, then she went back in the mercantile and I saw her go and stand behind the counter and wait.

Rose took my hand as we headed for the store, pale blue eyes so much like her pa's staring up at me. "She looks like Mother Long," she whispered, breathless, and I almost asked, "Who?" but we were already at the mercantile.

I couldn't help looking about in shock at how much they had for such a small town: on the floor, barrels of flour, white and middling; next to that, a barrel of molasses and another of vinegar and one of salt pork. Hams, shoulders, and breakfast bacon hung from the rafters. Toward the back there were pickle jars and milk crocks, and beyond that the farm tools. The side of the counter where the woman stood had big glass jars of striped candy that Rose eyed with longing, and behind her on the shelf were crocks of honey, coffee, and tea.

Mrs. Audrey, as she introduced herself, appeared young at a closer look. I say *appeared* because, though her blonde hair was fine-looking and there didn't seem to be a single line under the dark eyes that pierced us, there was something *old* about her, something almost bitter. A smallish man stood behind the counter, too, a ways down, filling egg baskets—three dozen for a quarter—and looked as out of place as a chicken in a wolf's den. Two young girls ran in, grabbed up some candy, and almost dashed back out before they could be introduced. Zora and Nora, the Audreys' twins, nodded to us, gave Rose the once-over with a kind of disdain, then left before you could blink. I went to say something to Rose, who was looking so crestfallen, but Mrs. Audrey was already there, leaning over the counter toward me with a look of alarm.

"Really, Mrs. McGregor," she said. "Puh-haps next time y'all should leave yo-ah *pee*-ple home." Rose and I turned to follow Mrs. Audrey's gaze, and we saw Jessie pointing out some goods to Lillie. I felt the blood go to my cheeks like it did when I got mad.

"We . . . well, we don't really allow . . . ," she lowered her voice, dipping her head toward mine, *"negras* in ah sto-ah," she drawled out, and before I could say a thing I heard a rustling from behind one of the shelves.

"Casting stones again, Leah?" a woman's voice called out. "I would have thought you had your hands full with me."

The woman appeared from the other side of the shelves then, slim and lovely, very refined, and not bothering to look our way as she set her few items down, took her gloves off, and laid money down for her purchases. She looked right at Mr. Audrey.

"You have so many customers you can afford to turn them away now?"

"No ma'am, Miss Cain," Mr. Audrey said, and I was surprised to see him smile until Mrs. Audrey huffed loudly. Then he dropped his eyes a bit.

"Well, Percy, I'm finished here. I believe you can tally *this* up," Miss Cain said then, and the way she said it made you think she wasn't sure he could do much else. Mr. Audrey's bald head flushed red under the few sparse hairs that were combed sideways, but he totaled her up and she was out the door before you could blink.

Lillie and Jessie joined me and Rose near the front, and we turned to watch the woman walk away from the mercantile with a kind of easy manner and light smile on her face—like she had a good joke but hadn't found the right person to share it with. I happened to glance back then, and I saw Mrs. Audrey was watching the woman, too, with a grim look on her face. I couldn't help but ask who she was.

"Ringleader of Sin," was all Mrs. Audrey provided, her face creased in distaste.

Jessie appeared to be enjoying her discomfort, but as I glanced at Lillie, I saw the frown on her forehead and the bolt of cloth she was holding hanging limp in her hands, and I knew she was thinking of her own past—and future as far as the *good women* of the town were concerned, and I felt my temper get the best of me.

"Ringleader, huh? Well, maybe next time you can introduce us, then," I said casually and saw Mrs. Audrey's face go sour on me. I grabbed Rose's hand, and she grinned up at me, then we all marched out of the mercantile without buying a thing on our lists. I know it's not right, but I confess wild horses couldn't have got me back in there as mad as I was.

Not long after that the men came back, and we told them what had happened. And Jack, being *Jack*, decided to go fetch the supplies himself, striding with purpose with his buckskins and hair long as an Indian's into the mercantile. "You can forget the castor oil if you want to, Uncle Jack," Patrick hollered as he leaned over the back of the wagon, and John-Charles laughed. I don't know what happened, but he came out with that grin of his, supplies stacked up near past his head, and we all pulled out shortly after that, having had our fill of town.

It wasn't until I turned to look back that I saw the pretty dark-haired woman again. She was walking toward the black-smith's, and I saw a young Indian woman sitting by the side of the dust-choked road, rocking a good-sized bundle in her arms. Neither of the women looked at each other, but as Miss Cain passed I noticed the cans of milk that fell from her bag— noticed, too, the Indian woman snatch them up quick and hide them in her blanket without missing a beat . . .

"Ringleader of Sin," I said under my breath, and I heard Jessie chuckle from the back of the wagon.

"She *would* be worth meeting, don't you think?" she said then, and Lillie burst out laughing. "You two beat all," she said.

"What's so funny, Mama?" Rose asked, always wanting to be in the know. I smiled at her. "Just a little family joke is all," I said, and when Lillie turned and smiled at me, I saw the unshed tears in her eyes. Saw the hope, too.

"That's what God put families together for, Callie, to believe in each other when we can't believe in ourselves . . ." Mama's voice whispers to me tonight as I write this. And the truth of it was in Lillie's eyes when I asked her to be the one to read from the family Bible tonight after dinner. How gingerly she opened that Bible, her voice soft but filled with emotion as she read each line of scripture with such care and gratefulness . . .

Lillie was still reading when the men went down to check on the cattle, her lips moving with the words as she rocked John-Charles in her arms. Seeing her like that, I couldn't help remembering the time she told me how she had gotten hold of our family Bible by accident, of how she had been so heart-broke when Jack had to leave Virginia City because of those outlaws. Then Coy's pa, Duel, had rode out to go help Jack. The next thing she knew, she had a letter in her hands from Jack, telling her Duel had been killed and asking her to see he was buried proper. The Bible had come back with Duel's body, so at first she thought it was his. Then one night when she was low, she opened it and saw our family page and knew it was Jack's Bible.

"I thought to myself only good families keep things like that," she'd told me. "So I was sure I wouldn't fit in—that you all couldn't love someone like me . . . But you know what I learned? I learned that because you come from a family that loved, that's why you could love me." I still remember her hopeful smile then. "So maybe one day John-Charles and my new little one will be able to say they had a good ma and pa. That they were loved . . ."

Lillie looked up once as we started clearing the dishes and made to rise, but I told her to go on reading.

It was Jessie that put to words what I was thinking as we walked to the spring together to get the water. "Never saw someone so grateful," she said, dipping her pail into the stream. "Makes a person ashamed to ask for anything more than what we've got."

"We have a lot, don't we, Jessie?" I said, and she cocked her head to one side and looked at me for a moment, thoughtful.

"Yes, I guess we do at that," she said finally and smiled.

The pretty Indian woman begging outside the blacksmith's today is the smith's *wife*. Stem says the young man is a pure whiskey soak if ever there was one, that "Mr. Carey" had only looked up once from the horseshoe he was tapping on, eyes all red and bleary, to ask Quinn and Jack if we had any horses to sell. Stem said he had ignored Stem completely—and his own wife, too, when she'd come in pleading with him over something.

Bless Miss Cain for giving the poor woman those cans of milk.

Later—Well, I have found out who "Mother Long" is. I overheard Rose telling Patrick a story tonight, whispering of "the perfect murderess" who became known as the "banditti of the plains." Rose must've thought over the "plains" part, because then I heard her add breathlessly, "Chubs, I think she's come to hide in these here mountains . . . to become the banditti of the *mountains*."

I have no doubt it was Jack that smuggled her another one of those awful dime novels.

It wasn't much later that I was woke by a stout little shadow leaning over me. "Mama? Are you awake?" Patrick whispered loud enough to wake the dead. "I come to check on you and Pa." He promptly climbed into the bed between us and whispered to me the whole sordid story, how Rose just *knows* Mrs. Audrey is really Mother Long. Even in the dim light, I could see his eyes were huge.

"Who's this Mother Long, then?" Quinn mumbled, turning over.

"The *bandanna* of the plains," Patrick whispered loudly again, and it was all I could do not to laugh as Quinn said, "The *what?*"

I'm awake now, and my two Irishmen, splayed out across the bed, have fallen sound asleep before they could hash out the whole story . . .

September 10, 1869 . . .

Lillie and I met the infamous "Ringleader of Sin" today.

It was shortly after breakfast when I heard the men talking amongst themselves about some of the cattle being missing as they hammered away, putting finishing touches to the new corral. Thinking it would give us a chance to see some of the countryside, I volunteered Lillie and me to go look for them. Jessie was quick to offer to watch our babes, so it was settled. They all grinned like it was a fine joke, then Quinn said, "Do ya think ya two can hannel the cattle alone then, lass?" and I said, "I did in California, didn't I?"

Then Jack says to Lillie, "What about wolves?" and she gave Jack a wry look before mounting up next to me.

"I worked in a saloon," she said, "so I guess I might know a thing or two about wolves." Lillie winked at me, and we both grinned at each other.

"I guess you see why I had to marry her," Jack sighed, and Quinn shook his head.

"Would've thought Callie to be enough for one family," he said, and I gave him a look and told him we would have the cattle back before dinner. As Lillie and I rode off, we could hear their laughter follow us clear past the spring and up the slope. Once we were out of sight, I turned to Lillie and asked her if she had a clue how to handle cattle.

"Well, I guess we'll figure it out once we find them," she said, looking at me with more confidence than I think she truly felt, and we both laughed. But it wasn't too long after that, we lost our sense of humor.

We found the stray cattle, but they didn't seem the least bit interested in seeing us. I reined my mount to the right and told Lillie to go left, and just when we thought we had them, two of the culprits went right between us, trotting off a short distance away and soon chomping on grass again. This went on so that I started wondering if the cattle were making a game of us. It was growing hotter and hotter, and Lillie and I were fit to be tied. The cattle had scattered everywhere, and our faces were smudged with dirt and sweat when we suddenly noticed we had an audience. We both turned at the same time to see Miss Cain, dressed as fine as the day we saw her in the mercantile, all embroidery and lace. Her hat—just as fine—was tossed to one side in the grass, and I saw her hair was darker than I remembered, dark and shiny like a raven's wing. She looked so pretty it still doesn't seem possible—because she was sitting astride a fallen log, corncob pipe clenched between her lips!

"Ladies, I was born and bred in Boston—intellectual hub of

the universe by most accounts," she speculated, tapping the pipe against her boot. "But this isn't Boston, so I'll give it to you plain. Best thing you can do is yell at them. They're dumb creatures— a bit like our two-legged counterparts," she said, winking. "Which is why I raise hogs now." She grinned at us then, hopping off her perch, and Lillie and I couldn't help laughing outright. She briskly introduced herself to us as "Willa," and shook our hands. Then she looked close at Lillie, squinting her eyes. "You look to be expecting," she announced, then didn't wait for a reply before she went on. "There is a doctor in these parts—or at least he says he is—he spends most of his time looking for gold. He isn't much of a miner, either, though, if that speaks for his character. But at the least, you know he's around if you think you might need him." She nodded to us and sauntered off toward her own horse, and within moments she was gone.

"Was she really here, or did I just imagine all of that?" Lillie said, turning to look at me. I shook my head in wonder.

"I'm a pretty big imaginer," I told her, "but I don't think even I could've come up with all of that."

Now, writing this, I *know* I couldn't have.

There *was* something about her, though, that seemed to inspire us. Without any more talk, Lillie and I turned back to the cattle, hawing and whistling at them like two old cowpokes, and rounded up the surprised mama and yearling in short time, leading them and the rest of the wayward little group home, tails tucked between their legs like kids caught playing hooky.

The men are impressed by us as well. I notice, too, that Lillie, who was so unsure of herself hours earlier, even has a bit of a swagger in her step as she walks by.

Later—I've been thinking a lot about Willa Cain this evening for some reason.

I feel almost like she flung that greeting out to us then retreated quick before we had a chance to say anything back. Like maybe she was afraid of what she might get in return. Lillie and Jessie think it's because of the women in town. "I've dealt with their kind before," Lillie said slowly. "It's a wonder she talked to us at all."

"Loneliness will tromp right over fear if the loneliness is strong enough," Jessie said. "Being out here all by yourself, that's got to be some kind of lonely."

Some kind of lonely . . . It's hard to imagine what would keep a Boston-bred lady out here, rising early day in and day out to feed stock and lug water, planting one foot after another all day long then heading back home to bed with no one to tell your worries, your fears, to . . .

I have to wonder how she does it. Does she turn her face up to the night sky and have her talks with You like I do, Lord? Or is she really alone? I hope not, but I can't help but wonder . . .

September 15, 1869 . . .

Sunny today, but windier than usual. Fall is coming. It's in the wind, in the grass that's already turning a honey color, and in our pace to get things done before winter sets in for good.

I've already carried two buckets of water from the spring, and I expect I'll have to make another run before all is said and done today. I noticed, though, my arms aren't nearly as sore as they were. Maybe I'm getting stronger.

September 18, 1869 . . .

We have all worked so hard today, pitching in to help the men dig a rough dirt dam to trap water from the spring for another watering hole. I'd just sat down to write this when Jessie came to tell me that Stem "'fessed up" that he had glimpsed Willa Cain's place while out looking for a stray. He said she had a small but pretty frame house, a milk cow, some chickens, and *the cleanest hogs you've ever laid eyes on.*

"He said she was high-stocked with brains, too—though he sounded suspicious of that part," Jessie said, grinning.

"A lot of detail for someone just trotting by," I said wryly, and Jessie chuckled.

"Ye'd never imagine it by looking at him," she said, shaking her head, "but that old man's got women beat for bein' in the know of things." We both laughed and looked toward the corral where Rose was following close on Stem's heels.

"Them two is a *pair*, ain't they?" Jessie said then, and I was surprised to see her eyes mist over a bit. "Just like family," she said, almost to herself, and I wondered if Jessie was thinking of the family she'd lost before the war.

"We *are* family," I said, smiling. "Jack says who else but us knows everything about each other—and loves each other anyway?"

"Jack say that?" she grinned, surprised, and I nodded, linking my arm in hers as we walked back to the cabin together to start dinner.

"And if *Jack* says it, you know it must be true," I said, and we both laughed.

Later—An old miner showed up at the ranch just in time for dinner this evening and to pass some news along as well.

It appears he and some partners are panning gold a short distance away. He saw the smoke and said he "thought to investergate." As it's custom in the "territory" to offer food and lodging to strangers that happen by, we invited him to stay. Over dinner he told us he had come west before the "wah" to hunt and trap. He made it well known to all of us that he'd been first to arrive in these parts and had "witnessed it as it all began." The question of Adam and Eve came to mind, but I bit my tongue, smiling to myself as he then declared himself as "the one who pioneered the territory." While his accent leaves no doubt of his southern heritage, he and Stem were soon thick as thieves, talking about old times.

"This dern place is on the verge of gettin' crowded," Stem said at one point, spitting tobacco, to which the old-timer tore off a great piece of his own tobacco and chewed energetically, nodding and spitting in agreement.

"Civilization is comin'," he declared somberly, and I picked that point to speak up and ask about the doctor Willa Cain had mentioned for Lillie. The old fellow nodded his head and told us there was a doctor-turned-miner in "these here parts." Wrinkling his crusty brow, he said, "I ain't sure how good he is with actual doctorin'. But he's a mite good tooth puller." He smiled big enough for us to see the "Doc's" handiwork.

He had no teeth.

Stem did tell us all later that our visitor had confessed on his way out that a traveling preacher is in town to hold a "tent meetin' on the morrow." He shook his head as the women of the group exclaimed, as if to ask what the world was coming to, but I could tell he was pleased at being the bearer of such news.

It's been nearly a year since any of us have heard a real sermon. Lillie, Jessie, and I talked it over then made quick work of the dishes so we could try to find Willa Cain's place before it turns too dark.

More later—

We found Willa Cain's place easy enough—but she made it plain to us that she isn't interested at all in going to hear the new preacher. "I have never benefited from such things before, so, no, I don't believe I'm interested," she said in a voice that was so proper I wasn't sure it was the same woman.

None of us knew quite what to do after that. I told Lillie and Jessie that in spite of her acting the way she did, I thought I'd saw a kind of longing in her eyes, too.

I wasn't sure if it was true or just imagined it—until I glanced back as our wagon pulled away and saw a feeling on Willa's face I can't quite explain. Now that I write this, I think I know what it was . . . the look of a dog that had been whipped so hard it would shy away from even a kind hand no matter how hungry it was . . . because it had been broke of hoping . . .

September 19, 1869 . . .

Such a blessing to finally be able to spend the Sabbath in a "church."

I admit I didn't know what to expect when we first came upon the tent the preacher had set up at the edge of town, surrounded by buckboards and bonnets as it was. The tent itself was huge—the oddest combination of skins and scraps of cloth I'd ever seen. There was a "barker," of sorts, standing outside the tent. "Th' rule is, Nothin' to be bought or sold hereabouts," he declared. "Just come an' hear the message."

The first thing that surprised me when we walked into the tent was the number of people who had gathered there. Good news travels fast—and far—by the looks of some of their trail-worn clothes. I saw Mrs. Audrey and her family—saw that Rose did, too, for she leaned over and whispered to Patrick and John-Charles, and I watched them stiffen and accept Rose's hand as she led them with a look of ultimate sacrifice to their seats. It wasn't until the rest of us got seated that I spotted the preacher who stood quietly reading his Bible at the front of the tent. He was quite large in size—six-foot-four or better—at least as big as Quinn, if not bigger. And he was handsome enough, with

brown, wavy hair and a strong but kind face. His suit was mod-
est but clean, maybe a bit worn, too. But when his eyes looked
up I felt as if they carried the knowledge of the burdens of the
world . . . and hoped somehow to ease them.

He cleared his throat, then without much ado, he began to
speak to all of us in a deep but gentle voice that drew us in.
Rose, Patrick, and John-Charles sat so still I had to keep checking to make sure they were there. They never took notice of me,
so spellbound they were with the preacher.

I will try to put the sermon to paper just as he spoke it.

"I want all of those that traveled the California and Oregon
Trails to stand and be counted," he announced, and nearly
everyone in the tent stood, chuckling, looking at each other.
Then he told us to sit again.

"Long journey, wasn't it?" the preacher said, followed by
"amens" all around. "Suffering along the way?"

Yes. Lord, yes.

"Sometimes you didn't think you could take another step.
Sometimes you thought maybe God didn't hear you anymore—
that maybe He was just too big and you were just too small."

There was tears in most of our eyes, quiet nods of heads,
and the preacher smiled a comforting smile that seemed to be
for each one of us personally.

"But just when you thought you were at your end, you came
up over that hill, into that land . . . that town . . . that tent, and
you found you had made it, you *had made it through* in spite of
what you thought."

There was a good amount of silence as everyone fell deep in
thought and memory. The preacher smiled again.

"It's the *journey* that I've come to talk to you about," he said.
"The journey of our lives." He stepped forward then with a look
of eagerness on his face, and Quinn looked over at me and
smiled. "Don't you see? We're just travelers here, just passing
through. Every day is another journey, but He's there to lead us

through it—if we'll let Him, if we'll listen." He held up a worn Bible in his hands for all to see, and I noticed how huge his hands were, and how callused, too, like he had worked at more than studying with those hands. "This book is our map, folks. The direction to get us home—to our *real* home, that is. And that home is called heaven . . ."

"What be yer name, young feller?" an old-timer called from the silence of the crowd, and the preacher dipped his head a bit. "Well, you can just call me Preacher, if you need to call me anything. Only name I hope for you to remember is Jesus'."

He spoke of other things, too. Of loving our neighbors as Jesus loved us. And he asked us to remember that it was the *broken* ones Jesus went to—not the "fixed."

He said most folks in the Bible that God used were broken, and that was exactly why God used them, because they understood what it meant to be broken—and knew how good it felt to be fixed.

The last thing he said was for us to remember Jesus had been broken, too. That He had been slandered and left alone in His darkest hour, that He had been laughed at and beaten, put in prison and even killed. He said God made sure Jesus was raised back up so we could have Someone to talk to Who understood . . . Then Preacher said we should be the ones to follow that example—that we should *understand* for others, too.

"Hebrews says it best," Preacher said, looking up from his well-worn Bible. "It says He can have compassion on those who are ignorant and going astray, since He Himself was also subject to weakness."

There was a whisper of a question then. "Aw, Harm, it jes means ya kin feel a feller's blisters better if ya've walked the road yerself," an old miner said to himself—apparently louder than he had planned, for the whole crowd overheard and tittered, but Preacher just smiled.

"I couldn't have said it better myself, brother," he said,

earning some chuckles. Then he told us to bow our heads so we could close with a prayer.

Afterward, I couldn't help thinking as everyone started a slow trickle from the tent that there had been something about the preacher that seemed almost regal while he talked to us, like he was out of place in his own humble surroundings. When he greeted us after the service, I thought putting my hand in his was a bit like shaking paws with a noble lion.

I turned and looked just as he took Stem's hand, and suddenly it seemed like everything had went quiet around us. I saw Stem look up into the preacher's eyes.

"Ain't had much book learnin', but what ya said sounded right t' these ears, young feller," Stem said abruptly, then he looked down at his dark old hand, still resting in the preacher's. I saw him nod then, like he'd settled something with himself. "My mama was a godly woman," he went on. "She didn't have nothin' t' speak of, bein' a slave an' all. But I recall how her eyes would shine, talkin' of seein' Jesus a'fore she died. She used to say, 'I don' have nothin', so I don' worry 'bout nothin' for this earth. I jes keep my eyes fixed on the Lord.'" Stem cocked his head sideways and squinted up at the preacher. "Ya kindly remind me of her, Preacher."

"I count that as fine company to be in," Preacher said softly, and I could see he was touched more than I expected—more than any of us imagined. "By the way, what do folks call you?"

"I was born Justice," Stem supplied. "But my friends call me Stem."

"Justice?" the preacher said, and Stem stood a bit straighter in defense, used to folks finding it funny for an old black trapper to have such a name.

"My mama knew humor well enough, I guess," he said finally, and the preacher looked into Stem's eyes as a kind smile came to his face.

"Or maybe she knew her *son* well enough," he said.

Stem looked at the preacher one last time before we all walked away, and I felt like they had understood each other in some way I can't exactly explain.

I don't think Stem can explain it either. "Don't know why I gave sech a speech," he said under his breath as we headed for our wagons. "Ye'd think I'd drew enough attention in my youth t' last a lifetime." Jessie glanced over her shoulder and smiled—we both did, for we knew *Who* had led Stem to speak.

Oh, thank You, Lord, for this day, for touching our hearts in the way only You know how to do . . .

I was writing in this journal when we were surprised by a visit from Willa Cain. She seemed to want to know how our trip had went, but it was like she wasn't sure how to ask—or how to get an answer without appearing to care. I think Stem sensed her feelings, for I saw him watch her from the corner of his eye as he talked partly to Rose—but mostly to Willa.

"Well, sis, I'll allow I ain't never seen sech a man that 'pears so fierce but kin hold a babe so tender in that big paw of his'n. He ain't the judgin' type, neither," Stem said, punctuating the thought with a stream of tobacco. I saw Willa's face was wistful. Then, catching me looking, she pursed her lips and cocked an eyebrow.

"What's this fellow's name, then?" she said, trying to sound casual, like she wasn't that interested.

"He says to jes' call him Preacher, said the only name that was important was Jesus'," Stem said, shaking his old head and smiling. "Ain't ever heard a man talk like him, an' I've heard a lot of jaw work in my time, that's fer sure."

Willa sniffed.

"Well, he sounds shifty to me," she said, rising from the table. "Let's take a walk, shall we, Callie?" she said then, real properlike, and Stem caught my eye and winked.

We took our walk down by the spring, just Willa and me, talking about little nothings, really, until she stopped for a bit when we were caught by surprise as a fish suddenly jumped up from the water, and we laughed. I saw Willa glance down at a ring she wore on her finger. It was a fancy gold affair, I could see that much. And I saw that the stone was missing, too, and wondered if she'd had to sell the stone. Willa caught me looking and got a secret kind of look on her face then brushed her hands through her skirt as if to hide the ring. Then, for some reason I don't think either of us knew, she just started talking.

She told me she wasn't as crazy as most folks thought—that sometimes crazy was smart.

"One thing that wasn't smart was me getting married," she said. "Some gentleman would start talking to me, start wanting to court, and I would think, *Well, it's the proper thing to do.* But for me there wasn't anything proper about it—no matter how much folks frown on a woman being on her own. I was just trying to replace something I had lost, and you can't replace people . . ."

She fell silent for a bit and we just walked, but I kept quiet, having a feeling she wasn't finished—and she wasn't.

She went on and told me she'd not been divorced from her second husband a month when men just started "happening by" her ranch to look her over. "Like checking a brood mare," she said with a grin.

"I read somewhere if Indians thought you were crazy, they would leave you alone, so I thought to try it out. I would spot some fellow coming down my road in a wagon or on a horse, and I'd say to myself, 'Okay, what's it going to be today?' Then I would greet him in whatever language I chose." She grinned again. "I'm fluent in five, so it made for interesting conversation." We both chuckled, then Willa went on. "Some decided to use the excuse of breeding their boars with my sows," she said. "So I washed them up good—even knitted booties for them to wear—and informed the poor gent standing there that his boar was too dirty for my 'girls.' Folks in town started saying I was crazy, that all my sinful ways had caught up to me . . ." Willa turned and looked at me thoughtfully. "So I decided I didn't need their religion."

"I didn't mean to offend you last night, Callie," she added. "I've taken quite a liking to you and your family."

Willa suddenly looked almost embarrassed at all she had told me, and she stood, shaking her skirts off then smoothing them over before she looked up at me again. "Well, this has been practically a speech for me," she said, turning toward her wagon. "So I guess I'll head home now."

"Come visit us anytime," I said, calling after her. "Not everyone thinks the same, you know." She stopped in her tracks, and I saw her look over her shoulder before she started toward her wagon.

"Perhaps you're right about that," was all she said, then she stepped up into her wagon and hawed her team on without looking back.

I don't know the whys of it, but there is something about Willa Cain that I feel drawn to, a yearning inside to show her things can be different—to help her, like the preacher said, to *understand* that God *is* there . . .

My mama used to say that sometimes we're the only Bible some folks will ever have the chance to read . . . *So, Lord, I'm asking You to help me. Help me to be Your Book so good she can't put it down until she's done . . .*

October 1, 1869 . . .

Well, my mama also used to say rudeness was the weak man's imitation of strength, too . . . I can see now why it's been so hard for Willa Cain to trust anyone around these parts. There are some folks that are mean just for the spite of it, and the man who came to buy one of our yearlings today is proof of that.

The man showed up as we were herding some of the horses to our new corral for branding. I was riding with Jack and Stem, coming down the slope at the west of the property, when I saw a short but thick-built man waving at Quinn in the distance. I don't know any other way to explain it than he looked seedy to me, and for some reason, I got a bad feeling in my stomach and nudged my horse on toward the corrals. Quinn had seen him, too, and hawed his team to a trot to catch up to him.

Somehow the filly Quinn had tied to the back of his wagon either balked or got tripped up, for as the dust started to settle around them, I saw she was tangled up in the lead rope and was nearly being dragged behind the wagon. I nudged my horse into a run and caught up with them just in time. Quinn started untying the horse and checking her out. He told me to go ahead and find out what the man wanted, so I did just that.

Mr. Carey, as he introduced himself, had been watching the scene from the yard. He laughed harsh as I rode up.

"Shoulda let yer man drag her," he said, looking up at me with bleary red eyes. "Horses are a lot like women—it's only the hard lessons they remember. You're a pretty thing, ain't ya?" he added then and grinned.

I admit I was shocked first, then mad, but remained cool as I asked him his business. He told me he'd come to buy a horse. He said, with a wave of his thick arm, that the horse he had was played out. I glanced over to his mount and saw the mare was in pitiful shape.

As a matter of fact, she looked to be so poorly cared for that I almost asked him to leave her, but then Quinn came up and I wasn't sure what to say. I did try my best to get Quinn's attention, to warn him not to sell the filly to the man, but he kept talking to the man, all but ignoring me.

So as not to cause a scene, I waited until they had finished their business and watched after Mr. Carey, trotting down the trail on his poor mare and leading the pretty two-year-old filly behind in a tight grip. As soon as he was out of sight, I turned and told Quinn what Mr. Carey had said, and he gave me a look of disbelief at first. Then I saw his handsome face turn grim and hard all at once. He said it was the last horse the man would ever buy from us. He said, "Been my experience a man who shows cruelty to an animal is sure to do the same to his own kind."

"I *tried* to tell you," I said again to make sure he understood. He pretended not to, talking about all he had to get done, but I heard him start to whistle as he headed back for the corral, and I knew he *had* understood. We've been married long enough for me to know when Quinn starts whistling, it's because he's worried.

I *am* aggravated with him. But I blame myself, too, and now I'm just wishing I had said something before that awful man led our horse away.

October 2, 1869 . . .

Rose churns tonight up and down with the dasher, saying, "Come, butter, come. Peter standing at the gate, waiting for a butter cake." But it sounds more like a growl than a song. She isn't too happy with her pa after finding out we sold Midnight out from under her. Even though we both told her awhile back the horse was too skittish for her, she feels wronged.

It's the first overcast day I can recall since we've come here. It suits my mood, though. I feel like I'm brewing as I write this, like those clouds hanging over the mountains, still troubled about selling our horse to that man.

Like Rose, I wish we *could* take it back—but for different reasons.

I'm sure Quinn thinks I'm blowing it all out of proportion, but every once in a while I feel like I've come up on a stranger living in my house . . . like he doesn't understand how I feel . . .

Later—Quinn just brought me a pretty bouquet of wildflowers, then we talked long into the night. The "stranger" has retreated to the shadows again, and we're together again, just like old times.

He told me tonight he hated when the silence edged in between us, and I agreed, but I told him something I'd remembered Mama telling me, too: Disagreeing is normal; it's lying to someone—to yourself—that's what's bad.

October 4, 1869 . . .

I was still having a hard time shaking the gloom of Mr. Carey's visit when Patrick brought me some flowers in this afternoon—a pretty but crumpled little bouquet of half-dead wildflowers. I put them in a little can of water and told him I would tuck some in this page to save. Just then Rose came in, taking it all in at a glance.

"They look pretty dead to me, Chubs," Rose announced with nine-year-old authority as she stood in the doorway, hands perched on her hips. Patrick gave her a withering look then looked down at his gift that, to him, had been ruined by her words. I could see his mind searching, grasping for something, *anything* to say back to her.

"Shut the door, Rose," he said, agitated, "'tis bloody windy out there!"

I didn't know whether to laugh or scold him. He had done

such a perfect imitation of his father that if it weren't for the voice, I might've wondered. Quinn, who had been stoking wood in the fireplace, coughed. Knowing that cough, I hurriedly tried to explain that "bloody" wasn't a nice thing for a boy to say, sending Patrick and Rose off quick to finish their outside chores.

No sooner than the door shut behind them, Quinn turned to me, shaking his head, and said with a grin, "Where *does* the lad come up with these things?" Then he saw my look and had the good sense to look sheepish before we both burst out laughing.

October 5, 1869 . . .

Beautiful day. Made breakfast, cleaned, baked three loaves of bread, and sent Rose and Patrick off to chores, then decided to ride out to help the men bring cattle down closer to the valley. Truth is, I was itching to see *fall* close up, and it didn't disappoint me. Everything seemed ablaze. The honey-colored meadows were like the flickering of the flame that gained heat farther up the slopes as I rode through the larch and aspens towering over me in a burst of orange and gold fire, and I felt awed by the beauty of it all. When I reached the men, I could tell they were a bit awed, too. They were all working in a kind of grateful silence, like they'd been given a chance at something so special they didn't want to mess it up.

Like being in love and wanting it to last forever . . .

I took a quick drink of water from my canteen and handed it to Quinn, and we smiled at each other, our eyes saying more than words. Then we went to work quick, helping drive the cattle down to the low meadows.

Later—My eyes are scratchy and I'm tired, but I felt I had to write about this day. I don't think I'll ever forget the beauty of what I saw, but if I did, I would want to have this to read and remember . . . Patrick just brought in another load of wood for me then asked if he could see the flowers he gave me that I'd pressed in the journal. When I showed him, he smiled, satisfied, and said, "And I ain't said bloody once since you told me not to say bloody."

"*Haven't* said," I corrected him, and he grinned up at me, all innocent, his blue eyes twinkling under those thick dark lashes.

"Haven't said bloody," he said.

Sometimes I could swear that Jack and I got our boys "traded" at birth; John-Charles always has his nose stuck in a book when he's not tending the horses . . . and Patrick is so rakish and charming . . . so much like Jack.

Ah, well, Mama said you never pay for your raising until you have one of your own. But I do have to wonder if I'm not paying Jack's share, too.

So much for poetry.

October 7, 1869 . . .

Patrick came barreling into the cabin tonight, yelling something about "that lady" being here and grabbing my arm until he pulled me out the door, and when I stepped into the yard, I saw it was Willa. She was coming down easy from her wagon, holding a good-sized bundle in her arms, and when she turned around, I saw fear in her eyes as they met mine.

"I found him in between our places, lying off by the side of the trail," she said breathlessly, then she pulled the blanket back to reveal a little Indian boy of about four or five, cuts and bruises all over his face, blood running from his nose and ears. He didn't seem to even have the strength to open his eyes but moaned a pitiful little moan that sounded like a cry for help.

"I don't know anything about children or doctoring," Willa said, her hands shaky as I took the boy from her. "I just assumed you and your family would . . ."

Once we were in the cabin, we made a quick pallet on the floor in front of the fire, and I had Rose go fetch the men. Then Willa and I went to work, trying to clean the blood from his ears and nose and giving him a bit of broth to sip. But he choked and coughed, hardly able to swallow a thing.

Jack got to the cabin first, and it wasn't long after he looked the boy over, studying his wounds first, then his clothes, that he announced the poor little fellow had been beaten by someone. He then told us that his moccasins looked to be Crow, but the beating had probably come from a white as most Indians don't beat their children—or their adults, for that matter.

"Best thing you can do is try to make him comfortable—but he might not make it," Jack said, low, his green eyes filled with pity—and something else, something I couldn't put my finger on as he glanced to where John-Charles was sitting. He left shortly after that to round up the men to follow Willa out and see if they could find anything or anybody around that might tell us who the boy belongs to. Lillie and Jessie came to help, too, but it seems like time will be the only thing to tell if this little one makes it.

I have him bundled on a thick pallet in front of the fireplace as I write this. He has been quiet all night except for just a tiny whimper of a word or two every once in a while in his sleep . . . poor little fellow!

Beaten. Who would do such a thing?

Lord, I won't pretend to understand how this could happen to just a child, but I do ask that You help this little one . . . I pray for his mama, too. I don't understand Crow, but I know the word he calls out every once in a while in his sleep is for his mama.

I know because I'm a mama, too . . .

October 8, 1869 . . .

No news about the boy's family. The children have been such a help, bringing up water from the spring, fetching wood—anything they can do, really. I think they're curious—at least Rose and Patrick are. John-Charles is a different matter, though.

Earlier, I was in my "room" when I heard Patrick and John-Charles bringing in a load of wood for me and the boy started talking again, delirious and mumbling. Then I heard John-Charles say, "What's he sayin'?"

Patrick answered, "Well, *you* should know."

There was a brief silence, then John-Charles said, "No *I* shouldn't, either!"

I heard stomping out of the cabin and came out from behind the curtain to find Patrick standing in the middle of the room with a bewildered look on his face. "I guess I'll stay in here and help, Mama," he said, resigned. "I'll never find John-Charles, anyhow. He always takes off for the woods when he gets mad, and he's been mad all day." He shrugged his shoulders and went over and sat down next to the boy, shaking his head like he didn't know what to make of his cousin.

I wasn't so confused. John-Charles takes after Jack in that way . . . going off to sort out his problems. I think there's a big war going on in that little body—a war of wondering just where he, half-Indian, half-white, fits into this world . . .

Patrick's always had a tender heart, but he has surprised me today at how he's taken it on himself to comfort this poor, sick boy, sitting with him, talking to him, and patting his head like I do when he and Rose are sick. He even got him to take some more broth, though he didn't open his eyes. The boy does seem to sense us sometimes, but he's made no other sound except for the pitiful little word he moans out every once in a while.

I was writing this when I overheard Patrick's voice, coming from somewhere outside the cabin, asking Quinn why anyone would hurt "a little boy like that" and "was it 'cause he's Indian?" There was a short silence that followed, and I knew Quinn was weighing his words. I went and peeked out the window then and saw that Rose and John-Charles were standing there, too. Rose had her arms crossed like she was ready to fight something or somebody, but John-Charles just looked wary, like he wasn't sure he wanted to be there for the answer.

"There is *no* good reason for it, lad," Quinn said, then looked to each of the children. "Folks can say that it's for this reason or that, but 'tis still wrong—in God's eyes and in mine."

"But people still do bad things anyway, don't they?" John-Charles said, then he turned and ran for home before Quinn could answer.

Oh, I hate this trouble, this awful thing that has taken not just one boy's innocence but all of our children's as well.

October 9, 1869 . . .

Another day with no news. At least the boy seems to be getting better. He sat up on the pallet today and drank quite a bit of broth then let Patrick show him his collection of bird eggs. His dark eyes were alight with interest until Patrick said "Mama" to me, then his little face crumpled, and he cried until I rocked him back to a fitful sleep.

The wind is picking up in the valley this evening, golden leaves and larch needles swirling everywhere in the air.

October 11, 1869 . . .

Sometimes when I see how quick God works, it amazes me to silence . . . I admit that's an amazing thing in itself, but what has happened is even *more* than that.

Here I prayed for that boy's poor, nameless mother, and Coy trots home tonight with the woman on the back of his horse, her little girl on the back of Jack's mount. Turns out she's the *same* woman we saw in town—same one who's married to that monster, Mr. Carey. She's pretty shook up, her and her daughter both, and wet, too—but they are delirious with joy at finding out the little boy has been in our care all along.

The daughter, Sarah, is about Rose's age and speaks pretty good English. But she's a bit skittish around us.

After hearing all they had been through, I can understand why. It seems Mr. Carey took to beating the little boy something awful the other day, and Willie—that's his name—ran out of their home to get away from his pa, then just kept running. Mother and daughter have been searching for nearly two days and were at their end when Jack and Coy found them near where the stream flows into the river.

"She was out in the river, trying to drown herself and the girl," Jack told us off to one side. "I got off my horse and was trying to talk to her, but she was having none of it at first. Just kept crying and saying she had lost her boy and didn't want to go back home because her husband would beat her and the girl, too. She told me she'd rather die and that it would be better for her daughter to die, too, than to go back home." Jack glanced over at Coy, who was standing in the corner, a bit shy like always. "Then I hear this splash and all of a sudden I see Coy in the water, too, easing out to her and talking to her real gentle-like. She looked shocked to death at first—I don't think she's ever seen a black man—let alone one built like a barn." Coy laughed softly, and Jack shook his head and grinned as he went on. "He don't know Crow, and she don't know much English but something happened because she got out and came with us."

Jack turned and looked at her, listening as she crooned to her little boy. "Wonder how she ever ended up with Carey . . . ," he said almost to himself.

Lillie, Jessie, and me took to the kitchen area so she could be alone with her kids . . . well, that and so we could try and sort out what was happening before our eyes. "For a mother to try and drown herself and her child was more than desperate," Lillie said, whispering.

"Can't imagine what the poor thing has been through," Jessie said, but when she looked at her, there was a knowing despair in Jessie's eyes, like she *could* imagine.

"Makes our lives look like regular picnics, don't it?" Coy said, startling us as we turned to see him standing nearer to us, holding his hat. What startled me most wasn't what he said, for he had just been voicing what we had all been thinking anyway. But it was the look on his face when he turned to watch the woman rocking her boy as Rose tried to coax her girl into playing. Like he was really worried about what might come of her. I saw she was wondering, too, her eyes darting fearfully to the door ever so often. She glanced over at me, and when our eyes met, I had the eeriest feeling that she wasn't in the water anymore—but somehow she was still *drowning*.

I couldn't bare to let her torment go on, so I went to her then and knelt down, asking Jack if he knew what her name was. He said something that sounded like "Awbonny," so I said, "Bonny, you're safe here with us. You're safe—do you know what that means?"

Jack looked doubtful that she'd understand, but she knew, for she looked at me with wide eyes then started to weep with relief.

"Well, I'll be," Jack said as I put my arms around her shoulders.

"Thank . . . you," she said slowly, but as plain as day, and when she raised her eyes, she looked at all of us shyly, gratefully, but she smiled at Coy.

It wasn't too long afterward that Coy offered up his tiny bunkhouse-cabin to "Bonny" and her kids, saying it was only right, being there was just one of him. Our moods lifted a bit until Stem appeared shortly after that. His face was somber with worry as he listened to all that had happened.

"Dern," was all he said at first, taking his hat off and rubbing his head like he did when he was worried. "I got a bad feelin' 'bout this—her bein' Injun and all could spell trouble." We all glanced at Jack—then to Stem, whose look was suddenly sorry. "Didn't mean no offense by that, Jack," he said, gently. "It's jes she ain't got no rights the way most folks see it, if'n he decides to come for her."

Jack nodded, his face grim. "No offense taken," was all he said, but I knew he was thinking of what John-Charles might have to face one day. He looked from Lillie to John-Charles, his green eyes troubled with a distant sorrow, like he was somewhere else. Then he clasped John-Charles's small, brown hand in his, and without another word to any of us, turned as if to walk away. Lillie got up slowly to follow, her own face confused and troubled, and I knew both of them were filled with haunts of the past. When I called after Jack he stopped for only a moment and turned back to me.

"It'll all turn out fine; you'll see," I said, trying in some way to make it better, but he just nodded like his mind was somewhere else.

"I figure we ought to let her stay, at least until we can decide what else to do." Jack glanced over at Stem. "We didn't ask for this . . . but then, neither did she," he added.

When Quinn came in I tried to fill him in the best I could, and he agreed she should stay, too. "But Stem's right about her not having much in the way of rights out here. We're a long way from California, lass," he said, and by the way he said it I knew he meant more than miles . . .

I stepped out only for a moment tonight to see if I could spot Jasper and Honey. That's when I saw Lillie standing off from their little cabin, just looking out toward the mountains. She's small as it is, but she seemed even smaller as I watched her standing alone like that. As I walked over to her, I saw she was holding an empty water bucket in her hand, almost like she had forgot about it. She turned and looked over her shoulder at me, trying to smile.

"Jack's out there somewhere," she said, and that was all she said for a while as I stood next to her, wondering where he'd gone. For as long as I can remember, Jack's always been like that, taking off on his horse whenever he needed to think. "He'll be back," I heard myself tell Lillie, remembering all the times my mama had spoke those same words as I stood with her on our porch in Missouri, watching the distance for Jack. *"It's how he speaks his piece with God,"* Mama had said. *"Some folks take to church, but your brother takes to the land, and it might be he has the right idea about that, too . . ."*

Lillie looked over at me and nodded, then she told me what Jack had said once they got back to the cabin, after he'd tucked John-Charles in for the night. She said he'd looked at her real sad and said, "What kind of life is my boy going to have?" She said the "my" part real hard, like she couldn't forget it. I tried to tell her Jack was just worried, that he didn't mean nothing by it, but she just nodded again.

"This land is something, isn't it?" she said after a while, then lowered her voice to a whisper. "You just fall in love with it, whether you should or not." She didn't say any more, but her silence could've filled a book of worry. I knew she wasn't really talking of the land. My feeling, considering all that had happened, was she was thinking of Jack and John-Charles, who she loved like her very own, and she was wondering where she fit in it all.

I told her that we all felt like that one time or another, that our lives could feel as far out of reach as this land, that the trouble that had happened had got us all feeling low. "We just need to have courage, is all," I finished and was surprised when Lillie looked back over her shoulder at me and smiled, wry. I saw a dimple in her cheek appear, and there was something in the way she cocked her head to one side, in the way her long brown curls straggled free from her bonnet, teased free by the wind, that made me realize how much I loved her like a sister.

"Don't you know, Callie?" she said, like she was laughing at herself as she turned to face the wind again. "Courage is just being the only one who knows you're scared to death."

We both turned back and looked toward the mountains, falling quiet for a spell.

"Well, I guess we blew that, then," I said finally, and we both laughed.

Lillie headed for the spring then, and as I walked back up the trail toward our cabin, a strange feeling stole over me all of a sudden. I felt—even now as I write this—struck by a kind of odd, sad feeling that I just can't shake . . .

October 13, 1869 . . .

Another "casualty" has appeared at our door today. The horse we sold Mr. Carey somehow found its way back here, bearing the telltale signs of being whipped—and whipped hard. Rose was the one who found her. She came running up to the porch where I was, her face streaked with tears, just as Patrick and John-Charles came up from the spring. Overhearing her story, they dropped their pails and ran for the barn. It took some doing, but I finally got them all back to the cabin and quieted down so as not to scare Bonny and her little ones. I found Lillie and Jessie first, then set off to fetch the men, who were out checking cattle. My heart hammered with dread as I rode out.

We decided to meet down at the barn to talk over the latest trouble.

"This place is becoming a regular hospital for Carey's handiwork," Stem said grimly, taking his hat off as he leaned over to take a look at the horse that had been put in a stall by one of the kids. She was lying on her side, panting, but her eyes looked almost human with the same look of relief that had been in Bonny's eyes when she'd looked up at me.

"Bet that sorry excuse was throwed while he was looking for 'em," Stem added.

Quinn was a mile past mad, pacing the barn, trying to figure out what to do, his accent getting thicker by the minute as he talked. "If it weren't for the woman, 'tis sure I'd be payin' the coward a visit, myself."

"Maybe we ought to go ahead and do just that, Quinn," Jack said, his temper getting the better of him. I felt my heart spring up in my chest, fearing the trouble might be enough to turn Jack back to his old ways. "Might be we should just go after him and give him a waylayin' like he did his woman and kids and this here horse."

"No, Jack," I said, not able to keep quiet anymore. "We all came out here to start a new life here. This will blow over. You'll see."

Jack looked doubtful, then Lillie stepped up with a determined look on her face. "You promised, Jack," she said. "We both promised. When we married, we made a promise to God that we'd live our lives different this time. You can't take that promise back just because there's trouble now." Their eyes met, and I saw something in Jack start to give under the weight of Lillie's stare. I was glad to see it.

"Look what He's done for all of us, giving us a new start and all," Lillie added.

"She's right, Jack," Stem said, shocking all of us—even Jessie, who looked as if she'd been suddenly frozen to the spot where she stood. He shook his silver head. "Ain't right t' go back on a promise—especially one t' the Almighty. He ain't played us wrong." Stem set his hat back on his head and looked around at all of us. Then, for some reason, his eyes met mine. "One thing I remember my ol' mama sayin' 'fore she died was, 'Don't give up on Him, an' He won't give up on you. No suh! No matter what it looks like, jes don't give up.'"

"Don't give up," I whispered back, and Stem cocked his head toward me and smiled. His soft smile made me remember all the times he had been there for me—for all of us over the years. A grizzled, old colored man dressed in buckskins, giving a bunch of white folks advice? Who would've ever thought? some people might say. But, again, I knew *Who*. I looked over at Quinn and saw that he knew, too.

"Don't give up," he said, soft, but there was strength in his words, too. Then Lillie was grinning, saying, "Don't give up." Then Coy and Jessie said it, too. Then we all looked to Jack, who stood looking at us like we were crazy but like he needed that kind of crazy more than anything. He took his hat off and ran his hands through his long hair and studied the floor, and I knew there was a war going on in him. A war between the man he was, and the man he wanted to be.

"Don't give up," he said, finally looking up at us, and I saw his eyes were shiny with tears.

I stayed for a while with Jack in the barn, helping him tend to the horse after everyone else had left, thinking it might give us a chance to talk in private. But he was so quiet at first that after he got her up on her feet again I took the salve and went about working it into the mare's hide after Jack cleaned her wounds. He stayed quiet, but I could feel him glance over at me from time to time, and I knew he was weighing his words.

"That was some speech Stem gave," he said after a while. "He was right with what he said—Lillie, too." He looked up at me for a moment, then his eyes went distant with thought. "Doing things the right way is hard, ain't it?" he said, turning back to me. The bewildered tone of his voice made me smile, and I told him I'd thought the same more than once in my life. Jack grinned that grin of his.

"I hope we make it, don't you?" he said then, and I nodded, remembering what Quinn had said to me that long-ago day when Jack had rode away from us, heartbroken, and I had feared I would never see him alive again. *"It's not death he's seeking,"* Quinn had said, understanding Jack more than me. *"It's life . . ."* Now I looked deep in Jack's eyes and saw the truth of Quinn's words, saw the lifetime of yearning and the newness of hope.

"I don't know why, but until all this happened, I'd pretty much put it all out of my mind, you know?" he said, and I knew he meant his life with Raven and the Blackfeet. He shut his eyes tight for a moment, like he was trying to shut out the pain of the memory. "John-Charles thinking of Lillie as his real ma . . . well, I guess it got me thinking it, too. I thought I had to let go of the past so's to have a future. Now I'm wondering if I was right. You know what John-Charles asked me tonight? He asked me if being part Indian made him part bad . . ."

"We're all going to make it, Jack," I told him, trying to swallow past the lump in my throat. "We've got each other. Most of all, we've got the Lord with us."

He looked doubtful for only a moment, then a soft smile came to his face and I saw his eyes go distant with the memory of something. "Believe in the Lord with all your heart and He will save you and your household," he said haltingly, like a baby taking his first steps. "Funny that I'd remember Mama saying that after all these years . . ."

Jack smiled kind of sheepish then and turned back to finish cleaning around the scratches on the mare's neck. The scripture wasn't perfect, but Jack remembering it left me speechless, and I thought of what the preacher had said about God using folks that were broke. I guess I was speechless too long, for I felt Jack swat me with his hat, "Cat got your tongue, sis?" he said. I shook my head and grinned.

"No," I said. "I just had this picture of Mama elbowing Pa up in heaven with that smirk of hers, saying, 'Hear that, John?' Remember how she used to look so good and pleased when she was right about something?"

Jack grinned wryly. "Yeah, it's about the same look you have on your face right now," he said, and we both laughed.

Lillie and I found the children tonight by way of their voices down at the barn—where they shouldn't have been. As we stepped inside, we could hear the children talking low amongst themselves, then I saw Bonny standing a short distance away, just watching. It wasn't until we came up beside her that we could see what was going on. Willie, still bruised and weak, was standing in the stall with Midnight, his thin arms stretched out as he offered his hand to the horse. I was afraid. But seeing the two together was like nothing I'd ever witnessed. Even John-Charles, who had an uncanny bond with horses, knew it was something special, for he, Rose, and Patrick kept their distance and just watched.

Midnight's ears flickered, then she sniffed the air and finally staggered over to the boy. With great gentleness, the horse began to nuzzle him, touching on each of his bruises with her velvet muzzle, like she was comforting his hurts. And he did the same, softly running his fingers over her scratches and scrapes, with a tenderness that brought tears to my eyes. It was as if they knew they had both suffered by the same hand, and it had forged a bond between them.

"I ain't ever saw a horse do that," Patrick said. Bonny said something in her own language that sounded like an answer. Patrick glanced to John-Charles for his take on it, but he just shrugged.

"Horses ain't like people. They have sense," Rose said with a sniff. "I'm gonna ask Pa if I can keep her now." Lillie and I grinned at each other then turned to Bonny, who had been watching her son and the horse with as much amazement as the rest of us.

"You look like Willie, kinda," Patrick said suddenly, looking at John-Charles, "'Cept for your eyes are green like Uncle Jack's. I wonder if your ma looked like Miss Bonny." Patrick just wasn't able to let go of his curiosity over his cousin being part Indian, especially now that another half-Indian boy was there to look at. I glanced over at Lillie, who suddenly looked like she had been struck.

"I know what my ma looks like . . . ," John-Charles started to say as he turned around. Then he stopped in his tracks, seeing Lillie and me standing there, and he smiled. "She's right over there," he pointed at Lillie, then ran headlong into her arms, hugging her around the waist. Lillie grinned at me with big tears in her eyes.

"Well, yes, I *am* your ma," Lillie said, petting his head. "But you had another ma, too. So that means you've been loved double, and there's not many people can say that." The happy way John-Charles looked up at Lillie made me wish Jack was there to witness it, and I couldn't help smiling, too.

It was as if in spite of all the trouble, we were being fit together, piece by piece . . . like the giant hand of Providence was putting the puzzle of our lives back into place.

"Good family," Bonny said, smiling at us.

I have to agree.

Quinn says Coy has planted himself in a tent outside his bunkhouse, and that when he rode by, he saw Coy sitting just outside the flap of the tent, cleaning his gun. I asked why he'd be there, even though I knew deep down that, without being asked, Coy had quietly accepted the job of protector over Bonny and her kids. Quinn smiled at me tenderly, and I knew he was thinking of when we first met and how he'd watched over me and my baby sister, over all our family, like we had always been his.

"A man can't help but want to protect those he cares for," he said. "Even if he isn't sure where it will lead him."

I hugged him tight, wishing I could stay wrapped in his big, comforting arms like that forever and wondering where those feelings would lead Coy . . . would lead us all . . .

October 15, 1869 . . .

Cold and windy today. The men are keeping an eye out for Mr. Carey as they bring strays back down from the high country. I feel like we're teetering on the edge of something happening, but I'm not sure what. Willa came to call earlier as I was packing up the noon meal for Coy to take out to the rest of the men.

"Something's happened, hasn't it?" she said, nearly running Coy over as she came through the door. Coy tipped his hat as he walked out, but she hardly noticed as she rushed on. "I had the strangest feeling I was being watched the whole drive over. It's too quiet, too. Where are your kids . . . where's the boy?"

I told her everything then, about the woman showing up with her daughter, how she'd been so filled with despair over everything that had happened she'd nearly taken her own life and her girl's, too. Then I told her about the horse showing up and how it had taken to the boy, even comforting him, and I saw tears fill her eyes—even though she was quick to blink them back.

"They've been through too much," I said. "We don't have any other choice but to help them."

"Oh, there is always another choice," she said, standing to her feet again. "There is the choice to stay out of the way of Jed Carey. He's not just a drunk—he's a dangerous drunk." She must have saw the stubbornness on my face, for she sat back down with a great sigh.

"Lunatics," she declared, then she bit her lip and looked at me.

"So, what can I do to help?"

October 16, 1869 . . .

True to her word, Willa has just come from town today with news of Mr. Carey, and we are not sure what to make of it. According to Mr. Audrey, Jed Carey is going around telling everyone that his wife's *people* "came like skunks in the night and made off with her, his kids, and his best horse."

"He's making quite a show of it, too," Willa said, standing in the yard with us all, "even going as far as saying he would pay a reward to get them back."

"He'll be gettin' a *reward* of his own when the good Lord gets a'holt of him," Jessie said, planting her hands upon her hips.

Stem chuckled, pulling her close to wrap his arms around her. "He surely wouldn't want to tangle with my Jess here. She's pret' near a force to be reckoned with herself," he said, then laughed again as she tried to shoo him away while looking pleased, herself.

"Why do you suppose he's made up such a tale?" Jack asked, dismounting. He wiped the dust from his face with the rag Lillie handed him then looked out to where the children were all playing together. We all looked. Bonny sat on the ground in front of the cabin, sewing contentedly on the goods she'd scrounged from us. For someone who had no real home, she looked so happy, so grateful, and I think every one of us felt the bittersweetness of it.

"He said it 'cause he's got somethin' up his sleeve, thet's why," Stem said. "Only conscience that feller has is when someone is lookin'. I know we ain't supposed to question God's creation, but a person does have to wonder sometimes . . ."

"We ain't gonna send her back," Coy said, then looked at all of us. "She has a right to *live,* don't she?" When he looked away from us all, I knew it was so he could try to hide his emotions.

"That boy was almost dead when Willa brought him here," Quinn said. "They were all almost dead. I don't think I could sleep, knowin' I sent them back to be finished off."

"Maybe it will all blow over," Willa said, but her face was doubtful, and so was Jack's. I saw it in his eyes mostly, how they were turned down at the corners that made him look so different than the Jack I had stood laughing with in the barn only a couple of days ago.

"Ma'am," he said to Willa then, shaking his head, "there's been a lot I've gambled on in my life. I'm not a betting man no more, but even if I was, I wouldn't bet on *that.*"

October 19, 1869 . . .

Jack was right about it not blowing over. Jeb Carey showed up at the ranch this morning, full of the devil himself.

Coy had spotted him as he was riding through the upper pasture and came racing to the cabins to warn us all. There was just enough time, thank the Lord, for Jessie to get Bonny and her children hidden away inside before he came trotting up. He spotted Midnight standing in one of the corrals, and I watched as he dismounted and fairly stomped to the fence where Jack, Quinn, and Stem were standing. They talked low at first, but I saw it was quickly getting heated, and I felt my heart come up clear to my throat. I started praying over and over, *Please Lord, just let him leave*, when I heard Stem say, "No, you ain't, either." Then I saw Jack hand him money, saw Mr. Carey throw the money on the ground.

"Thieves! I bought that horse fair and square," Mr. Carey hollered, and I could see the muscle in Jack's jaw jump clear from where I was standing. Then Mr. Carey started looking around, his gaze going to where Coy's cabin stood, and Lillie said under her breath, "Oh, please, God."

Coy came around the side of the corrals with his rifle, and I felt my heart drop. He said, "We don't want no trouble, mister, so you best git now." He picked the money up and tried to hand it to Mr. Carey, who looked at Coy like he was crazy.

"I ain't takin' nothin' from you, *boy*," Mr. Carey said, then Quinn took the money from Coy and handed it to Mr. Carey, the sound of his voice deadly calm.

"We don't deal with folks who mistreat their animals," Quinn said. "'Twould be best if you take your leave now."

Mr. Carey glanced back to his horse, and when I saw him eye his own rifle I ducked my head quick to pray, "Please Lord, You can't let this happen, not after we've come all this way."

I heard Lillie say "Amen" softly, and when I opened my eyes I saw her knuckles were white from squeezing the porch rail so hard. We watched Mr. Carey eye the men for a tense moment, then he got back on his horse.

"Horse thieves are hung in these parts, in case you don't know," Jeb Carey said, wheeling his horse around one last time to face Quinn.

"Maybe you should remember that, in case you think to

come here again," Quinn said evenly. "There's nothing here that belongs to you anymore."

Mr. Carey rode off, and as soon as we saw he was gone, Lillie and I headed for Coy's cabin. It was dark inside so we couldn't see nothing at first, but then Jessie, seeing it was us, lit a lamp, and we saw Bonny and Sarah over in the corner, tears rolling down their faces as they hunched over Willie, trying to calm his shaking.

"Lord forgive me for sayin' it, but I think I would have fought him with my bare hands if he'd come in here and tormented these folks again," Jessie said, looking up at us with an aching sadness in her eyes . . .

Willa came back tonight, and after hearing all that happened, she shook her head then walked over to where Bonny was sitting in front of my fireplace.

She eyed Bonny close—and Bonny eyed her, too—and I saw something pass between them, like a silent understanding of sorts.

"It might be best if Bonny and her children came to stay with me for a while," she said, more a statement than a question. Much to our surprise, Bonny readily accepted the offer. So, with heavy hearts, we helped them pack up what little they had acquired since they'd come to our place. Rose, Patrick, and John-Charles were angry, then forlorn, as their new friends climbed into Willa's wagon. Bonny hugged each one of us then surprised the children by giving them each a pair of moccasins she had made special for them.

We were all near tears. Somehow, without our really realizing it, Bonny and her children had become like family. Even the men went over to the wagon to say their good-byes. Bonny politely shook all of their hands—except for Coy. Shyly she offered him the necklace she had been wearing, reaching up gently to put it around his thick neck then turning quick to climb in the wagon. Willa watched us all with something akin to wonder on her face.

"I've never seen people care so much for folks like your family does," she said, accepting Quinn's hand to help her climb up onto the wagon seat next to Bonny. "It sure makes a person wonder . . ."

She didn't finish the thought but hawed the team on. When I turned to walk away, I saw Coy standing off to one side by himself, watching them leave with a tumble of emotions in his dark, thoughtful eyes. He didn't say anything but just watched until they were long out of sight. Suddenly that verse of Longfellow's played through my mind:

He speaketh not; and yet there lies, a conversation in his eyes. . . .

I had just got Rose and Patrick to bed (wearing their moccasins) and set down to write this when I overheard the men talking outside.

"'Been my experience that hard-boiled eggs are mostly yeller on the insides," I heard Stem saying, and I knew they were talking of Mr. Carey.

"You might be right," Jack said after a while, "but I still have a bad feeling about him leavin' so easy. There's something your pa told me awhile back, Coy, and I ain't ever forgot it."

"What's that?" I heard Coy say.

Jack cleared his throat then, and I heard him answer, "Never trust a wolf 'til it's been skinned."

Quinn must have showed up about then, because I heard his voice, then I heard them all moving away.

Oh, how I wish this trouble hadn't come to our door!

Lord, I can't say I understand why all of this has happened, just when we thought we were through with the bad times for a while. I would be lying if I said I did understand, and I know You aren't keen on liars, so I'll just ask You to please help us. Mama told me more than once that trials come to test our faith, but I recall her saying, too, that You always light our way through the darkness. Seeing the worried look on everyone's faces, and now, hearing what I just did . . . I pray Your help comes soon.

October 22, 1869 . . .

It's come as no surprise to us that Coy's decided to stay in Willa Cain's bunkhouse, as restless as he's been the past few days. "Ain't good for them ladies to be alone out there like that," he told us, shaking his head worriedly as he packed up after dinner. Jack told me once that Coy, like his pa, was the type to walk through fire for those he cared for. Selfless to a fault, is how he described him.

"You're a good man, Coy Harper," I said suddenly, and he turned and looked at me with a kind of surprised smile on his face. Then before he could say anything I ran up and hugged him, whispering I'd be praying for him.

"Why, I guess I'd appreciate that 'bout more than anything," he said, tipping his hat and smiling shyly before he mounted his horse.

Watching him ride away, I didn't know quite how to feel. I think Quinn sensed my uneasiness because he walked over to where I was standing and put his arm around me, smiling gently. "Everything's going to work out, Callie. You'll see," he said. I felt better just having him there, like everything wasn't so bad after all.

"It's a good thing seein' that young feller doin' fer 'em like he is," Stem said wistfully. "Makes an old man feel real shiny 'bout things agin."

I looked over at Jack and Lillie then and saw them smile at each other.

"Ye feel that shiny, I guess ye can get down to our cabin and finish that quilt frame for me," Jessie said, and Stem shook his head.

"Why, Jess, ye just took the poetry out of the moment," Stem said, grinning, and we all laughed. The laughter sounded so good.

Maybe things *will* get back to normal . . . A person can hope, at least, can't she?

Sabbath. Too bad we haven't heard any news about Preacher. I'm not that keen on going to town right now, but I think it would do me a world of good to hear one of his sermons—do us *all* a world of good.

November 1, 1869 . . .

It's a good thing we had Bonny and the kids go to Willa's. Mrs. Audrey came to call today with her fellow "sufferettes," as Rose calls them, and I have a feeling they would've fairly *ran* back to town with the news if they'd found Bonny here, the way they carried on about "poor Mr. Carey" at first.

Lillie, Jessie, and me were sitting on the new porch, watching the children play, when we saw the wagon with Mrs. Audrey and her twins coming our way, followed by another wagon and a buggy. Rose glanced up then stood like a startled rabbit, spotting Mrs. Audrey. Then she got a considering look on her face when she saw the twins were with her, like she was thinking the trouble of tolerating Mrs. Audrey just might be worth it for a chance to have some playmates. She and the boys watched warily as Mrs. Audrey stepped down followed by a smallish woman, dressed poor but tidy, in the other wagon, then an older, plumpish woman who groaned loudly as she stepped from her buggy. The buggy leaned dangerously side-ways as she lowered her bulk to the ground, and I saw Rose, Patrick, and John-Charles's heads lean with it as they watched. I quickly called for them, suggesting they take the twins to see the new foal down at the barn.

Mrs. Audrey was the first to reach us. "Mrs. McGregor," she said, nodding to me and then to Lillie and Jessie, "Mrs. Pumphrey, Mrs. Spence, and I thought it would be nice for us ladies to get togeth-uh—since there ah so few of us out he-ah."

"What I thought was I would be bored to death if I didn't get out of my house," the plumpish woman said, huffing past Mrs. Audrey. "I'm Mrs. Pumphrey. Do you mind if I sit a spell?" Mrs. Audrey pursed her lips, and Mrs. Spence didn't say any-thing at all. Jessie and me went and fetched the chairs from around the table, and we no more than got seated on the porch when the talk began.

"I suppose you've *hud* 'bout po-ah Mr. Carey losin' his wife and little ones?" Mrs. Audrey said, then went on before any of us could answer. "Just a puh-fect tragedy. He is offerin' a reward, you know, though I don't suppose it would have to be much— I've heard savages like that can be bribed for next to *nuth*-in'."

I thought it odd that they didn't know of "poor Mr. Carey's" visit to our place the day before, but I didn't say anything. Mrs. Spence cleared her throat and looked pointedly at Mrs. Audrey then tilted her head slightly toward Lillie.

"Oh, Delia, Mr. Wade was *captured* by them—that doesn't make him one," Mrs. Audrey said, then turned to look at Lillie. "Isn't that right, Mrs. Wade?" But before Lillie could ask what they were talking about, Mrs. Pumphrey leaned toward me.

"It's a pure wonder your brother turned out as well as he did," she said, shaking her head. "I mean, to be captured by Indians at such a young age! Then those years with the wolf pack—how did he ever manage to find you again, dear?"

It wasn't until that very moment that I realized Jack had done more than get our supplies for us that day in the mercantile. I honestly think I heard my whole family turning over in their graves. "It was surely a miracle," I said, thinking it *would* be a miracle if he wasn't struck by lightning for lying. I tried not to look at Lillie, who was coughing—or laughing—into her handkerchief. Jessie rose abruptly, saying how she had to "go check something," and I saw her shoulders shake as she went out through the door.

"Well, what I would like to know is, how did he *ev*-uh learn English?" Mrs. Audrey said.

"Oh, he always has had a way with words," I said. At least *that* wasn't a lie. Lillie got up and fetched the ginger cakes I'd made earlier while I brought out the coffee, but neither of us looked at each other for fear of laughing. Jessie stayed absent— and I'm glad now she did, the way the conversation turned then.

"You have quite a spread here," Mrs. Pumphrey started, taking a healthy bite of cake. "I imagine it takes a lot of work, though."

"A wise decision to bring yo-ah pee-ple along," Mrs. Audrey sniffed. "I'd have one of my own if Mr. Audrey would just relent."

"Stem, Jessie, and Coy are *not* our servants, Mrs. Audrey," I said, unable to put up with her hateful ways any longer. "They own their home and part of this land, too, just like we do— we're all *partners*."

"Well, I nev-uh *hud* of such a thing!" Mrs. Audrey said, her cheeks turning pink. I saw her glance over to Mrs. Spence, who looked like she had sunk so far back in the rocking chair she might disappear any moment.

"Well, the war *is* over, Leah," Mrs. Pumphrey allowed, taking another ginger cake.

A commotion caused our heads to turn as the children

came running around the corner of the house, piling in, hungry and dirty. Mrs. Audrey's twins, Zora and Nora, looked happy until they saw the horrified look on their mother's face. "What have you two . . . ," she started to say.

"Why, he looks a lot like Mr. Carey's boy," Mrs. Pumphrey said, eying John-Charles, but Mrs. Spence "reappeared" from the rocking chair long enough to elbow her.

"This is *my* son, John-Charles," Lillie said then, and I could see she had had her fill of the women, too. She put her arm around his shoulder protectively and looked straight into each woman's eyes like she was daring them to say another thing. I couldn't help thinking that her claiming him out loud like that had done something good for her. Something good for both of them.

The ladies' eyes went from Lillie to John-Charles and back to Lillie again as if trying to figure it out.

"Ma'am," John-Charles said politely to each one of them, dipping his head in a gentlemanly bow just like he'd been taught.

Patrick grinned, standing next to him. "His grandpa is a *med-cin* man," he announced proudly.

"Enough said," Mrs. Audrey announced, rising abruptly as she and the ladies quickly said their good-byes. The twins were the only ones of the bunch who looked sad to leave.

"Enough said!" I repeated sternly, then I turned back to Lillie. "First time since I met that woman that we agree on anything."

As the women climbed up into their wagons and buggy, Lillie smiled at me, but in her eyes I saw a fleeting look of hurt that she tried to hide. We watched the kids run back out the door in silence, then she turned to me again. "Why do people act like that, Callie? Like you have to be a certain way or you just don't measure up. I never have understood it," she said, shaking her head.

"I don't think God understands it, either," I said, watching the dust clouds swirl behind the departing women. Then I thought and added, "But He does say to pray for those that hurt you."

"He really says that?" Lillie said with such an earnest but worried look on her face, I had to chuckle.

"Yes, He really does," I said. "But I don't think He'd mind us asking for the strength to do it." Lillie looked at me for a long moment, then squared her shoulders.

"Well, let's pray for some strength, then," she said, and we both grinned at each other like young girls as we joined hands.

"Well, will ye look at all them teeth," Jessie said, announcing her return from her cabin. Then she must've realized why we were standing like we were, for she looked suddenly sheepish. "I guess I missed more than I thought," she added, then came and joined us in our "strengthening" prayer.

The men thought it was the funniest thing they'd ever heard when we told them over dinner what the ladies from town had said about Jack. They laughed, shook their heads, then laughed again.

I admit it was good to hear them laugh. But I did try my best to look fierce, telling Jack it wasn't the Christian thing to do, making up outlandish stories about our family and all.

"Aw now, sis," Jack said, wiping the tears from his eyes from laughing so hard. "I didn't mean nothin' by it—I just figured they'd be so busy tryin' to figure out my story, they wouldn't have time to pick on no one else." He looked over at Quinn and Stem and winked. "Like I said earlier, we're all in this together, ain't we?"

"What's this *we?*" Stem said, unable to hide the smile on his old face. "Ye got a tapeworm in there with ye?"

We all laughed at that, then talk soon turned to the ranch and what work still had to be done before winter set in for good. Stem, Jack, and Quinn took their leave not long after, to finish up with the cattle before nightfall, and we women had set to doing the dishes when Rose pulled on my skirt to get my attention.

"I asked Nora, Mama," Rose told me, her voice like a whisper as she dried one of the dishes. When I asked her what she meant, she winced and put her finger to her lips like it was a grave secret.

"I asked Nora if their mother was from the *plains*," she said with her usual flair. I looked at Lillie and Jessie, who were smiling as they dried dishes, too.

"Aw, Rose, Zora said it ain't so. She said her mama ain't a Long *or* from the plains," Patrick said, looking up from his game of marbles with John-Charles. He shook his head. "Their pa just got her in the mail, is all."

"You weren't supposed to tell," John-Charles said, looking up with a frown.

"The *mail?*" Lillie, Jessie, and me said at the same time, and Patrick shook his head at us, too.

"He-ordered-her-in-the-mail," he said then, sounding out each word slowly like he was talking to a child. "From the United of States."

"Why, he means she was a mail-order bride," Jessie said, a wide grin breaking out over her face. She winked at Lillie, who was looking a bit relieved to not have to worry about "measuring up" so much.

"Now, honey, that is news sure enough. But it *still* don't beat being kidnapped or raised by wolves," she said wryly, and we all laughed.

Stem just told me that he stopped by Willa's to "check up on things." He said Willa had went to town for supplies and Mr. Audrey just so happened to mention that the blacksmith had up and closed his shop along about noon and told Mr. Audrey he wasn't sure when he would be coming back—or if he would.

Oh, I pray that man is gone for good. We could sure use the peace.

November 2, 1869 . . .

We woke this morning to find the windows iced over with thick fingers of frost tempting us outside for a look. Opening the door brought a bitter wind, sweeping Jasper and Honey in with it, looking relieved, then confused, as Quinn and I stepped outside, shutting the door behind us, sharing a cup of coffee and the silence. It felt like we hadn't been alone in months, so we talked. About little things, really: the cattle, the horses, how they'd fare when winter set in . . . we talked about things we'd like to do to the cabin next spring.

When we fell quiet again, it was like we were still talking, but in a different way. We just stood looking at everything—the valley, the mountains, the sky—and I couldn't help thinking how close we'd become in spite of the work, in spite of even the trouble—or maybe it was because of it.

The door flew open shortly after that moment, and Patrick and Rose stared out at us much like Jasper and Honey had stared *in* at us as they shivered in the cold.

"What are ya lookin' at?" Patrick asked, and Quinn smiled at me before looking over his shoulder.

"Old Man Winter is coming," Quinn said, and I saw Rose and Patrick look up at him then peer out the door, past the yard.

"I don't see no old man," Patrick said, and we chuckled, turning to go back inside.

Rose laughed, too, like she understood, but I saw her take one last look before she shut the door. Just in case.

November 7, 1869 . . .

Stem just finished attaching the ropes to our cabins, linking us together so we won't get lost in the snow that Jack says is sure to come soon. I was sitting on the porch, taking a short break despite the cold, and was struck by the sweetness of Stem and Rose's talk, so I thought I'd write it down—if my fingers don't freeze in the meantime.

"Brains in the head saves blisters on the feet," I heard him say as Rose followed close on his heels while he nailed his end of the sturdy rope to each cabin. "Or frostbite on the toes, I shoulda said."

Rose giggled.

"But it's not snowing *yet*," she added, and he nodded, cocking his old head to one side as he looked at her.

"An' it weren't raining when ol' Noah built his ark, either, sis," he said. "That be lesson number seven hundred ninety-nine, I'm thinkin'. Do ye know what it means?"

Rose's chin tilted up in nine-year-old indignation. "Of course I do," she said. "It means you get ready for something that's coming instead of waiting 'til it's too late."

Stem conceded then. "Well, it's a good thing yer smart," he said, and Rose beamed up at him. Stem smiled, too, as he finished tacking the last of the rope. Then I watched him reach down and gently take Rose's hand in his.

"If I had a daughter I'd wish her to be smart like you," he said, and I saw Rose look up at him thoughtfully, saw her eyes go tender all of a sudden.

"I can be your daughter, too, Stem," Rose said. "I know my pa wouldn't mind sharing. He's real good like that."

I felt tears spring to my eyes then, and though I couldn't see Stem as he and Rose headed off toward Stem and Jessie's cabin to fasten the other end of the rope, I knew he must've had tears in his eyes, too. I heard him clear his throat a bit and say, "Well, yer right about yer pa bein' good, sis."

My cold fingers feel raw and sore as I write this. I have cleaned, cooked, and cleaned again today, and I just finished my mending. I'm tired to the bone, but I can't *not* write.

It's times like these I never want to forget.

Just when I think Rose is one person, she surprises me once again. Tonight she proved it by presenting us with her finished sampler after dinner. It says

> For my mama.
> One thing I know:
> I hatd evry stich I sode.
> But I love my mama,
> Pa and evin Patrik to.

It was all we could do not to laugh—Quinn almost undid me, trying to look so sober and thoughtful as he studied her work—which was surprisingly neat—but all the time laughter lighting his blue eyes.

We *did* laugh after she went off to bed, then Quinn went out to the barn and promptly made a little frame for it. I have hung it next to a sampler I did when I wasn't yet fifteen. It says

> How does the meadow flower its bloom unfold?
> Because the lovely little flower is free

down to its root,
and in that freedom, bold.

Quinn says they're a fitting pair. And I can't help but agree.

November 17, 1869 . . .

Slow morning. We've been working so hard around here to get ready for winter that I've hardly had time to take a breath. Purple-looking clouds hanging over the valley seem to bring a stillness to the air that no one can figure. It's not just the cold, but something about its looks that feels like winter.

The men have set out to try and find a wild turkey—or two. Jessie says the way they rode out of here you'd think they were desperate for something besides beef . . .

I best put this pen to rest now. There is so much to do for tomorrow!

November 25, 1869 . . .
Thanksgiving Day

And such a good day it's been, too. I feel like everything has finally settled down, no whispers or signs of Mr. C (I don't even like writing his name). Coy drove the wagon over here to bring Willa, Bonny, and the kids, and we had a fine time of it, everybody hugging or shaking hands like we hadn't seen each other in forever. The kids even got in on the hand-shaking, which sent them into a fit of giggles. They bundled up not long after and took off outside to play while we moved the furniture back and set up a long plank table in front of the fireplace that I covered with a linen tablecloth to spruce things up a bit. Then the men went to fetch more chairs from the other cabins to seat our "guests."

By the time they got back, with all the little ones trailing in behind them, we had the whole center length of the table covered with fixings. Everyone had brought something to share, so there was more than plenty. The men had given up on finding turkeys, but they supplied plenty of meat, just the same. We had roasted antelope, roasted sage hen, and—imagine!—roasted rabbit. There was beans and squash. Jessie made the gooseberry sauce, and Lillie surprised us with apple dumplings she'd made out of dried apples.

Stem, being the oldest of the group, said grace, his voice filled with great emotion. Surely there wasn't a more grateful group to say "amen" and mean it, than us. Even Bonny seemed to understand what our thanks meant as she cast a look at each of us, tears in her eyes. Willa tried to appear casual about the whole thing, but I could see she was touched, too.

Everything was so good—the food, the fire crackling in the fireplace, the laughter bursting out in all directions—that for a moment I wanted to weep, wanted us all to stay just the way we were. But too soon we were clearing the first of the dishes away while everyone complained about eating too much but kept eying the desserts anyway.

Willa, with her notorious sweet tooth, had brought two pies *and* one of the lushest cakes I'd ever seen. Quinn said it made his teeth hurt just to look at it, but that didn't stop him from going back for seconds, saying he was, "storing up for winter." Coy seconded the idea, and Willa, standing between the two, just shook her head, saying she felt like she was in the "land of the giants."

Stem struck up a lively tune on his fiddle soon after and had the children dancing a little jig as we clapped for them, laughing until our bellies ached at their antics. Then Stem played a sweet tune for Jessie, so haunting and pretty. I thought it sounded familiar, but I couldn't place where I'd heard it before. I mentioned a few tunes, trying to guess, then gave up.

"'Course ye ain't heard it. I jes made it up," Stem said

smugly with a twinkle in his rheumy eyes. "'Ode to Jessie,' it's called."

Jessie beamed a smile at Stem, and he took up the fiddle and started playing again.

"You trying to make the rest of us look bad or something?" Jack said, and Stem grinned.

"Ain't no tryin' to it," he said, and we all laughed. "Ye get as old as I am, ye better have learned at least one thing well."

"Gettin' old ain't so bad, if I handle it as good as you," Jack said.

Stem thought for a moment then answered, "Only one drawback I know of t' bein' old. An' thet's havin' sech a young memory."

"What's wrong with that?" Quinn asked, smiling.

"Why, bein' able to remember thet my body once *fit* the memory," Stem said, like it should have been obvious, and we all laughed again.

"I'm glad I met ye when ye was older," Jessie said, shaking her head. "I don't think I'd been able to put up with ye as a youngster."

"I'd a jes been fightin' the swarm of beaus tryin' to get at ye," Stem said. Jessie sniffed, but we could all tell she was pleased. Then I saw Jack look at Lillie, and I felt that odd twinge of sadness again, knowing the night was starting to end as he scooped up John-Charles's sleeping little form off the pallet in front of the fireplace. Rose and Patrick never moved a muscle when Coy went to pick up Bonny's little ones and carry them to the wagon.

Outside, Willa hugged me tighter than usual. "You take care of that family of yours, you hear," she said stepping up into the wagon.

Coy, taking extra care to help Bonny into the wagon, didn't go unnoticed by us, either. Quinn and I watched Jessie and Stem walk hand in hand back to their cabin, then he put his arm around my shoulders as we took a quick stroll back into the house.

"You'd think it was spring and not winter coming, with all this love in the air," Quinn said. I grinned up at him.

"So, the honeymoon *isn't* over yet, then?" I said, and we both chuckled.

"'Tis far from over," Quinn said after a while. Then, before we stepped back inside, he hugged me to him, wrapping his arms around me to warm me and maybe to blot out the world for a while, so it could be just me and him.

"Would God that it would always feel like this for us, lass," he whispered in my ear, and there was such a wistful note to his voice. Then he said, "Look at that," pointing to the moon that seemed to hang, bold and bright, just above the tops of the mountains, looking so big and close that it awed me—and scared me a little, too.

Every time I've thought I had a handle on this land, it overwhelms me with its grandeur, making me feel small again and unsure . . . almost like the feeling of holding a newborn in my arms for the very first time. One minute I'm so awed by the gift from God, so in love . . . then, the next minute, I'm scared to death I've been given too big a test to pass.

I almost told Quinn what I was feeling, but when I looked up at him, he was still looking at the moon. "Sometimes it doesn't seem real, does it?" he said then. "It doesn't seem possible this is our *home* now." He leaned over and kissed me so tenderly I lost what I was going to say . . .

November 26, 1869 . . .

Strange weather this afternoon. The sun shone bright while a heavy rain fell down over the valley. Some of the cattle hightailed it up the slopes for the woods, and the men had to fight to bring them down again.

By the time I went to fetch some more water from the stream this evening, it had turned bitter cold. Quinn said they could feel their own sweat freezing on them as they drove the cattle back down the mountain.

During dinner indoors tonight the men barely lasted through the meal as tired as they all are. I read Rose, Patrick, and John-Charles the "fiery furnace story," as Patrick calls it, and could barely keep my eyes open to finish. Lord help me, but I'm not done yet. Mending to finish tonight before I shut my eyes . . .

November 28, 1869 . . .

Cold, cold day.

I found Stem down at the stream when I went to fetch the water this morning. He was just sitting on the bank with his silver head cocked sideways, his breath coming out in slow streams of steam as he studied the mountains and the sky beyond. Something about the way he looked touched my heart, made me remember, too, the nights he'd sat up with me on the trail and told me stories about his life. He must have sensed me, for he suddenly turned and looked.

"I declare, I was fixed t' thinkin' I'd seen it all, 'fore I seen this here spread, Callie," he said, motioning toward the mountains and the thick clouds suspended above them. When he turned to me I saw that there was a serious but kind look to his rheumy old eyes as he smiled. "Get as old as I am, an' ya start wonderin' if all there is to see has done been seen. Good thing t' find out there's still good land *and* good people t' be knowed before yer lamp gets blowed out."

He struggled to his feet then and took the pails from me, filling them for me, "so as not to freeze them purty hands," he said. As I watched him bend over, slow and stiff like that, it was if I suddenly noticed how old he really was, how thin his shoulders looked, how the shock of silver hair seemed wispier, how his old, leathered face looked frailer as he turned back toward me. Slowly I felt something like fear fill me. Why hadn't I noticed it all before? I thought.

"I think your lamp has plenty of light left, if you ask me," I said, trying to joke past the lump in my throat. Stem chuckled, and the sound of his laugh made me feel a bit better. Watching him dip his own pails into the water, I felt myself shiver a bit.

"Ya got that right, Callie," he said with a sudden mischievous glint to his eye. "Lots left to do—ol' Jess's quilt frame fer one thing. If'n I don't get it finished soon . . . well, I don't think heaven itself could hide me from that kind of wrath," he added, and we both grinned, walking up the path to our cabins.

It's dark now and so much colder tonight. We saw a herd of deer walking past the cabins earlier, easy as you please, then while we were eating dinner, a big buck came up to our front window and pressed his face right up against the glass to look in. It scared Jasper and Honey so that they yipped and ran for cover under our bed, causing us all to laugh. Our laughter seemed to offend the buck, for he suddenly jumped at the noise and bolted into the brush.

November 30, 1869 . . .

Another cold day. The thick layer of frost this morning upset Stem's horse as he was heading out to check on the cattle and sent him tumbling, scaring Jessie half to death—scaring us all. Stem just laughed it off. "I got more lives than a cat, Jess, ye ought t' know that by now," he said and got right back up on his horse.

Best close for now. The wood box is getting low again, and I still have some baking to do.

Later—We had no more than laid our heads down when a hard wind picked its way through the valley, moaning against the cabins. The noise got louder, and all of a sudden I felt the cabin shudder. Quinn and I sat up at the same time, then we heard Lillie's frightened voice come from way off shrieking, "Jack, where's John-Charles?" We scrambled then, throwing our clothes on, lighting lanterns. Rose was standing in her shift with the cabin door wide open when we got to her.

"Look, Mama," she said, her voice hushed with awe. We followed her gaze in shocked silence as we looked upon the herd of wild horses huddled amongst our cabins. Then we saw John-Charles, plain as day, right in the middle of the herd, holding his hand out to one of the horses, smiling.

"I'll distract them, Jack," Quinn called. "You grab the boy."

Quinn eased himself out the door as Stem appeared and headed for the opposite side of the herd. Strange enough, the wild horses didn't seem the least bit frightened. We all watched them in awe as they pawed the ground, throwing their heads back and snorting puffs of steam as if to let us know they had laid claim to the yard.

"Dern if they don't act like we're the ones trespassin'," I heard Stem say, and for some reason the sound in his voice made me uneasy.

Jack finally got ahold of John-Charles while Quinn and Stem worked for nearly another hour, trying to run the horses off from the cabins by waving their arms and coaxing them to go instead of having to use their guns and startle our own herds.

The uneasiness that settled over me when I first saw the horses has stayed with me tonight as I write this. I get these kinds of feelings sometimes. My mama and her mama before her had feelings about things, too. Mama used to say it was just God giving His children notice about things, but I'm not exactly sure what this feeling means . . .

I just wish I knew . . .

I decided to take a walk after everyone else went back to bed tonight since I couldn't get to sleep. I couldn't help thinking of Stem's words as I looked out across the valley, and I did feel like a trespasser for some reason, felt like maybe it wasn't our promiseland after all and those mustangs had every right to resent us.

Are we supposed to be here? I asked the land—asked God.

I didn't get an answer. But as I hugged the blanket around my shoulders, feeling the bite in the air that promised the snow to come, I knew the land would have its say before it answered my question.

And so would God . . .

Oh, this beautiful, awful land . . . Lord, how can I love something and, now, fear it, too?

> *Why art thou cast down, O my soul?*
> *and why art thou disquieted within me? . . .*
> —PSALM 42:11

PART TWO

Out of the Wilderness

Then the peple got scairt an forgot
everthing. They evin forgot wich way
they was goin and got lost in the
wilderness. Moses liftd his arm agin and
askd God to show them The Way.
And God did.

By Rose McGregor
age 9 1/2
Mountana Teritery, 1869

I feel like we woke up in a different land today. It's almost *balmy* outside, the big, wide sky so blue it doesn't seem real after the days of cloudy, snow-choked sky and chilled wind. Jack says it's a *Chinook* wind but that the miners back in Virginia City called it the *fickle lady* because it blows into your life one minute, all sunny and warm, and the next, it leaves you back out in the cold without so much as a good-bye. I hope she doesn't change her mind for a while.

I feel so much better about everything—I think we all do. Lillie, Jessie, and me had such a good visit at Lillie's cabin. She showed us a quilt she had made, calling it her memory quilt. We had never seen such a pretty quilt and told Lillie so. She fairly beamed at us then told us how it came to be. Each scrap, she said, had come from a part of her life, some parts good and some not so good. There was an embroidered handkerchief of her mama's, pieces of her pa's overcoat, scraps of an old linsey-woolsey dress her friend Ely had given her right after her pa had died when she was just a girl. Another scrap was from a dress that must've held a bad memory, for she passed right over it and didn't say where it was from. In the middle of all of these delicately sewed pieces was two appliquéd wildflowers, one yellow and one blue, for each of the dresses Jack had bought her when they first met.

"I was going to sell it in a church raffle back in Virginia City," Lillie told us, smiling softly, "a kind of send-off to my past . . . But then a preacher's wife came to look at it, and she said something that made me think I ought to keep it."

"What?" Jessie and me both said at the same time, and we looked at each other and grinned. Lillie smiled, too, then gazed down at her quilt.

"She told me that a good quilter doesn't choose the pieces with her eyes but with her heart. She said if you do that, then no matter how ugly it might seem at first, how bad the colors clash, the quilt would always turn out good in the end when you put the whole thing together." Lillie looked back up at us then. "Suddenly I didn't want to give my memories away. I wanted to keep them, because I knew I had chose the pieces with my heart."

"That's about the prettiest story I've ever heard," Jessie said softly, and I couldn't help but agree.

December 2, 1869 . . .

The "fickle lady" has decided to stay on another day.

I went to fetch some water from the spring this afternoon and found Stem and Rose sitting close on the bank of the stream as they tried their hands at fishing. I almost joined them when I heard Rose talking about how she hated "that Mr. Carey fellow through and through for hurting the horse and his own little boy." I stood back a ways then and watched Stem set his own pole down gently as he peered over at Rose, real thought-fullike.

"Hate makes ye a black heart, and it don't change the other feller none either," he said, then cocked his head to one side. "That's lesson—what number be it, sis?" There was a pause as Rose cast her line in, then she nodded to herself.

"Eight hundred and ninety-nine," she announced gravely, and I couldn't help but smile to myself.

"Thet many, eh? Well, I ain't one to dispute sech a figger—not with a smart whip like you as my counter, but there's more to be had. If anything ever happened to me, I'd want to make sure ye'd be ready for the world."

"Ain't nothing ever gonna happen to you, Stem," Rose said, her voice so sure. "The preacher said God gives us whole new bodies, so I'm praying for you a new one. I thought about just praying for you a new leg, but I figured if you could get a whole body, you'd probably want that."

I saw Stem smile then, and he cleared his throat. "I thank ye for that, sis," Stem said. "I always figgered I'd have to wait to git the whole package once't I got t' the pearly gates."

"Well, you can't go to heaven just yet," Rose said matter-of-factly. "God's too smart for that, Stem. He knows we need you here."

"Well then, thet settles it, don't it, sis?" Stem chuckled and Rose giggled. I felt my heart swell with love for the dear old man who had loved all of us like we were his own.

I left them like that and came back to the cabin, thinking of how I might thank Stem without giving it away that I'd overheard their little talk. It wasn't until a few hours later, when Quinn and Jack said they were wanting to take a trip into town, knowing the good weather wouldn't last forever, that I found my chance.

I asked Stem if he was planning on going into town, too. He shook his old white head at me and grinned. "No, I promised Jessie I'd finish that quilt frame, and today I aim to do jes that," he said amiably. "Might as well jes leave the young'uns to me, too. The little britches ain't been too keen on me jes takin' Rose fishin'. If'n I git Jessie's quilt frame done, I might ought to take them all down to the crick for a day of it."

Stem was smiling with his head kind of cocked to one side like he always did, as if he was already imagining the afternoon, and before I knew it, I had leaned over, hugging him tight as I planted a kiss on his leathery old cheek.

"What's thet for?" he said, shocked, but I could see he was touched, too.

"Because as hard as I try, I can't find enough words for how I feel in my heart," I said then, feeling my eyes mist over.

"Well now, honey, ye don't hafta. I feel the same 'bout you, too." Stem grinned then and touched his hand to the cheek I had kissed, shaking his head. "Said it before, and I'll say it agin: If'n I was younger I would've give that Irish whelp a run for his money," he declared, and we both laughed.

December 3, 1869 . . .

The worst thing has happened. Oh, Lord, I would pray for courage to get through this, but I don't think even courage is enough to keep my heart from breaking to pieces.

We were coming home from town and had only pulled into the yard of the ranch when we heard the awfulest crying—heart-wrenching keening that I will never forget until the day I die. I ran through the door of the cabin to find Rose holding Patrick and John-Charles tight in her arms, rocking, the awful crying I'd heard coming from her. I asked her where Stem was, feeling an awful foreboding in my body, like my legs wanted to give out, like I didn't really want to hear. Then she told me, her voice shaking as Quinn held her and the boys. Bonny's husband had come back, had seen Midnight in the corral. Stem and the kids were in the house and hadn't heard him ride up. He'd slammed open the door and stood there looking at them with an angry smirk on his face. Then his eyes had fallen to their feet, and he saw the moccasins Bonny had made them.

"He took his gun out, Mama, started waving it at us," Rose sobbed. "Stem stepped in front of us and told him they'd step outside. I yelled at Mr. Carey not to hurt my uncle, and he just laughed and said I was blind. He said white girls couldn't have Negroes for uncles."

Rose was crying so hard the words poured out of her in a gush of sobs and hiccups. "Mr. Carey shoved Stem when he went through the door, and Stem shoved him back. Then Stem turned to me and said for me not to ever forget, said sometimes it's a good thing to be blind . . . Mr. Carey pushed his gun up against Stem's back and made him walk up the hill. You know Stem can't walk fast, but Mr. Carey kept pushing him with the gun. We couldn't see after that, but Mama, we heard a shot! Then Mr. Carey came back, and Stem wasn't with him. We wanted to hurry to find Stem and help him, but Mr. Carey told us to stay in the house and keep our mouths shut or we'd be even sorrier than we already were. Then he got back on his horse and rode off. Mama, you gotta find Stem and help him! I'm afraid Mr. Carey hurt him!"

"Which way did they go, lass?" I heard Quinn ask her gently, but I was already out the door, running past Jack and Lillie and Jessie, who had just pulled into the yard behind us in the other wagon. I ran blindly, but somehow I found Stem. He was lying just over the hill that sloped down to the stream. His clothes were still smoking from the gunshot when I got to him.

I knelt down, trying not to cry as I waved the smoke away from him so I could unbutton his vest, but he put his shaky hand on mine. "Don't," he rasped. "Too late."

"It don't seem right, someone so young'd have so much hate," Stem said then, almost like he was talking to himself. "Whenever I thought to hate, I'd jes look at this land God made—or some sweet child, like little Rose, with so much God in her new eyes—and I'd think, 'What's to hate?'"

My tears were falling on his face as he drew in a quick, sharp breath. "What's to hate?" he said again, a bare whisper, and I looked up and saw Jessie running toward us, her skirts flying. Quinn, Lillie, and Jack weren't far behind. The whole world was running, but none of us were quick enough.

"Lord Almighty, Callie," he whispered, "I wish this was a bad dream an' I could jes wake up."

I believe Stem did wake up . . . just not for us . . . not for us.

Stem died in my arms just as Jessie reached us, sobbing, "Not before me! Oh, Lord, don't take *him* before *me!*" She knelt down and touched his face, and he looked at her one last time with love, then regret. And then he closed his eyes, and there was a hush that seemed to still the air around us. When I looked down at Stem the regret was gone, and he looked younger somehow. There was a softness to his face I'd never seen and a smile that looked a bit like relief and joy mixed together.

It was like he was remembering . . . remembering how good it was to see God's face again . . .

I'm not sure how much later it was, but after we'd gotten Stem's body back to his and Jessie's cabin and were beginning the sad work of laying him out, I looked up to see Jack, Quinn, and Coy saddled up and riding out. I knew they were going after Stem's killer. All I can think of as I write this is, no matter what happens, it's not enough. It won't bring him back. It *won't* bring him back . . .

How long ago was it that you told me I'd get used to death, dear friend? After all these years that's passed, I still haven't, Stem. I guess it's like you always liked to say, this might be one trick even a young pup can't learn.

December 4, 1869 . . .

Early—They tracked Mr. Carey to one of the meadows in the high country. Quinn told me he was so busy looking over his shoulder, galloping his horse and shooting wild at them, that he failed to see the bluff ahead. His horse saw it, though, and all of a sudden it balked and reared, and Mr. Carey fell off. He was still holding the horse's reins, though, trying to get back on, but the horse was wild. And right on the edge of that bluff, the horse reared again, and Mr. Carey backed up to miss getting trampled—and slipped over the edge. They found him at the bottom with his neck broke and ended up burying him where he lay.

I don't know what to write, what to feel. God's justice? That's what Jack says. But I don't feel any sort of justice about it, and I won't pretend to know the Lord's mind. But I couldn't imagine Him feeling good about any of this, either.

Knowing Mr. Carey is dead doesn't bring Stem back to us, and that's the *only* thing that would make me feel better right now.

I have just returned from helping Jessie get Stem's body ready for burying. We could hear Jack's awful hammering of the coffin as we worked at the grim task, and I looked up once to see Jessie staring at an object shadowed in the corner of their little cabin, a large wooden ring standing on two stout legs. "He finished my quilt frame, just like he promised," she said, her voice soft. When she dropped her head and looked at me her large dark eyes were so full of the hurt I felt, I wanted to run away.

"I went looking for Stem this mornin'," she said softly. "Sounds crazy, I know, but I kept thinkin' maybe somewhere outside he'd be able to come to me, tell me he was okay." She shook her head. "I kept walkin' and walkin', and I started thinkin', *Where is he that he can't tell me he's okay—and who is God not to let him?*" She was silent for a long while, then she looked at me, looked right in my eyes and said, "You think God only answers white folks' prayers, Callie?"

If I hadn't been sure my heart was already broke her words would have done it for sure . . . "He didn't answer about my baby sister, Rose, or my pa—or my ma before that," I said slowly. "I think He's color blind to us, Jessie, when He chooses to say yes—and when we don't want to hear His no."

"Jes seems like more no's than yes's, don't it?" Jessie said as I helped her dress Stem in his Sunday best, trying so hard not to cry that my hands trembled. Jessie looked down at him for a moment, then at me, studying my face for a long time. I don't know what she saw, but when she started talking, her eyes took on a faraway look.

"Yes, ma'am, I've been told no before . . . ," she said softly. "I asked the Lord, begged Him, not to let them sell my man and little ones away from me—but they was sold anyways. When I got my freedom, I asked Him to help me find my family. But I never found them, not a one, and oh, how I searched! It was in one of the last of those towns that I gave up on life. White man in town caught me by the sleeve and told me my free papers didn't mean nothin', said any of my kind would serve him as he pleased and if I felt to say anything, he'd just shoot me."

Jessie sighed and told me how she'd got away from that man, how she ran and ran until she got all the way out of town, how when night fell she found some thick brush to hide in. "I was sittin' in that brush when it struck me. I thought, *Oh, what's the use?* I remembered stories my own mama told me about the Lord comin' for folks on fiery chariots, and I looked up in the night sky and said, 'Why don't Ye jes come get me, then? There ain't nothin' good come of my life, and now I can't even find my family. So jes come get me. It don't even have to be a fiery chariot. Amen.'" Jessie turned to me then, smiling a wry smile.

"As ye can see, He didn't come. Well, I got to cryin' real pitiful-like when I saw He wasn't comin'. I was cryin' over all I'd lost, and suddenly this big voice comes up inside of me, getting so loud I felt it on the outside, too. Scared me something silly. The voice say, 'Jessie, yer not finished yet. Ye ain't lost yer family. This is just part of the journey ye gotta walk without 'em.' So I got up and started walkin' again.

"One night I set down to rest, and I was struck by how lonely I was, so I decided to try talkin' to the Lord again. I said, 'Lord, I've walked a goodly part of this journey now alone. I sure would appreciate some company.' Didn't think any more about it. I got up next mornin' same as always and started walkin' again. 'Bout noon was when I came across yer wagon train. Then Stem showed up on that horse of his'n, with that smile a mile wide, and I knew the Lord had sent him. But I tested the poor man all the way to California." Jessie chuckled with the memory, but then her smile dimmed, as if she suddenly remembered Stem was gone.

"I must be a fool," she said suddenly, startling me.

"Why would you say such a thing?"

"Because I fixed it my mind the Lord was done tryin' me," she said, frowning. "Ain't none of us gonna be done with trials 'til we die." She looked at me, her smile trembly. "I just didn't want to be alone in the trials no more, is all."

"But you aren't alone, Jessie," I said in a rush, trying not to cry. "You still have us."

"Yes I do, at that," she said, walking slowly over to the beautiful quilt that had been spread so proudly over the little bed in the corner. She pulled the quilt off and tucked it gently around Stem's still, cold form.

"It just doesn't seem right for ye to be so quiet, husband," she whispered.

When she looked at me again, she tried to smile, but the smile seemed lost in the lines and wrinkles that were etched in her face like a living map of pain and endurance.

Later—Just woke up from a bad dream. I was holding Stem in my arms again, yelling up at the sky, *No, No, No!* over and over again . . .

Why is it that we yell *No*, knowing good and well how useless it is? Do we think if we yell loud enough that God will listen? Or is it so we can't hear the horrible sound of our own hearts breaking?

We'd laid Stem out on his and Jessie's kitchen table. The men had carried Jack and Lillie's table in, too, to support his cold, rigid form now covered with Jessie's beautiful quilt. Then, as night fell, we'd gathered around him to begin the long, sad vigil until dawn, huddling together like calves lost in a storm. Jack tried to lighten things. "Remember when Stem . . ." I can't *remember* now what he even said, but I remember we kind of laughed at first, then we all cried. Everyone of us.

Finally the men sent us women away, saying we should put the kids to bed and get some sleep ourselves. Sadly, Lillie and I hugged Jessie as she slipped into the bed she and Stem had shared, then we went to our own cabins, leading the weary youngsters along the dark paths.

I sent the kids to their beds and fell asleep almost immediately myself but awoke just as quickly when the dream stirred my thoughts. Quinn heard me crying out just as he'd stuck his head in the door to check on us. He settled beside me on the bed, trying to comfort me, wrapping his big arms around me, arms that had been there to hug me when I lost my pa and baby sister . . . when Jack rode away and I feared never seeing him again. All I could think was *Why?* I didn't even realize I'd said the word out loud until Quinn turned me to him.

"There are no reasons I can find fitting, lass," he said softly. "Never will be—none ever good enough, that is." I couldn't see his face, but I heard the horrible grief in his voice and the sigh that followed. "'Tis sure the devil's boots don't creak when he sneaks up on us," he whispered, and I knew by the tone he was thinking of his brother, the one we named Patrick after.

Suddenly I felt the need to have Rose and Patrick with us. I scooped Patrick out of his bed and put his sleepy body in between Quinn and me, then I went for Rose, too, but she refused to be comforted. "Go away, Mama," she said, turning her back to me, giving the wall her grief instead of me as she sobbed quietly in the dark.

I thought to go back to bed, but instead I lit the lamp and settled at the kitchen table so I could write this, hoping I might feel better if I got the feelings out of me and onto paper, but I don't.

I feel like Elisha tonight, running from the evil that's at my heels, like I'm just running and running to that desert place— only it's in my mind that I'm running. I have to wonder, If I was running for real, would I come back . . . ?

Oh, Lord, sometimes I just want to climb out of my skin, just shake it off like a dirty overcoat. Just climb out and call to You, Lord, like Jessie did, to come get me, come take me away from all this ugliness I've seen.

Where's your faith? a small voice whispers, and I say, It's here. See, I know that You are here, God, I know You are creator of all. I know You're a God of love that's so pure, like when I looked at Stem, dying, and saw him looking back at me—that love, that's You . . . It's just that sometimes this world dirties that love, and it's so hurtful to witness . . .

December 5, 1869 . . .

The sun is dawning over the mountains in the distance, and I feel like it has no right.

I slept no more last night. Occasionally, looking out our cabin's window, I could see the glow of a cheroot in the dark outside Jessie's porch, and I knew it was Jack's. When it got light enough for me to see him, I watched him walk slowly to the barn. Through the open doors I saw him bend beside the coffin he'd built and lift it onto his shoulder. He looked up and spotted me watching him through the window then, his eyes so full of sorrow. He carried the coffin into Jessie's cabin then emerged again and trudged slowly my way. I opened the door and motioned toward the coffee I'd poured for him at the table.

"Seems like no matter where we go, sis, we always end up makin' a trip to the grave," he said softly, and I felt the tears start fresh tracks down my cheeks. Tears for Stem, tears for us.

"It's been too many trips, Jack," was all I could manage to

say, and he just nodded and headed back down the path to Jessie's cabin.

I went to the spring to fetch some water, and when I came back, Patrick was already up and about. As I opened the door, he looked startled, then said, "Shut the door, Mama. It's . . . it's cold out there!" Then he burst into tears.

We buried Stem just before sunset, and if there were any days I could erase from my mind, it would be this one. It hurts to write about this, but it hurts more not to. I'm not sure if that would make any sense to anyone but me.

I know it was cold, but I can't remember *being* cold. I remember Patrick holding my hand so tight as he squared his little shoulders, trying so hard to be strong for me like his pa. Willa kept taking a few steps forward, then she'd stand still for a moment, only to take another few steps, like she wasn't sure where to stand. Bonny wept softly as her little ones clutched her skirts. Her beautiful hair, cut off to show her mourning—not for her husband, Coy told me earlier, but for Stem.

"She's no hypocrite. I'll give her that," Quinn said under his breath as he stood by my side. When I looked at her, I saw her eyes catch mine and tried to smile, but I couldn't seem to get it right. Jessie saw me struggling, and she started crying, then I did, too.

Then I wondered whether people knew if they were going out of their minds. If they did, I hoped I would, so I could pretend I wasn't there.

Jack shifted then, standing on the other side of me beside

the grave—as he had done twice before. But this time he didn't run. He remained, firm and unmoving, with Lillie on the other side of him holding John-Charles's hand. I couldn't help thinking that Jack was like those wild mustangs, so determined to keep the ground they had found—no matter what. He cleared his throat, but a sob escaped anyway as he opened the family Bible.

I felt Quinn's arm go around my shoulders as Jack began to read the Scripture verse—but I don't recall which one. Then I heard him say good-bye to Stem, heard everyone saying good-bye but me, and I looked away, trying to escape it . . . My eyes rested on Willa, who had been standing silent through the whole thing, her gaze fixed on that freshly turned mound of dirt.

"I guess no one knows he came and helped me from time to time. No, he wouldn't have told it," she said to no one in particular, shaking her head.

"He was too good for this world," she blurted out suddenly, almost angry, surprising us all. Then she burst into tears and fairly ran for her wagon. We all stood there, just watching her go, too weary to do anything about it.

The men began to lower the coffin, and I saw Jessie take a sudden step forward. She was looking down into the hole, and suddenly I knew what she was thinking.

"Jessie," I said softly, and she hesitated, looking at me.

"No, yer right, Callie," she said, almost a whisper. "I don't have to climb in there to feel dead, do I?"

Quinn, Jack, and Coy hurried to cover the grave after that, worried that Jessie might try something if they didn't. But I could see that she was played out. Lillie and I went over and stood by her side as they finished up. Even after Coy and Bonny left, we stayed with her.

"I just can't leave yet," she told us more than once, so the men took Patrick and John-Charles back to the cabin, and Lillie and me stayed, wrapping ourselves with the blankets they brought out. Then they brought us coffee, and we still stayed with Jessie, watching as the little light that was left dipped down behind the mountains.

Jack finally came and fetched Lillie, saying it wasn't good for her or the baby to be out in the cold. He handed me the Bible as he left. Then Quinn was walking toward us, carrying something in his arms. In that quiet way of his, he showed us the good-sized stone he'd carved Stem's name in, just like he'd done on that rock in Nebraska for Pa. He couldn't fit much else, so underneath Stem's name, he simply put "John 15:13."

I held the lantern up and read the scripture out loud to Jessie. "Greater love hath no man than this, that a man lay down his life for his friends" is what it said.

We watched Quinn dig another, smaller hole and settle the stone in it at the head of the grave. "It's fitting, isn't it?" I said gently, and I saw Quinn turn and look up at Jessie, hoping he had done something to help somehow. Her eyes met his with such gratefulness—and such heartache.

"More than fittin'," she said softly.

I felt something wet hit my face and looked up to the sky to see the first thick flakes of snow falling hard and heavy, spiraling down toward us through the sky, and for some strange reason, I couldn't help hoping it never stopped.

Later—Still snowing.

I just came down from trying to comfort Rose, but she's having none of it. I don't understand it, but I can't shake the feeling she's blaming herself in some odd way . . .

Quinn told me that he heard Rose crying softly from her little loft room while I was with Jessie. He said he climbed up to comfort her but found Patrick leaning over her bed, patting her back softly with his chubby little hand, saying, "Don't cry, sister, don't cry." He said he noticed John-Charles on the other side of the bed then, watching intently for a moment before taking his side of Rose's back and beginning to pat her, too.

Quinn crept back down the ladder before any of them noticed he was there.

"'Twas a sacred moment," he said with tears in his eyes. "One I won't forget as long as I live. If you could have seen them comforting her . . ."

"I just can't understand why she wouldn't come to his grave with us," I said, tears in my own eyes. "She loved him as much as any of us, maybe more."

"You've just answered it yourself, lass," Quinn said then. "'Tis said that the chief mourner is rarely found at the funeral. Our Rose, her feelings have always run deep. So deep it worries me sometimes. I fear one day they could lead her wrong."

"She wasn't wrong to love Stem," I said, looking up into his worried eyes, and I saw a gentling come in them.

"No," he said softly. "If loving such a man as him were wrong, we'd all be at fault, wouldn't we?"

He hugged me to him then, and as he did, I silently prayed that God would see Rose through this terrible time—see us all through.

He is our only hope. I know *none* of us have the strength ourselves.

December 8, 1869 . . .

Cold wind today. I keep wishing I could tell Stem just one more thing. What would it be? My mind races, I think of so much: *I love you. I miss you, miss your laughter and your love* . . . I suppose I could write things forever, so maybe I don't wish I could tell him one more thing, I just wish he was here. I know we're not supposed to question God, but I can't help it. Can't help wondering why. My faith feels so shaky . . .

Rose finally came down from the loft this evening after everyone else had turned in. I was sitting up by myself, mending Quinn's trousers, when I heard her step quietly down the ladder and pad her way over to the rocker where I sat sewing. She stood, watching me in silence for a bit, then stepped in front of me. I set my sewing aside, and she came to me, curling up in my lap just as she always did when troubled.

I told her I'd tried to run from pain, too, tried to hide, but I'd found out hiding was lonely.

"It's my fault, Mama," she blurted out, and then it was as if a dam had broke open and she started to cry. "It's all my fault. I prayed for Stem to have a new body—but I didn't mean for God to take him to heaven." She sobbed harder, and I hugged her to me, whispering comfort in her ear the best I could, feeling tears of my own trickle down my face. "It's not your fault, honey," I whispered. "God just chose to take him home."

"But I thought *this* was his home," Rose said, the misery of trying to understand so strong in her blue eyes. Then her eyes turned angry.

"I hate Mr. Carey," she said then. "And I don't care if I have a black heart for it, either. Stem, Jessie, and Coy are *all* black, and I'm gonna be just like them!" She burst into a fresh round of tears then, leaning against me, saying, "Why, oh why, Mama?" until I felt another rip in my heart, wondering just how much a heart *could* take.

I didn't try to tell her the whys of it, for I didn't know myself. But I kept her hugged close to me, and we rocked for a long while like that, not just mother and daughter, I thought, but two hurt souls, trying to find comfort the best way we knew how . . .

He will swallow up death in victory; and the Lord GOD will
wipe away tears from off all faces. . . .
—ISAIAH 25:8

Promiseland

I wish I could describe how I feel. Sometimes there just isn't the words . . .

I look at the words I've just written, and they are nothing—mean nothing. Just dark scratches on a page.

Please help me, Lord.

December 11, 1869 . . .

I saw the preacher pull into our yard just as I was coming from the spring this morning, my hands almost froze to the pails as I walked slowly up the hill toward him. I saw Preacher look toward the corrals where the men were, then to me, and he smiled a sad kind of smile and headed in my direction. He took the pails from me like he needed to busy himself as he talked. He said he'd heard about Stem as soon as he rolled back into town and it hit him nearly as hard as the deaths of his own parents. He shook his head, like he was trying to understand, then looked sideways at me.

"There was something about him," he said softly. "Something I saw that first night, like he was there to comfort me—not the other way around."

I felt my eyes burn a bit, nodding. "Stem was always a rock to all of us," I said. "I don't know what we'll do without him—what Jessie will do without him . . ."

He looked down at me then, his dark eyes so full of sorrow and compassion that I felt I could look into them forever. "Trials come to test our faith," he said, setting the pails down, and he turned and looked toward the mountains that loomed in the distance. "Beautiful country," he said, and I laughed kind of a harsh laugh that surprised even me.

"We thought it was going to be our promiseland here," I said. "And Stem believed it more than anyone."

Preacher looked at me thoughtfully, then said, "Sometimes I think of all those poor souls Moses led out of Egypt. They saw the Red Sea part, ate bread from heaven, and still, when the trials came, they forgot. They ended up wandering year after year because they forgot God was God . . . They forgot that all they had to do was step forward and reach their hands out and God would've led them home. Don't let death take your hope from you, Mrs. McGregor," he said, turning toward the path that led to Jessie's cabin. Then he stopped for a moment, looking across the land again, and he turned back to look at me one last time. "This *is* your promiseland. Stem wouldn't have wanted you to forget."

I stood outside a long time after dinner, just as the sun was starting to dip behind the mountains, and I felt my eyes drawn to the sky . . . so much sky. As I looked up into that ocean of blue, I couldn't help thinking on what Preacher had said. *Stem wouldn't have wanted you to forget.* The words whispered to me again, and as I lifted my arm up and held my hand to the sky, watching the fading sunlight filter through my fingers, a peace came over me that I had never felt before, warm and comforting. I shut my eyes and prayed then. "Don't let us forget, Lord," I whispered, and I could've sworn I felt the firm grasp of a hand covering my own . . .

Rose asked if she could go down and see Jessie tonight. I had so many chores to catch up on, but it was the first time since Stem died that she had mentioned going anywhere outside the house, so we went, trudging through the fresh snow, Jasper and Honey tagging along, strangely silent and nuzzling Rose's hand as if they understood.

As Jessie opened the door to us, we stepped into the warm little cabin, and I saw Rose's eyes go to the spot where Stem always sat to play his fiddle. The fiddle was still there, gleaming by the light of the fire, and I saw her face start to crumple as she looked Jessie in the eye for the first time.

"I'm so sorry, Jessie," Rose sobbed, great tears streaming down her face, her little shoulders shaking. She told Jessie about her prayer then, and I saw Jessie smile, but it was a grim kind of smile.

"There, there, sis," Jessie said, her large, callused hand patting the small of Rose's back. "Ain't no one's fault. The Lord jes allowed this to be Stem's time, is all. Preacher said there ain't nothin' the Lord don't know. We jes got to trust He knows best." I saw Jessie's eyes go distant then, to that place we go when we give up looking for the answers the world gives us. The look was sad and questioning, then finally accepting.

Rose wasn't so accepting. "Well, if I was God, I'd know it wasn't best to take Stem from us," she said hotly, and it was on the tip of my tongue to correct her when I saw the barest hint of a smile cross Jessie's face.

"Well, ye ain't God, child, so don't go talkin' like that," she said sternly but gently, like she understood. Rose looked up at her, sensing that, then placed her hand in Jessie's. She looked around the little cabin with a kind of longing.

"Can I stay the night with you, Jessie?" she asked suddenly, and when Jessie's eyes met mine we both knew without saying she was trying to get as near to feeling Stem as she could. Because Jessie understood that, she agreed.

"Can't think of any way better to spend my evenin'," Jessie said.

When I left them, they had their heads bent over a small, leather-bound box that Stem had carried everywhere he went. As I trudged back up to our cabin, Jasper and Honey in tow, I remembered something Stem said long ago. "Sometimes the reasons fer things happenin' don't seem good," he'd told me, "but the Almighty has a way of makin' good of it all in the end."

December 13, 1869 . . .

It's a mystery to me why things panned out like they did tonight. My reasons for going out to Willa's place were purely selfish, but I think the good Lord had other plans . . .

I'd told Quinn when he hitched the team for us that the trip was for Rose, but I think it was for me, too. No sooner had I bundled the two little ones in the back of the wagon and hawed the team away from the ranch than this strange, childish thought came to me: *If you don't see it, it isn't real.* I thought I could almost pretend Stem's death hadn't really happened. In spite of my praying, the look of Rose's forlorn little face looking up to the sky from time to time throughout the day had got me down, and all I could think of was to get away from it all. By the time we reached Willa's place, I started pondering why I'd felt so drawn to come when I hardly knew her at all. I saw Coy's rig and knew he would be visiting with Bonny. Life went on, I thought, whether we felt like it should or not. I considered leaving, but then I spotted Willa standing on her porch, like she was expecting us.

She watched me help Rose down and gather Patrick into my arms, then she said, "Seems like everyone had the same idea today." Without another word, she reached to take Patrick from me. He looked at her, wide-eyed, then something in his face showed he liked what he saw, and he went to her. Willa acted like it was nothing, but I could see it touched her as she led me and Rose into the house wordlessly.

The kitchen was filled with the smell of fresh coffee and fresh-baked bread. It was decorated pretty, too, with little engravings and dry flowers on the wall and a floor so clean you could eat off it. As I sat down at the table with Willa, I couldn't help thinking everything seemed made for company, like the house had just been waiting. Willa poured us each a cup of coffee, and not long after Rose and Patrick had scampered off to find Bonny's little ones, we started talking—or I should say I did. I told Willa about Stem's headstone, and about Rose, then I told her about the preacher coming and what he'd said. Willa nodded through most of it until I came to the part about the preacher. Her eyes fairly sparked with fire then.

"Well, that's fine to *say*," she said. "But where's the proof of it? Seeing is believing, I always say. And I haven't seen much proof in my life . . ." I saw the spark in her eyes dwindle a bit, and she looked down at the gold ring she wore, rubbing it softly with her finger. The prongs where the stone should've been were smoothed over by wear, and I wondered how many times she had rubbed her finger over that ring.

"I used to believe in a lot of things, Callie," she said, not looking up at me. "The reason I wear this ring is to remind me why I don't believe anymore." She told me then about the girl she was before the war, about the handsome young boy she used to race every day after school until she realized one day she *wanted* him to catch her. How he'd become a soldier for the North and how her mama had given her the ring when they announced their engagement.

"Have you ever looked in someone's eyes and it's like you *know* him and he *knows* you and you don't even need words because you feel like you've come home somehow?" Willa looked at me, and I nodded, thinking of Quinn, realizing all I had as her lonely eyes turned to look out her window.

"Shawn's grandmother lived in Kentucky and had written to him of a beautiful diamond that had been passed down from generation to generation—that he should have it to give to me. She was afraid to mail it, with the war and all, so he decided he would ride to her house when he was given his next leave." Willa smiled, but her smile was sad. "I was so afraid for him that I tried to convince him to go west with me, but he wouldn't. He had given his word, he said, so he would stand and fight. He was like a great lion of a young man, big and strong, and I always imagined he had to be made big to hold such a heart as his . . ."

Willa looked up at me, and I saw the tears in her eyes even as she tried to blink them away. "He said he would come back—but he never did. I prayed and prayed, but he never came back. So I quit praying . . ."

She sighed, then she glanced over at the little table under the window and said, "There are my advice-givers, now." She pointed to an old silver-edged double frame propped up on the table holding a picture of a distinguished-looking man on the left and a petite, smiling woman on the right. The woman looked so much like Willa I knew the people in the pictures had to be her parents.

"I talk, and they listen," she said matter-of-factly, and she smiled wryly. "I suppose I shouldn't complain about the arrangement—at least I never have to worry about disagreements."

"It sounds lonely to me," I said softly, feeling my heart go out to her, having just two old photographs to keep her company. Willa shrugged, like she was trying to shrug off my sympathy, too.

"It's better than nothing," she said, trying to sound casual. Suddenly I felt a surge of love well up in me for her that I didn't know I had. It was like I could see her as she truly was, lonely and hurt and trying to find her way . . . and I thought, even as hurt as I was, and as much as I'd been through, how lost I'd be without God.

"God is real, Willa," I said, feeling my own faith start to lift a bit as I spoke—like I was talking to me as well as her. "He answers us. It's just sometimes the answers aren't what we expect."

Willa didn't look at me but picked up the coffeepot and poured another cup for each of us. I might have thought she wasn't even listening if I hadn't seen her hand shaking a bit as she poured.

"I don't know how you can talk so sure after what happened to Stem. God is good, they say. What's good about that?" she said, then raised her chin a bit, defiant. "Like I said before, seeing is believing, and I haven't seen anything good yet."

I'd started to tell her sometimes we can't see His reasons, right off, but just as I did, Coy and Bonny and the kids came tumbling into the kitchen to tell us it had started snowing again, and since I didn't have runners on the wagon, Coy thought it best for me to head home. I hugged Willa and Bonny and her kids and made my way out to the wagon, and as I turned the team to head home, I glanced at Willa and was shocked by the longing I saw in her eyes as she stared after us. Like her eyes wanted what her mouth couldn't yet admit . . .

Her look kept with me as I pushed my team into a fast clip through the icy wind and large flakes of snow that had already blanketed the ground in white. The look made me think of something my mama had told me long ago when we had been so worried about Jack: *"Doesn't matter how much a person denies believing in God or Jesus,"* she'd said. *"They believe, all right. We were all born believing. All you have to do is look in their eyes, and you'll see the truth of it."*

I had seen the truth of it in Willa's eyes tonight. I just wish I knew how to help her heart. And why does this have to happen now? Why, when I'm fighting to understand things myself?

Lord, there's so much I don't understand . . .

Will I ever?

December 14, 1869 . . .

Lillie's condition left her feeling poorly today, so Jessie and I decided to lend a hand, making sure a good fire was stoked and filling the copper tub on her stove with plenty of water to last the day before we got to our own chores. As we walked back from the stream a second time, I told Jessie about me and Willa's talk, how I went out there to "hide from it all" and ended up hearing myself telling Willa to have faith in spite of my own faith feeling so shaky.

"Funny thing is," I told Jessie, "I *did* feel a bit stronger after we talked."

Jessie nodded. "Sometimes I think the Lord gives us others to think on so we can't think on ourselves so much," she said. "Did me good havin' Rose come spend the night. Just before you two came, I was lying in bed, fixing to cry myself silly when the Lord spoke to me. He say, 'Jessie, I ain't give up on you, so you don't give up on Me.'" Jessie looked over at me. "I say right back, 'I'm just sad, Lord—but I ain't gave up on You.' Then I say louder, so the ol' devil can hear, 'I ain't gave up!'"

Jessie shook her head a bit. "Next thing I know, I'm lying next to Rose, pattin' her little back in the dark 'til she falls asleep, and I say, 'Well, Ye made sure I couldn't give up, didn't Ye, Lord?'"

We smiled a bit at each other, then Jessie said, "Good Lord sure don't let us stay quitters long." I saw her look at the cabins, her eyes trailing over the land, and it struck me that out of all of us, Jessie had the hardest road to walk. But she'd kept on walking. She turned back to me then, studying me with those large, soulful brown eyes of hers, and in them I saw a lot of tragedy, a little triumph, but most of all, I saw the will to survive.

"How did you ever get so strong?" I asked then, and she looked at me curiously.

"Why, I ain't strong, Callie," she said matter-of-factly. "The Lord's strong for me. He know. Get as old as I am, ye get used to losin' a lot of things in yer life. But I lose my faith, I lose *me*."

I couldn't help thinking, as I watched Jessie working by my side until nearly dusk, how much like old Joshua she was, fighting the giants of her life, pressing on with that enduring faith of hers . . . as if her spirit senses what's over the hill even if her body doesn't . . .

Cold and windy tonight. There's just a dusting of new snow that came this evening—but enough to make the cattle work for their food. Quinn heads out for more wood as I write this. I told him to make sure Jessie is well stocked, too. She's a mighty woman of faith, but that takes a mighty heart, too . . . I pray the Lord will be with her tonight and comfort her in His arms.

I'm more tired than usual. I wish I could wake up and have it be spring already.

December 15, 1869 . . .

More snow. Quinn and Jack told me it's only the beginning of our winter as they headed for the barn this morning.

Rose, Patrick, and John-Charles are lying on the hill making snow angels.

I'm worried about our supplies getting low.

Later—We had no more than laid our heads down tonight when Jack came barreling into our cabin, Jessie already in tow, his voice hoarse and shaky, telling us Lillie was fixing to have the baby. I was up and dressed in no time. Jack grabbed my hand tight as we stepped into the deep snow, and it scared me in a way, for he hadn't held my hand like that since we were kids, when we lost our mama. The awful words, *It's too early, it's too early,* kept running over and over in my head as Jessie and I stumbled through the drifts in our skirts behind him. I felt Jack squeeze my hand once, like to remind himself I was still there. It wasn't until we got to the door of their cabin that he seemed to realize he was holding my hand like that. "The snow . . . ," he said, as if to explain, but I knew it was more than the snow.

Lillie tried to put on a brave face as we looked her over. Jack paced back and forth across the room until Jessie finally ordered him and a frazzled John-Charles down to our cabin. As Lillie watched the door shut, the tears she had been holding back filled her eyes.

"I should've listened to Jack," she said, her voice shaky. "He told me over and over to take it easy. It's all my fault if anything happens to our baby . . ."

"This baby's just decided to meet ye sooner than ye thought. Jes wantin' its own way, is all," Jessie said, patting Lillie's hand gently. "Now, that shouldn't surprise ye, honey, knowin' how Jack's always fixed on doin' things *his* own way . . ."

Lillie smiled a trembly smile, and Jessie and I did our best to comfort her when the pains came.

Their baby girl was born less than an hour later. So tiny . . . just a little slip of a thing. She hardly cried at all, and when she finally did cry, it was so soft, I felt like she was just a whisper away from leaving us. Lillie felt it, too, for she kissed the tiny cheek as tears coursed down her face. "Don't leave me," she whispered, trying to smile. "We've only just met."

I felt as if whatever was left of my heart was going to shatter into little pieces. I looked over at Jessie, who stayed quiet as she tidied up the room. But the sorrowful look in her eyes said it all.

Jack came in soon after, so I waited until we left the cabin to talk, to ask Jessie what she thought the little one's chances were. "That child don't need *chance*. She needs the good Lord to deliver her," she said. "He did good by Moses and Daniel, as I recollect. I figure He'll do the same for her." I saw Jessie's chin go out like it always did when she set her mind on something. "All we gots to have is faith."

I watched Jessie tromp with purpose through the drifts of snow down to the empty little cabin that had once been filled with fiddle music and laughter, and I couldn't help thinking I'd never seen someone so selfless, so willing to give in spite of all that had been taken from her. So determined to believe . . .

I wish I could be as determined. This last trouble is like a ruthless thief, coming back to steal the last of our resolve . . .

December 18, 1869 . . .

Cold, cloudy day. So quiet around here. The snow just keeps piling up, leaving us no chance of finding the doctor now . . . We were amazed when Willa came riding through the snow. She offered to help however she could, but Jack ended up asking us all to leave, saying he and Lillie just needed some time alone—that the quiet might help the baby nurse better.

But his words held more hope than his eyes. He stood there in the door of their cabin, looking so hurt, so lost, that I wanted to put my arms around him. He must have sensed it, too, because he held a hand up to me, like he didn't want me to come any closer. Or maybe he was just afraid of what I might say.

"He can't take her, sis," he said. "He just can't take her, too." It was the way he said it—like he was talking to someone else, like he was begging as he looked up to the cold night sky.

And I just knew it was God he was talking to.

Later—And a little child shall lead them . . .

I'm reminded of those words tonight as it was Rose who brought me our family Bible to read, looking so solemn as she sat down at my feet with Patrick and John-Charles planted on each side of her. I had thought to turn to Daniel, for we were almost to the story of the fiery furnace, but was surprised when I went to open it and it fell open to a page with a *another* little dried flower tucked in the crease that I never recalled seeing before. There was scripture underlined, too: "My grace is sufficient for thee: for my strength is made perfect in weakness," it said. My eye caught some writing off to one side, and I was shocked to see it was Pa's spiky handwriting, not Mama's. Pa had wrote: "I am weak, Lord. Be strong in me for my family, for those I love."

No sooner had I read it out loud to Quinn and the children, I felt in my heart it was meant for Jack to hear. I tucked the Bible under my arm and trudged out in the snow to Jack and Lillie's cabin. Jack looked haggard when he answered my knock and let me in then went right back to the little stool he sat on next to Lillie's bed, his shoulders hunched over like he was carrying the weight of the world on them. Lillie looked up at me then, and I saw she had been crying.

"Jessie was just here," she said, then lowered her voice to a whisper of awful hopelessness. "She won't nurse, Callie. It's like she doesn't have the strength."

Can a heart die a thousand times? I didn't know what to say, so with trembling hands, I opened up the Bible, telling them what I'd found, and as I read the scripture, read Pa's words, I saw Jack's head raise up a bit.

"I wonder when Pa wrote that," Jack said, never taking his eyes off Lillie or their baby, but I saw something new pass between them then, like a spark of a memory. Then we prayed, all of us holding hands around the bed, trying to drown out the baby's silence with our pleas.

As I turned to leave, I saw the look on Jack's face had changed, Lillie's too, like they were willing to hope again. Jack stood like he wanted to say something, the Bible hanging from his hand as he just stared. I saw the tumble of emotions cross his handsome face, and I realized what he was trying to say. We weren't brother and sister for nothing.

"I love you, too, Jack," I said, and he smiled a relieved kind of smile before I shut the door behind me.

There is something I have never written about. It happened long, long ago, but sometimes it feels like it was only yesterday when the memory of it comes to me like a sharp, bittersweet pain that washes over my eyes and I see the baby twins that were only allowed to lie in my arms for just a few short days. I remember the agony of Quinn and me having to bury them with no minister, no comfort from any family but each other . . . and Rose asking questions and being too young to understand . . . It's a pain I wouldn't wish on my worst enemy and cannot bear for my brother.

There is a part of me that worries that Jack's faith—that all of our faith—can't hold up under this flood, Lord, that we've tread this water 'til we're so weary that all we can think to do is give up . . . Yet there's another part of me that's afraid to let go of Your hand, that deep down knows You will be the One to pull us out if we can just hang on . . .

December 23, 1869 . . .

I just haven't had the heart to write lately. Each day seems such a struggle, like walking through molasses. The weather is so bitter, yet we trudge out and make our way down to Jack and Lillie's cabin, we breathe our relief and thanks that the sweet baby has made it through another day. Then we pray.

Oh, how we pray.

December 24, 1869 . . .
Christmas Eve

I admit my heart was not in the celebrating mood when I woke this morning, but so much has changed . . .

It was Quinn's gentle nudge that got me up and going, saying how the children needed it—and we did, too—whether I thought so or not. Quinn bundled up, going to pick a tree with Rose, Patrick, and John-Charles, and I had set to cooking when I realized I needed water. Dutifully I pulled on the old wool overcoat and boots and trudged out the door.

I didn't seem to even notice the cold, my heart was so heavy as I walked to the spring, thinking on the baby, wondering how much of a chance something so small could have. I can't say how long I stood there, just thinking, when suddenly I heard the wild horses, the sounds of their pounding hooves and snorts startling me as I glanced down the canyon. I saw the herd was turning toward the stream, puffs of steam trailing up from their noses in the cold air.

I scrambled up onto an outcropping of rock to look as they trotted along a trail in the canyon below, and for a moment, the world was just me and those wild horses, and I felt my breath catch in my chest. There was such a beauty in that small moment, so much that it almost hurt, like being given a gift you weren't expecting.

Oh, how I wish I could describe the feelings that welled up in my chest, watching the sun glinting off their shiny coats, hearing their whinnies filling the air, blotting out the bad of the world and making me think good could come again. For just that moment, there were no worries or tears or darkness, just beauty, and it awed me to think how big God truly is. I realized what I was seeing was just a small part of His making, like looking at a few stitches on a big quilt. Then the thought struck me how sad He must be that we forget how big He really is . . .

I bowed my head right there on that hill and prayed for Lillie's baby. But my prayer was different than the others I had cried or stumbled through the past several days. *Giving this baby a chance at life is a small thing for You, Lord, so I won't doubt anymore that it can be done . . .*

After a while, the horses turned and made their way into the distance again, and I climbed down the hill, filled the water pails, and headed back toward the cabins. It wasn't until I came over the last rise that I saw Quinn coming for me at a quick pace.

"Gotta get back to your brother's cabin, lass. There's something you should be seein'," he said, all out of breath. Then he took the pails from me like they were nothing, and we fairly ran the rest of the way.

It wasn't until I got into the cabin, my heart beating out of my chest, that I realized something had changed. The heavy feeling of sorrow was gone, and I saw Jessie standing to one side, a real fine smile on her face for the first time since Stem died. Lillie grinned at me big and motioned for me to come over to the bed, and as I looked down at the baby, tears began to spill down my cheeks. The baby's fine, petal-like skin had pinkened, and she was nursing hungrily like I had never seen a baby nurse.

"I opened that Bible of your mama's this morning, Callie, and right in front of my eyes was the prayer I knew I was supposed to pray," Lillie said with big tears in her eyes. She laughed a little, too, then looked over at Jack, who was standing in the corner, holding John-Charles with a sheepish look on his face. "When I told Jack I thought we were supposed to pray it for the baby, he said, 'Well then, let's say it out loud so the good Lord will be sure to hear us.'"

Lillie scooted the Bible to herself with one hand, her voice taking on a soft note. "'Unto thee lift I up mine eyes, O thou that dwellest in the heavens,'" she read. "'As the eyes of servants look unto the hand of their masters, and as the eyes of a maiden unto the hand of her mistress; so our eyes wait upon the LORD our God, until that he have mercy on us. Have mercy upon us, O LORD, have mercy upon us . . .'"

"The doctor showed up right after that," Jack said then, with a kind of wonder on his face, and pointed in the direction of their little kitchen area where for the first time I noticed a stranger standing, warming his hands at their fireplace. The stranger turned to me and smiled like he knew me, and I felt a tiny shiver go up my back.

"I opened the door when I heard the knock, and he just walked right past me to the baby, took her out of Lillie's hands, and started looking her over with his back to us," Jack went on, still looking shocked. "Then he handed her back to Lillie, and she was all pink and crying—and not sick crying like before, but like she was hungry." Jack looked at the man, his eyes misting. "I don't know what you did, mister, but you saved my little girl, and I can't thank you enough for that."

"Well, now," the stranger said, his deep voice so humble. "The Lord always makes a way when there seems to be no way, doesn't He?"

We all stood there, motionless, for a bit, the silence so peaceful and heavy that we all jumped a little when the baby up and cried. Then we laughed, looking at each other with such joy as she took to her mother's breast again with such gusto.

"We named her Mercy," Lillie said, looking down at her daughter with love, "because that's what God gave us, Mercy."

"Can't think of a better name for a Wade to have, can you, sis?" Jack asked, and we all laughed again—even the doctor, who seemed to take as keen a liking to us as we did to him. He even helped Quinn get the tree set up in our cabin while I finished up dinner and carried it down to Jack and Lillie's cabin. Even Jessie laughed a time or two, then we noticed it was snowing again, and the doctor said he had to go.

Jessie helped him on with his coat and then surprised even

herself by hugging him. "I'm jes so grateful to ye for helpin' like ye did," she said, wiping her eyes. "I just thank the Lord for ye, sir."

The stranger had his hand on the door by then, but stopped and looked at Jessie for a long moment, then he smiled. "Blessed are those that mourn, for they shall be comforted," he said like a whisper, then he was gone.

"We didn't even get to ask his name," Jack said, looking over at Quinn. They both headed out the door to catch the doctor, only to return a short bit later. Willa was with them, coming to tell us the news of a Christmas service that was going to be held in town, but the doctor had up and disappeared. "No tracks or anything," Quinn said. "The snow is over two feet deep. How can there be no tracks?"

"Well, it wasn't Doc Eddy. Percy told me he took off for Deer Lodge over a week ago," Willa said, looking around our stunned little group. After we told her all that had happened, she crossed the room quickly and peered down at Mercy, who was now sleeping peacefully in her mother's arms.

"Well, I'll be. Mercy Wade," she said, swiping at her eyes, "you just might be the one to make me think there really is a God after all."

As one soul leaves the earth, so another comes into it . . . I keep thinking of that saying. I know it may sound strange, but somehow, I think little Mercy and Stem's souls must have brushed past each other, that somehow an old fellow in buckskins was able to add his prayer to ours. *"Ain't never left you in a lurch yet, Callie,"* I can just hear him laugh. Quinn thinks that doctor was an angel sent by God, and as crazy as it might sound to outsiders . . . well, if they were here, if they saw what we saw, they would understand there's really no other answer but that.

When I held Mercy in my arms late tonight, those eyes that looked up at me seemed so wise for such a tiny, elflike creature . . . as if she's already seen the best of us all and isn't so worried about tomorrows. I said a little prayer for her then, and when I bent down and kissed her tiny cheek, I whispered, "Fight, little one. Fight for all you're worth." And I got the eeriest feeling as she stared up at me with those eyes of hers that seemed to speak to me like a gentle rebuke from heaven itself: *"It's you I'll be teaching how to fight."*

Later—"Mama," Rose whispered, looking up at me so pensively as I tucked her into bed. "Is the baby gonna live?" When I told her yes, she hesitated and drew her doll close to her. "Is it a boy or girl?"

"A girl," I said, and I told her how Uncle Jack and Aunt Lillie had named her Mercy, for the mercy God had given them.

Rose let out the breath she had been holding in, like she had been carrying the weight of the world on those tiny shoulders of hers. "Then God gave me mercy, too," she said solemnly. "When I was praying, I told Him I understood he needed Stem, so maybe He could understand how I needed a girl in this family. I said I'd sure like a girl for Christmas, for if it was another boy, I felt I was done for."

"Aw, Rose," Patrick said sleepily from under his mountain of covers.

"Well, you're not done for, are you?" I said, feeling myself start to grin. As I climbed slowly down the ladder, I could hear Quinn's soft chuckle, and I saw him sitting in that big old rocking chair before the fire. I walked over to him, and he pulled me down on his lap, hugging me to him.

"You know, I was thinking that our darkest hours aren't our darkest hours—they're our *dawn*," he said, and then he smiled softly when he saw my curious look. "I was sitting here thinking, and I wondered if sometimes those hours are like a light God shines into our hearts, showing us what we are made of . . . what we are made *for*. Think of it," he said. "Jessie, standing by Lillie in spite of her own grief, praying . . . you taking that scripture to them when they needed it the most, even when your heart was so down . . . Jack and Lillie—you all gave your cares to Him, and you *believed*. And look what has come of it, lass . . . look what has come of it." He shook his head in wonder. "'Tis a miracle . . ."

"*My strength is made perfect in weakness* . . ." The words of the scripture Pa had underlined all those years ago whispered to me.

I looked up at the clock we'd hung above the mantle, saw the time, and turned back to Quinn, feeling love and gratefulness for the gift of such a husband like him that even now is hard to put to words.

"Merry Christmas, Quinn," I said, and those pale blue eyes stared back at me with love and warmth and unshed tears, and I knew he understood.

"Merry Christmas, Callie," he said softly.

I thought I was through writing for the night when Quinn came in and surprised me with a beautiful new headboard for our bed that he had carved special for me; two hearts interlaced with each other so that you can't tell where one ends and the other begins.

"Just like us," he said, smiling softly, and I started crying. It was as if some dam had been broke open by his gift, and I cried about everything. I cried sad for Stem and Jessie, then I cried my relief for little Mercy surviving. Last I cried tears of gratefulness to God for being so faithful even when I had felt almost faithless and for blessing me with a family, with a husband that loved me so . . .

Quinn held me close and kept patting my head, saying, "There, there, lass," and for some odd reason, I suddenly got the picture in my head of him patting Honey's head like that, and I felt myself begin to smile as I looked up at him. A smile that was so long overdue that my face felt almost strange in the pose—but good, too. Quinn seemed to understand.

"I couldn't have asked for a better gift," he said, "than to see you smile like that again."

December 25, 1869 . . .
Christmas Day

And what a joyful day it has been. We had such a good time of it, getting started for town this morning after all the "girls" gathered in our cabin to visit and get things ready while the men set the wagon boxes on the sleds and hitched our teams. Everyone made over Mercy as we worked. She looked perfectly sweet in the little gown Jessie had made for her with its puffed sleeves and fine stitching. Bonny seemed as taken with her as Willa, who couldn't seem to help herself from looking at her again and again. Soon enough, the wagons were filled with straw, hot rocks, and blankets, everyone was bundled up, and off we went through the deep snow. If I wasn't so overjoyed for us all to be together, I might have been scared, for the snow had covered everything so that you couldn't tell where a gully or wash wasn't or the road was. But God smiled on us, and we made it to Audrey in good time.

I admit, I was surprised to see that, in spite of the weather, there was just as great a turnout as there'd been in September— if not more. We filed into Preacher's tent, stomping our feet and grinning at each other like kids. Even Willa seemed pleasantly surprised as she looked around at the crowd clustered around the little wood stove in the middle of the tent. I was amazed that a tent could be filled with such warmth on this icy cold day.

We sang "There Were Shepherds" and "Away in a Manger" then lastly "Silent Night"—which brought the sound of familiar sniffles around the tent.

After the singing, we finally settled down for the sermon, and I glanced over and smiled, seeing Willa motion to Lillie to ask if she could hold Mercy. Willa kissed Mercy's cheek, so tender, then looked up with a contented smile on her face as Preacher stepped up to the pulpit, and suddenly the smile changed and she looked stunned for some reason.

"I would like to thank everyone for being here today," Preacher began. "It's a hardy bunch that can brave weather such as this, so I hope you'll accept my gift to you this Christmas Day . . . it's the story of a man and a room full of gifts."

There was excited murmurs amongst everyone—especially some of the miners who had been sitting stiff, waiting for the sermon. Children even forgot their squirming and leaned forward in their seats as Preacher began. I felt Willa squirm next to me, but I was already caught up in the picture Preacher had begun to paint of the man who had lived his whole life working and praying but never really living.

He said the man grew old and one day he died, and when he opened his eyes again, he was standing before Jesus. The man was overcome with joy to realize he was in heaven because his life had been so miserable—and he told the Lord as much. Jesus took the man's hand, his smile sad but kind as he led the man into a huge room filled with gifts.

"These were all for you," Jesus said, and the man looked at him, startled. Then he went over to the largest gift, wrapped fine with bows and such, and when he opened it, he saw it was the day of his birth.

The man started tearing into all the boxes then, Preacher told us. He started crying as he saw himself being hugged by a loved one in one of the boxes, heard the laughter of a child in another one. He opened box after box, showing him all the gifts of life—gifts he had never took the time to open . . . never took the time to *see*.

Preacher grew silent for a moment, and I could hear sniffles coming from all over that tent. Then I saw something had caught Preacher's eye, and I saw his eyes widen in surprise, too.

I followed his stare, and I saw Willa suddenly spring up from her seat. She handed Mercy back to Lillie quick, then without a word to any of us, she was out of the tent in a flash. I glanced over at Quinn, who looked as shocked as I felt, then I turned and followed after Willa as fast as I could. I found her just as she was getting ready to step up into her wagon. She must have sensed me, for she looked over her shoulder then. "Please, just go back in, Callie," she said. Seeing her tears, I put my hand on her shoulder softly and asked her what I already knew. Preacher was Willa's long-lost love . . . the man she had waited for to come home from the war.

"All of these years," she said after a while. "Well, *someone* has a sense of humor. Shawn becomes a man of the cloth, and I become the Ringleader of Sin. She laughed then, but there was no humor in her laugh, and I couldn't help thinking it was like watching a delicate piece of crystal fall off a table and you're not sure you can catch it in time before it shatters.

"God's bigger than a bunch of foolish lies," I said. "If it's meant for you and the preacher to be together, there's no one on earth that'll stop it. Least of all you." Willa turned back to me then with a hurt but hopeful look on her face.

"When I saw how that baby was healed I almost believed . . . ," she said softly. Then she frowned. "But if God is real, why doesn't He ever talk to me, Callie? Why didn't He stop me from making such a mess of my life?"

I couldn't help smiling, she sounded so much like me. "We're not puppets, Willa. We have a little thing called choice," I said, then I looked at her close. "Tell me, have you ever really waited—have you tried to listen to see if you'd get an answer?"

"No," she said softly, looking away. "I'm scared." When I asked her what she was scared of, she turned back to me for just a moment.

"Don't you see, Callie?" she said. "If I listen and He doesn't talk—if there really isn't a God—then I really am alone." When she looked at me so sad, it struck me that I was seeing the real Willa Cain for the first time after all the months I had known her . . . a woman who was lonely and so very scared.

"Did it ever occur to you that maybe it was God that brought you here today?" I said. "Wouldn't you like to know if this day is one of your gifts?"

Willa didn't answer me. Instead she climbed onto the seat of her wagon, took up the reins, and hawed her team on down the snowy trail that led out of town . . .

When I turned around, Preacher was standing there, his face grim but determined as he folded his arms across his chest. The rest of the congregation milled behind him, trying to figure out what had caused such a stir, but he didn't seem to notice.

"She should have known better than to run," he said, almost to himself. "I always caught her in the end." He turned and walked back into the tent, the rest of us trailing back in to find our seats again. And as I sat there listening to the deep rise and fall of his voice, as he spoke of what the true gifts were that God had given us, he told us the greatest gift of all was the gift of love. "That was why the Christ Child was born this day," Preacher said, "to give us a chance . . . to give us His love . . ."

Preacher looked down at his Bible then and slowly turned the page. Then he read these words: "And though I have the gift of prophecy, and understand all mysteries, and all knowledge; and though I have all faith, so that I could remove mountains, and have not charity, I am nothing. . . ."

The words made me think of Stem and then of Jessie, how she had kept on loving in spite of her hurt. Then I thought of *all* the people who had loved me—and who I had got to love back—and I thought how poor my life would've been not to have had that love. When I looked at Quinn there was tears in his eyes, and I knew he was thinking the same. I think everyone was feeling that way. There wasn't a dry eye to be found as we all moved slowly out of that tent after the service. There was a difference in the air, too, like everyone had changed somehow in the short space of time. I even overheard Mr. Audrey invite Doc Eddy to their home for Christmas dinner. Mrs. Audrey's smile was wan, but she nodded her agreement just the same.

Pretty soon we had our wagon loaded with Coy and Bonny and her kids, since Willa had already left in the wagon they'd come in. I smiled, seeing the preacher behind us in his own rig with Jessie perched on the seat beside him. As Jack and Lillie took the lead, turning their team down the winding, snow-choked trail that led home, Quinn and I grinned at each other like kids . . . it *felt* like Christmas. Then I thought of Willa and wished with all my heart she could be with us, too.

It wasn't until we all rumbled into our little valley that I saw my wish had come true. Willa was there, standing by her wagon, shivering, like she had been waiting on us awhile. As I stepped down, I saw her eyes go wide as she spotted Preacher helping Jessie from his buggy. She backed up a little as Preacher headed over to her, but he didn't seem in the least bothered by her reaction.

"I can't think of a better Christmas gift than to be standing here with you, Willa, after all these years," Preacher said, smiling big.

"All these years is right," Willa sniffed. "I guess I should say it's nice to see you're alive, but I'm still trying to figure out how you ended up in the very last place on earth I would imagine *you* to be."

"Don't you see God's hand in this?" he asked, but she refused to look his way.

"No," she said, shaking her head. "I see a poor sense of humor—a bad joke played on the wrong day." Willa paced. "I've decided there are no real happy endings, Shawn Michaels. I've told everyone who would listen that fairy-tale endings were for the weak. Then you show up and try to ruin my speech."

The preacher threw his head back and laughed then. "Same old Willa," he said, then he started to say something else but was overcome with laughter again, and we all found ourselves chuckling, too.

"Go ahead and laugh," Willa said, trying her best not to smile as she looked around at us all. "It was a good speech."

We went inside then to feed our hungry bunch, and after we sang every Christmas song we could remember, we pulled out our surprise for Jessie. She looked up from the stack of goods for quilting, her lips trembling as she thanked each of us. Then it was the children's turn; Patrick gave Jessie a pretty little wooden cross he'd carved for her, and John-Charles gave her a wooden frame with braided horsehair edging for the only picture she had of her and Stem. Sarah and Willie shyly presented her with a little beaded purse. But Rose's gift surprised us all. It was a sampler she'd made for Jessie. "Mrs. Jessie Dawson" was sewn prettily in the middle of a pale piece of linen with a tiny border of flowers and flounces surrounding her name. Hard work for any young girl—but especially for Rose, who avoided sewing like the plague. Amazing what your heart can push you to do.

"I sewed that because you said you never wanted to forget the day you became Mrs. Jessie Dawson," Rose said, a smile hovering on her lips as she waited for Jessie's reaction.

"Why, that's the finest thing I ever seen, sis," Jessie said, smiling past the tears in her eyes. "Thank ye all. Thank ye kindly."

I have a gift to give, too," Preacher announced suddenly.

"But it's for Willa." All heads turned to see Willa give a start, looking up from Rose's sampler.

He tried one pocket, and it appeared there was something in it, but he looked like he thought better of pulling it out. Then he went to scrounging in his other pocket, finally coming out with a small square of tissue paper that looked like it had been open and refolded so many times it was near brittle.

He offered the paper to Willa, who looked at it like it might bite her, then he sighed and opened it himself and we saw it was a set of the prettiest hair combs we'd ever seen. They looked to be a green enamel of sorts inlaid with tiny white flowers and vines.

"I meant for you to have these years ago," he said, handing them to her. "For that beautiful raven hair," he added.

Willa touched a hand to her hair, then caught herself. She cleared her throat and looked over at Rose. "Beware of the flatterer," she said. "He feeds you with an empty spoon."

Preacher put his hand to his chest then, as if injured. "Ah, but the thorns which I have reaped are of the tree I planted," he said, smiling.

"He thinks quoting Byron is going to impress me," Willa said to no one in particular, but I saw that her cheeks had turned a pretty pink in spite of her words and a soft smile curved her lips. I looked at Lillie and Jessie, and by their looks, I knew they had seen the same thing.

When I glanced over to Rose, who had been so quiet during this exchange, I saw her lips were pursed and a tiny frown wrinkled her brow as she looked over at Willa, deep in thought, as if the weight of the world were on her mind.

"Miss Willa, why would anyone *feed* you with an empty spoon?" she asked, and we all busted out laughing.

Preacher followed Willa out to her wagon when she abruptly announced it was time for her to go. She had the strangest look on her face, like she was scared to death, but maybe glad, too.

From the window, we watched them talk a bit in the yard, then we saw her fairly run to her wagon, watched as Preacher stood in the middle of our yard, watching too, until her rig was far out of sight. Then he shook his head and climbed into his buggy, a determined look on his face.

"You know, I was a lot like her when I first met your brother," Lillie said as we turned from the window. "I always told myself if I didn't care, then I wouldn't have to worry about getting hurt again.

"But I cared, no matter how hard I tried. I just had a mask I wore that said I didn't." Lillie shrugged her small shoulders and looked down at Mercy, smiling. "I cared . . . I always cared."

"Well, now we'll just have to say a prayer for that girl, won't we?" Jessie said, looking from Lillie down to Mercy. "Jesus ain't no *suspector* of persons, ye know. A very good friend of mine told me that, and I'm inclined to believe her."

Rose fairly beamed as she looked up into Jessie's smiling face.

"That friend was me, wasn't it, Jessie?"

"It sure was, honey," Jessie said, smiling too, and soon after, we all joined hands to pray.

Are You out there tonight, God? If ever I could imagine You being close enough to look over my shoulder it would be tonight, beneath this huge bowl of cold, clear sky littered with stars . . . Thank You so much for this night, Lord, but if You don't mind my asking one more thing of You, I pray that You help Willa, too. Let what she thinks is her dark hour be her dawn. Let her know You are there, like I do . . . like we all do . . .

December 27, 1869 . . .

Back to work today. I've finally got the cabin back in order and have just finished putting in my last pan of bread. The stack of mending before me is enormous—which is why I chose to take a breath and write—if only for a moment.

No new snowfall, which is good as the cattle were having a hard time of it, figuring out how to dig their noses through the snow to the grass underneath. Rose, our staunch little *horse-woman*, says if it weren't for the cattle watching the horses paw and nose their way to grass, they would have starved "dumb."

Patrick looks like a little bear bundled up as he takes Jasper and Honey out with him to fetch some more wood for me. Jasper and Honey just look none too thrilled about the trip.

Later—Jessie came for dinner this evening. Then, not long after she arrived, Quinn went out for more wood and came back in with Preacher, who said he'd just stopped by for a little visit. A long way through cold and snow for just a little visit, I thought, but I didn't say it. Truth is, we have all taken quite a liking to Preacher. Not just for his preaching, but for the man himself. He has an easy way about him that makes you feel like you've known him forever, so kindhearted and smart, too—not just with books, but life. I could tell Quinn enjoyed his company, too. As I watched them sit and talk in front of the fireplace while Jessie, Rose, and me finished up with the dishes, I couldn't help thinking how they reminded me of two solemn warrior-giants, meeting to talk about the sad ways of humans. I suddenly heard Quinn asking Preacher about his family, and my ears perked up, curious.

"When my family found out I was going west to preach, they thought I'd lost my mind," Preacher said with a wry grin.

"My father said, 'You leave, and your money stays.' I told him what I was doing wasn't about money, but he never understood that." Preacher shook his head. "He believed doing anything—or speaking to anyone outside of their 'circle of money'—was going beneath our class."

Quinn looked up from studying his work-worn hands. "Ah," he said. "I imagine your father never played much chess then." Preacher raised a brow, and Quinn grinned. "He would've known, if he had, that the king and the pawn, they go in the same box when the game is over."

Preacher laughed outright then. "I'll have to remember that, McGregor," he said fondly, and Jessie and me smiled at each other. Then there was a knock at the door, and Rose and Patrick ran to open in. *Willa* came in, looking half-froze but pretty in a windblown sort of way. She also looked mortified.

"Well, I didn't know you had company," she said, her eyes sliding Preacher's way, and I saw her put a nervous hand to her hair. "I just thought to come by for a little visit." We all glanced at each other then and grinned.

"I should probably go," she added. "I didn't mean to interrupt anything."

"Well, I do have to be real careful about who I'm seen with," Preacher said with a teasing look, but he stood and offered her his chair.

"You best step lively, then," Willa retorted. "I would hate to be the cause of your downfall." But she sat down anyway, and as I went to fetch her some coffee, Jessie winked.

"What is it that I hear they call you in town?" he asked.

"Ringleader of Sin," Willa deadpanned, but there was a flicker of hurt in her eyes, too. I knew Preacher saw it, too, for he softened a bit from his teasing her. We all gathered around the fireplace with our chairs and had a good time talking and drinking coffee. But as most good nights do, it came to an end too soon. Rose and Patrick had pleaded for Jessie to be the one to tuck them in, and she went up the ladder behind them with a smile as Preacher and Willa began to bundle up for their trips home. As Quinn and I stood at the door with them I saw Preacher hesitate all of a sudden and turn back to Willa.

"Would tomorrow be too early to call on you?" he asked, and we all turned to see what her answer would be.

Willa looked stunned at first, then some of the wariness eased from her eyes and she laughed. "Are you trying to save me, Shawn Michaels?"

"Maybe," he said smiling—but looking at her thoughtfully, too, before they both headed out the door. "Or maybe God's trying to save us both."

Willa looked back at me for the briefest moment, and a tumble of emotions crossed her face that I had never seen before. "Thank you, Callie," she said, shutting the door behind her.

I told Quinn after they left that I hoped Willa would relent—and soon. That if it was so easy for me to see how much Preacher cared for her, why couldn't she? Quinn just smiled at me, one dark eyebrow raised.

"How soon we forget," he said, and I suddenly felt sheepish, remembering what a time he'd had trying to convince me—and thinking, too, how much I would've lost had I not listened to God instead of myself.

"*Maybe God is trying to save us both,*" Preacher had said.

I pray that You do save them, Lord. I guess I've lived long enough to admit we all need saving from ourselves one time or another in our lives . . .

December 31, 1869 . . .

The eve of our new year . . . Jessie didn't mention that, but I wonder if something in her sensed it was time for a change. If maybe her wanting us to help her pack up some of Stem's things wasn't God's gentle nudge to get her back to the "land of the living," meaning living for *Jessie*—not just us. As Rose and I quickly finished our chores and bundled up to walk the path to Jessie and Stem's place, I couldn't help thinking on that, how Jessie just charged on, helping all of us with no thought to herself. And yet every night she had to trudge back to that cabin and sit alone with her thoughts of what could have been.

Jessie opened the door as quick as I knocked, and it touched my heart to see how eager she was for our company as she ushered us in, taking our coats and herding us over to warm ourselves by the fire. "This place is a sight," she declared, trying to busy herself making coffee as Rose and I glanced around the little cabin that fairly sparkled with neatness. I saw two packing boxes in the corner that looked to be filled with Stem's things, and I wondered what help she was needing when I saw the new quilt that was spread on her bed. It was one of the finest-looking patchwork quilts I've seen. Jessie smiled as Rose and I went over to take a look. Then she joined us, telling us how one day she had been sitting just staring at the quilting frame Stem had made, when she remembered about Lillie's memory quilt.

"I think the Lord brought it to my mind because I was having a hard time thinking of packing his clothes away," Jessie said, smiling. "But that's how He works. I got me a quilt I needed and something of that sweet man's to hold on to when I fall to sleep, too," she added. I saw Rose look up to Jessie then down to the quilt as she bent forward and ran one hand softly over the fabric almost longingly.

Jessie saw the longing, too, for she reached down and took Rose's hand in hers. "I got something for ye, sis," she said, and she led Rose over to the table. Something was hidden there under the tablecloth. Jessie pulled the cloth off, and there sat folded neatly on top of the frame a smaller version of Jessie's own quilt.

"That's yours," Jessie said, and a wide-eyed Rose grabbed up the quilt and hugged it to her chest, the look on her little face so sad and sweet at the same time that it brought tears to my eyes.

"Oh, thank you, Jessie!" Rose said, hugging Jessie's neck while she held tight to the little quilt. "Now we can *both* have something from Stem to hold on to at night."

After we had all dried our eyes, we took to the kitchen and had ourselves some coffee and little sweet cakes Jessie had made. Then Rose shyly asked Jessie if she could look through the boxes of Stem's belongings, and when Jessie said yes, she quickly left us to our talking, quilt clutched tightly in one hand as she sifted through the boxes in the other.

"You didn't have to let her do that, Jessie," I said then, and Jessie sat her cup down and looked at me.

"Why, Callie, it don't hurt me none. Those are just his *things*," she said simply. "Who Stem *was* made up a lot more than them pitiful boxes."

It hit me then, as I glanced back over at those two boxes, maybe that was why they were so meager, that Stem had been so busy in the *doing*, in always helping others, always taking pleasure in *people*, that he'd rarely had need of *things*. I told Jessie I hoped my boxes would be just as small.

"Me, too, honey," Jessie said. "Me too."

Not long after that was when Rose brought us a slip of paper she'd found tucked in one of Stem's old buckskin jackets. She handed the paper to Jessie, and we both watched as Jessie opened it gingerly, squinted her eyes at it, then made as if to tuck it away. I was confused for a moment until it suddenly struck me that maybe she couldn't read.

"It's a mite dark in here," I said so as not to embarrass her. "Maybe we should light that pretty lamp of yours."

"Oh, I'll do it. You hold on to this," she said, fairly shoving the paper into my hand as she pretended to busy herself with the lamp. I opened the paper and glanced at it, then looked up to see Jessie watching me carefully. "Might as well read it," she said, fiddling with her lamp. "Looks like I'll have to add some oil."

"Read it, Mama," Rose said, pleadingly.

I opened the paper gently, then felt a lump come to my throat as I saw that the date was only two weeks before Stem had died. I touched the indents he'd made with his deliberate, shaky handwriting.

"If yore reading this, then I figger I'm gone. I always did like to have my say, so you might guess I ain't done yet," I read, then I looked up at Rose and Jessie and saw Rose take Jessie's hand, saw a smile tremble on Jessie's lips as she nodded to me. I went on in spite of the lump in my throat. "I ain't no judge, but I figger this can serve as my will. If anyone thinks to dispute it, they kin take it to Quinn McGregor or Jack Wade. They've been like sons to me and know my mind, too. I'm sorry I had to leave you, Jessie, but the one comfort I hav is knowin who I left you *with*. Callie and them have been more family than the folks I was born to. With that sed, I hereby leave all my worldly goods to my wife, Jessie Dawson. They ain't much, but she's loved me better than anyone, and the least I kin do is make sur she's squared away til we see each other agin.

"Lastly, I figger someone had to tell this to Jessie as she can't yet read. I say *yet* not to embarrass her but because I'm countin on her keepin her promise to learn. Not for me, but for herself.

"You never know, Jessie, it might just come in handy one day.

"Love, Stem—or Justice Dawson, for any of them legal types.

"P.S. And tell Rose not to ferget lesson numbr nine hundred."

We all were quiet for a bit—especially Rose, who had walked slowly back over to where the boxes sat. Then, as if a thought suddenly came to her, she came back over to us and took Jessie's hand, asking her if she could be the one to teach her to read.

"Why, that would be right kindly of ye, sis," Jessie said, looking up at me with a distracted kind of smile, and I sensed by the smile that she wanted to be alone in her thoughts for a while. We helped Jessie with the few dishes then began to bundle up again for the walk back home. We hugged each other long and hard. I asked Jessie if she wanted me to take the little letter and read it to the others for her, but she got a funny look on her face and held the paper tight. "If ye don't mind just telling 'em, Callie," she said. "I'd kind of like t' hang on to it for a while." Then she surprised us again by giving Rose one of the boxes of Stem's things.

Rose and I took our leave then, each of us silent in thought as we headed back up the little hill that led to our own cabin. After only a bit, though, I sensed Rose looking up at me as she carried her box along, quilt tucked neatly in at the top, and I smiled down at her.

"So what was lesson nine hundred?" I asked, and Rose cocked her head to one side and smiled up at me with tears in her pale blue eyes.

"When life leaves you bitter, do something to make it better," she recited. "I'm doing it, too," she said proudly. "I'm gonna teach Jessie how to *read*, Mama. I'm *gonna* make it better."

So quiet tonight. Quinn and Patrick were off to bed after the last load of wood. Rose is up in her own bed, "working on something" as I can see the dim light of her lantern still flickering against the cabin walls.

And I write . . . just as I always have, to think, to hope, to remember . . .

Promiseland

Our new year rang in with the sound of an ice storm battering the cabins, bringing us out of our beds and to the windows, where we viewed what looked to be our entire herd standing in the front yard, bawling for help. Quinn and Jack slipped and careened to the barns to gather enough hay to tide them over for a while, then slipped and careened back to the cabins. Quinn is bundling up now for the second round, and I worry about him going out again—he and Jack were very nearly stampeded the *last* time.

Now that the day is nearly done the storm has quit, and Jessie, Lillie, and I have been standing on our porches, calling out to each other from time to time as we are icebound. We think the men must have decided to stay in the barn and wait it out until the next round of feeding.

"It seems if it's not people trouble, it's weather trouble. How do ye beat it?" Jessie called out just awhile ago. Lillie held up her hand like an idea had come to her and went back into her cabin. I wonder what she is up to—

Later—Well, now I know what Lillie was up to. We have just come back from our little New Year's celebration down at Jessie's cabin.

It all started when Lillie came back out of her cabin with what looked to be the bottom of one of their packing crates with a rope tied to it. She threw it on the ground, eased herself down to sit on it, reached for the large bundle (Mercy) in John-Charles's arms, and then instructed John-Charles to sit in front of her and hold fast to the rope. Before we could blink, they were headed past our cabin in a flash. "See you at Jessie's, Callie!" she called as I saw a blurred grin go past me and heard John-Charles laughing like I'd never heard him laugh before. Jessie leaned out from her steps, grasping a porch post, and caught them just in time to help stop the contraption.

When pigs fly! I thought at first, then found myself scrounging with Rose and Patrick for one of our packing crates in spite of the thought. Before I knew it, I was sitting down behind Rose and Patrick, wrapping my arms around them tight as we slipped and slid down toward Jessie's cabin on that little scrap of board. I saw Jessie and Lillie standing on the porch, laughing as we headed their way.

Jasper and Honey barked and chased after us, then slid down the hill themselves, legs splayed out like newborn calves. Rose and Patrick whooped for joy, and I felt the laughter begin to bubble up in me, too. Then I heard myself say to Jessie as we came to a stop, "I guess this is how we beat it."

Jessie looked at me, surprised at first, then slapped her leg and laughed. "I guess it is," she said, helping us up and into her warm little cabin.

The men joined us later, and what a good night we all had together . . . and bless Lillie for thinking of such a scheme. Lillie laughed as we bundled up to leave, the men trying their best to scowl over our foolishness, mumbling about us throwing caution to the wind.

"I know Jack thinks I was being reckless," she whispered to us, "but I just wasn't in the mood to give in to another bad day."

We all looked at each other, and it was as if we understood without speaking what Lillie meant by that. I think we all felt we'd had to give in too much already, and as simple as it seemed, our *not* giving in had lifted our spirits, had made us feel like we had a choice again.

"Besides, who is Jack to lecture *us* about being reckless?" I whispered back as I headed out the door with Quinn and the children, and "us girls" couldn't help but chuckle.

The popping, cracking sounds of tree branches breaking and falling to the ground under the weight of the ice and snow echo loudly in the night as I write this. I'd like to imagine it's fireworks that I hear, celebrating our new year . . .

And Lord willing, a new page in our lives.

January 2, 1870 . . .

The Sabbath. The weather has come in almost gentle over the valley today, as if nature is paying its respects to God as well. The sun shines bright, brighter than it has in days, making the Absaroka Mountains look so bold as the sunlight sends slivers of light and warmth across the white blanket of valley.

We have had a good day of prayer and fellowship together, the weather, being as good as it was, seeming to lift our spirits even more.

As Quinn began from the Book of Joshua, I found myself looking out the window as he read, " 'So the sun stood still in the midst of heaven, and hasted not to go down about a whole day. And there was no day like that before it or after it, that the LORD hearkened unto the voice of a man: for the LORD fought for Israel.' "

I looked to the sun shining bright over the mountains then turned back to the faces of my family sitting in our cramped little cabin, and I saw that the light of faith had begun to shine bright in their eyes again. And I wondered if it could be possible that God had given us the day as it was to show us His love, to show us He was fighting for us, too.

None of us were exactly "Joshuas," but then, I remember something a very wise little girl reminded us all awhile back.

She said Jesus wasn't a *suspector* of persons . . .

January 3, 1870 . . .

Back to work today. Sunday seems to have not only lifted our spirits, but our energy as well. Quinn is already out and about with Jack, tending to the animals, and I have finished all but my mending for this morning.

Patrick is off to cut wood and check the coop. Rose made a quick job of helping me get the bread kneaded before she was off to help Jessie begin her "learnin' to read."

So much to be done. Ah well, what is it Stem used to say? *"A wishbone ain't no substitute for a backbone."*

And now I, little journal, must get back to work myself.

January 5, 1870 . . .

Jack and Quinn came in with the news this morning that we lost four head out of the herd. It breaks my heart to hear of any of those poor beasts freezing to death, but the men say it's a very small loss. I'm sure I will get used to being a "cattlewoman," but right now any news of loss is not *small* to me. And yet, there is a new strength in me—in all of us, I think, that keeps us looking past what we see and on to that place where hope for better is . . .

When Quinn came in this afternoon for a quick bite to eat, I noticed he was in one of his talking moods as he mentioned that Rose had told him of the quilt Jessie made, saying he'd never heard of a memory quilt. I told him Lillie's story, then asked if he wanted to see Rose's quilt, and soon we were up and climbing the little ladder to the loft.

We both fell silent as we stared at Rose's bed and discovered what all those nights of her "working on something" were about.

It was the queerest-looking doll I had ever seen: dark burlap face with what looked to be shocks of white horsehair standing out on its head, with a piece of buckskin sewed around its body for a coat. One of its legs was a stick.

"It's Stem," I said, feeling a lump in my throat.

"'Tis enough to spook a man, is what it is," Quinn said, his accent thickening like it always did when he was unsettled. "Looks as if it has the mange . . ."

"It's *Stem*," I said again, and as we looked at the doll we smiled at each other—but neither of us had the heart to laugh. There was something oddly poignant about that odd doll sitting in its place of honor on Jessie's "quilt of memories."

Later—Another snowstorm has blown into the valley tonight, stronger than any we've had so far. Though I hate to admit it, it feels like the storm hasn't just thrown its shadow over the land, but over us as well.

January 6, 1870 . . .

More snow. Worry comes tonight like a hand squeezing our throats, trying to choke our faith . . . our hope. Quinn stood at the window for a long time after dinner, just looking out and not saying a word. He didn't have to. His eyes said enough . . .

He's carving on a piece of wood now, sitting by the fire.

"Mama?" Patrick called from his bed to me this evening as I was writing this. "Yes, Patrick," I said, then there was a brief silence. "That man that was in the fiery furnace with Shadrach, Meshach, and Abednego, that was *Jesus*, wasn't it?"

"Yes," I said and glanced over at Quinn, who had set his carving down and was listening, too.

"Jesus stood in there with them so they wouldn't be scared,

didn't He?" This time Patrick didn't wait for my answer, but went on. "Because I know I wouldn't be scared of no fire or *nothing* if Jesus was standing there with me."

"You're right about that, honey," I said, then fell silent for a moment.

I got tears in my eyes, and Quinn did, too, as he looked over at me and whispered, "Out of the mouth of babes, eh, lass?"

All I could do was nod.

How soon we forget to trust, Lord, when some new trouble comes our way . . . And how much more I understand now Your words when You said:

> *Verily I say unto you,*
> *Whosoever shall not receive the kingdom of God*
> *as a little child shall in no wise enter therein.*
> —LUKE 18:17

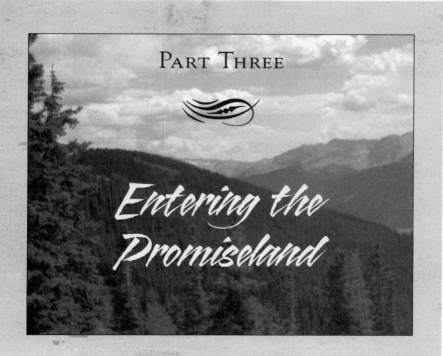

PART THREE

Entering the Promiseland

Some people were scairt of the gients.
But Joshwa and Kalib wernt.
They knew God was bigger.
So they kept going.

By Rose McGregor
age 9 1/2
Mountana Teritery, 1870

*Patrick's sweet words are still ringing in my years, and yet once again
we face another trial. I'm almost afraid to write the words, Lord, but
You know my heart. I am afraid of what will come of all of this. Of
all of us. I'm so weary of trouble, but when I think of quitting it just
doesn't seem to be a choice for me anymore. If my steps falter, will You
hold my hand and lead me on?*

If we weren't living this, if I wasn't seeing it for myself, I
would hardly believe another trouble has come to our door so
soon.

It all started when Jack and Quinn, seeing a break in the
weather, decided to go for supplies this morning and came back
with bad news.

It appears that while they were in the mercantile, Jack overheard some part-Indian fellow bragging about being paid to
guide a military party against the Blackfeet—declaring to the
Audreys that he was going to help see to it that the Blackfeet
would be "herded onto a reservation where they belonged."

We all just stood there, looking at Jack, then I glanced over
at Lillie, and I never saw her look so scared in all my life. I'd be
lying if I said I wasn't scared, too, because I know Jack, and I
knew by the way he was avoiding Lillie's eyes that he was going
to ride off to warn the Blackfeet before he said it out loud.

"I can't pretend I didn't hear it, Lillie," he said, low, like he
was trying to soften the blow of his leaving with his tone.
"They're my friends—our boy's *kin*," he added.

"What about us, Jack?" Lillie said, looking down at Mercy
sleeping in her arms. "What about *our* family?" She looked up,
startled, then, like something had just occurred to her. "You
aren't taking John-Charles!" she cried.

We all looked back at Jack again, and he looked down at
John-Charles, putting his hand on his son's head. "It might be
the only time he'll be able to see them free," he said quietly.

Then he asked Quinn if he would help him get the horses ready. Quinn looked over at me with a quick, sorry look then turned to follow Jack out the door.

Just like that, he was going. I knew there was no arguing with him, either. I had seen the look in his eyes before, that kind of faraway look that said he was already gone to the Blackfeet in his mind but was just waiting for his body to catch up.

"Ain't nothin' gonna happen," Jack said, trying to comfort Lillie when he and Quinn came back. "I know where their winter camp is. It'll only be a week, Lillie—two at the most—and then we'll be back home." He hugged her tight to him then, and I saw Lillie relent, and I knew that as mad as she was, it was because she was scared not to let him go.

Jessie and me helped to finish packing the food for him, and the whole time we were wrapping things up, I felt low, like I was helping my brother go to his grave. Jack kissed me on the cheek then grinned at me like he understood. I tried not to cry as I watched him hug Rose and Patrick then Jessie, shaking Quinn's hand before he hugged Lillie to him and kissed Mercy's head. John-Charles waved to everyone like he was going on a picnic, and that made me want to cry even more.

"I thought we had made it, you know?" Lillie said as we all shivered on the porch together, watching him ride away with John-Charles. "What if he doesn't come back?"

"He'll be back," I said, and as I did, it was like I could hear the sound of my voice mingling with the faraway sound of my mama's. "Our hearts always lead us home."

"Where's home?" Lillie said dully as she turned to me. Her eyes were full of sorrow and doubt, and I saw Jessie reach over and pat her back.

"We're home, honey," Jessie said. "We jes got a little more walkin' to do, is all, to get across that ol' Jordan."

Before they walked off toward their cabins, I heard Lillie ask Jessie if she would mind staying the night with her, and her voice sounded so young and lost it broke my heart to hear it. Jessie, of course, was more than happy to oblige.

I've thought and thought tonight. Thought about all that's happened, about the prayers and the shining moments of seeing answers . . . thought about what Patrick said and Jessie's words, too. I would think after all we've been through, I would've known better than to get so comfortable so soon . . . that I would've remembered that winning a battle doesn't mean you've won the war. And yet I *did* start thinking that way.

All of this talk of our promiseland made me remember what Preacher said about the Israelites and their journey to the Promised Land. Made me remember, too, how downright foolish I thought they were for complaining and getting scared after all God had shown them.

And now, I guess I'm acting no better.

January 8, 1870 . . .

Finished my washing early this morning. I hung everything outside as the sun was shining at first, then by noon a bitter wind began to blow, freezing the clothes, so I brought them back in and have them draped around the fire now.

It is snowing again, and all I can think of is Jack and John-Charles.

Why is it that I can't hear that still, gentle voice that speaks to my heart tonight? I keep paging through my Bible, looking for a scripture to ease my worries . . .

January 10, 1870 . . .

Cold but clear today. Quinn has rode out to Willa's to ask Coy to come help until Jack gets back. Yesterday was the Sabbath, and we spent it reading scriptures and praying. We all are trying our best to keep Lillie's spirits up.

It was so hard—I never have been much of an actress when it comes to hiding my feelings.

I feel so far away from everything, like I'm just going through the motions as my thoughts stray to Jack. My worries. I tried reading scripture again but couldn't seem to find the patience to sit still long enough . . .

I overheard Patrick asking Quinn tonight when John-Charles would be home and heard Quinn telling him soon—that his Uncle Jack knew the calving would be starting shortly and that he hadn't ever left them short-handed yet.

Yet . . .

Jessie and Lillie have been spending a lot of time together, talking, like there's something they share now that they hadn't shared before.

I—no, I won't even think it.

Later—I've just woke up from a dream. I dreamt I was standing alone, surrounded by nothing but blue, when I saw a hand hold something out for me to see. I knew somehow it was Jesus' hand. So I squinted my eyes to try to see what He was holding, and then I realized it was a key of some kind. My only thought was I had to get that key, that it would help me in some way, so I reached forward to take the key, and suddenly Jesus closed His hand over mine, holding it still.

"I am the key," He said, and then suddenly I was awake, looking around my room, and now here I sit writing this, Preacher's words coming back to haunt me . . .

"When the trials came, they forgot," he'd said. "They ended up wandering year after year because they forgot God was God."

Thank You for reminding me, Lord. Help me to be strong, to not get so caught up in my worry that I forget You are in charge of all. I pray that You keep Jack and John-Charles in Your loving arms and that You bring them home safely.

January 12, 1870 . . .

Where has the day gone to? I feel like I just opened my eyes, and now it's time to shut them again. I am so tired, but I feel stronger, too, if that makes any sense. I looked in my mirror tonight as I brushed my hair out and was surprised at the woman who stared back at me.

She looked determined, like she could handle just about anything.

January 14, 1870 . . .

From every cut springs new growth, my mama used to say, and though it's the middle of January I feel like we've all been budding in spite of the cold, in spite of our worries for Jack and John-Charles. It's like we've all begun to be of one mind, not just in our work, but most important, in our prayers. Like a row of wheat that springs up out of the ground to reach for the sun at the same exact time . . .

Coy has been helping Quinn quite a bit around the ranch, although he tries to get back to Willa's every chance he can to "help the women." Lillie spends a lot of time between Jessie's and our cabin now, and Mercy gets so much attention Lillie fears she will be "spoiled silly" by the time Jack and John-Charles come home.

Patrick is lost without his cousin. He asks, "When is John-Charles coming back?" so many times that as I write this Rose is telling him to hush. She is taking teaching Jessie to read real serious, her little red head bent down next to Jessie's as they pore over an old reader of hers. "No, Jessie," Rose says, "it sounds like *this*."

Jessie, with her beautiful, old, dark face screwed up in concentration, glances up suddenly, and I see her cock her head to one side as she looks at Rose, sizing her up.

A determined gleam has come to Jessie's eyes, and it's almost like I can hear her thoughts: *If that little slip of a thing can do it—I can, too.*

And I have no doubt she can.

January 20, 1870 . . .

I was the first to wake this morning and so went to fetch some wood to get breakfast started. I was almost back to the cabin when I had the strong feeling come over me to pray for Jack and his boy. So strong that I took no thought of dropping to my knees in the snow as I bowed my head and prayed.

I'm not sure how long I prayed, but when I opened my eyes I saw Jasper and Honey sitting together right in front of me, just staring. They didn't jump around or try to play as I stood up but followed me quietly back to the house, like they understood.

January 27, 1870 . . .

We have been so hard at work, trying to keep ahead of this bitter weather, that I haven't had a chance to write until now. I have so much to tell you, little journal, and I'm sure you will be as pleased as me to find out it's good news.

Jack and John-Charles have finally come home!

We were laying out some wild hay for the cattle when I saw Quinn kind of cock his head to one side, like he sensed something. Then Coy straightened up and shaded his eyes against the glare of the snow, looking toward the distance. "Rider comin'," was all he said. Then Jessie said excitedly, "It's Jack. I just know it, Callie."

I dropped the hay I had in my hands and pushed my bonnet almost clear off my head so I could see, then I started walking, then running through the snow toward the rider heading into the valley. Even from a distance I could see Jack's wide grin when he spotted me running for him. By the time he trotted up and dismounted to hug me, everyone had surrounded us, laughing and slapping him on the back. John-Charles was so worn out he could just open his eyes a crack to look at Rose and Patrick, then I told my two to run and let Lillie know Jack was home.

We all walked with Jack the rest of the way to his cabin, and as we did, I couldn't help noticing how thin he'd become. But the smile that suddenly appeared on his face when he saw Lillie standing on their front porch with Mercy in her arms was something to behold.

They just stood staring at each other, then Jack turned to lift a sleeping John-Charles from his saddle.

"This the Wade place?" he asked, and I saw Lillie had tears running down her face, but she grinned, too, as she tried to smooth her windblown curls into place quick.

"Sure is," she said as a dimple appeared in her cheek. "You're welcome to come in and try the fare if you like."

"Well now," Jack said. "How do I know it'll be worth the price?"

Lillie shrugged. "You don't. But I guarantee you, it's the only place around that'll give you a square deal," she said, and then they both chuckled like it was an old joke between them.

As I listened to their easy banter, I couldn't help thinking the picture they must have made back in Virginia City: the lady dealer and the gentleman gambler. I told Jessie as much as we stood there, and she nodded.

"I imagine they were a sight," she said as we watched him climb the steps, and he and Lillie shut the door behind them. "Only I never in my life heard tell of a gambler that had tears running down his face like that—unless he lost. And your brother sure don't look like he's lost."

Quinn said tonight I was so pretty in my "happy state" that he would've rode out and carried Jack back on his shoulders if he'd have known the "gude" outcome of it.

"I haven't looked *that* bad, have I?" I asked, and he smiled and wrapped his arms around me.

"It wasn't your looks I was speaking of, lass," he said soft. "'Tis one blessing you Wades have, is that you look good even when things are bad. What I was talking about was your heart, the way your eyes shine your happiness for others. I think I would work double my whole life if I could keep your eyes shining like that."

"You probably will," I said, teasing, and we both laughed. Then we hugged and kissed . . . and well, the rest, little journal, is not for you to know . . .

January 28, 1870 . . .

We have had everyone at our cabin tonight for dinner to celebrate Jack and John-Charles's return. John-Charles seemed so quiet tonight. But it wasn't until our little ones had tuckered themselves out and fell asleep on the floor in front of the fire that we had the chance to hear what had happened on Jack's trip—what happened to John-Charles.

Such a sorrowful, horrible tale . . .

Jack said he and John-Charles had only been with the Indians one night when the military attacked the encampment at daybreak on the *twentieth of January*, the day I'd prayed out in the snow. His voice grew hoarse as he told how the soldiers killed more than 173 Blackfeet, how they captured nearly 140 women and children and led off more than 300 horses. He said the military report was a lie—that they claimed all who were killed were "able-bodied men"—except for fifty or more women and children that were "accidentally killed."

He said, "And I'd like to know how it was 'self-defense' when only one soldier was killed in the battle." Then his face hardened even more, and the muscle in his jaw twitched.

"God forgive me, but I wanted to kill them all for what they did," Jack said then, looking away from us for a moment. "But we were outnumbered and outgunned from the get-go."

Jack said he and John-Charles lay next to Medicine Weasel, John-Charles's grandfather, in the gully to hide. And as they were hiding, he looked down at John-Charles then, expecting him to be hiding his face, but he was looking straight ahead, his eyes growing old as he watched the battle before him. He said when the soldiers had finished and rode away, John-Charles scrambled up the embankment and headed for the village without looking back once. When Jack finally reached the encampment, he said he spotted John-Charles standing in the middle of the smoke and dead bodies littered through camp, just staring. He stared so long and hard Jack said he thought his heart would break for his son.

He looked at all of us, grim, then went on with the telling of it. Something eerie happened next. He said as he was standing there, he noticed the camp had grown strangely quiet, then out of nowhere a group of horses that had been turned loose came stampeding through the camp. Jack said before he could call out to John-Charles, he was already off and *running* in the midst of the herd. Jack watched him, stunned, unable to reach him, as he ran and ran right along with the wildly pounding horses—and to everyone's amazement after the dust settled, they found him without a single scratch.

Later that night as the elders gathered around the fire, amid the wails of grief and cries for revenge, Jack said the old men kept turning to study John-Charles as he slept peacefully in Jack's lap.

"They told me they had named him Runs-with-Horses and that what he had done was a sign to them," Jack said, "a sign that white men might take their lands—but the white men would never own their hearts."

"Why would they talk like that to *you?*" I said then, and Jack's smile was grim.

"They don't see me as white, Callie," he said, "not after living with them like I did."

But by the troubled look on his face, I knew there was something that had bothered him about it.

Lillie sensed it, too. I saw it in her eyes as she looked over at me, like she had seen, too, that something had been taken from Jack, making him appear suddenly unsure of what might be next.

I saw him watch the fire for a long while, glancing to John-Charles from time to time with such a sad look on his face.

When I finally got the chance to ask him in private what was the matter, he said, "When Raven died, Medicine Weasel told me that no person is ours alone, that they're with us for however long it takes us to learn from them. He told me that's why he wouldn't fight me taking John-Charles away from the tribe. He said there would be things we'd teach each other." Jack ran his hand over his face then, and when he looked at me his eyes were so sad. "But you know what, sis? I think that old man just knew John-Charles would be coming back to him anyway, that maybe all he had to do is wait."

The grief on Jack's face was like he'd already lost John-Charles. As much as I wanted to tell him it surely wasn't that bad, I couldn't.

John-Charles *does* seem changed. I'll never forget the look in his eyes when I hugged him tonight . . . Those green eyes, so much like Jack's, stared back at me with the look of an old man . . . and so distant. Jack and Lillie hadn't missed it, either. I know by the way Jack was so quick to turn and take Mercy from Lillie's arms, like he was already trying to comfort his loss in some way.

Tonight, after everyone had left, I told Quinn it didn't seem fair, after all that Jack had been through, with how hard he'd fought to be a godly man, for this to come to his door now.

"Seems none of us are through battling our giants, yet," Quinn said. "But if any family is up to the fight, I'd say we are." There was a gentling in the lines at his eyes, and he sat down next to me then put his arm around my shoulders, like he always did to comfort me.

Oh Lord, I come to You again and ask that You see us all through this, that we somehow find Your rest . . . There's so much I hope for my children, for all those I love . . . I guess that's why I understand Jack's worry.

Even as I write this, I wonder if that old Indian was right. Is anyone really ever ours to keep? Even our children? Or are they merely on loan from You, just long enough to see how we'll treat the gift?

May we never lose sight of what a gift each and every one of us is to each other.

January 29, 1870 . . .

Back to work again. Quinn goes to tend the cattle and horses with Jack, Rose milks, and Patrick is off with Jasper and Honey to fetch some more wood. He said to me when he bundled up to go, "Mama, I hope it gets warm soon or we're gonna run out of trees."

I can safely say, looking out the window, that I don't think we're in any danger of running out of trees anytime soon.

It is a bright blue day but so cold. White clouds drift around the mountain peeks and seem to hang just above us, almost like you could reach up and touch them . . .

I just spotted John-Charles and Patrick walking toward the woodpile together. They don't appear to be talking much. Patrick has put his arm around John-Charles's shoulder . . . so much like his pa, he seems to sense that sometimes a touch is better than words.

Lillie and me took a trip to Jessie's cabin tonight for a little "mending" party. "Makes a quick work of sewin' when ye have conversation," Jessie said when she'd told us her idea earlier in the day, and we couldn't help but agree. It was a real treat, too, for us to be alone together, to be free to talk and not worry who might hear.

It was no surprise to any of us that as soon as we began to sew, we started talking on all that had happened with Jack and John-Charles.

"Jack's just sick about the whole thing," Lillie said as she jabbed a needle into a pair of worn trousers. "He said he begged Medicine Weasel and some of the others to come with him, but the old man told him he had to see to his people. Now he's just worrying on what it's done to John-Charles to see what he's seen."

"I don't think any of us can imagine what's going on in that little head of his right now," I said as I sewed on one of Rose's dresses.

"You know, I cared for John-Charles that time after his mama was shot . . . when Jack couldn't . . . well, you know. Anyway, sometimes it scared me that he never cried for her. Never cried for nothing, for that matter. He'd just look at me with those eyes of his, like Jack's but different, too . . ." Lillie looked up at me and Jessie then, and I saw the worry in her eyes, and I knew she was wondering what would come of all of it.

"And now I see that look again. Like he knows everything and he hasn't made up his mind whether he likes this world or not."

"Well, honey, I still haven't made up my mind on *that,* either," Jessie said, looking up from her own sewing, and we all smiled softly at each other. "But one thing I do know for sure is the Lord is faithful, and He's done seen us through so much, He'll see us through this, too."

"*If any family is up to the fight, ours is,*" Quinn had said, and I felt strengthened by the memory of those words. "We just can't give up," I said then. "I remember my mama saying once that life wasn't one long race but a bunch of little ones strung together by time . . . I can't help thinking this is another one we've been given to run."

"Seems like we've been given an awful lot of them races since we've been here, doesn't it?" Lillie said, then she looked between Jessie and me. "Do you ever wonder if God's testing our faith?"

"I've thought on that lately," Jessie said, biting a piece of thread in two. "I don't think He's the one sending the troubles—but I do think He's curious to see what we do with them."

Lillie was quiet for a bit, then I saw her glance away for a moment, a thoughtful look on her face.

"I asked John-Charles to say grace this morning at breakfast, and he said he didn't want to. Said he didn't believe no more. Said he was mad at God. You know what Jack said?" she said softly. "He said, 'You can't be mad at Someone you don't believe in.'"

"What did John-Charles say to that?" Jessie asked, and Lillie smiled a bittersweet kind of smile.

"He said, 'Well, I'm still mad at Him, and you can't change my mind about *that*, Pa!'"

Lillie smiled softly. "All of a sudden I got this real peaceful feeling, and I looked at Jack and said, 'Well, we've been mad before, too, haven't we?' Then he and I bowed our heads and joined hands to pray. You know what? About halfway through Jack saying grace, I felt John-Charles's hand suddenly come to rest on top of ours. All I could think was I had felt just like that before. I mean, how many times have we *all* felt like that, torn between not wanting to believe but knowing deep down He's there, tugging at our angry hearts?"

"Ain't that the truth...," Jessie said. "Ain't that the truth."

I just nodded, and Lillie and Jessie fell silent with me as we went back to sewing. Sometimes the comfort of being with folks that understand the deep-down things in you is enough. Any words after that would've just gotten in the way.

January 30, 1870...

We had a good day, just being together again. Jack read scripture for the Sabbath, ending his reading with a verse he picked from the Song of Solomon: "Many waters cannot quench love, neither can the floods drown it."

I recall it being one of Mama's favorites.

It's funny that it's only now that I'm beginning to under-stand why she liked it so.

January 31, 1870 . . .

It's been such a mild day for January—which is why we girls took advantage of it—scrubbing our wash *and* our hair, so we could "hang" both out to dry. We had no idea it would cause such a commotion . . .

Lillie and I had been sitting on the porch, letting our hair dry in the sun, when the Indians appeared in our yard out of the blue. We had been talking (I can't even remember what we were saying, now) when I'd happened to turn and saw this old Indian grinning back at me. It struck me odd that his teeth looked so white set in such an old, leathered face. He was dressed in buck-skins, wearing what looked to be an ancient pair of cowboy boots on his feet. The young brave standing next to him was a bit stockier, his long hair black instead of silver, but his smile was the same. Next thing we knew, they were stepping up onto our porch, easy as you please.

I'd almost caught my breath when I noticed they weren't really looking at us, but at our *hair*. I saw Lillie put a shaky hand on the arm of her chair as if to rise, but I stopped her. "I'll go get Jack," I said, rising from my own chair. Somewhere around the back of the cabins I could hear the children playing, and I thought to go in the opposite direction. I turned and made like to pass the Indians—and almost succeeded until I felt my hair being grabbed up by strong hands at the nape of my neck. I glanced sideways and saw the older one smiling at me, and I felt the younger one tug on my hair, moving his hands downward, to where my hair fell past the back of my knees. I drew in a deep breath to scream or faint, I'm not sure which one, but then I heard Lillie say, "Why, aren't you—"

Suddenly Jack was there, with Quinn and Coy standing in

the yard. I heard Jack say something in a strange language then heard him laugh, and I thought if I wasn't so scared I would have took off after him.

"Callie, that there is Medicine Weasel," Jack said, trying to keep a straight face. I heard the older one say something and then felt the younger brave move his hands off my hair. "One Shot was just measuring your hair," Jack said then. "He ain't ever saw hair so long as yours and Lillie's—but yours is a curiosity. They ain't ever seen red hair."

Jack stepped up on the porch after grasping first Medicine Weasel in a bear hug then the brave called One Shot. Finally he turned and made his introductions. I tried my best to act casual, but the old man stared at me close, then turned and said something to Jack, and they both laughed.

"Medicine Weasel says not to worry, Callie. They don't like to scalp family. It makes for bad feelings."

Well, everyone laughed at that, and I found myself starting to smile too, after I'd gotten over my shock. Pretty soon everyone was filing into our cabin to share some lunch together, and I found myself actually enjoying hearing their laughter as Jack spoke to them then translated for everyone. John-Charles seemed so happy, sitting close to his grandfather's feet as he spoke, but Patrick was almost beside himself with excitement.

"A real live medicine man in our house!" he exclaimed to anyone who would listen, then he turned to his sister. "It's just like in those stories, Rose."

"Oh, Chubs, you're such a *child*," Rose said with all the dignity of a nine-year-old, and we all laughed at that.

We talked and visited all afternoon, Medicine Weasel and One Shot sitting on the floor as they didn't take to chairs for some reason. Then at one point I noticed Medicine Weasel watching us all closely for some time, like he was studying each one of us separately. After a while of that he appeared suddenly satisfied, and I saw him turn and start talking in Blackfoot. I watched Jack's eyes fill up with tears.

"What's he saying?" I asked.

"He says he feels comfortable here," Jack said, listening to the old Indian intently. "He says he thinks we are like the Blackfeet, like him." Jack turned and looked at us then. His smiled was sad. "He says that as he was studying us, he was able to see under our skin and into our spirits, and he saw that our hearts had been broken like his."

The old man looked over at Lillie, who was holding little Mercy in her arms, and he gestured to her. Lillie looked from him to Jack with a little fear in her eyes.

"He's asking to hold her," Jack explained. Then gently he took Mercy from Lillie's arms and placed her into Medicine Weasel's hands. Medicine Weasel looked down at Mercy, and for the second time that day, we saw him smile. He spoke to Jack, and Jack spoke back in the strange tongue, then the old man laughed—a wry kind of laugh.

"He asked her name and what it meant, and when I told him, he said *mercy* is what everyone seeks. He says it's funny he found Mercy in a white man's camp."

Medicine Weasel struggled to his feet and walked slowly over to where Lillie stood. He handed the baby back to her, and when their eyes met, I felt like a kind of peace had settled between them. When he spoke again, it was in English, which startled us all—all but Jack, that is.

"She will give mercy to many," Medicine Weasel said, looking down at the baby and then to John-Charles, who stood close enough to be his shadow. He put his gnarled old hand on top of John-Charles's head with a tenderness that touched my heart. "But she will give the most to her brother."

Our guests have refused the invitation to sleep in the cabins but instead have set to erecting a tepee in the yard—sending the children into whoops of joy.

"Mama, do you think Medicine Weasel would be my grandpa, too?" Rose asked, her face pressed against the window, and it hit me that Rose's curious draw to Medicine Weasel wasn't just because he was an Indian. It was because of losing Stem.

"Me, too," Patrick chimed in, and Rose gave him a look before turning back to me. "Well, Mama?" she said, and I told her I didn't rightly know.

"If you get to, I get to," Patrick said. Rose ignored him until she glanced over and saw the sorrowful look on his little face. I watched her irritation turn to pity, seeing the big bottom lip that stuck out, the pale blue eyes like his pa's, now watery with tears.

"Oh, come on, Chubs, you can sleep with me tonight," she said then, all benevolent. I followed them up the ladder into the loft to tuck them in and watched as Rose set her "doll" off to one side to draw her little memory quilt back and let Patrick in beside her.

Watching Patrick snuggle in with his sister, I thought of how truly blessed we were to have our family together. It made me think, too, of how cruel it was that Medicine Weasel had lost so much of his own family—even his home, by what Jack says. And for no other reason than greed for the land.

After Rose and Patrick finished their prayers, I found myself back downstairs, staring out the window to where Medicine Weasel and One Shot stood with Jack and Quinn, talking. I saw the old Indian glance around to the cabins, then to where some of our cattle were nosing through the snow, and I saw a look come over his face like he was trying to figure something out. His eyes followed the slopes up to the mountains, then back to the valley, and I realized he was wondering why there wasn't room enough for all of us. It was the same kind of look I'd seen on Jessie's face before, like you can't quite understand the cruelty of some people's hearts.

I admit I can't understand it either, and I know God doesn't like it.

What was it Thomas Jefferson said? "Indeed, I tremble for my country when I reflect that God is just."

February 1, 1870 . . .

So bitterly cold today. Rose, Patrick, and John-Charles haven't left the front of the fireplace since they finished their chores this morning. They're playing a game that One Shot taught them, spinning "tops" made of birch wood. Whoever's top, after they smack against each other, can spin the longest, wins.

John-Charles is in the lead, but Rose and Patrick don't seem to mind. I think they're just glad to see him smiling again.

I know I am.

Back to cooking, little journal. We're planning a potluck tonight, and if I don't get to cooking, my *pot* isn't going to be too lucky.

Later—We had such a good time over dinner. Medicine Weasel is about as interesting a person as I have ever met. And, it appears, he was the "talker" of the group tonight.

First thing he shared as he came in was that he didn't "have much respect for cows." He said when they all rode out this morning to check on some of the herd that had drifted toward the slopes, looking for something to eat, he was shocked to see two cows pretty near dead. Just standing there, he said, *starving*.

"Buffalo have better manners than to die like this," he said in English, with a hint of disdain.

"Do Indians believe in God?" Patrick said out of the blue then. Rose tried to nudge him, but I noticed John-Charles looked up at Medicine Weasel, curious to see what he would say.

"Some do," Medicine Weasel replied. He glanced over at Jack and Lillie, then to John-Charles, who was sitting next to him with a considering look on his face.

"Big Plume, a great warrior, told me once how the Lord saved him," he said. Then he smiled, looking over at Jack. "It is a good story."

"We want to hear it, then," Jack said, and everyone agreed.

There was once a young brave, Medicine Weasel told us, who got lost during a raid and ended up alone in the enemy camp. When he realized he was alone, at first he cried, then he remembered about the Lord of the "black robes." As he ran away from the enemy camp, he began to pray. When dawn came he hid in a badger hole until night, then he started running again and praying until morning came, and he hid in the brush, where he fell asleep. As he slept, he dreamed of a handsome white Man who wore a canvas shirt. The Man said to him, "Don't cry, and don't be afraid. You will get home safely." The next morning as he hid and slept, the Man came to him again, this time wearing a blue shirt and saying the same comforting words to him. The third morning, he dreamed of the Man again; this time He wore a red shirt, and He smiled at Big Plume . . .

The fourth time the Man came to him in his dreams was when Big Plume reached the mountains. This time the Man was wearing a skin shirt with holes in it and crosses painted on it. The Man said, "Don't be afraid. I am the Lord, and I am sorry for you. You will get home, and you will live to be an old man."

"As soon as Big Plume made it home, he had a skin shirt made, just like the one he saw in his dream, with holes and red crosses painted on it," Medicine Weasel said. "He wore it in battle and was never injured. When he got too old, he prayed to the Lord and then passed it on to Bear Chief, who also was never injured while wearing it. To this day it is called 'the Lord's shirt.'"

"I sure wish I had that shirt, Grandpa," John-Charles said suddenly, looking up at Medicine Weasel earnestly, and the old man smiled.

"I wish I had that shirt, too," he said with an almost sad note to his voice. Then he looked around the table at all of us. "Big Plume taught me a prayer. Would you like me to say it?"

We all smiled through our tears, nodding as we joined hands around the table, and I saw John-Charles grab first his grandfather's hand, then Lillie's. Medicine Weasel bowed his head and prayed in his humble old voice:

"God Almighty—

"The Blackfeet are all His children.

"He is going to help us on earth;

"If you are good, He will save your soul."

A fine dinner it turned out to be. I think it was the first time in my life I saw someone glad to be wrong. Lillie fairly beamed at Medicine Weasel the rest of the evening, and the poor old fellow, not quite sure why she was doing all that smiling, kept glancing from Jack to One Shot with a puzzled kind of smile, then he'd go back to watching the children spin their tops.

February 3, 1870 . . .

Medicine Weasel still hasn't gotten over my red hair. Tonight after dinner he told Jack he wished for me to give him a lock of it to keep.

I whispered to Jack he could wish all he wanted but he wasn't getting any of my hair, then Jack went and told him and One Shot what I said, and they all had a good laugh about it.

I couldn't help but grin, too, and when my eyes met with Medicine Weasel's, I saw in his look that he was as curious about me as I am about him.

February 7, 1870 . . .

More visitors today. I'm not complaining, though. It's nice to have a break like this to share laughter and food over a warm fire with friends.

Willa, Coy, Bonnie, and the kids were the first to arrive. Willa stepped down from the wagon, took another look at Medicine Weasel's tepee, and said, "I had a feeling there was something interesting going on."

"Makes ye get up early jes to see what might happen next around here," Jessie laughed, and there was something in her laugh that touched my heart.

I think Jack was worried about an argument breaking out as he's told us the Blackfeet and Crow have always been enemies, but Bonny, Medicine Weasel, and One Shot all got along fine, as if there was a silent understanding between them that they had all lost enough.

Then Preacher arrived, looking surprised but pleased at our crowd as we all once again crowded into our cabin to visit. Medicine Weasel seemed eager for the visit as well, hobbling in behind everyone on his threadbare boots—boots, I'd learned from Jack, that he'd taken in trade all those years ago for nursing Jack back to health.

Rose helped me in the kitchen, and I made tea and some sweet cakes, then put on a pot of beans and had Quinn fetch a chicken for me to bake for later.

When Jack told the story of what happened to the Blackfeet, I saw Willa's face growing suddenly sad, the old doubter in her rearing up again.

"Where is God in that, Shawn?" she asked, glancing over at Medicine Weasel and One Shot, and Preacher shook his head like he'd had the conversation before.

"Those soldiers had a choice," Preacher said. "God gives us that choice—He doesn't want us for puppets, you know."

Willa glanced up with a thoughtful look on her face. "Don't you wish we were—puppets, I mean? Wouldn't it be easier?" she asked, and Preacher looked at her for what seemed a long time.

"No," he said finally. "That would be like forcing someone to do something he doesn't want to do. It wouldn't be real, Willa. You can't force people's will—or their love. It wouldn't be worth much if you did."

We all nodded at the truth of his words—even Willa—and Medicine Weasel, who I know had been listening, chose that moment to turn to Jack and ask him something in Blackfoot.

From the moment Medicine Weasel learned that Preacher was a "holy man," the old Indian had taken a keen interest in what Preacher had to say. So much so that he had chose a spot on the floor close to where Preacher was, for better study of him.

Jack told Preacher then that Medicine Weasel wanted to hear a story from him, and we all smiled. We'd been quick to learn the Blackfeet loved a good story. I remember Jack telling me once that they enjoyed a story better than most anything and would drop whatever they were doing to hear a good tale told. He'd said they figure the work will always be there, but the storyteller might not.

"Why don't you tell us how you got to be a preacher?" Jack asked, and after several of us pleaded, he finally relented.

"Not everyone from the North was good—or the South bad," Preacher started, looking about the faces of our group. His deep voice was both gentle and strong, causing us all to lean in as though we *felt* his words as well as heard them. "Just people caught in a war is all . . .

"*I* turned bad, though. Seemed the more battles we fought, the more death I saw, the more I drank. I drank and drank, until I wasn't worth much to my men—or to myself.

"One day as I was fixing to start my drinking for the evening, a traveling preacher showed up in our camp. I wasn't too happy about the interruption and decided if I had to be there, I was only going to pretend to listen. Then he starts talking about a war going on . . . a war we couldn't see, a war between God's forces and Satan's. I don't like admitting it now, but I made fun of him. I can't remember what exactly he said to get me to quiet down, but one thing I won't forget is what he told me later as he packed up to leave. He said, 'Son, you got a lot to learn about what's real and what's not. That liquid you pour down your throat isn't real—but God's going to show you what is. He sure is going to show you—and once He does, you aren't ever going to be the same.' "

Preacher was quiet for a bit, then he smiled a wry kind of smile as he glanced over at Willa before going on.

"About a month later, we were in the heat of another battle when I saw one of our boys—his name was Loyal—stand up from behind the barricade. 'Buddy!' he yelled and started running across the field. I saw another soldier then, a Confederate, and his head kind of snapped up, a huge smile broke across his dirty face, and he started running toward us all, yelling, 'Loyal!' over and over. Everything was so confused, with all the smoke and guns going off. One of our men must have thought Buddy was going to kill Loyal . . . he didn't know they were brothers.

"He shot Buddy just as Loyal reached him. But it was what happened next that I'll never forget as long as I live—none of our men will, if they were ever to admit what they saw. Loyal knelt down, crying, brushing Buddy's hair back from his head, and all of a sudden a stillness came over the whole battlefield. Then all of a sudden, there was these men standing around the two brothers—not soldiers, either, but big men, dressed in simple clothes. And they looked, well, clean—cleaner than anything I've ever seen. One of the big men knelt down next to the brothers, and we saw him take Buddy's hand. Loyal looked right up at the man, tears streaking his face, and said, 'He's going home, ain't he?' The man nodded, and then just like you blinked, they were gone—all but the two brothers—and bullets started flying past us again, smoke pouring across the field like it had never happened . . ."

"What happened to Loyal?" Jack asked, and Preacher smiled a small smile.

"Loyal carried his brother all the way across enemy lines to make sure he would get home for burial, then rejoined our unit that night. Not a scratch on him, either.

"All I could think of that night was that old traveling preacher's words, how God was going to show me what was real. I started thinking if I was going to choose sides, I wanted it to be God's side."

"Angels unaware," Patrick declared, looking up from the circle of children that sat by the fireplace, and we all smiled.

"I believe so, Patrick," Preacher said, nodding, and Patrick beamed at the other children with a satisfied look on his face.

Medicine Weasel sat back, seeming satisfied with the story, too. He turned to Jack and told him in Blackfoot that Preacher's angels made perfect sense to him. Jack told us he'd said if God is our Father, then it was only right that He would send bands of warriors to protect and defend His children.

"It is what any good father would do," Medicine Weasel said finally in English with a shrug of his thin shoulders.

It was then that I turned to see Willa, listening so close she was almost leaning out of her chair. I saw the look on her face, and I could have sworn that it looked like hope. Jessie and Lillie said they saw it, too.

"They say all things work together for good," Jessie said as we stood watching them leave tonight. "But who would have ever thought up a night like this, an old Indian talkin' church as good as Preacher?"

"Well . . . God would!" Lillie said, and we all grinned at each other. Then I said, "Makes you get up early just to see what might happen next around here."

We all laughed. Then Jessie said, "Well, it's truth, ain't it?" then we laughed again, and Jessie shook her head.

"Crazy as loons," she said, shaking her head again, but the way she smiled said she was glad of it.

I'm glad of it, too. I can't help thinking how strange the twists and turns of life's road are, how everything can seem so jumbled and tangled that you're almost sure there's no way to sort it out. Then all of a sudden, a mighty Hand seems to reach down and work those roads smooth so they cross each other at just the right time.

It's funny how the thing Jack and Lillie feared in John-Charles's ties to the Blackfeet is what brought them together closer as a family. I don't think I'll ever forget that old Indian and how he took to Mercy so quick, how with just a few words, he wove a cord that connected them all . . . and how he spoke of the Lord just when his grandson needed to hear it the most . . .

February 8, 1870 . . .

Quinn and Jack came in this afternoon for a quick cup of coffee and to tell us of our latest loss: One of the cows that had just calved had dropped dead right in front of them. They said that, as fate would have it, another one of the cows had lost a twin the night before, so they had set about the task of trying to get the cow to take to the orphan and nurse it, when they found they had an audience.

Rose and Patrick, they said, soon lost interest and went to

feed the horses, but John-Charles stayed on, watching until they were pretty sure the cow was allowing the calf to nurse.

Jack said what unnerved him most was when John-Charles had asked what would happen if the cow decided she only wanted her "real" calf.

"Oh, Jack," Lillie said, looking distressed. "My poor baby has been through so much."

If ever there was any doubt to anyone how much Lillie loved that little boy, it was forever erased by what we saw happen just before dinner as Rose, Patrick, and John-Charles all came tumbling in, their faces red from the cold.

The sudden wary look on John-Charles's face wasn't hard to see as he came skidding to a halt in the front of the room, watching Lillie as she rocked Mercy in her arms.

But Lillie, being Lillie, just looked up from Mercy and smiled at him. "Come on over here, and give your mama a hug," she said softly, and he shook his head, pointing to Mercy.

"Oh, honey," Lillie said. "I have enough room for two." She shifted Mercy to one side to show him, and after what seemed an eternity, he finally went to her. "I have room enough here," Lillie said, pointing to her lap and . . . here, too." When she pointed to her heart, something in John-Charles gave, and we watched as he climbed onto her lap and then leaned his head on her shoulder.

Jack had just carried in a pail of water from the spring for me. "I don't guess I could love anyone more than I love Lillie, sis," Jack said, watching the scene, his voice thick with emotion. I saw him look over at Medicine Weasel, who was smiling, too, in spite of the tears that stood in his eyes.

Jack crossed the room quickly then, catching Lillie by surprise as he leaned down and planted a kiss on her lips in front of us all. I felt like all the stiffness went out of the room as we chuckled.

Rose said, "Uncle Jack!" turning a shade of pink I never saw before, but Patrick just smiled.

"Aw, it's okay, Uncle Jack," he said, with a wave of his hand. "My mama and pa, they do's that all the time."

Everyone had a good laugh at that—except for Rose, who did her best to look fierce until Jessie put a friendly arm around her.

"And one day ye'll 'do's' that, too, sis," Jessie chuckled, and Rose couldn't help but laugh, too.

February 14, 1870 . . .

Patrick's birthday today. It's so hard to imagine my sweet little fellow being six years old already. I made him his favorite cake, and Quinn gave him a fine-looking fishing pole he had made himself. Jessie gave him a little wooden box with a lock on it that had been Stem's, and Jack gave him a little knife that Patrick thought was "first rate."

But Medicine Weasel outdid us all, giving Patrick a beautiful little drum that had bright red fish painted on it and feathers hanging from some of the straps.

No sooner had Patrick started his drumming than Jasper and Honey began to howl woefully to the "music," putting us all in stitches.

John-Charles didn't seem to mind at all as he sat and listened to Lillie, Medicine Weasel, and One Shot talking. But our sweet little Rose was green with envy.

"Can't he see that's hurting their ears," Rose said, a bit grumpily.

Jessie, who knew the green monster when she saw it, went and put her arms once again around Rose's shoulder, and I couldn't help thinking how close the two had become since Rose's decision to teach Jessie to read.

"Now, sis," she said to Rose gently. "Is that any way to carry on? Look at all the good Lord's given ye! Why, ye have a memory quilt *and* a fine doll, and it ain't even yer birthday yet. What's it hurt that yer brother have a little drum to play on?"

I should be used to Rose's moods changing like the wind by now, but she still surprised me—surprised us all—by going over and hugging Patrick.

"I'm sorry, Chubs," she said earnestly, then planted a kiss on his cheek.

Easygoing Patrick just grinned happily. "You were right, Jessie. Now she 'do's' it, too!" he declared, and we all laughed— even Rose.

February 17, 1870 . . .

Another cold day. The men and the boys have been hard at work trying to keep the stock alive, which has left us women to pick up the slack. The need for firewood seems endless, and our "mountain" of larch looks more like a hill now. It's so cold that the firewood sounds as if it's being split when I carry it into the warm cabin. My fingers feel as though they've been split, too, lugging water from the freezing stream, washing clothes that seem to take forever to dry inside the cabin . . . Rose has made me so proud lately, helping with all the chores, then bundling up for the trek down to Jessie's for her lessons. Quinn has decided she needs a "treat" for all of her hard work and is making her a surprise for her birthday this spring that he won't even tell me.

Rose breezed in tonight to tell us that Jessie is coming along "just fine" with her learning. "Jessie does try to get ahead of herself sometimes," she said with a weary sigh as she helped me set the table for dinner. "But I told her patience is a virtue. Isn't that right, Mama?"

I said yes it is—and then pretended to check the biscuits so she couldn't see my grin.

February 18, 1870 . . .

Rose has been coughing up a storm tonight. I've doctored her as best I can, making up a mustard plaster for her chest. Of course, there's no doctor to be had—even if the weather wasn't as bad as it is. It's times like this I feel we are so fragile out here . . .

I think Quinn must have sensed how I was feeling earlier, for he came to me when I was sitting in the rocker, mending and listening for Rose, and he gently took my sewing from me and pulled me to my feet.

"I'm thinking our Rose will be fine, lass," he said softly. "She's made of tough stock, but if it's a doctor you're wishing for, we have one." He took both of my hands in his and smiled. "All we have to do is ask."

We both bowed our heads and prayed, and after we were done, we both looked up at the same time to see Patrick standing at the bottom of the ladder, rubbing his eyes.

"Maybe God will send Rose an *angel unaware* like he did for Mercy and Preacher," he said. He padded across the floor and sat in my lap, looking straight ahead as if he were deep in thought. Then he said, "If God does, Mama, I want to know right away. I don't want to miss it this time."

Our "angel unaware" has turned out to be Medicine Weasel. Not long after Quinn went out to the barn and I had finished up the morning dishes and put another fresh plaster on Rose, I heard a knock at the door and found Jack standing there with Medicine Weasel.

Jack said Medicine Weasel had heard about Rose's cold and offered to doctor her in his tepee. As sick as she was, Rose hollered a quick, "I want to go, Mama!" from the loft, and soon Jack was carrying her down the ladder for me to bundle her up.

When we turned around, it was as if Medicine Weasel had disappeared. Then I spotted him climbing slowly down the ladder of the loft, holding Rose's "Stem" doll in one of his hands. He looked almost embarrassed to be holding the doll, but I was touched by his thoughtful old heart.

"She'll be in good hands, sis," Jack said, his eyes meeting mine, and I saw the love in them.

"She already is," I told him.

Jessie was beside herself with worry this evening when I told her that Rose had been taken to Medicine Weasel's tepee for doctoring. No matter how much any of us tried to put Jessie's fears at ease, she wasn't having any of it until she saw Rose for herself—which was odd, because Jessie had developed a strange fear of going near the old man's lodge, often walking a wide circle around it most of the time.

"All my fault," Jessie said as we made our way toward Medicine Weasel's tepee. "If that child hadn't come out in the cold every day to help me with my learnin', she wouldn't be so sick."

I tried my best to convince her it wasn't her fault, but it was as if she couldn't listen to me until she saw Rose for herself. Then when we got to the tepee, she told me she'd wait outside, that if Rose could just call out that she was fine, that would suit her.

I entered the tepee and got so caught up with all I saw that I forgot for a moment that Jessie was standing outside in the cold. I was surprised to see there was a settee of sorts propped against one of the hide walls; the dirt floor had been swept neat and had furs and rugs spread across it. I think it was even warmer than our cabins, though the fire in its center was small. I glanced over at Medicine Weasel and One Shot, and they smiled. Then I looked over at Rose, who was snuggled under a thick buffalo robe, her face still looking a bit flushed, but pleased.

I went over and hugged her and asked her how she was feeling, then I told her Jessie was outside, and for her to say something so Jessie could hear her.

"Make sure Jessie doesn't quit her studies, Mama," she said, before breaking down into a fit of coughs, then, louder, "You hear that, Jessie?"

Jessie, who had been standing outside the tepee, wringing her hands in the cold, leaned over and peeked her head just barely through the flap of the door.

"Ye promise to get well, sis," Jessie said, her voice cracking just a bit. "And I'll promise to do them studies. I'll do them *all*, or my name ain't Jessie Dawson."

When I told Quinn tonight what had happened, he just shook his head in wonder.

"I'm thinking she's plucked more than our Jessie's heart-strings," Quinn chuckled. "When I went to check on her this evening, she looked to have about run Medicine Weasel and One Shot ragged with all her questions. The funny thing of it was, they couldn't seem to help themselves, almost like they enjoyed her too much to complain."

We both laughed, then Quinn's eyes turned thoughtful.

"I'm thinking we should be counting our blessing to be in

such a caring family," he said softly, and I hugged him then and told him I couldn't agree more.

Sabbath in a tepee . . . who would have ever thought?

Rose is very near well—although I wonder if she will be willing to admit it. When I went to check on her today, she was sitting up with a buffalo robe tucked around her little legs like a tiny queen holding court as Medicine Weasel told a story that sounded to be in part Blackfoot, part English to her, Patrick, and John-Charles.

I had a feeling by the way he waved his hands through the air that he was telling some kind of a war story. "What's that?" I asked, and Rose put her fingers to her lips to shush me. "We're fightin' them dern white-eyes," she said somberly.

Medicine Weasel looked up at me and grinned. I couldn't help grinning, too. "Don't say *dern*, Rose, it isn't nice," I said, and the old Indian gave me a look of something akin to appreciation before he went back to telling the story . . .

Finds Rose home at last. Jessie, bless her heart, seemed happiest of all, spending nearly the whole day up in the little loft talking with Rose. It wasn't until just before she came down to help me get dinner started that I realized how lonely she had been without her little friend, and I felt ashamed that I hadn't seen it sooner.

"I sure did miss our times together, sis," I overheard Jessie say. "I used t' think I liked the quiet, but I don't. Guess having ye with me reminded me of how happy I was when I had my little ones around me."

"Where are they now?" I heard Rose ask.

"Don't rightly know," Jessie said. "But the Lord do, and I reckon I'll jes have to trust Him to watch over 'em."

"I love you, Jessie," Rose said then, and I heard a slight pause. Then, by the sounds, I knew Jessie had leaned over to hug Rose.

"I love you, too, honey," I heard her say, her voice a bit shaky.

It took all I had not to break down crying in front of Jessie as she came down the ladder to help me cook.

Quinn called me outside at sunset to show me something, and I still haven't gotten over the beauty and awe of what we saw.

"I've never seen anything like this," he said as I bundled up and stepped out on our porch next to him then followed his gaze to the sky.

It had been dreary and overcast most of the day, but I noticed a stream of gold light had pressed its way through the clouds forming an upside-down V over one of the mountain peaks, illuminating these tiny ice crystals in the air and making them flash and sparkle with its warmth. Just a breath of a breeze came then, and Quinn said, "Listen." As we did, I could make out a faint tinkling sound, like wind chimes, or the clinking of glass as the ice crystals hit against each other in the breeze.

"'Tis like the sound of heaven celebrating," Quinn said.

"I wonder what they're celebrating," I said, and Quinn smiled a bit.

"Maybe they're celebrating us, that we've made it this far," he suggested, and I nodded as we both fell silent again to listen.

It was as if in spite of the cold, in spite of the dreary clouds choked with snow that hung above the mountains, God was still showing us He was God. That no matter how dark things could get at times, He would always be there to shine a light through.

February 28, 1870 . . .

Another long day of work, which made our surprise tonight even more special, more worth cherishing forever . . .

I should have known something was up. If Rose's grin was any bigger you wouldn't have seen her face for all the teeth, but I had no idea what was to come until I saw Jessie suddenly stand up after dinner was finished and ask Quinn to see our Bible. She glanced around the table at all of us, and I saw there were tears in her eyes. Then she smiled a big smile at Rose before she opened up the Bible, bent her head, and began to *read*.

"'In the beginning was the Word, and the Word was with God and the Word was God.'" She stopped then and closed the book, and only then did she look up at us, great tears of happiness in her eyes.

"Now Jessie Dawson's got the Word, too," she said. "And there ain't no better thing to have, far as I can tell."

PART FOUR

Season of Rest

After God helpd them whip the gients
Joshwa and Kalib wer tired so God
said, "Take A Rest" and they did.

By Rose McGregor
age almost 10
Mountana Teritery, 1870

March 2, 1870 . . .

The promise of spring has tugged us all outside today. The sun is bright, and the snow is melting, pouring off the cabin and barn roofs like little waterfalls, running down the mountainsides and streaming from the branches of the trees like teardrops. It's like the whole valley is weeping—but for grief or joy?

I feel a difference in us with this thaw that's come. Looking to the corrals where the men are working with the horses, I see Quinn take his hat off to wipe his brow, see him glance over to Medicine Weasel and Jack as he tells them something . . . I hear them laugh. One Shot is trotting his horse around the yard, a big smile on his face as he tows a muddy ball of skins behind him with a rope so Rose, Patrick, and John-Charles can try their hands at shooting arrows into a moving target . . . Jessie is sitting next to me here on the porch, rocking Mercy with such a look of love on her sweet old face as Lillie stretches her back and looks to the mountains hooded in blue, smiling . . .

And I, little journal, can't help feeling like we're somehow connected to this land now . . . like our trials have weathered us in the same way winter has weathered the land. And like this land, we are ready for the waters to recede, ready to feel the warm sun shine down upon us again. Ready to feel life again.

If the valley *is* weeping, then it must be for joy . . .

Just found this scripture:

> *In his favour is life: weeping may endure for a night,*
> *but joy cometh in the morning.*
> —PSALM 30:5

It's fitting, I think.

March 3, 1870 ...

Much excitement with another new calf found in the far meadow today. Patrick and John-Charles came in this afternoon, muddy and grinning, to announce their "find," and I was on the verge of scolding them after an entire morning of cleaning when Patrick said, "And it don't look nothin' like Mercy did when she was born. It's already got hair *and* teeth, too."

I admit I was caught off guard. But there was something so touching in the way the two headed out the door together, talking in earnest over the finer points of being born *with* teeth, that I just didn't have it in my heart to scold them for tracking in mud.

March 4, 1870 ...

My poetic little "waterfalls" from the other day have turned the valley into a huge bog of mud—mud that's been churned up by our herd of cranky, expectant mothers as we all pitched in to move them in closer this afternoon s*o as to keep an eye on their calving.

The "ladies" wanted no part of it, of course, and tried every way they could to aggravate our progress, and *I* was trying every way I could to be gentle with them, seeing how poorly they looked after the hard winter.

Though no one spoke it, we were all determined to do anything we could to hang on to what was left of our herd. So the men whistled and hollered, slapping their ropes against their thighs as they herded the contrary cows into the pens. We women helped with the strays and opened and closed the gates as each reluctant mother-to-be was finally cajoled and threatened into entering, and the kids reached through the fence to keep the troughs filled with hay, hoping to soothe the cows' ruffled feelings. Everyone of us was working together as a family, and pretty soon, I felt our spirits rise in spite of the trouble—especially Jack, who watched me with amusement as I tried to shoo one particularly stubborn red heifer away from the thick pool of mire she had just been pulled from. The large brown eyes of hers looking at me so obediently were foolers. No sooner had I got her turned away than she let fly a back leg that would have connected with my head if I hadn't dove out of the way.

Everyone ran to see if I was all right as I landed squarely in a rather large puddle of mud. Once the mud was wiped away and it was determined I would live, Jack teased, "Why, look, I think Callie's met her match—and *she's* got red hair, too!" which caused a hearty round of laughter.

Later—It seems Jack hasn't finished with me, yet. Rose told me in a burst of excitement tonight as she was helping me get dinner ready that "Uncle Jack just named that red cow 'Callie.'" And, she added excitedly, "He said I could name her calf if I wanted and I told him if it was a girl I think 'Tulip' would work. Don't you, Mama?"

"Why not 'Rose'?" I asked dryly, glancing at Quinn, who grinned then pretended to stoke the fire. Rose pursed her lips for a moment in thought.

"Well, I don't want an old cow named after me," Rose said, sniffing in an almost haughty way. Then, realizing her blunder, she added with a sweet smile, "But *Tulip* is a flower—and that makes it almost like Rose."

I'm thinking that was supposed to make me feel better.

I just woke from a dream of Willa. Oddest dream . . . Willa was running through the mercantile dressed in rags, saying, "I can't find my dress" over and over. Then I saw Preacher, and he was trying to hand her a bolt of white cloth but she wouldn't take it. "It will get dirty if I wear it," Willa said, wringing her hands, and then I woke up.

I wonder what it means. We've been so busy I haven't had a chance to go see her. I pray everything is well with her . . .

March 8, 1870 . . .

The sun just keeps working its wonders on this land, shining over the mountains, tugging leaves from their buds, waking the wildflowers to sing their color through the valley again. Jasper and Honey are so relieved that the snow is gone that they almost look like deer bounding through the valley. Even our cows appear friskier, munching on the new grass for all they're worth—all except for the infamous Callie, who is long overdue and looks so woefully huge she has earned everyone's pity.

Medicine Weasel nearly shocked the life out of me today when I overheard him ask Rose how Callie was doing.

March 18, 1870 . . .
Jack's birthday

Hard to imagine him being thirty-one already—maybe because I don't want to imagine *me* being twenty-nine. Ah, well, at least we had a good celebration this evening in spite of our "advanced years."

Everyone made a quick work of their chores and gladly gathered at our cabin for the party. With our hens laying again, I was able to make him a sponge cake with icing flavored with just a touch of rose water, and Lillie went all out, making his favorite baked chicken and sweet cornbread. Jessie surprised him with a buckskin shirt of Stem's that she'd worked over to fit him. Quinn gave him a fine box to keep his gun in with a buffalo head carved on the lid that Patrick and John-Charles admired greatly, and Rose proudly presented him with a horse-hair whip she'd braided herself.

"But not for Midnight," Rose added. "She's real good at listening now."

Medicine Weasel and One Shot weren't exactly used to the notion of "birthdays" but were eager to celebrate anyway. They gave Jack a saddle made out of buffalo hide that was stuffed with elk hair. It looked odd, but Jack seemed more than pleased to get it.

In spite of all of that, I think it was little Mercy who gave Jack his best gift. We were all laughing and talking when she let out a holler (she's lately discovered she likes the sound of her voice), and Jack went over and picked her up from Lillie, brushing a big but gentle hand over her downy head of curls. She looked up at him with wide eyes and gave him a grin that beat anything I'd seen from a baby that small.

I wish I could describe the delight on Jack's face as he smiled down at her. "Why, bless her little heart, she's smiling at me, Lillie," he said softly, and suddenly we were all crowding around for a look. It was as if Mercy was our living proof, our little bundle of God's grace that would always be there to remind us of that cold winter day a stranger had appeared to show us that we weren't so alone as we thought.

I happened to glance over at Jessie, who was looking down at Mercy with a satisfied look on her face, and I saw Jack suddenly turn toward her, too.

"I sure wish Stem could see her," Jack said gently, and Jessie cocked her head to one side and smiled a kind of half-smile that was full of memories and something I couldn't quite put my finger on.

"Why, I kindly like to imagine he can, Jack," she said softly.

March 22, 1870 . . .

Mild, sunny day today.

Coy showed up at the ranch late this afternoon just as we were finishing up dinner at our outside table. He was grinning before he got off his horse, answering me that Willa was fine and telling us that Preacher would be holding an Easter service in town—but I soon sensed there was more, and Lillie did, too.

"You're looking awful shiny, Coy Harper," she said. "Is there something you have to tell us?"

Coy just laughed and tipped his hat back from his head. "I got some more news," he admitted, then smiled a kind of mischievous smile until Jessie gave him what-for.

"You'd do well to answer 'em quick," Quinn said wryly. "The three of 'em together are a force to be reckoned with." Coy laughed again and then finally announced that he had asked Bonny to marry him—which sent the men into hearty handshakes all around and us girls into several rounds of questions about the wedding plans. So much so I think the poor man's head was swimming with it all by the time he finally took his leave. Jack even said as much, grinning as he stood next to me, watching Coy trot his horse back off toward Willa's again.

"I *am* happy for them," I said then, turning to Jack. "I just hope other folks can be happy for them, too."

Jack nodded and looked at me thoughtfully then, glancing once toward his cabin where Lillie sat on their porch, rocking Mercy and John-Charles side by side, and he smiled softly. "People can get some funny thoughts in their heads sometimes, sis," he said, "about what's right or not. I recall one of the Blackfoot elders pitching a fit when they found out I was marrying Lillie and we'd be the ones to raise John-Charles. He said, 'A fish and a bird can fall in love, but where will they build their nest?'"

Jack's smile was wry. "I knew he was tryin' to say it would

never work . . . But it was Medicine Weasel who held up for us. He said there *was* a place for us."

"Where?" I asked, looking up into those green eyes of his and seeing something in them that reminded me of our pa.

Jack smiled then, and he swept his hands through the air, holding them out toward the distance as if he was leading me somewhere special—not with the flashy way of a gambler, but with the way of a man sharing his hard-earned wisdom, the kind of wisdom that comes from someone who has loved, lost, and learned to love again.

"Montana," he said, like he was introducing me to the land for the first time, and we both smiled.

April 7, 1870 . . .

Rose came barreling into the house this evening, tears streaming down her face, hollering that Tulip was going to die if I didn't help. By the time I dried my hands and got out to the yard, I saw that she had rallied the whole family together like a tiny general and set off to lead us to the spot where the newborn calf lay.

When we finally reached the calf, I could see why she was so distraught as the poor thing was too weak to even stand. The strange thing was, the thought of that little calf not making it seemed to grieve us all in a way that I can't quite explain. Before any of us had a chance to say anything, Quinn picked Tulip up and began to carry her to the barn, knowing Callie would follow. The new mother wasn't happy about our carrying off her baby, but as weak as she was she could only trot slowly after Quinn, mooing worriedly for her calf.

First thing we did as soon as we got them into the barn was try to get the calf to nurse, but it was too weak to stand long enough to suck. Jack and Quinn finally held the mama still so I could get some milk from her for the calf, then Jessie made a quick work of fashioning a "teat" like we'd give to a sick baby from a scrap of old cloth, all the while trying to comfort Rose, who was wringing her little hands with worry.

"It's all right, little sis," she said gently, and I was surprised to see Quinn's eyes a mirror image of Rose's worry when I looked up at him.

Once Tulip finally figured out what we were trying to do, she took to the teat quick, bringing whoops of joy from Patrick and John-Charles. We all stood grinning in silence for a while, just watching that little calf perking up with each passing minute, finally standing, then wobbling around on little legs that seemed to point in four directions at once. Even Medicine Weasel managed a smile, pointing to the milk dribbling down her chin, and One Shot laughed.

"She's a sight, ain't she?" Jessie said, stepping back with a relieved smile on her face, and I couldn't help agree.

There is nothing quite like seeing one of God's "newcomers," as Jessie calls them, being given a chance at life . . . and deciding to take it.

April 17, 1870 . . .
Easter Sunday

And a fine Easter it has been. Preacher outdid himself on the service, and giving one of the most beautiful sermons I've ever heard, too. I hope and pray I can remember his words just as he spoke them to us so I can keep them in this journal to read on . . .

We sang "Rock of Ages" and "Amazing Grace," and once we finally got seated, Preacher stepped up to the front. He looked all about the tent, smiling at people, nodding, and as soon as everyone got settled and quiet he began.

"I come from a long line of storytellers, my granddad being the king of the tall tale when we were kids, leaving us laying wide-eyed in our beds at night, dreaming of adventure," Preacher said. "Then there was my Aunt Sadie, who lived such a life in her mind that when she told you of it, you almost doubted the *truth*." Everyone chuckled, and Preacher smiled easily; then his face turned more serious. "There *are* those who use their gift of gab for evil, painting pretty words to hide dark intentions . . . But the best storytellers are those who fire your soul with their words, who leave you with, not just a story to remember, but a different way of looking at *life*—of living life. Jesus was such a man, and it's in His honor that I bring you my story for this Easter Sunday.

"Over the years a lot of folks have asked me the same question: *Why?* Why did He go through with it? Why didn't He just call out to God and tell Him to stop all of the madness? After reading the Scriptures more times than I can count, I came to the same answer every time. He did it for love.

"Now remember, this is just a story of sorts. I pray it does justice to His name. So now, I want you to close your eyes, and just imagine . . .

"Imagine Jesus walking up that lonely hill called Calvary . . . . Memories begin to fill Jesus' head as He forces His pain-wracked body on. He stumbles once but rights Himself and continues to walk, remembering. He sees anger, then brokenness and doubt, through the eyes of men desperate for a forgiveness they feared they would never have—the very men who would walk with Him. Then comes the memory of fishing . . . He can hear the slap of a net against the water again, see the childlike amazement on His friend's faces, hear the laughter of a wedding, and remember the loving sister who fell at His feet, weeping pitifully for her brother. So beautiful was the human spirit when it loved . . .

"So many more images come to Him in His memory, and He realizes He has fallen in love with each and every one of them . . . He stumbles again under the heavy burden on His back then feels the grasp of a firm hand and sees His Father's love staring out at Him through the eyes of a man dressed in a soldier's uniform.

"There are so many who are lost, He thinks, *so many who need to be found* . . . My *life for theirs, Father* . . . And with that thought He is given a vision of what would come to pass through the ages. He sees an old man who drinks too much because he's seen too much ugliness in the world. The old man wakes in a snowdrift one night, lying on his back. He begins to cry, calling out for Jesus. A drop of blood falls upon the man, and Jesus sees him being helped up by a scraggly looking boy—a boy who would later give him a Book that would open his eyes to beauty again.

"Jesus takes another step, and as He does, He sees a fallen woman who cries herself to sleep at night when no one else can hear her—but *He* hears—and as she drops to her knees, another drop of blood falls, and suddenly the woman is a laughing mother of four who travels at night to the worst brothels around to tell young girls she understands their life—and she knows Someone who will treat them better—a man called Jesus . . .

"Jesus nods, thinking yes, He understands. Then He lies down willingly as soldiers begin to nail Him to the cross. They begin to hammer, and the pain must be unbearable, but it's as if Jesus is distracted by something. His head is turned, as though He's listening. Somewhere in the distance He can hear the laughter of a child, drowning out the sound of hammering, drowning out the pain, as a lilting little voice sings strong and sweet, echoing throughout the centuries: 'Yes, Jesus loves me . . .'

"As the hours go by, Jesus feels His heart swell with the love that so many would ponder over for years to come. *Why?* they would ask. But, then, they hadn't seen what He had seen. He closes His eyes and with a great sigh, He says the words that would make it happen, the words that would give us a chance to be all God meant for us to be.

"'It is finished.'"

Preacher, who had a distant look on his face as he was telling the story, seemed to come to us then, and he looked around the tent. It was so quiet you could've heard a pin drop.

"But He wasn't *finished* with *us*," Preacher said, his voice thick with emotion, and I saw his eyes travel the crowd, finally coming to rest on Jessie, then all of the rest of our family, and when his eyes caught Willa's, he smiled. "He had only begun to show His love. Peter found that out. I can only imagine how heartbroken he was, sitting in that boat a few days later, tormenting himself over *denying* Jesus. Then he spotted a man standing on the shore. *'It's the Lord!'* he heard John exclaim— and yet he didn't flee. Instead, he plunged into the water and began to swim *toward* Him for all he was worth. Because Peter knew . . . that no matter how bad he had messed up, he would be forgiven, he would be *loved* . . .

"My prayer for all of you this Easter is that the next time you feeling like running away—you dive into the water instead . . . and that you love each other like Jesus loves us. Love like you've never been hurt before."

Handkerchiefs seemed to suddenly spring up in hands throughout the tent. I heard a lot of sniffing—Willa being one of the snifflers—then I heard someone blow his nose loudly and saw it was the grizzled old southern man that Stem had befriended.

"Ain't never heard the likes," he said to no one in particular. But I'm sure everyone agreed. I glanced up at Preacher, who was walking slowly toward the door of the tent, stopping to shake hands, to pat someone on the back, and I couldn't help thinking, like I always thought when I looked at him, how he didn't quite fit the picture folks had in their minds of a man of the cloth. Willa told me his family had "groomed" him in hopes he'd be a senator or maybe even president one day. Then I remembered the words the old minister had told him, *"God is going to show you what is real, son . . . and once He does, you aren't ever going to be the same . . ."* And I wondered if that man had somehow known what Preacher was meant to be.

Preacher had chosen a beautiful spot for the church's Easter picnic on the outskirts of town, not far from the tent, near a stand of cottonwoods that lined the riverbank. Nearly everyone from the service came, with wagons and buggies spreading out across the hillside as folks started emptying baskets or pails of food and spreading them over sheets and tablecloths spread on the soft spring grass. Like with Preacher's other sermons, kindness seemed to flow out afterward, the haves inviting the have-nots to join in. An odd combination it was to see, but good, too. Preacher stood and called for grace to be said, and it touched my heart, seeing practical strangers join hands to pray.

I know it touched Quinn, too, the way he looked about him as he helped me set the food out on the blanket. It was like Preacher's coming had done more than get us together on the Sabbath. It was knitting us together as a little community, too.

"Fine idea, you had, Preacher," Quinn said after we had all settled our hunger. The Preacher smiled then looked at Willa. "I couldn't have done it without Willa," he said, and she blushed prettily but didn't say a thing—which surprised me.

But it didn't surprise Preacher, for he cleared his throat then. "I told Miss Cain this morning that I had something important I would be telling her today," he said, his smile getting wider. "Which probably explains her pensive silence."

"Oh, for goodness' sakes," Willa said, jumping to her feet as she pretended to dust her skirt off. "You haven't changed a bit—still as ornery as the day is long."

"It's not orneriness—it's spring. And spring is for getting

things out in the open, airing them out, so to speak," Preacher said. Patrick and John-Charles, who'd developed a strong liking for Preacher, laughed heartily, like they understood—even though they didn't—and that got everyone else laughing, too.

Preacher stood then, facing Willa, and we all waited with bated breath to see what he was going to do. "As most of you know, I lost most everything I had during the war . . ."

"I have never cared for money; you know that," Willa said suddenly, and he smiled patiently.

"There is one thing I never parted with, though," he went on, looking at all of us then back to Willa. He reached into his pocket and withdrew a handkerchief—a lot like the one he had had at Christmas. Then he silently opened up the handkerchief. We all bent in close to see what he held out, and I felt a lump in my throat as I stared at the single, sparkling diamond that lay in the center of the cloth.

I looked over at Willa, who had been leaning in with the rest of us, and tears were already working their way down her cheeks. She looked up at the preacher and smiled, holding out her hand to turn the little gold ring around on her finger to show the empty setting. She had kept the ring, and he had kept the stone, I thought then. The both of them had never really let go of their love, of their hope that, in spite of miles and hardships, they might be reunited someday.

"You aren't the only one who holds on to things," Willa said thickly, then her breath caught in her throat as we watched Preacher kneel down in front of her.

"I've had to hold these words in me for years, and I'm not holding them in any longer," Preacher said. "Willa Cain, will you marry me?"

I know we were all holding our breaths because as soon as she said yes I heard a huge exhale. Then there was a collective inhale when Preacher asked how long their engagement would be. Willa said, "Long enough," and suddenly that dream I'd had suddenly came to mind for some reason, and I said a quick prayer for them both.

"How long is *that?*" Preacher asked with a tone of frustration we had never heard before, and we all suddenly laughed. Willa did, too.

"Well, not as long as before," she said, grinning, and Preacher couldn't seem to help himself from grinning, too.

When I looked over at Jack, he was grinning as well but seemed to be looking past us all.

"Well, what do you know?" Jack said as he rocked Mercy in his arms. "Here comes ol' Mother Long herself."

Lillie whispered, "Shame on you," as we turned to see Mrs. Audrey and her brood coming toward us. "I wonder if I should do my wolf howl," Jack added under his breath, grinning. Quinn, Jessie, and I were quick to look away so as not to laugh. Anyone who's been around Jack long enough knows he has that affect on you.

Preacher looked curious enough to ask, but then Mrs. Audrey, Mrs. Pumphrey, and Mrs. Spence were nearing, looking like they had a specific purpose in mind. All but Mr. Audrey. He just looked uncomfortable, like he wasn't sure what was going to happen.

Mrs. Audrey nodded to us all briefly before turning to Preacher. "Quite a little group you have here, Preacher," she said, and he just smiled.

"So, you've already met my friends then?" Preacher said evenly, and there was such a genuine kindness to his words that Mrs. Audrey's face suddenly got a bit contrite, like she was trying to figure which way to lean. Mrs. Pumphrey nudged her, but Mrs. Audrey was looking to where Coy and Bonny sat, watching the children play near the banks of the river.

"Why, isn't that Mr. Carey's sq—," she started, but then Mr.

Audrey nudged her, too, and she said, "For goodness' sakes, Percy!"

Then Mrs. Pumphrey cleared her throat. "What Leah is try-ing to say, Preacher, is your preaching has done us all some good—enough that we know it's high time we started acting better toward our *neighbors* and all . . ."

Suddenly Mrs. Pumphrey seemed to lose steam—not to mention words.

"'Do unto others as you would have them do unto you' is what we should've been practicing all along," Mrs. Spence said, as clear as a bell, shocking us all. "I just hope it ain't too late."

"Hear, hear," Mr. Audrey said then—another shock. He glanced toward his wife and the rest of the group then back to Preacher, squaring his small shoulders a bit as he said a quick "Have a good day, now," even smiling at the rest of us before he turned away to follow the rest of them as they quickly made their way back to where their wagon was waiting.

"Why, Preacher," Jessie said, breaking the silence, "I think the Lord's showing ye that all yer hard work is startin' to pay off."

Preacher looked dazed for a moment, then grateful, and then a soft smile formed on his handsome face. He glanced over at Willa.

"In more ways than one," he said.

As I read over what I just wrote, I can't help thinking that it hasn't been just Preacher's words but his ways that has touched us all. Seeing how kindly he treated Mrs. Audrey and her group in spite of their troublesome behavior didn't just touch my heart. It also taught me something, too, made me want to be more like Preacher, too.

I told Quinn tonight that it just goes to show that some-times we *are* the only Bible some folks will ever have a chance to read. He smiled softly.

"And what a tragedy our lives are," he said, "if we never allow them to do so, lass."

May 2, 1870 . . .

It has been raining nearly all day. But the thick, gray storm clouds hanging over the mountain peaks haven't dampened our spirits at all. As a matter of fact, I've wondered often today if us girls aren't as excited as the bride- and groom-to-be with all the fun we've had, decorating for the wedding tomorrow.

We've swept and cleaned the barn out as best as we could and made an archway with greenery in the center above the door for the bride and groom to walk under. Then we had the men set up some makeshift tables and spread fine-looking linen cloths over them for the food. Rose, thankfully, gathered as many bunches of wildflowers as she could find this morning before the rain, and we've placed them all around the inside of the barn in little cups and tins of water, and it's looking almost pretty in a quaint kind of way.

Mr. Audrey came out to deliver the rest of the supplies Quinn and Jack had ordered, and in wanting to practice broth-erly love, we decided Coy and Bonny would want us to invite the Audreys to the wedding (which seemed to please Mr. Audrey a lot). We told them to bring Mrs. Pumphrey and Mrs. Spence, too.

And now, little journal, I am off to do some cooking.

I pray as I put the finish to this page that Coy and Bonny will be as blessed as Quinn and I in their new life together and that the Lord leads them always.

Because I can't imagine anything better than that.

Promiseland

What a beautiful wedding day for Coy and Bonny—and not just in weather but in spirit also. As I watched the two of them standing before Preacher today, Bonny looking so pretty in her beautiful antelope-skin dress and the little sprays of flowers Willa had tucked into her hair, and Coy, so handsome and strong, his dark face beaming love, I couldn't help being awed by the beauty of the moment. There is something poetic, almost like hearing a sweet song for the first time, seeing how God is able to put souls together that link so perfectly.

Coy and Bonny, two people so different yet so alike, both so alone in the world . . . so willing to take a chance at love.

We were all beaming happiness for them as Preacher read from Scripture about love. The Audreys, Mrs. Pumphrey, and Mrs. Spence were almost decent, and Mrs. Pumphrey even got a little teary-eyed when Bonny shyly said, "I do."

About the only time I felt sad was when the old-timer Willa knew struck up his fiddle-playing for a dance. I felt a sharp, bittersweet pain go through me then, remembering Stem playing his fiddle the very first time Quinn and I danced together. He'd taken the fiddle from some young fellow trying to scratch out a tune saying, *"Give me that fiddle, son! Yer playing them strings like they's still in the cat!"* How we'd all laughed, then smiled with joy, as he played a tune slow and sweet.

Memories of Stem seemed to be with everyone as I looked around our barn.

I saw Coy and his new bride look at each other when the music started. Coy bent over and whispered something in Bonny's ear, and I saw her nod and smile. Then Coy turned and walked slowly over to the corner where Jessie sat, her eyes closed with a kind of sad smile on her face.

I saw Coy reach down and gently take Jessie's hand, and she opened her eyes in surprise then smiled as he drew her up and into his bearlike arms. They turned round and round across the swept dirt dance floor, and I felt tears come to my eyes as I watched Coy press his hand gently against Jessie's back and saw how Jessie closed her eyes with such a sweet smile of pleasure and gratefulness for that touch—the kind of human touch we were all meant to give, I think. And it hit me with the memory of what Lillie had said all those months back about how frail we really are. But I remembered, too, what the Good Book says about love never failing . . .

And it didn't—didn't fail us once as we laughed and celebrated long into the evening, twirling round and round that dusty dirt floor of the barn as the sun set in golden glory behind the mountains in the distance.

Quinn was stoking a small fire in the fireplace as I was writing this, and when I looked up at him, his face was so deep in thought that I asked him what was the matter.

"If you could turn back the page, lass, would you do it the same?" he asked then, his pale blue eyes searching my face. "Would you marry me again?"

"No," I said abruptly, then grinned as Quinn's head snapped around to look at me, and I laughed. "I would've married you sooner," I added. "After all, I know how it all turns out now."

Quinn grinned. "And you wonder where Rose gets her ways," he said, chuckling as he leaned down and kissed the tip of my nose. Then he whispered in my ear, "But you can't know how it *all* turns out—we've only just begun."

Promiseland

My sweet Rose's birthday today . . . If ever there was a girl who's loved, it's our Rose. Seems all of Montana Territory showed up just to let her know that, too.

Once the table was set, we all joined hands and sang, and somewhere in our song, Quinn's eyes met mine, and the love and pride in them for our daughter made me remember what he'd said the night before about not knowing how it'd all turn out. It hit me then that the knowing of it didn't matter so much anymore—that being together, being loved, was all that really mattered.

Rose beamed bigger than I'd ever seen, hanging onto the little journal I gave her in one hand as she opened the rest of her gifts.

But it was her Pa's gift that made her cry.

She had just finished opening the last of the gifts when Quinn stood and smiled softly at her, then he went out the door without another word. We all knew something was about to happen, so we crowded out onto the porch to watch. Soon we saw Quinn leading Midnight from the barn, smiling softly as he neared Rose, who was waiting patiently on the bottom step of the porch.

"Fair Rose," he said, his voice thick with emotion. "T'day Midnight is officially yours—and the saddle too, lass. But not so you can ride away from us—so you will always have a way to get home."

We all watched with tears in our eyes as Rose looked first at Midnight with such love and then to the saddle that Quinn had spent so many hours hand-tooling himself. Then, much to our surprise, Rose walked right past her gift and over to Quinn. She grabbed his hands, rubbing her small fingers over the cracks and calluses, over the new scratches that lined his work-worn palms.

"I love you so much, Pa," she said, tears streaming down her small face, and I saw everyone glancing at each other in surprise at Rose's reaction.

I wasn't surprised, though. Because I knew as much as my daughter loved that horse and the new saddle, she loved her pa more.

May 8, 1870 . . .

I have been thinking all day on this. Through cleaning and cooking, lugging water from the stream, those words of Preacher's has come to me over and over about us loving like we've never been hurt before. I thought of how hurt I was when Pa and our sister Rose died and how I almost didn't marry Quinn because of the hurt. Then I thought of Jack and Lillie, of Bonny, then Willa, wanting so bad to believe but struggling against her fear, and of Jessie pressing on in spite of it . . .

And I couldn't help but wonder if all we have been through was part of finding our promiseland—and I don't mean a place, but our promiseland *inside* of ourselves.

If maybe once we learn to love like the Lord loves us, like we've never been hurt before, then that's when we find our home . . . our promiseland . . .

May 9, 1870 . . .

Another warm day, which found me making several trips to the stream, the last of which was when I found John-Charles there. He was standing near the banks as he stared off to the distance, and though I knew he sensed me, he didn't turn around right off. When I followed his gaze, I understood why. The wild horses had returned, spread out across the meadow in a breathtaking blanket of color as they tossed their heads and whinnied from the opposite side of the stream.

"They're so beautiful," I said, almost to myself, and I saw John-Charles turn to look at me then.

"Yeah," he said, then looked at me close, like he was wondering if he could trust me with something.

"They let me pet 'em," he said finally. Then I saw him glance over his shoulder quick. "I don't tell Pa, though. He'd want to catch 'em." His eyes grew thoughtful as he looked back out toward the herd, and something about the way he looked made me think of Jack when he was young. "They were here first. They should be free."

For some reason I sensed he wasn't just talking of the horses—but of his mama's people . . . of his grandfather who would soon be leaving for the reservation to search for whatever family they might have left.

"They *should* be free," I said, and he smiled at me almost like he was seeing me for the first time.

Before we could talk anymore, Patrick showed up with their fishing poles, and John-Charles was waving good-bye to me as he ran to catch up with his cousin, a little boy again, looking forward to a day of fishing.

I stayed out there for a while after they tromped off down the stream to their "secret" fishing hole, drinking in the beauty of the land and of the wild horses that were as much a part of the land as the mountains that stood dark against the brilliant blue sky.

I know the horses sensed me, but for some reason this time they didn't run off right away but lingered. I saw the leader of the herd toss his head then, and for a moment, I almost imagined he looked right at me before he whinnied and the rest of the herd turned to follow him as he began to slowly trot away. I watched them until they were far out of sight, and for the first time since we came to this land, to Montana, I felt I had been accepted in a way.

Felt maybe I was no longer a trespasser . . .

Blessed be the Lord, that hath given rest unto his people
Israel, according to all that he promised: there hath not failed
one word of all his good promise, which he promised by the
hand of Moses his servant.
— 1 KINGS 8:56

May 11, 1870 . . .

I found Jessie in her garden this morning—or, I should say, I
heard her first, for her deep voice carried across the valley as I
was walking back from the henhouse with my apron full of eggs,
and I stopped for a moment to listen to her sing. I'd never heard
the song before, but it was beautiful, full of hope as she sang
about loved ones waiting for us on the other side of the river . . .
Though I couldn't help smiling to myself when I finally spotted
her, hunched over, her skirts swaying sideways as she sang and
tilled the ground.

Jessie looked up then and smiled good-naturedly. "I'm sure
I'm a sight," she said, pushing back her bonnet. Then she
stretched her back and looked out over the land, her eyes turning thoughtful.

She said, "Remember when I told ye I like to stay outside
because I felt closer to Stem somehow? Well, all these months I
never felt him once, no matter how long I'd stand outside."
Jessie shook her head. "This morning I woke up, and I decided I
was gonna come tend this here garden for *me*. No more looking
or waiting, I said. I come for me, just to feel my hands in the
dirt, feel the sun."

Jessie looked over at me with a shy kind of smile. "I was
hunkered down over these here rows, Callie, and I know it
sounds crazy but I could've sworn I heard Stem. He say, "Bout
time, old woman. Ye ain't been waitin' on the Lord? Well, He's
been waitin' on *you*.'" She cocked her head sideways. "Now,
what do ye think that means, Callie?"

"I don't know," I said slowly, then I found myself grinning. "But it might be fun to find out, don't you think?"

Jessie chuckled. "You are something else." She gazed up at the sky for a long moment, then she reached over and pointed to a new sprout of what looked to be tomatoes. "Wasn't no more than a tiny green spot over a week ago," she said. "Sure is somethin' to watch things grow, ain't it?"

I found myself crouching down in the dirt to have a look and felt the same awe I'd always felt seeing that first tiny shoot of a plant begin its life. "It has always amazed me, seeing something grow so big from such a little seed planted in the dirt," I said then, and Jessie cocked her head to one side again and looked at me like some thought had just occurred to her.

"Kindly like a tiny miracle, ain't it?" she said.

She smiled at me then, a warm comforting smile that seemed a mile wide, and I smiled, too, thinking her smile, to me, felt just like summer.

We had a fine string of trout that we pan-fried for supper tonight, and Patrick, so deliriously happy to have been the one who caught them, is already after Quinn to take him fishing again in the morning.

"We'll go if we get up early enough in the morning, lad, so to finish our chores," Quinn said, smiling. "'Tis the early bird that gets the worm, you know."

"Oh, I know, Pa," Patrick said with a grin. "I saved them in here so that bird *wouldn't* get them."

He dug into the pocket of his trouser and produced a handful of some very wilted-looking worms for us to see. Rose tried to poke fun, but he was having none of it, turning his back to her as he looked up at Quinn so seriously.

"They'll do, right Pa?" he asked, and Quinn bent down, pretending to inspect them in earnest, and I was struck as I watched the two of them with their dark heads bent together, how much alike they really were.

"They'll do," Quinn announced finally, and when he looked up at me, his pale blue eyes were filled with a little laughter—and a whole lot of love.

May 12, 1870 . . .

Mr. Audrey paid us a visit today. But what surprised us even more than his visit was the letter he had carried all the way out to the ranch for *Jessie*. It appears our Stem, or "Justice Dawson," had spent a great deal of money, placing ads in newspapers all over the country, telling of Jessie's search for her family. And there's no doubt in any of our minds that it was God who made sure her family found them.

"He's never early, never late . . . but always on time," Jessie said as she looked up at me after reading through the letter from her eldest daughter for a second time. "Canada—can ye imagine that? The good Lord knew, He *knew,* I was to read this here letter myself, Callie." Jessie began to cry then, and I did, too, tears running down both of our cheeks as we stood together on the front porch of her cabin.

"He put Stem after me to learn to read . . . then had our little sis help me finish with it. I never could figure out why it was so important for an old woman like me to learn readin' . . . But now I know. Yes, Lord, I surely know . . ."

Jessie pressed the letter to her heart gently, her large brown eyes filling with tears once more as she looked toward the distance where the little grave sat beneath two towering willows. "Oh, Stem. Oh, my sweet man," she said, smiling and crying at the same time, and I was struck how I had never seen such a beautiful face in my life.

None of us could think of anything else but Jessie's letter tonight, as excited as we all are for her.

Jack said, "What are the odds?" as he shook his head in wonder for what seemed the twentieth time, and Lillie looked up from rocking Mercy with a smile.

"Jack," she said. "You and I, of all people, could testify to just how much God likes to show folks He tends to favor those with bad odds—kind of leaves them no doubt of Who's really in charge."

May 13, 1870 . . .

It's been decided that Quinn and I will be the ones to take Jessie to Helena. Her daughter's letter says they all plan to arrive on the twentieth, so that gives us a week to get there, and I have never seen a more excited person in my life.

Jessie has come up to the cabin at least four times already as I was packing to ask me if I thought "this dress" or "this bonnet" would look better for meeting them at the train.

Rose and Patrick aren't too happy at being left behind. They have joined forces, sitting side by side to grace Quinn and me with their injured looks.

May 14, 1870 . . .

We are off! May God grant us a safe journey.

May 19, 1870 . . .

We've only just made it into Helena, and it's the first time I've had a chance to sit and write. This city is such a surprise after living out in the valley so long. There are people everywhere, wagons and buggies on a constant move up and down the streets as I gaze out this window of the hotel we're staying at—so many storehouses and cabins, saloons and gambling dens, the sounds of saws and hammers working at even this late hour. The odd thing is, I'd thought I would enjoy seeing so many people again, but I find myself missing home instead, missing the valley and watching the sun set behind the mountains . . . missing our little ones.

I guess that's why the sight of Jessie rocking in that rocker on the front porch of this hotel seems so touching. When Quinn came back from checking on some buyers for our cattle, we joined Jessie on the porch, and I soon saw a smile come to Quinn's face as he watched her rocking back and forth for all she was worth.

"I'm thinking if that rocker had wheels, Jessie," he teased, "you'd already be back to the valley by now."

Jessie grinned big, but there was a determined look on her face, too—the look of a mother who would die before she lost her children another time.

"No sir, I won't be leavin' jes yet," she said after a while. "Not without my babies, I won't."

May 20, 1870 . . .

We took Jessie to the train station in Helena today, and I think I was as nervous as Jessie as she stood as still as a statue, watching for that train to pull in. Just as the train neared us, a heavy rain began to fall, pouring from the sky, but Jessie stood her ground—and so did I.

Through the sheet of rain I watched the train come to a halt and saw the conductor open the door. That's when I spotted a young woman of about my age as she fairly burst through that door and down the steps with what looked like the rest of her family pouring forth after her. I heard Jessie cry out the woman's name then, like it was the only name on earth, and I started crying when I heard that young woman yell, "Mama! Oh, my mama!"

They ran to each other, hugging and crying, and as the rest of Jessie's long-lost family surrounded her, those words that the stranger had spoke to Jessie all those months ago came to me like a whisper: *"Blessed are they that mourn, for they shall be comforted . . ."*

They all hugged each other tight, swaying together as the rain poured down around them so hard that they slipped and fell in the mud. But they only laughed harder, not caring about the rain or the mud.

I didn't care, either. Because I knew God *had* heard Jessie's prayers all along. Heard all our prayers, really. And somewhere up there, I just knew there was a certain angel looking on as an old man dressed in buckskins stood with a smile on his face a mile wide, holding his hand out to Jesus . . . And Jesus taking that hand, saying with a chuckle,

"Well done, thou good and faithful servant."

May 28, 1870 . . .

It feels so good to be back home I don't think I ever want to leave again. What surprises me more is that I think our children have decided they don't, either . . .

Earlier, as I was hanging some of the wash out to dry, I spotted Rose, Patrick, and John-Charles all tromping up the hill behind the cabins, Jasper and Honey trotting close behind. And as I heard their voices carrying in the clear air, I stopped what I was doing to watch them. There was something about the way they walked together . . . I don't know . . . like they weren't new to the land anymore, but born to it, and I couldn't help thinking it was as if their roots had been sown deep—not by time, but by the struggles they had endured alongside the rest of us . . .

"Jessie says living out here will give us gumption," Rose was saying as she spread a blanket down for them to lie on at the top of the hill. I saw Patrick hesitate then, looking around the grass. Rose looked, too. "What are you doing?" she said, and he looked up at her.

"I already had gumption once," he said. "And it made my legs itch. I don't want it again if I can help it." John-Charles started looking around warily then, and Rose laughed.

"You sillies," she said. "Gumption means you stick to something even if it gets hard."

John-Charles nodded thoughtfully, and Patrick said, "Like Jessie learnin' to read?" I heard Rose tell him yes as they all three plopped down on the blanket, Rose in the middle, as the talk soon turned to the business of making out shapes from the clouds.

"That one there looks like a buffalo's head," Rose said, starting the game, "and over there is a man's face. He looks just like he's smiling."

Jasper barked then, and Patrick said, "Look, Jasper sees a squirrel."

"Well, that one looks like a cow chip," John-Charles teased, and both boys laughed boisterously. Rose laughed, too, then she sighed.

"I wonder what I'll be when I grow up," she said out of the blue as she peered up at the sky.

"I just want to be here," John-Charles said, then Rose sat up and looked at him, and Patrick did, too.

"You can't be a *place*," she said indignantly, but John-Charles made like to wave her off.

"I can be anything I want to," he said, reminding me so much of Jack as he plucked a blade of grass then and put it in his mouth.

"I want to be *here*," he said again, "with the mountains and the horses. I don't think I ever want to leave."

"Me, either," Patrick said with a surge of conviction, lying back down. Rose followed, looking up at the sky again.

"I don't want to leave either," she said softly. "I want to be here 'til I die, then I want to be buried next to Stem. On his left side, though—Jessie says she gets the right side 'cause of holy matrimony."

They went on talking like that for a goodly while, and as I went back to hanging out clothes, I felt tears spring to my eyes, realizing that somehow along the way, our three little ones had formed a bond among themselves that was more than just blood.

When the men trailed in this evening, I heard the same sound in their voices, too, heard it in Jessie's low, sweet voice as she proudly read Scripture this evening, looking up from time to time to her children and grandbabies. I saw it in Lillie's peaceful eyes as she handed Mercy to me to hold. I saw it in Medicine Weasel's smile as he hugged John-Charles to him and patted him on the head with a gnarled old hand.

Quinn looked at me and smiled then with such a love, and I felt it roll over my heart like a warm balm. And suddenly I heard something whisper deep within me, telling me that balm was God, spreading His love over us just like the sun had soothed the winter-weary land, knitting us into the family we were always meant to be.

June 1, 1870 . . .

My last page, little journal . . . soon I will be opening the new one Quinn has brought home from the mercantile. Funny, but I feel almost like I'm leaving an old friend behind as I take a last look at these pages that have kept my thoughts such company over these past months. So *much* has happened . . . and yet I look forward to what's to come.

I feel a quietness in us all now, like we've all, in our own way, begun to make our peace with God, begun to trust Him with not just a bit of our lives but with *all* of our lives . . .

Christians, having to make peace with God? I can hear some say, but then I don't imagine they're being truthful in their hearts if they ask such a thing. If they were, they'd know it's just part of the journey. They'd know what it takes to learn going through the worst of times can make you a better person for it, can make you see things you would've never seen in the good times. They'd know that making peace doesn't mean forgetting . . .

I don't think He *wants* us to forget. For if we forget the storm, how can we relish the calm that comes after?

Of course, I'm not so foolish as to think this is the end, either—but I do think it's a new page of our lives.

There is still so much more work to be done . . . but I refuse to complain. We're a *family* now, a real family that has its ups and downs but that also has its times of joy, too, and I can't think of a finer gift from God than that.

I don't think I'll ever forget the look of sheer happiness on Jessie's face tonight at dinner, surrounded by her daughter and two sons and their families . . . of Coy and Bonny holding hands as they walked down by the stream together . . . or of Willa and Preacher catching each other's eyes just before Preacher bowed his head and said grace over our dinner.

And what a spread it was! Jack couldn't help himself from teasing Jessie, saying she had enough family now to make up almost a whole town on their own.

Jessie just cocked her head to one side and looked at Jack. "Funny you should say that," she said. "We've been thinking on doing just that."

She looked up at the evening sky above us, thoughtful then, almost like she was having her own private talk with God. I saw her glance over at her children, and they all nodded, then Jessie looked back at us and smiled a smile that spoke of one that had run a long, hard race and had finally begun to just make out the finish line in the distance. "When we get the land to do it," Jessie said, almost like she was talking to herself, "we're gonna call it 'Justice.'"

"Well, I can't think of a finer name than that," Jack said softly. I looked over at Quinn, and we smiled at each other. I happened to look up then, and I saw that the stars had begun to come out, sprinkling the dusky sky with thousands of sparkling lights that seemed to hang so close over our heads that I felt I could almost touch them.

"Will you look at that?" I said, and everyone glanced upward, smiling, and I heard Jack suddenly speak something in Blackfoot to Medicine Weasel, heard them laugh.

"Hey, sis," Jack said, grinning mischievously. "Medicine Weasel says if you're ready for that crow, he's got a good recipe, says the way he makes it, it ain't so tough to chew."

Well, everyone laughed at that—even the children, who probably weren't so sure what they were laughing about but were just caught up in the joy of laughing. I was, too, and as I sat there, letting their laughter wash over me, I couldn't help thinking how funny life was. How God's answers to our prayers aren't ever what we expect them to be.

They're always better.

Acknowledgments

I TRULY BELIEVE the people God puts in our lives are for reasons far beyond what we could ever imagine. For writers, it's a true blessing to have friends and family who support them during the journey of writing a book. I couldn't imagine the journey of writing *Promiseland* without all of the dear people the Lord has put in my life. So these pages are for all of you who have been such shining examples of what family and friends are all about . . . what *love* is all about.

My cup runneth over . . .

To my family . . .

My son, Mitch: You are and will always be the "wind beneath my wings." I am so blessed to have you in my life, to laugh with, to love, to pray with . . . I thank God every day for blessing me with you. *My parents, Diana and Joe McClure,* whose witness brought me to the Lord: You have been there for me more times than I can count. Thank you for your love, for believing in me, and for all of your prayers. *My grandparents, Doug and Dorothy Vance:* You've always been there to listen when I needed to talk, to support me, to love me, and to make me laugh when I needed it the most . . . I love you all so very much . . .

To my friends . . .

Dawn Fansler, my prayer-warrior buddy and fellow author: Thank you so much for your help, for showing up at my door at just the right time—and for your friendship. *Shelly Guy:* Thank you so much for all your help, for your kind heart, and for all of our late-night chat sessions—they meant more than I can say.

Linda Glasford and Greg Johnson, my agents and friends at Alive Communications: Thank you both so much for believing in me, for all your help and support—it's so wonderful to work with two such godly people. *Sue Ann Jones:* Thank you for being the best editor a girl could hope for. Your hard work and encouragement are appreciated. *David Moore:* Thank you for your prayers and your sincerity. God has great things in store for you! *Ann Pals:* you've been such a true friend and champion of Callie's story. Thank you, thank you, for always being there. *Joey Paul, publisher, Integrity Publishers:* Many thanks to you, Joey, for believing in *Promiseland* and for your patience and your true commitment to uplifting God in the written word. *Chelsea Perry:* Thank you so very much for praying, listening, for believing in my work, and for your calls that seemed to always come at just the right time. Our God *is* an awesome God. *Roy Quest,* fellow writer and friend, you are a true example of what it means to "walk the walk." Thank you so much for being there for me. *Terry Romeo:* Thanks for all your words of encouragement, for your prayers, and for your friendship. *Laurie and Joe White:* It seems as if we've known each other forever, and I am more than grateful for our friendship. You are the best of what true friends can be. I am so blessed!

To my pastors . . .

Jeff and Patsy Perry: I could fill more than one book on just what the two of you have done for me, for helping to change my life in such a radical way through your messages of what it truly means to live a life for Jesus. I wish everyone could have the chance to witness what I have witnessed: to see such humbleness, grace, and love in action. You have made such a difference not only in my life but in my son's, and that means more to me than you will ever know . . . Thank you for being such an awesome inspiration in my life.

Pastor Don Henning: I can't thank you enough, Pastor Don,

for your prayers and compassion. Your gentle spirit and giving heart are true gifts from God. *Pastor John Moore:* Thank you for your prayers and for your mentoring spirit; your legacy lives on in our children—and what a blessing that is for us all. *Pastor Virgil Nelson:* Thank you so much for your unwavering support, for your prayers, and for caring so much. *And for all the staff and members of St. Louis Family Church who are too numerous to mention:* I cherish you all; it is an honor to be a part of such a great group of people!

Finally, to all the dear readers who continue to take the time to write me such wonderful words of encouragement and praise—your letters have meant more to me than you will ever know.

The Other Side of Jordan

The Other Side of Jordan

By

Dawn Miller

INTEGRITY®
PUBLISHERS
Nashville

THE OTHER SIDE OF JORDAN

This book is dedicated to my son, Mitch . . .
I can think of a lot of words, but there aren't
enough to describe how much I love you.

PART ONE

On the Other Side
of Jordan

Here's your new journal Mama!
I asked Pa which part of the jorney we are
on now, he said the Other side of Jordan.
But Preacher says we still got to Pozess
the Land. He says peoples toes curl when
they think of facing The Enemy so they quit.
I asked Preacher if Joshua's toes curled
and he said no. He said God told Joshua
not to be scared. I said if God told me not
to be scared I'd go ahead and wade
through that ol river and climb on up to the
other side and not quit til I got my land.
I'd even go barefoot.
Your daughter,
Rose
PS. Pa said for me to write on the next page
too. He said it's a tre-dition.

So God told Joshua and the people to
GO FORTH and get what's yours. Be of
GOOD COURAGE, God said,
I got you this far, didn't I?

By Rose McGregor
13 years old
Montana Territory, 1873

Are you out there tonight, God? Because I could sure use some of your advice right along now. I know my mama always said if we looked hard enough, we would see you working even in the worst of people, but I admit I'm having a hard time of it.

Sometimes I feel like we've all lived ten lifetimes since we came to Montana four years ago, and sometimes, like today, I feel like we've come no further than that first shaky step we took out of our wagons—like we're still that ragtag group of drifters, still wandering, still looking for that place where we belong . . . especially after what happened in town today.

Quinn, of course, says I'm taking it too much to heart—that we all should remember who we are, not who someone *says* we are. He has always been that way with me, a great oak who's always there, always strong, always sturdy enough to stand against the battering winds that blow into our lives. But for all his sturdiness, my husband doesn't always understand everything about a woman's heart. And he wasn't in the mercantile when Leah Audrey said all she did, either.

We had all been so eager to take the trip to town, hoping for a little relief after the summer we've had . . . If the grasshoppers wasn't enough, those awful, greedy fires that swept through our valley over and over again through the summer had scorched more than just our grass but our spirits, too, and the proof of it was on every face as we climbed down from our wagons onto Audrey's hard, dusty main street. *Battle-weary* comes to mind . . . like soldiers searching for anything familiar to hold on to so they can leave behind the trying world they're in, even if it's only for a moment.

Even our little ones looked to be searching for something familiar as I watched them climb out, one by one: first John-Charles, then Patrick—but especially Rose, who hitched our baby, Mara Lee, on her hip, took Mercy by the hand, and made a quick beeline for the mercantile with a determined look on her face as she set off in search of the Audrey twins.

Once we were inside, me, Jessie, and Lillie got so busy gathering up news about the new church everyone was pitching in to build for Preacher, and dreaming over the bolts of goods we might get to buy one day, that I think we forgot our troubles for a moment. I say a moment because it wasn't long before we noticed Mrs. Pumphrey and Mrs. Spence—or Widow Spence, I should say—standing before us with excited looks on their faces.

Mrs. Pumphrey took a deep breath, her plump face set with determination, then went on to tell us that the ladies of Audrey had got together and decided it was high time a group was formed to get us all together once a month. "I figured we'd just call on each other like we've always done, but Mrs. Audrey says now that town's starting to take shape, we ought to do it up the *proper* way," she added, a slightly amused look in her eyes as she passed me the sheet of paper she held in her hand. "Sign here if you're up to it." Widow Spence smiled shyly like she always did, her salt-and-pepper bun bobbing at the back of her neck as we took turns signing our names to the paper. And it was right after Lillie had signed and turned to hand the paper to Jessie that Mrs. Audrey appeared, and for reasons I still don't understand, she was bent on being nasty.

"Ah see you have the *whole* brood heah today," she said to me. Her dislike for our *brood* has gone from bad to worse since word of Jessie and her family trying to buy land for their "town of color" has spread throughout the territory. Jessie finished signing anyway, a look of grim satisfaction on her old brown face as she noticed Mrs. Audrey's surprise that she could write.

"Yes, we do tend to travel in *packs*," I said, feeling my cheeks burn as I watched Mrs. Audrey take the paper from Jessie's dark, leathery hand by pinching its edge between two fingers like it was dirty. She made what might pass for a smile, then turned abruptly toward Lillie like a cat about to pounce on a bird.

"Oh, and Miz Wade," she drawled, brushing back an invisible strand of blonde hair, "Ah believe ah met an old friend of yoahs the other day. She said she knew you in Virginia City. Lillie Lee—that was your *maiden* name, wasn't it?"

Lillie squared her small shoulders, said it was, then got straight to the point, asking Mrs. Audrey if the woman happened to work in the same gambling den as she had. Inside I cheered my sister-in-law's gumption, but I saw that it had cost her, too. Saw her smile had gone and bright pink spots had appeared on her cheeks.

"Ah'm not sure . . . but she did say you were so much more than just a dealer, dear," Mrs. Audrey drawled again, her dark eyes going mean. "*And* she seemed to think you were quite a shot with a gun, too. Said there was even a newspaper account of it."

I saw a sudden look of alarm cross Lillie's face as she glanced around for her stepson, John-Charles, my brother's quiet little half-Indian boy. But John-Charles was out front with my Patrick, helping the men load the supplies we'd be taking home. Rose and Mercy looked up only a moment, then turned back to their chatter with the Audrey twins.

"It's been said that a rumor without a leg to stand on will get around some other way, too—especially in this town," came Willa Cain's voice from behind us, and we all turned to see her standing there, looking like a pretty picture right out of *Harper's Weekly*—except for the way she had her arms folded across her chest and frowned at Mrs. Audrey. Mrs. Pumphrey looked amused again, and Widow Spence, shocked—although I don't know why. Even being engaged to Preacher hadn't softened Willa's sharp tongue when it came to dealing with gossips.

"It's all right, Willa," Lillie said, straightening herself up as she headed for the door, the rest of us not far behind her. "It's all right . . .

"Of all the times for trouble," I said once we were outside, feeling the lowness of it all creep over me. "But I guess that's when trouble does its best work."

"Ten minutes in that place, and *I* start feeling sorry for myself," Willa said with a sniff as she shut the door of the mercantile.

"Uh-huh," Jessie said, folding her arms across her chest like she always did when she was aggravated. I saw Mrs. Audrey had gotten to her, too.

"I know it sounds crazy," Lillie said as we stood together and watched the men finish their loading. "But all those years of living like I did in Virginia City, of seeing real ladies pass me by on the street without so much as a nod my way . . . well, I always promised myself one day I'd be one of them fine ladies, maybe even the head of some ladies club or such."

She stood there looking across the town, and there was such a little-girl wistful look on her face that I felt my heart want to reach out and hug the lonely young woman she had been. Lillie finally turned back around and gave us all a sheepish grin. "Don't matter how much I've tried to talk myself out of this foolishness. That girl is still inside me, and she won't give in."

"Well, maybe it's time she had her way," Willa said, a thoughtful look on her face. "I told Shawn just the other day that folks ought to stop trying to play God. Judging is his job, and I don't think he takes kindly to those who forget that."

"Well, it *is* my past," Lillie said with a frown. "No matter how far I've come, it seems to always find me."

"We all have pasts, Lillie," Willa said. "It's just that some have skeletons in their closets . . . and some have live bodies."

"I think I prefer skeletons. Skeletons can't *talk*," Lillie said with such childlike earnestness none of us could help smiling a bit at each other.

"Preacher says be of the world—not in it," Jessie said, speaking up. "An' that always sounded good to me, not to care what the world thinks. But I reckon sometimes it's hard not to care."

We all fell silent then, and I knew each of us in her own way was wishing the day had turned out different—or wishing that we *didn't* care. We watched Quinn and Jack lead one of our best heifers over to Mr. Audrey to pay for our meager supplies, then the men had the wagons ready and we were climbing in, waving our good-byes to Willa as she stood on the dusty boardwalk where the Audrey twins had joined her. The twins waved a reluctant good-bye to Rose, caught somewhere between their mama and pa's ways, as we started to roll past.

Rose finally turned from them, and I felt her watching me close for a bit, pursing her lips as she righted the bonnet that would be gone as soon as we were out of sight of town. But it was Patrick, who could sense my moods sometimes even before Quinn, who leaned forward from the back of the wagon, the baby cradled in his arms. "Mama," he said, soft-like, "will you look at Bird smile . . . "

I reached for my baby girl then, her toothless grin reminding me of Willa's words the day she was born: "I've never seen a baby come into the world so *merrily*," she'd said as we all wondered over such a smile on her face. A smile that had caused me to think so many times since then that she'd came to us knowing the end of some great story . . . and thought it might be fun to watch us all get there.

"*Mara Lee*," I corrected him like I always did, but Patrick had refused to call her anything but Bird since the day she'd peeked her little head of tousled curls over the rail of the crib at him and he'd said she looked just like a bird, waiting on supper.

"What an absolute bunch of outcasts," I heard Mrs. Audrey say as she joined her daughters outside the mercantile, watching our wagons roll out. I literally bit my tongue trying hard not to say anything. I glanced back down at Mara Lee, shiny black curls framing her little heart-shaped face as she stared up at me with those blue-gray eyes of hers. Then she laughed a huge belly laugh for such a little baby and grinned up at me again, and it was like she was saying, *The joke's on them, Mama—not us.*

I held on to that grin of hers the whole way home, through the bone weariness that settled in again from those long months of summer, from the disappointment of our trip gone bad and the hurt of Mrs. Audrey's hateful words . . .

But I felt the memory of Mara Lee's smile slip away from me as we pulled into our valley and I saw again the scorched hillsides standing stark against the setting sun. I felt Quinn studying me, remaining by my side even after everyone else had piled out of the wagons.

"What is it you're thinking, lass?" he said, pulling me close to him as I held our sleeping baby in my arms.

"I was just thinking this is the first time I'm actually wishing for an early snow," I said, and he followed my gaze to the hillsides.

"'Twould be a better sight, to be sure," he said gently, as if he sensed my hurt mood. Then he cocked his dark head to one side and turned me to look at him, his pale blue eyes searching my face. "But the grass would still be gone, wouldn't it? And an early snow would only make it worse on the cattle. Covering something up doesn't make it go away. Sometimes it makes things worse."

Now, as I write this, I have to wonder if that's what I'm doing, Lord, trying to cover up my fears so no one can see. I'm wondering if my sad turn of thought is really about the grasshoppers, the fires, or Mrs. Audrey—or if these are just the final straws.

Lately, it seems I am plagued more and more by fears I can't shake. Like a nightmare that has come to stay, returning again and again, I get these odd feelings . . . and find myself looking around expectantly for a great hand to snatch what I love out of my reach. *Trust in the Lord,* my heart says, and I do. But I'm ashamed to admit there is that small part of me that hesitates after I hand all that I love over to him. In my mind I see my hand still in midair, ready to pluck everything back just in case . . .

Just in case? How you must shake your head over me and my ways, Lord. But if I can't be honest with you, who can I be honest with? Who better to help me be honest with myself? You are my mirror that never leaves my side, forcing me to take a look even when I don't want to.

And that, I think, just might be one of my greatest blessings of all—even if I might not admit it to anyone else . . .

Help me to see what I need to see, Lord. Help me to have the faith of a child again . . . to, like Rose says, climb to the other side and not quit until I get there . . .

And maybe even do it barefoot.

October 18, 1873 . . .

Willa came to call this afternoon like she always does, in a flurry of dust and purpose. With Preacher gone for another week and our old friends Coy and Bonny off scouting land with Jessie's kids, it was clear to me that Willa was looking for company—or maybe something to take her mind off her worries . . . which is something we understood all too well.

We were hurrying to finish the canning, saying like we did every year that fall in Montana means looking over your shoulder for winter while you work as fast as you can to beat its coming. But I think we were trying to keep our minds busy, too, trying not to think of that bad visit in town or anything else that seemed to lie just under our small talk. Willa took one look at us from the door of the cabin, rolled up the sleeves of her fine dress, and pitched right in. Our talk, of course, ended up turning to town and Mrs. Audrey.

"Well, you can suit yourself, Lillie, as far as joining that group of Mrs. Audrey's," Willa sniffed. "But I think I'd prefer to stay the topic of lively gossip myself."

"Speakin' of gossip, when *are* you gonna marry that fine man of your'n?" Jessie asked.

Willa arched a brow, but Jessie didn't budge in wanting her answer. Willa sighed finally, knowing like the rest of us that with Jessie, she wouldn't be able to help herself from giving in.

"I told him we would marry as soon as the church is finished," she said, avoiding our eyes as she looked out the window and gazed toward the mountains in the distance. I don't know why, but there was something in the way she said "finished" that stilled my hands from what they were doing as she went on. "He has someone who's going to take over the mission field once the church is done, you know. That way, he won't have to go away anymore." She turned back to us then and smiled. I guess it was her smile that made me remember the day she had shown me those pictures of her parents that she had always kept with her and how she said she would talk to them when she was lonely. "I talk, they listen," she'd said, but by the look in her eyes she could've added, *And they don't ever leave my side.*

I think Lillie sensed what Willa was feeling, too, for she said, "Life can be shaky, can't it, Willa?"

"If you're waitin' on life to quit bein' so shaky, chil', you're in for a long wait," Jessie said to no one in particular. I felt her words go through every one of us then, for I had no doubt they were meant for us all. And when Jessie turned to look back at me, I saw in that sweet, dark face of hers a lifetime of big trials and little triumphs in its lines and wrinkles, and I also saw that she understood.

Because she is one of us, too.

Quinn told me tonight while we were lying next to each other that he and Jack were going to have to bring the cattle down from the mountain pasture soon, that they had already stripped off what little grass there was left up there. He said if the cattle stayed up there much longer they would starve to death. He said he hoped the wild hay they had managed to cut before the fires would last. Then he asked me how much food stores we had left, and when I told him, he eased closer to me. "The Lord will see us through this, lass," he whispered, and we both fell silent. "Everything is going to be fine," he added after a while, breaking the silence.

I felt him search the covers then until he finally came to my hand, and when he took it in his own huge hand, covered with calluses, I heard him sigh.

I feel like we are all searching in the dark like that right now, Lord, reaching out to find your hand again . . . holding our breath until we do.

Sabbath morning, and everyone is still asleep . . . All but me and little Mara Lee here, draped under the little cloth I usually use to hide her nursing when company is around. For some odd reason, she has grown fond of it and gets too restless to nurse if I forget to cover her face . . . My funny little Bird, I wonder what your life will be like. I wonder if you will get as much joy as you give. I pray so . . .

This is the scripture I was led to just now: "Many waters cannot quench love, neither can the floods drown it"—Song of Solomon 8:7.

As I read it again aloud, Mara Lee pulled the cloth off her face to grin up at me . . .

October 20, 1873 . . .

I had quite a scare today—enough that my hands are still shaking as I write this. I don't know exactly how the team got so spooked, but it seemed to happen along about the time I was heading back from the spring with the water barrels for our wash. Patrick and John-Charles had just finished helping load them and had turned to go fetch their horses so they could join Rose with the cattle when the mules spooked for no reason I can explain. One minute I was hawing them up the hill, and the next thing I knew, Sassy, our oldest and gentlest mule, decided to take off in a dead run, giving Worthy no choice but to join her. Quinn ran out from the stables, hollering and waving his arms, trying to get them away from the deep ravine they were headed for, then Jasper and Honey joined in barking, even trying to bite at the mules' legs, but it felt like nothing was going to stop them.

Everything I saw seemed to me to slow down then. I remember feeling my bonnet fly off, felt the wind pulling the pins from my hair as I was jounced and jolted all over the front seat of that wagon. I remember seeing the shocked faces of the ones watching me as I flew past them, holding on to those reins for dear life, their helpless looks reminding me so much of the day we watched those flames roar through the valley.

It was Quinn who finally got close enough to dive onto the mules, yanking at Sassy's bridle as hard as he could while they dragged him along for a bit. Quinn finally jerked so hard on them that they swerved, then they stopped so quick the wagon tipped sideways and I was dumped to the ground.

Quinn picked me up and hugged me tight to him, and I know he must've felt something in me was ready to break because he kept holding me, saying, "Easy there, lass. All's well that ends well."

But when does it end? went through my mind to ask, but I didn't. Instead I let him lead me back toward the cabins, and when I saw how terrified the children were, I tried my best to smile.

"I didn't know ol' Sassy still had it in her," I said, trying to force cheer into my shaky voice. "Just goes to show you what an old lady can do when she sets her mind to it." I forced a chuckle then that I didn't exactly feel, and I heard Mara Lee chime in, laughter bubbling up out of the homemade baby buggy her little cousin Mercy had been pushing her around in.

"Oh, Mama," Rose choked out, her face streaked with tears. Patrick looked like he might get sick any minute, and John-Charles, like always, sat on his horse, the stoic little Indian, his mouth set in a thin line—but I'll never forget the tears I saw in his eyes.

"Well, it looks like Quinn here was the man for the job," Jack said, trying to joke away the bad of the moment. "He's always had a gift for dealing with stubborn ladies."

"Oh, hush," Lillie said, swiping at him with the dishtowel that was still in her hands as everyone crowded around me.

"Lord, chil', I think them guardian angels of your'n don't get a moment's rest," Jessie said then, hugging me. As she did, Lillie's eyes caught mine, and I saw by the look on her face she understood that life had went and gotten shaky on me again.

I waved them all away finally, saying I was fine. It wasn't until I shut the door of our cabin that I allowed myself a good cry. Then I cried for everything. I cried for our gardens that had been half ate up by grasshoppers, for our hay lands and the four years of work the fire had stole, I cried for the worry I'd seen in Quinn's eyes about how we were all going to survive the winter, even though he tried to hide it. I cried because it seems everything keeps going wrong no matter how hard we try . . .

But it was when I splashed some water on my face and took a quick glance in the mirror that I was so unnerved. For some reason the face that stared back looked almost like a stranger to me. Oh, my red hair was still there, and so was the spattering of freckles across my nose, but the glint of the fighter that I was used to seeing seemed to be gone.

How do I fight, Lord, when it seems like everything's been taken out of me? I thought then. *How do we possess this land like Preacher says when everything that's happened lately seems to tell us to leave?*

"Would to God that we had been content, and dwelt on the other side of the Jordan," Joshua had said when it seemed everything was going wrong, and I felt like I could've been the one who said those words myself. That's when Mercy's little voice startled me out of my thoughts.

"Aunt Callie, are you scared?" she said. I turned to see her standing in the door of my room, her golden curls so much like Lillie's, shining around her head like a little halo. Mara Lee, who is near half her size already, was perched comically on her hip, and I reached out and took her, trying to busy myself with her changing so I could think of how to answer. As if sensing my mood, Mercy watched me with a kind of patient understanding that always amazed me for one so young. If being born too soon had made her small, God had made up for it by the giant heart she had for others. It never ceased to amaze me how perceptive and well-spoken this child, not yet four, could be.

"Sometimes I get scared," I said finally, and Mercy nodded and walked around the bed, running her fingers over the stitching of my quilt.

"Mama says God doesn't give us fear," she said, then she came back over and sat down next to me, putting her little hand in my own as she looked up into my eyes with such a thoughtful look to her tiny face. "So, if he doesn't give it to us, that means we don't have to keep it, right, Aunt Callie?"

"No, we don't," I said, trying to blink back my tears. Mercy smiled, satisfied with my answer, and then she took her leave, a child again, skipping back outside to find Rose and the others.

To have the faith of a child again . . . my own words, my own prayer, has come back to me again today as I put this all to paper. I do pray, Lord, to feel that kind of faith again in me—the kind I saw shining in Mercy's eyes. There is such a simple beauty in that kind of trust. It's no wonder you say those are the kinds of hearts that will enter heaven. I know I couldn't think of better company myself . . .

I read another Bible story to the children tonight after dinner. I admit, I was so weary from all that happened I could barely keep my eyes open—but it is "tre-dition," as Rose likes to say, and I sensed their needing something familiar to hold on to, too, by the way they wordlessly gathered to me after dinner. Truth is, there was something comforting for me as well, having them sprawled all around me on the floor as I rocked Mara Lee to sleep. Patrick was the one to pick the story of Gideon and the angel, but after I finished it, it was clear he wasn't happy with Gideon.

"Well, Gideon must've been crazy," Patrick said, always right to the point. "If a real live *angel* showed up to me, I think that'd be enough proof. I wouldn't have to set out no ol' piece of sheepskin to see if it got wet."

"I think Gideon was just scared," I said, patting Patrick's arm. Then I looked over at Mercy. "But you know what? A real good friend of mine told me that God doesn't give us fear, so that means we don't have to keep it—and Gideon learned that, too."

"I bet that friend was Mercy," Rose said knowingly, brushing a hand over Mercy's curls. "I can tell because Mercy's cheeks are all red now."

"'Bout as red as your hair," John-Charles teased, and they all laughed—even Rose—and I noticed something new in their laughter: a strength I hadn't realized before. I wonder even now as I write this if their wanting to be read to was a way of moving on, too, past the bad of the day.

"I still say he should've knowed better," Patrick said, unwilling to give up his point, and it was along about that time I looked up to see Lillie standing in the room, watching us, and when our eyes met, she smiled a wry kind of smile that said, *We should all know better.* I watched her bundle up Mercy to send her on her way to their cabin with John-Charles, and I couldn't help thinking again how pretty Lillie was with her little turned-up nose like Mercy's and her golden-brown curls that always seem to escape her bun. Rose and Patrick climbed the ladder for their own beds not long after, and as Lillie and I sat talking quietly, I confessed to her I wondered if I hadn't been waiting on proof myself instead of just having faith.

"I had a room I kept above the saloon where I worked," she said then. "And every morning I used to stare out the window, watching people going up and down the street below." Lillie got up and added a piece of wood to the fire, talking with her back to me. "Everyone seemed to be going somewhere but me. Seemed like the whole world knew how to live their lives but me . . . But you know what I found out, Callie? I found out there ain't a one of us that really knows how—we're all just learning along the way . . . I almost told Mrs. Audrey that, too. I almost said, 'You don't know where I've been, how I got there, and you don't know where I'm going, either.'" Lillie looked over her shoulder at me then and smiled a small kind of smile. "But something kept me from saying it. Maybe *Someone.* I think I know why, too; I think it's because Mrs. Audrey's learning, too."

I admit I felt humbled by Lillie's forgiving heart . . . by her goodness . . . but I felt grateful, too, to have her in my life, and I couldn't help going over and hugging her. "I hope I'm learning, too," I whispered then, feeling my eyes well up with tears. When she pulled back from me, I saw her eyes were shiny, too, and it hit me that it was the first time we'd been able to share such a moment since all the trouble.

"We're all learning," she said, taking a shaky breath as she smiled. "It's like Jessie says, 'You're not dead until you die, so you might as well live.'"

"Jessie *would* say that," I said, shaking my head, but before any more could be said, Quinn came in from checking on the cattle with Jack. He took one look at us then went to busying himself with carrying the water into the kitchen, whistling as he did it. Lillie smiled as she shrugged into her shawl—common knowledge was that Quinn's whistling was a sign he wasn't sure what to do next—and we walked to the door together. As I watched her make her way down to her own cabin, I thought of what she had said.

It seems at every turn lately, the Lord has been speaking to my heart. I said a quick prayer of thanks to him for that, and when I stepped back inside the cabin, I saw Quinn standing in the middle of the room with a surprise for me: tiny yellow-hearted daisies he had found growing in a split of rock on the side of the mountain. The only place, he informed me, where the wind wasn't blowing and a bit of sun shone.

"Do you remember the first time I gave you flowers like that?" he said, smiling softly, and I nodded, trying to blink back the tears. Then I got the idea to fetch my first journal and find the entry that told of that first day he gave me flowers all those years ago on that wagon train headed west. We sat like kids, cross-legged, in front of the fireplace as I turned the pages of that old journal, finally coming to the entry I was looking for. I was surprised to find the daisy he'd given me that day still tucked safely in the crease of the page. I held it up, letting the firelight dance off its dried petals, and saw Quinn's wind-burned face go soft with memories.

"Do you remember what I said to you that day?" he asked softly as he reached forward to touch my hair.

"Well, yes, it's right here," I said, looking down at the pages so as not to cry.

"But do you remember, lass?" he prodded again, and I felt a single tear slip down my cheek as he hugged me to him.

"Yes, I remember," I whispered finally. "You said they were tiny but tough—just like me."

"I didn't remind you to make you cry," Quinn said, and I heard the emotion in his deep voice. Then he pulled back from me, and when he looked down into my eyes I felt like we were back on that trail again, just him and me under a dark, dark sky that went on forever. "I reminded you because I thought you might have forgot."

I'm pressing this new flower in this page . . . so I don't forget.

October 21, 1873 . . .

I guess my crying the other day didn't go as unnoticed as I thought. If there hasn't been enough excitement around here lately, it seems the children had to try and make some more, but if nothing else, it's made us all laugh again. Now that it's over, that is . . .

It all started when I accidentally overheard Rose, Patrick, and John-Charles talking. I was coming back from Lillie's with a thimble of hers I'd borrowed to do some mending when I caught a movement out of the corner of my eye just behind the corrals and saw just a peek of a dark head of hair as Patrick took off his hat.

"Mama was *crying*, I'm telling you," Patrick was saying. "Mercy told John-Charles last night, and he told me. Didn't you, John-Charles?"

I saw another shadowy figure, hands shoved in his pockets, and heard John-Charles clear his throat. "Yes, but I wasn't supposed to tell it. She just said pray because Mama and Jessie looked sad and Aunt Callie looked like she'd been crying. Mercy's always sayin' things like that."

"Yeah, but *she* never lies," Rose said knowingly, and I saw her skinny elbow come out to rest on the fence railing. "I think it's that ol' Mrs. Audrey's doing. I *still* say there's something about her. I read that desperadoes on the run sometimes go into hiding and pretend to be someone else so's they don't get caught." She took a breath then said, "But livin' the lie catches up with 'em 'cause all the meanness don't have nowhere to go, and it just comes bustin' out all of a sudden."

"Aw, Rose, she's just spiteful, is all," Patrick said, impatient after three years of suffering through Rose's insistence that Mrs. Audrey was the "Banditti of the Plains" she'd read about in those awful dime novels. But then with a bit more gruffness than I've ever heard in his voice, he added, "But she *does* need to be taught a lesson."

"Pa says women need us to look out for them," John-Charles added with a note of duty. "And Mama, Aunt Callie, and Jessie are about the best ones I know of."

"Well, don't you even think of leaving me out of what you're planning," Rose said, insisting on being a part of what she thought might be a great adventure. "I might be a girl," she said, "but I can ride better and faster than either of you."

It didn't take long after that for me to hear that they figured riding into town at night and scaring the daylights out of Mrs. Audrey was a pretty good start—nor did it take long for me to find Quinn and Jack down at the barn and tell them of our children's plot. But instead of confronting them like I thought they would, the two men decided it would be "first rate" to follow them out and wait until they got good and lost.

"That's about the best time to close in on 'em, too," Jack said, "when they're scared half out of their heads." He grinned at me, and Quinn matched the grin with one of his own. When I told them it was no wonder our children acted the way they did, they grinned again . . .

We are now waiting for the prisoners to be brought in, Jessie, Lillie, and me. Mercy is wheeling a dozing Mara Lee around in the carriage, looking almost half-asleep herself.

"Sakes alive, Callie, put that pen down," Jessie says as I write this. "I'm on pins and needles 'bout them little ones, an' that scratchin' sound don't help."

I'll say this, then end it: I think our Jessie is on "pins and needles" more about Rose than anything . . . that her "little sis" could do such a thing is more than Jessie can imagine. I just looked up to see Lillie smiling at me like she knows what I'm thinking. Most likely, she does.

More later . . .

Our wayward group has returned, and never was there a more forlorn-looking bunch than Rose, Patrick, and John-Charles as they shuffled into the cabin with Quinn and Jack behind them. Rose looked like she had been through a war, her long, honey-red hair all askew. Patrick and John-Charles just looked white from fear.

It was then that Mercy woke up from the settee and spotted them.

"Rose!" Mercy yelled, running to her like a little mother to help her up the stairs to the loft.

"I think I can make it," Rose whispered dramatically, not daring to look at me or Lillie—but especially avoiding Jessie, who had crossed her arms the minute the door opened and was tapping her foot against the floor.

It wasn't until we got Patrick and John-Charles off to bed as well that we got the full story of what happened.

Quinn and Jack waited until the kids were almost out of the valley before they stepped up their pace, following just a short distance behind the little group. And that's when it seemed Rose (the fearless leader) started to lose her sense of direction. First she led them off to the left then edged a bit to the right and finally, realizing she was lost, resorted to making a deal with God.

"Put your hands together," Rose had suddenly announced, holding a hand up to stop the procession, then she put her own hands together and began to pray: "God, if you help us find our way out of here, I promise I'll be good," she said, then hesitated for a moment. "But let's make me bein' good start tomorrow because if we *can* find town, I'm going to tell that ol' Mrs. Audrey what we think of her hurtin' Mama's and Jessie's and Aunt Lillie's feelin's—*after* we scare her real good."

"I think we should say amen real loud, Rose," Patrick added. "Just to make sure he hears."

"Well, what if he doesn't agree with the deal?" John-Charles said, and Patrick let out a loud sigh.

"Amen *seals* the deal, don't it, Rose?"

"Near as I can tell," Rose said. "So let's do it."

They all hollered, "Amen!" and that's when Quinn and Jack came galloping in, scaring the life out of them all. Quinn said Rose's first words after she caught her breath were, "Don't scalp me! My cousin's an Indian."

I don't think any of us laughed so hard in our lives. Even after Quinn and I turned in for the night, we'd fall silent then start laughing again. Then the silences got longer, and I thought he had finally fallen off to sleep when I felt him turn to his side suddenly and peer at me in the dark.

"Lord, I promise to be a good husband to Callie," Quinn whispered gravely. "But I promise to be good startin' *tomorrow* because tonight—" He turned and started to tickle my sides unmercifully, and as I began to laugh, so did he. We laughed and laughed like kids in spite of everything that had happened, and as we did, I realized again how much I loved the sound of our laughter together—and how much I had missed hearing it lately.

When I got up to check on Mara Lee, hearing Quinn's and my laughter still echoing in my ears, I couldn't help but come and write this. To remember. Even an echo of laughter can make you smile like you hadn't smiled in a very long time.

October 23, 1873 . . .

Cloudy and cold this morning. There's a mist coming off the mountains that stretches down across the valley like long fingers. Jasper and Honey bark, snapping at the mist, then they run back to where Quinn, Jack, and the boys are saddling up. Patrick and John-Charles look tuckered out from the work load their pa's have heaped on them, but neither of them has complained. Paying penance has made it a very quiet two days—but busy just the same. Rose and I have just finished churning five pounds of butter and are making ginger cakes for Jessie and Lillie's visit. We've decided to spend the afternoon together sewing. Rose, who usually would rather be hung over a cliff with a mess of snakes crawling over her (Rose's own words) than sew, is handling her dilemma bravely. She's even managed to smile a weak smile at me a few times as she stirs the batter . . .

I suppose I spoke too soon on Rose. We were maybe a half-hour into our sewing when I saw her mask start to crumble—even in spite of Mercy's efforts to cheer her.

Rose, looking like she couldn't bear it anymore, sighed and set her sampler on her lap, looking from me to Lillie and finally even to Jessie. "Well, doesn't it say *anywhere* in the Bible that we're supposed to protect our family?"

"Protecting your family isn't plotting to scare someone half to death, Rose," I said, trying to keep a straight face as Lillie glanced my way with a twinkle in her eye.

"'Vengeance is mine; I will repay, saith the Lord,' it says right here," Jessie said, tapping her gnarled old finger against a page in the Bible.

"Yes ma'am," Rose said, trying to blink back the tears of a prodigal daughter. We watched her jab at her sampler with the needle, and when she looked up again it was as if a thought had suddenly occurred to her.

"I'm sure glad I taught you how to read, Jessie," she added, then bent her head back down over her sewing. Jessie, Lillie, and I couldn't help but smile, for everything in her voice said at that moment she wasn't very glad at all.

October 25, 1873 . . .

I spent the better part of this evening filling and refilling and heating water for the washtub so we could all be ready to leave early for church in the morning. I was so looking forward to hearing Preacher speak again that I didn't mind the work—neither did Quinn—even as tired as we both were. Rose and Patrick, on the other hand, acted like prisoners facing the gallows come morning. Even after we had sent them off for bed, faces scrubbed and prayers said, Quinn and I could hear them whispering worriedly amongst themselves up in the loft. Then we watched as Patrick climbed back down first, Rose following reluctantly.

"Mama, do you think God told Preacher what we did?" he said, looking from me to Quinn like he wasn't sure he wanted to hear our answer.

"I think if God wants Preacher to know, he'll tell him," Quinn answered somberly, and Rose and Patrick looked at each other with dread. Mara Lee slapped her hands in the water, then laughed when it splashed against her face, looking at all of us as if to ask if we had seen her new trick.

"Well, at least Bird's happy," Patrick said with resignation.

"Sure, *she* can be happy," Rose said with a large sigh of resignation herself. "She's a baby—she ain't done nothin' yet."

October 26, 1873 . . .

Sabbath. Jessie is forever saying she thinks God whispers straight into Preacher's ear, the way he knows just how to plant the right seeds in our hearts to grow, and I have to admit, today seemed to be proof of that. Such a full day. I will try to record everything as it happened . . .

Before dawn even broke, we were hurrying to get on our Sunday best. We had mended our clothes over so much that I worried they wouldn't survive another wash, but thankfully, they did. Mercy and Mara Lee looked like little china dolls in the matching dresses and bonnets Lillie and I had cut down from one of Rose's old calicoes. Rose looked pretty as a picture as well, but her eyes were solemn. Patrick and John-Charles were somber little affairs, too, with their slicked-back hair and too-tight shoes. Every one of us needs new shoes—my own being stuffed with so much paper at the toes to make up for the hole in the soles that Quinn teased me that I "crinkled" when I walked. Or tried to tease, I should say, for I saw the hurt of it in his eyes when he said it, and I put my hand on his arm and patted it.

"At least you'll be able to tell where I'm at," I said, trying to get him to smile. He cocked his handsome head sideways, looking at me before he pulled his hat down.

"'Tis a comfort knowin' you canna sneak up on me," he said, smiling a small smile as he hawed the team on.

I don't recall much about the trip, other than we were fairly warm in spite of the chill—that, and I wondered what Mrs. Audrey thought of her proper town with two huge bull elk standing in the middle of the road, pawing and snorting and refusing to let folks get by. But we did get by finally and made our way, quick, inside Preacher's tent to get a good seat, along with everyone else in the territory. Mrs. Pumphrey and Widow Spence were already seated alongside Mr. and Mrs. Audrey, the twins next to them. I saw Rose glance over toward them briefly, then she spotted Preacher coming from the back and motioned for Patrick and John-Charles to hurry and sit before he saw them. Mercy hurried, too, though she didn't really understand why.

Preacher walked to the front of the tent with his Bible in one hand, touching shoulders and saying his hellos, then turned to face us with a smile once he got to the front. Willa sat in the second row of chairs with us, looking up at him like he hung the moon, and judging by the feelings of the rest of the crowd, you might wonder if he did. Preacher started right in, like he always did, his deep voice strong and gentle, causing you to feel his words. And we did . . . every one of us did. Lord, help me remember exactly what he said . . .

"I've been wondering about some things I'd like to share with you all, if you don't mind," Preacher began, looking around the tent.

A few people called out, "Go on, Preacher," and he smiled again.

"I know most of you well enough by now to know you thought coming to this territory was like finding your Promised Land. I know, too, that these last months have left a lot of doubts in your minds about that thought. But what I want you to ask yourselves now is whether you've really crossed over to that other side of Jordan to the Promised Land yet. *Have* you left your old lives behind—left behind any old fears or old ways of looking at things? Or are you still standing on the banks, afraid to move forward, afraid to take hold of what God has promised you? Sometimes I wonder . . ."

He looked around the crowded tent. "Now, don't get me wrong," he said. "I know everyone's been through some real tough times this past year. But the truth is, I don't think God puts us through as much adversity as we like to think. I think we put ourselves through more by not letting go. Tell you what else: I think he just waits for us to get so sick of wallowing in our trouble we're finally willing to take the risk—the risk that his plan might just be *better* than ours . . .

"The children of the Israelites were born risktakers. They had cut their teeth in the wilderness, and they knew with every fiber of their beings that God had something better for them. They didn't look back because they already knew what was there. Instead, they followed God toward their future . . . and when they snuck into Jericho, they found another risktaker.

"Her name was Rahab."

Preacher kind of leaned his elbows on the pulpit then, like he was getting ready to share something good. "Now, the funny thing is," he said slowly, "most people would think the children of God might have a problem striking a bargain with a known prostitute . . . "

I glanced over quick at Lillie and saw her eyes go wide as Preacher went on.

"But you see, her title meant no more to them than their old address. All they saw was another child who had been a slave to the wilderness—another child who had the faith to believe God would set her free, too. The good Lord honors faith like that, too.

"I know most folks don't like reading down that line of 'begats' in the first chapter of Matthew, but if you did, you just might find that some impressive descendants came from Rahab the prostitute . . . " Preacher ducked his head and looked at his Bible. "Let's see: It says Salmon begat Boaz by *Rahab* . . . Then Boaz begat Obed by Ruth, and Obed begat Jesse, and Jesse— why, he begat David the king." Preacher smiled with satisfaction then ducked his head again, looking back to where he'd marked his place. He ran his finger down a ways then rapped the

Book with his finger. "Now, here's a name that comes a little farther down that same line—I think you might just recognize it."

Preacher looked back up at us, his eyes passing over every single one of us in the tent.

"His name is Jesus. '*Jesus*, a descendant of Rahab the prostitute?' you ask. He was . . . and, my friends, he was one of the greatest risktakers of all times. He risked everything on a world that had fallen so far down its people forgot that all they had to do was look up and reach out their hands to God.

"Jesus knew God is almighty. In the Gospel of Luke, it was Jesus himself who said he had stood and watched Satan fall like lightning from heaven. And yet Jesus 'made himself of no reputation' . . . and came 'in the likeness of men: And . . . as a man, he humbled himself, and became obedient unto death, even the death of the cross.'

"Have any of you ever really thought about Jesus' death? Have you thought about what filled his mind as he faced the cross? Well, I think He was *afraid*."

Preacher paused then, looking around the room again, and for just a moment I could've swore his eyes met mine. Then he went on talking.

"Think about it: The Son of Man, knowing what's to come, is all alone, kneeling in the garden to pour out his fears to our Father. Scripture says he was sorrowful and deeply distressed, but that in agony he *prayed more earnestly*. And his prayer was, 'Not my will, but thine, be done.'

"Jesus looked past his fears and took that risk because he knew who God was, who God *is* . . . "

As Preacher fell silent, I glanced around the tent and saw that Mrs. Audrey's cheeks were bright red—but so were mine, judging by the hot feel of them, because Preacher had spoken to my heart as well. He'd touched all our hearts. I saw Lillie looking like she'd just been told the best news she'd ever heard.

Jessie was nodding with big tears in her eyes, and Willa looked more amazed than I ever saw.

"Until we can understand that the same God who made this earth is the same God we pray to," Preacher went on, "that he's the same God who promises us victory if we only believe . . . until then, none of us will cross over to the other side of Jordan. And know this: There are some who may even drown in the crossing." Preacher looked around with a sad look to his eyes then finished his sermon.

"My prayer for you is that you *don't* drown. But instead, you lift your hands up out of that water and let God pull you out. Take the risk, folks. Take the risk!"

We waited, silent in our own thoughts about what he'd said, until Preacher had walked past us down the aisle, then we began to file out. I felt Quinn take my hand, and when I looked up at him, he smiled. Then I saw Lillie fairly pull Jack with her to join us in the line shuffling out.

Jack was the first to speak. He cleared his throat and reached out and shook Preacher's hand. "That was a fine talk, Preacher," he said. "Ain't every day an ol' risktaker from the wrong side gets to hear what it would be like to take a risk for something right."

"I felt the same way some years back," Preacher chuckled, and that's when Lillie stepped up, looking from Preacher to Willa with tears in her eyes.

"Did you say anything?" Lillie asked, and Willa beamed, shaking her head.

"Didn't have time," she said. "I suppose that makes it even better, doesn't it?"

"It didn't even matter," Lillie said softly, shaking her head in amazement. "God didn't even care what Rahab was. He just saw her faith . . . and he remembered her for it . . . "

"Well, I seem to recall a little girl sayin' once that Jesus ain't no *suspector* of persons," Jessie said from somewhere behind us, and we all laughed. I saw Rose cringe then as the attention was turned to her, and she quickly grabbed ahold of Patrick and John-Charles, scampering out of the line before Preacher could see them. Preacher shook his head, looking at us all like he wasn't sure what he had missed, then he caught sight of Mercy and smiled.

"Well, Mercy Wade," Preacher said, bending down to shake her tiny hand. When his large hand covered her own, Mercy's eyes went wide as if she was seeing her hand disappear for good. "So this is what a miracle looks like in a bonnet and dress . . . " We all smiled, and Mercy smiled proudly along with us. She knew the story of her birth now as well as the rest of us.

I didn't say a word about the fear part of Preacher's sermon—but I don't think I had to, the thoughtful way Preacher caught my eye as he looked up from Mercy.

We had to move on then to allow Preacher and Willa to tell the rest of the congregation their good-byes, and that's when I saw Mr. and Mrs. Audrey standing behind us. Mrs. Audrey gave us a long kind of considering look, like she was trying to find how she really felt, then she shook her head and turned away. I could've sworn I saw Mr. Audrey look at her, sad, like he understood more of what was going on than she thought.

We headed for the wagons not long afterward, and that's when we saw Peach in his usual spot, waiting on us. Peach, like everyone else who'd stumbled into our lives—and maybe even for reasons I still haven't figured—had decided he liked us well enough to come calling when he saw fit. And Sunday was one of those days. He never set foot inside the church. Instead he waited for us outside the tent, sitting in his old wagon, whittling on a piece of wood.

Today, though, he had company. At first I thought the boy to be about sixteen, seventeen years old, but when he looked up, I saw it was just his size that had fooled me. His face was as young as Rose's, but now that I think on it . . . maybe old, too, like he had seen more than his fair share of life. He looked up at us briefly, his dark eyes taking in our whole group, then he slowly walked away, and it wasn't until we got to our picnic spot that I found out anything about him. And that was after we got over the shock of seeing Peach with his new teeth.

Jack was the first to notice, and as is Jack's way, he couldn't let it go without saying something.

"Why, Peach, you're looking real shiny with them new teeth," Jack teased. "Who you gettin' gussied up for?"

"Maybe it's Widow Spence," Lillie said, the dimples in her cheeks coming out as she grinned.

Peach looked at Lillie, startled, like she might have guessed his secret, then was quick to compose himself as he turned back to Jack. "And as far as gettin' gussied up, ain't nothin' doin'," he said, shaking his grizzled old head. "Last feller I heard of went all out with a full dippin', ended up gettin' his ears so plugged he never heard a drop of sound agin."

We all laughed then, and it wasn't until Jessie, Lillie, and I had made plates for everyone that I thought of the boy again and asked Peach who he was.

"The Norton boy—can't tell ya much 'bout him," he said. "But what I kin say is, he's a real hard worker. Been up to my place to help me a time or two. Wouldn't give a plug nickel for his folks, though."

"Zora and Nora, they say he's next door to a perfect heathen," Rose offered, and Patrick grinned, tipping his hat back from his head in a way that reminded me so much of Quinn. Escaping the possibility of Preacher being disappointed in them had put them all in a better mood.

"Those ol' twins don't know nothin'," Patrick said, crossing his arms. "He lives on the old Posey ranch, Rose. Ain't nobody *next door* to him for miles."

"I don't know anything about him being a heathern," Peach said.

"What *is* a heathern, Peach?" Rose asked, taking on his slang like it was second nature, and Peach cleared his throat, trying not to smile.

"Well, Miss Rose, I'm figurin' you're lookin' at one."

"But I thought *heathen* meant you didn't believe in God," John-Charles said, studying Peach with new interest, and all the children's heads turned to stare at Peach then.

"Well, I reckon I don't," Peach said, avoiding their stares.

"Well, who do you talk to, then?" Rose pressed him, ignoring Quinn's and my looks.

"I talk to myself," Peach said, and Rose looked at him curiously.

"Well, I always have a lot to talk about," Rose said. "But I think even I'd get pretty bored if it was just me doing all the talking *and* the listening. And lonely, too."

It was then that I saw Mercy quietly slip her little hand in Peach's, saw Peach's eyes crinkle at the corners with what might have passed as a smile as he looked down at her, and suddenly there was a different look on his face, kind of thoughtful, but something else, too.

Of all things, it was precocious little Mercy who broke the mood. She stared up into Peach's kind old face with such a wistful look that I thought she was going to say something real sweet, like she had done to me before. Instead she said, "Can you take them teeth out, Peach?"

What remained of our proper little picnic was over as our children jumped up and surrounded the dear old trapper, exclaiming with the kind of oohs and aahs usually reserved for a traveling circus as a fine set of snowy new teeth were extracted and shown about with all the flourish of a magician producing a rabbit out of thin air.

Thank you, Lord, for this day. For Preacher's words and for this wonderful, crazy bunch I call my family. I couldn't imagine my life without them.

October 27, 1873 . . .

It's a cold, windy day—a lot colder than yesterday, in fact, colder than it's been all month. Fall appears to be on its way out a lot quicker this year—which is why I decided to make a quick work of lunch so I could ride out with the men to start rounding up our cattle. Lillie got the same idea as me, but Jessie was having none of it.

"No ma'am," Jessie said, shivering as she eyed the men adjusting their saddles down by the barn. "The good Lord gave me feet to use, and I reckon I'll keep them on the ground today. You just leave me them babies, and we'll both be happy."

We knew Jessie had been lonely with her own family gone and Rose back in the saddle now that her punishment was over, so we obliged, bringing her an ecstatic Mercy and Mara Lee (who wasn't sure what Mercy's excitement was about, but was glad to join in), and off we went.

I don't think Lillie and me have ever been so cold in our lives—but so glad we went, too. As we moved away from the dull, burnt hills of the valley and began the steep climb to the mountain pastures, color sprang up everywhere, from the reds and oranges in the trees to the wide blue-gray sky that hung over us like a bowl to the dark black peaks of the mountains proudly sporting their first caps of snow. The horses got friskier as we climbed, too—especially Midnight, who is almost as comical as her mistress, Rose, when it comes to antics. She pawed the earth and rubbed her nose in it so often that she soon had what looked like a brown, shaggy beard on her face, causing us to laugh.

When we got to the mountain pasture, we didn't find as many of the cows as we expected, but the ones we found were work enough. Some tried to double back, and some went for the ravines while others dodged us, squeezing their bulky bodies through stands of lodgepole pine that defied the imagination. By the time we were to the halfway point of the mountain, I was getting good at feeling when they were going to try and make a break for it. Lillie was, too, and we grinned at each other from time to time when we'd bring a straggler back in. Rose, Patrick, and John-Charles were old hats at it, and I couldn't help marvel at their horsemanship, as young as they are, whipping around the herd, hawing them like old cowhands. I noticed something else, too. I noticed that without us even trying, we were all moving and working together, wordlessly, like we sensed each other's moves.

I think Preacher's sermon did us good, too, for we all seemed determined to keep our spirits up in spite of the worry over where the rest of the herd might be.

"You look just as pretty as the day we first met," Quinn said, sidling up next to me with his horse as he reached for a wayward strand of my hair. Jack picked that time to come trotting up.

"Yes, she's always been a looker," he said, grinning his slow, easy grin, "but them lookers are hard to handle—I should know."

"Should know what?" Lillie called out, and we all laughed. Lillie frowned prettily. "Never mind," she said. "Maybe I *don't* want to know." Which made us laugh harder.

Such a good day in spite of the work . . . I wish I could capture it to paper, what it was like watching us all walking together to the corrals once we made it in—Rose, Patrick, and John-Charles's tired laughter rising up to mingle with the

churned-up dust tinted orange by the low afternoon sun . . .
Jack draping his arm over Lillie's shoulder as they walked
together . . . and Quinn, turning to look over his shoulder to see
where I was . . .

Jack asked if I would go with him after dinner to watch John-
Charles with the wild mustangs, and as tired as I was, I was still
eager to go with him. It had been a long while since I'd taken a
walk with my brother, and it brought back old memories of us as
kids, walking the farm in Missouri together. We talked about
those times as we walked, about how he had planned to be a rich
and famous gambler and I had planned to travel the world and
write my adventures as I went.

"We weren't too far off, Jack," I said as we walked. "You
gambled, and I wrote journals—still do. God just changed our
minds about what you gamble on and what I write about."

Jack grinned. "It's a good thing he did, too, sis," he said. "It's
a good thing." And then we stopped just a short distance away
from where John-Charles sat, patiently watching the herd. It
never ceases to amaze me how the mustangs always find their
way back to our ranch just before winter hits. This time,
though, they were staying closer to the river, with the grass as
poor as it is, munching on anything green left to find near the
banks.

We watched John-Charles slip off his seat on the outcropping of rock and cross over the little gully as he headed for the
river, armed with just a halter he would use to bring one in. He
only brought in what we needed and no more, Jack said. What
we saw next was like watching poetry.

John-Charles edged closer to the herd, and I could see by
the way he headed for some of the horses to the right that he
had an idea which one he was going to pick. The horses imme-

diately sensed him, and I saw that one of them in particular kept its eyes right on John-Charles. Jack told me that would be the one. We watched as John-Charles took what he called the lead-mare stance, squaring his shoulders to the horse as he stared eye to eye with the horse. The mustang immediately cantered off a short distance, and John-Charles turned to him again, standing between it and the rest of the herd and silently telling the horse he was calling the shots and that it could rejoin the herd when John-Charles said. Finally the horse slowed its trot and dropped its nose to almost an inch above the ground. Then we saw John-Charles turn sideways, looking slightly away from the horse. Suddenly the horse stopped and turned to face John-Charles. Then it walked right up to John-Charles, its nose just inches away from my nephew's shoulder. John-Charles gently slipped the halter over the mustang's head and then turned around and began to slowly lead the horse toward us, smiling easily as he spotted us from the distance, like what he'd done was the most natural thing in the world.

Rose had learned some of the same moves after watching John-Charles one full summer and studying what he did. One day she led a horse right up to the cabin, haltered by the drawstring from her petticoat. The memory still makes me smile. Made Jack smile today, too, when I reminded him of it.

"I never did figure out how she managed to do that until I heard John-Charles explain it one day. Still, it doesn't seem real," I said, and Jack smiled, soft-like, then looked back out toward the river where John-Charles was still making his way toward us.

"He says they talk more with just a look than we do with a whole lot of words," Jack said. "Sometimes I think he's so used to being around them he forgets how to talk around us." He turned and looked at me then and said, "I know it sounds crazy, but I was almost glad that he went with Rose and Patrick like that."

"Well, when you put it like that, I guess I'm glad, too," I said, and we both smiled at each other. "I'm glad you let him do as he saw fit with those mustangs, too," I added. Jack nodded.

"I did it for me as much as him, sis," he said, "to make him feel a part of this land."

I didn't say anything then, but I knew Jack meant a part of the family, too, with John-Charles being torn between his real mama's family—the Blackfoot—and ours.

"I've been thinking on what Preacher said," Jack said after a while. "And I think he's right that we need to be risktakers about trusting God. I think this land is worth the risk—that we're worth it, Callie. I know it's been hard, but when hasn't it? If you think about it, we've been risktakers all along and didn't even know it. Jessie trampin' all the way west with nothin' but a bundle on her back . . . Quinn goin' it alone after losin' his whole family, and you and me losin' Pa and our sister, Rose, like we did." Jack glanced over at me and smiled a wry kind of smile. "And I think Lillie took the greatest risk of all, marrying me . . . "

"Not so big a risk as you think," I said, feeling the love in my heart swell for my brother. He smiled.

"You know what John-Charles told Lillie today?" he asked then, and when I shook my head, he chuckled. "Well, you probably wouldn't guess it, but he told her that he didn't want her worryin' over him findin' out how his real mama died. He said he knew a long time ago that a bad man had shot her and that when the bad man went to shoot me, Lillie killed him. He said, 'Mama, you're a hero to me no matter what Mrs. Audrey says.'"

"How did he ever find out?" I asked through my tears.

"He found the newspaper article," Jack said, shaking his head. "God sure has a way of working things out, don't he, sis? That's why I know he'll work out our troubles with the ranch, too. We just got to ask him."

Then Jack did something that surprised me. He asked if we could pray.

As we joined hands, I felt Jack's hand tighten around my own, and I remembered then all the times we had taken each other's hands as kids, through the good and the bad, and I couldn't help thinking there was a different feeling to the way he held on. Like he wasn't just making sure I was there with him, but that he was there for me, too.

"What are you all prayin' about, Pa?" John-Charles said, coming up just as we said amen.

"Why, your inheritance," Jack answered easily. John-Charles seemed to think on that a moment, then he took his hat off and wiped his brow tiredly.

"Well, can we just start with dinner? I'm awful hungry," he said, and we laughed.

Not long after we got the horse to the corral, I stood and watched Jack walk away with his son, his hand resting on John-Charles's head with such love. And for some reason I remembered a time on our old farm back in Missouri, watching Jack and Pa walking together in much the same way. I remember how Jack had looked at the ground as the afternoon sun glared down over them and then how he had looked back up to Pa.

"Pa, when do you think my shadow will be as big as yours?" he asked. And I recall Pa looking down at him with a soft smile, touching Jack's head as he did.

"Why, when you become a grown man—like me," Pa had said simply, and Jack had looked worried all of a sudden, like he wasn't sure if he would make it to being like Pa.

A worry he had carried in him over the years, I thought then, and I had the strongest urge to yell after him then, to tell him how much his shadow looked like Pa's now . . .

October 28, 1873 . . .

Another cold day. The sky is choked with heavy gray clouds that hang so low over the valley I feel like I could take a needle and stick it into them to make them rain . . . Instead, I'll be mending the mountainous stack of clothes sitting before me as I wait for another loaf of bread to come out of the oven . . . and there goes the poetry right out of me.

Quinn came in tonight, and I knew right off something was troubling him, whistling like he did while he helped Patrick carry in another load of wood. I had to ask a couple of times before he finally came out with it, sitting down at the table with a long sigh.

"Truth is, Jack and I are about at our wit's end. With Coy gone right now, we're short a hand—and we need the help more than ever with the cattle straying every which way to find grass," Quinn said tiredly, and I saw Patrick and Rose's eyes meet across the table, worried for their pa.

We joined hands then to pray over our dinner, and as soon as we said amen Patrick reached over and touched Quinn's arm, patting it the same way I did his when he needed comfort.

"Don't worry, Pa," he said. "God's sure to send help, now. I told him while we were praying that in case he hadn't heard, you needed help and that I didn't think I'd ever heard you ask for anything in my whole life."

"Well, I'm not so sure that I haven't asked God for things," Quinn said with a slight smile on his face. "But it's a fine thing to pray for your family, Patrick."

"I prayed, too," Rose said, not to be outdone. "Patrick just said it first."

Mara Lee suddenly let out a yell right out of the blue, startling herself more than she did us, and we all started laughing. She looked toward each of us, unsure what to do for just a moment, then it occurred to her she already knew what to do— and she laughed.

Quinn laughed, too, leaning over to pull Rose and Patrick

to him, hugging them as if to say it would all turn out fine. But tonight, just before he nodded off to sleep, I felt him search in the dark for my hand again, heard him sigh when he found it.

This time, though, it was me that whispered, "Everything is going to be fine."

It has started raining tonight as I'm writing this, the big drops of water hitting our roof like heavy drumbeats. I can't say how many times since we've been here that I've sat hearing that sound . . . but I can say I never get tired of listening. Sometimes I've even thought how good it would be to climb into the loft and lay on Rose's or Patrick's bed with a lamp and a good book and just escape from everything while it's raining like this. But I've never done it. Seems my only free time is spent with you, little journal, and I just can't bear to trade our visits for anything. Makes me think of Willa's pictures—I talk, you listen—but there's more to it than that . . .

There are times when I hear God's voice whisper to me as I put all these thoughts to paper, and those are the best times of all . . . Only right now, I keep hearing those words of Rose's, and it makes me wonder if he doesn't whisper to her, too.

Be of good courage, I hear. *I got you this far, didn't I?*

October 29, 1873 . . .

Rose has scared us nearly half to death today. It was around noon, when the men came in from rounding up more cattle, that I first noticed she was missing. I had looked up from setting the table and for some reason, it dawned on me that I hadn't seen her in a while. I could see Patrick and John-Charles with the men down at the barn, so I went out on the porch and called for her, then I went to Lillie and Jessie's cabins—but she wasn't there, either.

By the time Quinn came up to the cabin with Patrick, I was starting to get scared.

Quinn searched the barn and corral then joined Jack and John-Charles, riding out to search the pasture. Lillie, Jessie, and I searched all along the riverbanks. By that time, we were all hoarse from hollering for her and thinking the worst of what any parent can think might happen, what with the grizzlies and moose that lurk in the willows near the river this time of year . . . And just as we joined up back at the barn, Patrick showed up and confessed that he knew where she went.

"She rode off that way on Midnight," Patrick said, pointing away from town as all heads turned to him.

"Where, son?" Quinn said, his voice as breathless as I felt, and I knew he had seen the fear in Patrick's eyes, too.

"To the Norton place," Patrick said, and no sooner had he said it than Quinn was up in the saddle and heading out again, Jack not far behind. "She wanted it to be a surprise . . . she was going to find you some help, Pa," Patrick called after Quinn, but they were already gone.

Jack told us later that Quinn had rode straight up to the porch of the old, run-down house and that just as he was dismounting, they all saw Mr. Norton careen out of a tall stand of weeds, a whiskey bottle in his hand. Before anyone could say anything, Quinn was inches from the man's face.

"Mr. Norton, you don't know me, so I'll get right to the point," Quinn said softly. "My name's Quinn McGregor, and my daughter, Rose, has turned up missing. The thought is she was headed this way."

"I might have seen her," Mr. Norton said, wiping his face with the back of his hand. Then he looked up, like he might have recalled some foggy memory. "She's a pretty little filly, right? With red hair?"

Something in the way the man said that set Jack's temper

off, and he stepped in front of Quinn then, talking real quiet. "Now, my brother-in-law here is what you call a God-fearing man," he said. "Don't get me wrong. I fear God—but I love my niece, too. Point is, I don't fear death . . . But mister, I have a feeling you do. So if you know anything, you best tell us now."

It was about that same time that Rose and the Norton boy came trotting up on their horses at *our* ranch.

Mercy took one look at the faces of Jessie, Lillie, and me, then walked slowly over to where John-Charles and Patrick stood. She tugged on John-Charles's trousers, and when he glanced down she said, "I think we ought to pray for Rose now."

Gale is the Norton boy's name. "But it's Gale like in a windstorm," he'd made sure to add, smiling a shy kind of smile at me as he turned and shook everyone's hands so politely. As I watched him, I couldn't help thinking there was something about him that was different, something almost gentle in spite of his large build, that made me think he was more the calm after the storm than anything else . . .

Later, after the men had calmed down enough to decide to hire him and we were all in the kitchen getting dinner ready, Rose told us she thought he didn't have the nicest of parents, that they had been arguing real loud when she had rode up to fetch him for Quinn. She said that something had crashed against the wall just as Gale had opened the door to her. She said Gale had just shut the door, soft-like, behind him and walked slowly out to the yard with her. And once they got away from the house, he had unwrapped a kerchief of his and took out a handful of toy soldiers and began lining them up on a stump—that even when the yelling got real loud, he just calmly kept arranging the soldiers in neat little rows until he was satisfied with how he'd placed them.

When she asked him what he was doing, he looked up at her and said, "This is one game I can win."

"When we were riding back here, I asked what he wanted to be when he grows up, and you know what he said, Mama?" she said then, looking at me with a puzzled but kind of sad look to her pale blue eyes.

"He just said, 'Someone who cares.' He can't be a heathen and say something like that, can he, Mama?"

Rose didn't wait for my answer but shook her head and started in on kneading the bread for me. "No," I heard her say, real quiet, after a while. "I don't think he's a heathen at all. I just think he got stuck with heathens for folks."

I looked over then at Jessie, who had been listening while she worked, and I saw her wipe her hands across her apron. "Well, that may be the case as far as that boy's folks," Jessie told Rose. "But you're the one we almost died worryin' over today. Don't you go runnin' off ag'in like that and not tell us where you a-goin', sis, you hear?"

Rose smiled her best charming smile at Jessie as she worked at the dough. Then with a little flip of her head she said, "Oh, Jessie, don't you know I can handle myself? I don't need no one worryin' over me."

"Don't need no one, huh? Well, there ain't much brag in that, sis," Jessie replied. Then I heard her say it again, almost like a whisper, like she was deep in thought over something or other. "Don't need no one." But when I looked over at her, she just smiled and smoothed over her skirts, real prim, like I'd never seen her do before.

Lillie, who had been sitting in my rocker bouncing Mara Lee on her knee, just looked up at me with one brow arched and said, "I'd hate to be on the other end of that thought."

It's been decided that Gale Norton will take over Coy's old place in the bunkhouse while he helps Quinn and Jack finish the roundup.

I think Jack has taken quite a liking to him, too. When I went down to the bunkhouse with some extra blankets for Gale, Jack was just leaving, and I noticed there was a look of amazement on his face.

"That boy's something else," Jack said, taking his hat off his head and worrying its brim with his fingers as he spoke. "I asked him if we should let his folks know where he was, and he said for me not to bother myself, that they probably wouldn't notice he was gone." Jack looked up at me and shook his head. "And he didn't even say it mean-like, either, sis—just said it like he was stating a fact. Then he told me he was willing to work hard for his keep. Said, 'Mr. Wade, I plan to be better than what I came from, and the way I see gettin' there is to work. So you can count on me workin' real hard for you and Mr. McGregor.'"

"Rose said his folks seemed rough," I said, suddenly wishing I had brought more than just blankets.

"Well, she was right about that," Jack said. "But he's different than them; I can tell you that already. You talk to him, and you'll see—he feels like family already," Jack said, smiling at me as he turned to make his way up to his cabin. "I think he might be one of them risktakers, too," he added, not bothering to look back.

I made my own kind of discovery in a way when I knocked real light on the bunkhouse door and heard the boy's voice saying to come on in. First thing I saw was Gale sitting on the little bed of Coy's, his large frame hunched over as he read from the Bible by the dim light of a single lantern. Coy must have left the Bible behind. Then I saw Jasper lying curled up at the end of his bed . . . and Honey, who never lost any time deciding if she liked someone or not, was lying right on the bed with him, her head draped over his leg.

"Well, I see you got company," I said, offering him the blankets. He set down his Bible and smiled.

"Yes ma'am," he said, taking the blankets. "Do you know when her pups are due?" he asked then, taking me by such surprise that I sat down on the bed next to him, stroking Honey's fur as I looked her over.

"I *had* wondered at Honey filling out so much lately—and even had worried a little about her moving so slow, thinking she might be sick," I said, almost to myself. Then I looked over at him watching me with a pleased kind of smile, and I couldn't help but smile back. "But it never occurred to me that she might be with pups."

There was something about his eyes, I noticed then, that reminded me so much of Quinn when we first met. Not the color, for Quinn's are blue to Gale's brown, but the haunting look that was in them . . . along with the endurance it took to get past the pain.

"Looks like you're going to have some company, then," I said. He laughed outright, and Jasper and Honey both barked, too.

"I don't mind the company," he said, patting them both on their heads. "I'm glad they're here."

I thought on what he said all the way up to the house—and how really glad he looked to be there in that little bunkhouse with just a lantern and two dogs. It made me wonder just what kind of life he had lived with those folks of his.

A *risktaker,* Jack called him, *just like us . . .*

I know Isaiah himself said your ways are unsearchable to us, Lord, but I don't think it would take much searching even for me to see that you have sent this boy to us . . .

October 30, 1873 . . .

It's a dark, cold morning.

Rose is back to working on her sampler again. Quinn says

she is to work on it until she learns to be a proper-acting young lady. Not long after he closed the door behind him and Patrick, Rose looked over at me with a forlorn look on her little face and said, "Well, how long is that going to take?"

Quinn killed an elk this afternoon after they had finished a day of "rounding up the ladies" . . . a good thing, going into the winter months, knowing we will have the extra meat. And it seems hiring Gale has been another good thing. Quinn told me tonight that the boy worked as hard or harder as he and Jack and that he never complained.

"He acted as if that meal you packed him to take along was the best gift he ever had," Quinn said, shaking his head.

"Maybe it was," I said, and when our eyes met, it was like we were both wondering what kind of gifts Gale Norton had ever got from his parents, if any at all.

I'm glad he is here . . . so is everyone else, judging by the steady procession that has gone to the bunkhouse since he came. Jessie gave him one of Stem's old overcoats and some trousers as well and demanded Gale's old worn-out pair so she could mend them. Lillie took him some more blankets then went back with some jerky and a fresh pitcher of milk, "just in case," then looked put out that I had already thought of the milk.

"Well, I don't know what all the fuss is about," Rose said as we were getting dinner ready—still grouchy over her imprison-ment. "He's just come to help with the roundup."

"Maybe," Jessie said, planting her hands on her hips. "But your ma and pa, your Uncle Jack and Aunt Lillie—even me, sis—we all know what it's like not to have nobody. An' truth is, *ever'body* needs somebody. Like I told ya before, there ain't much brag in sayin' otherwise."

"Yes ma'am," Rose said, ducking her head as tears filled her eyes. I saw the anguish in her eyes of once again being put in her place by Jessie—*Jessie, who had always favored her so!* But Mercy was quick to sidle up to Rose, patting her on the back.

"It's all right, Rose," she said softly. "I know you're not *really* bad."

At least Rose had the good sense to look contrite when Gale came to join us for dinner with a little wood carving of Midnight he had done for her.

Me, Jessie, and Lillie grinned amongst ourselves; we knew Rose didn't mean what she said. She had been making over Gale along with the rest of the children. But it doesn't hurt to let her chew on a little piece of humble pie, either . . .

Jasper and Honey are going crazy outside as Quinn drags the elk to the barn, barking and doing zigzags around him, hopping like rabbits, making me smile.

I'm surprised Honey can manage, fat little bug that she is now . . .

October 31, 1873 . . .

Cold again today . . . or maybe more chilly than cold but *that* will come soon enough. Rose watches out the window as the men ride out. Mara Lee sits on the floor, slapping the tin plates I've given her to play with. Sometimes I wish I could turn back time, and Rose would be Mara Lee's age again. When I confessed that to Quinn this morning he said, "What would you do different? Make her not *Rose?*" I told him I couldn't bear that, either . . . and he smiled and kissed my nose. But I *do* worry over her reckless ways sometimes. I don't understand why she takes off like she does, not telling anyone where she's going. Going off on a whim to fetch the Norton boy wasn't the first time, and my heart of hearts tells me it won't be the last . . .

I have to stop this, have to put Rose in the Lord's hands just as I've promised to put all of my other worries and fears.

Take care of her, Father. Talk to that heart of hers and show her your way . . . she means an awful lot to me.

Patrick came in tonight nearly beside himself with excitement as he told us how Gale is showing him and John-Charles how to carve figures out of little pieces of wood.

Rose appeared unmoved, but the bother showed true in her eyes. Patrick, with ways that are beginning to remind me so much of his father, was quick to sense her hurt.

"Don't be sour plums, Rose," Patrick said softly as he sat down next to her on the couch and leaned his dark, wavy head against hers. "You'll be carving with us soon enough."

Quinn and I both glanced over at each other questioningly—then we both grinned as it dawned on both of us at the same time what he had meant to say.

Grapes or plums, Rose seems to have been gentled by her brother's love tonight, and I know I have you to thank for that, Lord.

November 1, 1873 . . .

So much for Rose staying gentled for long . . .

We had a hard enough day as it was, the men being so cold and weary from driving the rest of the cattle in, that the rest of us pitched in to get just a bit of the cut hay to them. By the time we finished, we were all dirty and tired. I guess I was too tired to think, because when Rose asked if she could "please just ride Midnight so she can stretch her legs a little," I didn't see the harm in it.

I should have known better. I think down deep I did, especially when I saw Gale speaking to her before she rode off and saw Rose wave him off with a little flip of her hand. Yes, I suspicioned something then, but it wasn't until the rain started that I noticed she hadn't made it back.

"I told her she shouldn't go so far, that it might rain," Gale said with a frustrated but worried sound to his voice.

And it was Gale who first spotted her coming down the slope in the rain, looking as relieved as I felt. We all leaned forward, squinting from the porch, catching only a glimpse of her going into the barn as a flash of lightning struck: no bonnet on, her long hair plastered to her back as she swung off of Midnight.

"Never knew a child to take off like she does—except for maybe your brother," Lillie said, smiling wryly at me as she released the breath she had been holding in. "I guess I spent so many years praying for a real home, I figured to stick to it once I got it."

"She wasn't hurting anything," John-Charles said, real quiet, always Rose's defender when push came to shove. Patrick looked at him like he shouldn't say any more, then Mercy, who was standing between the two of them, tugged on their trousers to get their attention. Patrick looked down and said, "I know, I know. Let's pray for Rose."

As aggravated at Rose as I was for scaring me again, I sent her to fetch some milk for dinner in spite of her being drenched. Rose gave me a pathetic look, then turned and shuffled back out the door without another word.

It wasn't long after Rose left that Jessie mumbled something about forgetting something down at her place, that she'd be right back. I was just about finished with dinner when I heard the most awful, blood-curdling scream come from somewhere outside the cabin. Quinn and I were up and running out the door with everyone else on our heels.

The rain had stopped, and we found Rose lying crumpled not too far from the barn, her face a mask of terror as she looked up into Quinn's and my eyes.

"A big man!" she croaked out as she took another great gulp of air. "He tried to *take* me!"

"Pa, look over there," John-Charles said softly, and when I saw Jack start off in the direction John-Charles pointed, I went, too. Jack whispered something about there being a big man out there lurking in the shadows and if I was going to be fool-headed enough to follow, I ought to at least stay behind him.

But it wasn't until we were almost upon the "big man" that I realized it was not a man at all—but Jessie wearing Stem's old hat as she skirted along the edge of the brush toward her own cabin, carrying a thick bundle under her arm.

"Jessie Dawson!" I hissed under my breath, and she started. Then she grinned, shifting the bundle of men's clothes to her other arm.

"Guess our sis might not be so headstrong no more 'bout handlin' herself," Jessie said with satisfaction. "Guess she might just figure she *does* need folks around that cares."

Jack burst out laughing. "I swear, Jess," he said. "I think I would've sworn off cards sooner if you'd been around to set me straight."

"I'd'a cured you from a lot more'n cards, Jack," Jessie said, wry-like, and we all laughed, heading back down to the cabin.

Rose, of course, played the perfect victim to Mercy as she hovered over her, wiping the tears from her face with a cloth. But it was Jessie who held her hand, murmuring in all the right places as Rose told her about the huge man that had dragged her behind the brush, "very nearly taking my life," Rose said, her eyes becoming as round as saucers as she looked from Patrick to John-Charles to Mercy, then finally to Gale, declaring she'd never doubt Jessie again "as long as I live."

"Well, that's an awful long time to be making such an oath, sis," Jessie said. "I think if you jes concentrate on *now*, you'd be doin' good."

"Oh no, Jessie," Rose declared solemnly. "I think I ought to stick with *as long as I live*. Just to be on the safe side."

"Well, who can argue with that?" Jessie said with a satisfied note to her voice, and we all couldn't help but smile—even Gale, who is new to our little flock but seems to feel as much exasperation over Rose as the rest of us.

Everyone is asleep now but me. Quinn is just the opposite, saying he would have to sleep on it before he could think of what we should do about Rose. But I find myself unable to rest, thinking of what she said when I saw her off to bed, when I asked her why she did the things she did . . .

"I don't know why, Mama," she whispered miserably, staring up at me with those huge eyes of hers. "It's like when I hop on Midnight and ride out, I go on an adventure in my mind, and I forget the time." She looked like she might cry at any moment, so I sat down next to her and hugged her to me. She buried her face in my neck, like she used to do when she was smaller, and she poured out her sorries into my neck. She sobbed that she was sorry about hurting me and Quinn . . . sorry for making Jessie cross with her.

She pulled back from me not long after that and looked up into my face, like she was trying to decide if she should say any more. "Sometimes I worry that all of those adventures I read about folks doing in books . . . that there won't be any adventures left by the time I get old enough to do them," she confessed. "I even prayed and asked God to keep some on hold for me."

I brushed my hands down the length of her still-damp hair, over and over again, trying to figure out what to say to my sweet, reckless daughter, but all I could think of to tell her was that I loved her . . .

I was wrong, little journal. It isn't Patrick who favors Jack when he was young. Rose has become so restless, so impatient with life lately, that she reminds me more and more of Jack, with her "I got to do it my way" and her eyes that always search the distance for something none of the rest of us can see . . .

Lord, I pray to you for the wisdom to handle this the way you see fit. Because right now I feel useless to know what to do.

And that's about the worst feeling I think a mother can ever feel . . .

November 2, 1873 . . .

Sabbath morning . . . Just me and Mara Lee again. I've become grateful for these mornings I spend alone with her, grateful for the way she looks up into my eyes with such happy trust that I feel like I must be doing something right . . .

There is a thick frost covering the windows; winter is breathing its first breath on our lives again.

With Preacher gone again, we decided to hold "church" at our cabin, filling it to the brim as everyone crowded in, shivering from the cold.

After we finished praying, Quinn opened the Bible, but instead of reading the Scripture like he usually did, he leaned over, pointing to the place he had marked, and asked Rose to read it. I was so glad he did and grateful, too—grateful to you, Lord, for leading him in that way.

He had picked a passage from the Book of Ephesians, and I thought I knew why as Rose began to read, her voice becoming more and more strained as she read the words before her.

"'Children, obey your parents in the Lord, for this is right. Honour thy father and mother; which is the first commandment with promise: that it may be well with thee, and thou mayest live long on the earth.'"

Rose paused then, thinking she was finished, and I admit, I did, too. But Quinn gently prodded her to go on. "'And, ye fathers, provoke not your children to wrath: but bring them up in the nurture and admonition of the Lord,'" she read, and then Quinn put his hand on her arm tenderly for her to stop reading.

"I would like to say something to my children now," Quinn said, looking around the room, and everyone waited, wondering, like I was, what he was about to say.

"I believe with all my heart that every word of the Lord is true. And in knowing that, I can keep the hope that my and your mama's dreams for you come true—that his promise comes true, that all *will* be well with your lives . . . and that you may live long and happy upon this earth."

Quinn glanced down at his large, work-worn hands then, and there was such a humbleness in the way he looked that it brought tears to my eyes. When he looked up, I saw there were tears in his eyes, too. "Rose, Patrick," he said quietly, "I hope that I've not provoked either of you to wrath . . . and that I've done as the Lord has asked and trained you up in his ways. If I have done anything wrong, I want to right it, because I love you . . . and I don't want you to lose that promise."

"Oh, Pa," Rose said, her voice barely a whisper, "you've never done *nothin'* wrong."

"Never," Patrick echoed. Then he and Rose looked at each other as if they couldn't imagine anyone saying that *their* pa had done anything wrong—most of all, to them.

I could tell those thoughts stayed with the two of them throughout the day . . . as Quinn's words stayed with the rest of us. Lillie was the first to speak of it, though, as she took Mara Lee from me so I could make a fresh pot of coffee.

"I wish I'd had a Pa like him, Callie, when I was growing up," she said out of the blue, and then another voice said, "I do, too," and we turned around to see Gale standing there, holding Mercy's hand. I caught a brief look of bittersweet longing on his face, and then it was gone, replaced so quick by a smile that I wondered if I had imagined the look.

"I guess we've all been orphans a time or two in our lives," Jessie said, rising from her chair then, and I saw her glance Gale's way before turning back to us. "That's why the Lord put us together *now*. So we could see what real family is all about."

I am so thankful we did witness what real family is all about today, Lord. A real family with you in it . . .

Quinn had done what any good father would do: He had put the burden upon himself, allowing his children to see the truth through humbleness and love.

But he did it because he trusted you, God. Without even realizing it, Quinn did the same as Jesus in that scripture Preacher read to us: He humbled himself and became obedient . . .

I pray we all can become more like that, Lord—more like you each day we walk through this sometimes troublesome but beautiful gift you've given us called life.

November 3, 1873 . . .

Back to work on this cold, cold morning. I've baked two loaves of bread, mended Patrick's pants yet another time, and heated the last pan of water to finish scrubbing the floors—although now I'm wondering about the wisdom of that; it's just begun to sleet outside, a fine mist coming to us in sheets through the gaps in the mountains. Already I can see where the muddied footprints will land . . .

Patrick did bring in enough wood this morning (aided by Rose, no less) before they all left to go help set out hay for the cattle. I think he and Rose are bent on proving to Quinn their wayward ways are not his doing—especially Rose. I've never seen her throw herself into housework with such eagerness—making beds, changing Mara Lee for me while I finished cooking breakfast. She even made the trip down to the bunkhouse to fetch Gale when it was ready. She really is a sweet little girl.

And Patrick, with the way he held his "Bird" in his arms nearly all through breakfast, just to see if he could make her laugh. They've only been gone a little while, and I miss them, miss Quinn . . .

Never mind the muddy footprints; I hope they come in soon.

Mara Lee is pounding on the rail of her crib, hollering with her newfound voice. I think if she could talk, she would say she misses them, too.

November 5, 1873 . . .

The warm Chinook wind that came in sometime last night has brought us beautiful weather. Some call it Indian summer—*why* I'm not exactly sure, but it seems to have brought the "natives" out to the ranch today to celebrate.

Peach was the first to show up, and by then we had already made up our minds to make a day of it, the general thought being that it would probably be one of the last times to enjoy the outdoors until next spring.

"I thought when I saw the sun shinin' like it was this mornin' there might be some shenanigans goin' on over here," he said. Then he took a second look as Gale came strolling out of the bunkhouse and added, "Guess I thought right," and we all laughed. Then we set about fixing what we could for our noon meal. Jessie brought a fine batch of biscuits she had just made, and Lillie the beans and some pickles she'd canned last summer, while I provided coffee and fresh chunks of elk the men roasted on sticks over a fire. It wasn't long after we'd started to set up our makeshift table that Preacher and Willa showed up.

We had such a good time of it, visiting and laughing, and I told Preacher as much as we watched the men start to set up the horseshoes.

"Always laugh when you can," Preacher said, grinning. "It is—"

"Cheap medicine," Gale finished, and we turned around. Willa's mouth dropped open as she looked from Gale back to Preacher.

"Did you hear that, Shawn?" Willa said, knowing full well he did, for he was standing right next to her. The humor of it wasn't lost on Preacher, either, as I watched him grin down at his pretty fiancée.

"Byron, wasn't it?" Preacher said, but Willa had turned back to look at Gale with a surprised but pleased look on her face, delighted to find such a "diamond in the rough."

"Quoting Byron," she said, smiling at Gale fondly. "I hope you like books as much as I'm guessing you do because first chance I get, I'm bringing you a stack from my own library. No sense letting a mind like that go to waste."

"I'd appreciate that a lot, ma'am," Gale said, smiling back at Willa like he couldn't believe what was happening to him.

None of the rest of us were surprised—Gale had gained more than a few admirers among us along the way as well.

Soon enough, the wind picked up, and we were heading back indoors, laughing again to hear the children beg Peach to take his teeth out for them again, which he did, to their delight—and it wasn't too much longer after that, that Peach came into the kitchen asking us if we had seen his teeth.

It seemed with all of their "funnin" around, poor Peach had forgot to put his teeth back in, and when he finally remembered, they were gone.

Well, we searched and searched all over the cabin, outside, then back in the cabin again . . . until we heard a horrified scream come from Mercy and went running to see what was the matter.

Mercy was standing stock-still, staring in horror at her stuffed bear sitting on his usual place of honor on the settee—a spot that we had passed back and forth more times than I could count during our frantic search. Our eyes followed to where Mercy's shaking finger pointed, and that's when we saw Peach's false teeth, grinning madly from the bear's mouth . . . and suddenly John-Charles was nowhere to be found.

Peach was the first to talk. He took one look at the bear and said, "Dern, them teeth look better on him than me!" and whatever we had thought to do to the culprit was lost then in our fit of laughter.

It was Rose who cornered John-Charles later, just before they were leaving for the evening.

"Admit you did it," she said, perching her hands on her hips.

"Did what?" he said in that quiet way of his, but as they squared off to outstare each other I saw John-Charles start to waver. First his eyes, then I saw his lip curve into what might have been a smile. Rose grinned triumphantly.

"I knew you did it," she said and flounced off with Mercy.

"How did she do that?" I heard John-Charles ask Patrick then, and I saw Gale ease closer, too, as if he was hoping for Patrick to shed some light on Rose's mysterious ways as well.

"I haven't figured it out, yet," Patrick admitted. "But it helps if you don't look at her."

Such a good day, all and all, Lord. And so good to see Preacher and Willa again. He says he will be in town for this next Sabbath, and we're all tickled about that.

Willa, I think most of all.

The Other Side of Jordan

I read another Bible story to the children tonight. Since Gale has never attended one of our little get-togethers, we let him choose. So it was Daniel and the lion's den again—one of their favorites.

The story, much to my surprise, went off without a hitch, most likely because they were all so tired . . . But I should have known the evening's entertainment wasn't over when I watched Patrick suddenly rise from the floor and stroll over to the window to look out.

"Looks like Old Man Winter is comin'," he said, his voice lower than I'd ever heard, and when I realized he was trying to be like Quinn, I had to bite the inside of my cheek to keep from grinning. Then Mercy was suddenly standing next to him, golden curls tossed messily around her wide, innocent face as she took a glance out the window, too.

"Old Man . . . like Peach?" she asked, turning to look at Patrick. When he nodded yes, she clutched her bear to her chest protectively. Patrick caught the move and looked over to where John-Charles sat and grinned.

"Yeah, like Peach," he said, and Mercy looked thoughtful for a moment then turned to look back out the window. But I noticed the ever so slight move of her hand as she covered her bear's mouth.

"Well," she said finally, "I'm gonna pray Old Man Winter has his own teeth."

Funny. I just came in from outside; I do smell snow in the air tonight. I used to think Mama was fooling us when she'd lift her nose to the wind and declare that she could smell rain or snow coming. But then, when I think about it, there were a lot of things she said when I was young that I doubted.

I wonder if Patrick and Rose doubt some of the things I say. I wonder if one day they'll say, "If only I knew then what I know now."

Probably. Who was it that said youth was wasted on the young? I can't remember his name, but I think he was right . . .

November 7, 1873 . . .

So cold today, bitterly cold—enough to take your breath away, is more like it—and now, after what's happened tonight, it's as if I feel that bitterness came to steal the peace in my heart away as well . . .

I can't remember what time it was, but I know it was late, for all the children were already asleep when Gale came to the door to tell Quinn and me that Honey had had her pups. I knew there was more by the look in his eyes—Quinn did, too, and it was a moment before Gale could tell us he wasn't sure they were going to make it.

As soon as we were inside the bunkhouse, I could hear Honey's tail start to slowly thump against the floor, as if she sensed we were there to help her. But sadly, there was no helping three of the six pups, who were already dead by the time Quinn picked them up to examine them.

It might sound silly to some, but the look in Honey's big eyes as Quinn took three of her puppies away from her nearly undid me. I wanted to say something, but couldn't find the words; feeling another's sadness like I do, has always turned me silent that way.

"'Twould probably be best if we didn't mention these little ones to the others," Quinn said to Gale, and he nodded his agreement, but I saw the hurt of it in his eyes, too.

"Have you ever wondered why stuff like this happens?" Gale said then, avoiding my eyes. "I mean, why did they have to die? Why *couldn't* they have just lived?"

"More times than you know," I said, nodding and finally finding my voice. "And I haven't gotten an answer yet."

Quinn glanced up at me then, and when our eyes met, it was with an unspoken understanding of two people who had been through those questions together over the years.

It was when Quinn went to go bury the pups that I suddenly felt the overwhelming urge to get away. Without a word to anyone, I grabbed up his old overcoat, went down to the barn, and saddled up the buckskin. I don't remember thinking about anything as I did it, and I can't really explain it now as I write this . . . But all I knew was that I had to get away . . . from Honey's sad eyes and Gale's questions . . . So I rode. I rode and rode . . . the only other time I remember riding like that was when I was just a girl, when we were on the trail coming west. I remember riding out with Jack to see my first glimpse of the Platte River and the endless stretch of land beyond it, and I remember, too, how much it scared me. The bigness of it all . . .

But this time I realized I wasn't scared but searching—as I dismounted on the crest of the upper slope leading to the mountains.

The moon was so full and bright that it almost didn't look real. It resembled a huge, shiny coin some great hand had set down in the middle of the picture . . . almost too big and so close that it made even the mountains look small. It made me realize how small we really are compared to all of God's creation. I think it amazed me, too, to think how much he cared in spite of that . . . and suddenly I knew then that all the tumbling and turmoil in my heart that I was trying to sort through, to explain, he already knew.

"I wish I knew the whys of things," I whispered up into the huge bowl of night sky filled with stars. "But more than anything, I wish I knew you better . . . "

And no sooner than those words were out of my mouth, I felt a strong but gentle voice say to my heart, *You will.*

I wish I could put to paper how I felt up there, just me, standing underneath all that majesty but suddenly feeling more a part of it than lost to it . . .

I don't know how long I stood there like that, but after a while, I heard footsteps coming and turned to see Quinn leading his horse and looking more than relieved.

"It's a good thing for the full moon and this frost," he said. "Otherwise I wouldn't have been able to find you."

"I don't know why I ran off like I did," I said, trying to find the words to explain. "It's not as if I haven't seen animals die before."

"What you saw was a mother lose her young, something all parents fear," Quinn said gently as he came to stand next to me, and it amazed me again, even after all these years, how well he knew my heart . . . sometimes, I thought, better than I did myself.

"You scared me, you know," he whispered into my hair finally, and I let him pull me close.

"I can take care of myself, you know," I said in halfhearted defiance. Quinn turned me around, taking hold of my chin as he looked into my eyes.

"So you can," he whispered, an amused look in his eyes, and it hit me then how very much I sounded like Rose.

"I sounded just like Rose then, didn't I?" I said, and he chuckled and took my hand as we turned to walk the horses the rest of the way down the slope together.

"Yes, you did," he said. "I expect that's part of the reason I love her so much."

We walked hand in hand like that all the way back to the cabin, and I can't help thinking even as I write this that my dear friend Grace was right in what she told me all those years ago about me and Quinn.

I think her words were, "God knew what he was doing

when he put you two together. One day you'll see the truth of that, too."

So I do, old friend. So I do.

—Early morning with Mara Lee again, and I just came across this scripture: *"Be of good courage, and he shall strengthen thine heart"*—Psalm 27:14.

And you have, Lord.

PART TWO

Tearing Down
the Walls

So after Joshua took his shoes off,
God told them to GO FORTH, march
around the city SEVEN TIMES and holler
like crazy at the Enemy. And when they
did what God said, the walls came
down and they were all pretty happy
about that.

By Rose McGregor
Almost 14
Montana Territory, 1873

Sometimes I think Preacher would have made a fine writer. Not that he's missed his calling, because he hasn't . . . he just has a way of telling things that makes it stay in your mind long after you leave. It's like reading a book that's so good you not only can't put it down but have to keep opening it back up to read it again. Today was proof of that, for I keep turning my mind back to the words Preacher spoke to us . . .

By the time we got to "church," the tent was already packed to overflowing. I spotted Willa, who had saved us a seat with her somewhere in the middle of the mass of people, and as I struggled with the rest of our brood toward her, I could feel something different in the tent.

Preacher even seemed different, the way he walked to the front of the tent with such a determined look on his strong face . . . like God had put something on his heart and there would be no rest for him until he told it. I saw him glance toward us and smile, his eyes even lighting up a bit at seeing Gale with us. He bowed his head, then said a quick prayer, and started right in to talking.

"As I was praying this past week, the one thing the Lord kept putting in my heart was to remember that the strength we need to get through the trials in our lives isn't our own, but his," Preacher said as he looked around the tent full of faces. "He got my attention on that one; I have a pretty strong hunch he knows what he's talking about when it comes to battles."

Everyone chuckled then, and Preacher smiled good-naturedly and went on.

"Well, you know, if you think about it, Joshua didn't do what he did on his own strength. Rahab didn't do what she did on her own strength . . . and neither did King David. Does anyone remember what David said to Goliath just before he slew him? 'Thou comest to me with a sword, and with a spear, and with a shield: but I come to thee in the name of the LORD of hosts, . . . for the battle is the LORD's.' Three very different people—Joshua, Rahab, and David—but the one thing they had in common was their faith in *God,* not in themselves. They believed that with God by their side they could defeat their enemies, and they could take the land God had promised them.

"Now, I know some of you might be thinking you can't compare yourselves to folks from the *Bible* . . . but that's just what the Lord wants you to do. He wants you to remember these were just plain folks: Joshua was just a poor kid without a home. Rahab, well, we all know what she was. And David? A shepherd boy, the youngest and smallest of the bunch. But all three of them knew they could make a difference in their lives by letting God's light shine *through* them."

Preacher paused for a moment, and as he did, I turned and looked at Gale, who was watching and listening as if his very life depended on it. Quinn looked, too, then turned back to smile at me.

"There was a great artist I happened upon while I was in Boston," Preacher said. "I'm not going to mention his name because, well, that's not important. But I want to tell you his story because in a way, it's our story, too."

I saw a lot of folks lean forward then when Preacher said the word *story,* for he was known throughout the territory to be a fine storyteller.

"See, I heard from some of my friends that this artist had created a real masterpiece," Preacher said, "and I got to thinking maybe I ought to see it for myself. So I went to this fellow's studio and asked if he would let me see it, and to my surprise he said yes. He ushered me into this room where a large painting stood on an easel, and I saw even from a distance that the painting was, well, good but pretty plain—just a landscape of rolling hills and trees with a small country church placed just in the distance. There was nothing grand about it, and it sure wasn't what I would call a masterpiece. To make matters worse, the closer I drew to that painting, the more I realized there was slashes and cuts all over that huge canvas."

"Well, I stood there thinking, *What in the world has he done to his painting?* Finally, I turned to him and said, 'Sir, did you know there is what looks to be knife cuts all over your painting?'"

Preacher paused again and leaned against his little podium. "Well, that fellow just smiled at me and real casual-like, he walked over to the windows of his studio and started pulling back the heavy drapes like nothing had happened. By this time, I pretty much figured the man was crazy. But then he joined me again, standing by my side, and we both watched as the light began to pour through those slashes that I had spotted.

"Suddenly, I saw that light fill the painted hillsides, sweeping the grass here and there with warmth as it moved slowly toward the church in the distance. Then I saw the light hit the tall steeple, illuminating a gold cross at the top that I hadn't even realized was there before. Folks, that painting had become beautiful to me and so real that I felt I could step right into it and be at that place.

"'You see,' the artist told me then, 'those slashes are how the light gets in. Once it begins to work its way through those cuts, it is able to illuminate the painting. The *light* is the key because it fills the gaps in with its beauty . . . making my creation more beautiful than it would have ever been on its own.'"

Preacher looked around the tent again, and when he did, I could have swore I saw tears standing in his eyes. I glanced over at Willa, and she looked teary-eyed, too, but as eager to hear the end as the rest of us.

"I can't tell you how many times I've thought about that artist and the freedom he had to look at his work as only half-done without the light. My prayer for each one of you today is that you can see your own life with the same eyes as that artist. That with every one of life's cuts, you open yourself to God's light. Because the more we allow God in, the more his beauty, his strength are able to shine through wounds and heal them . . . once and for all."

Preacher went to step down then, but something else seemed to occur to him, and he held up his hand to get our attention.

"If you can't remember anything else from today, remember this: Jesus said, 'My strength is made perfect in *weakness*.' He was saying, 'I am shown strong in your weakness.' Let him be your strength, folks."

It was a quiet crowd that filed out after that. More, I think, because we were all thinking on what he had said . . . and how badly we did want God to fill those scars in our life with his light.

I know I was thinking it. And as I watched my family's faces—Jessie, Lillie, Jack, Quinn, and even Gale—as they took turns helping to bundle up the children and then slowly climbed into the wagons to head for home, I knew they were thinking it, too.

It's snowing again, harder, like it's serious about staying. I just got back from checking on Honey and her three little pups. They were all nestled in a blanket on Gale's bed, Gale on one side and Jasper on the other, like two sentinels keeping watch over them. Gale sat up quick when I came in, but he didn't leave Honey's side. It was the sweetness of his worry over her that caused me to reach out and start to brush the dark hair back from his forehead, just like I do with Patrick, but Gale flinched, like he thought I might strike him.

"I'm sorry," he said, looking embarrassed, and all of a sudden a peace came over me, and I knew it was God's love for the boy, because for once I knew just what to say.

"Sorry for what?" I said, smiling like nothing had happened

out of the ordinary, and I saw the relief come quick to his eyes. We sat next to each other for a while like that, just petting Honey and looking at the pups. Finally, Gale set one of the pups down next to Honey and turned to me, a pensive look on his handsome, young face.

"Do you think Preacher was right about God healing our scars once and for all?" he asked quietly, and when I told him yes, he nodded again and seemed to go somewhere inside of himself, deep in thought.

"We all have scars, honey," I said, rising to leave so he could be alone in his thoughts. "It's just some's already been healed by God and some . . . well, he's just waiting for them to ask him to heal them . . .

I'll never forget the look in those brown eyes of his as I turned to leave . . . reminding me of that poem I read once:

> Thanks to the human heart
>   by which we live,
> Thanks to its tenderness,
>   its joys and fears;
> To me the meanest flower
>   that blows can give thoughts
>   that do often lie
>   too deep for tears . . .

Still waters run deep, my mama always used to say. I pray for that boy tonight, Father, that you reach out to him and let him know that you are waiting to heal his hurts . . . just as you have done for me more times than I could ever count . . .

November 10, 1873 . . .

I have to wonder at the timing of Preacher's message with Medicine Weasel and One Shot showing up here tonight, nearly froze to death and so sick—with what, we're not completely sure. But if Jessie's right about what they have, we're all going to need every bit of strength you can give us, Lord . . .

Rose had been out in the barn with Gale, seeing to a calf, when she heard riders coming and had run out to see who it was, delighted to recognize the visitors were her old friends Medicine Weasel and One Shot. It wasn't until she got right up on them that she realized they were bad sick.

"Scared me to pieces, Mama. They looked like dead men riding horses," she said breathlessly as she followed us all down to the bunkhouse, emptied of Gale and the pups the minute we found out the sick men had come to stay awhile. Quinn lifted One Shot out of his saddle and carried him easy as a baby into the bunkhouse as Jack helped Medicine Weasel down from his horse and half-carried him, too.

"No, Rosie," Jack said gently as Rose tried to follow him in. "You can't come in here until we find out what's wrong with them. You keep John-Charles back for me, too, you hear? He's going to put up a fight once he finds out his grandpa is here. And you're the only one I know who can help with that."

Rose nodded, taking her new duty seriously as she planted herself outside the door while the rest of us went in.

It wasn't until Quinn turned up the lantern that we got a good look, and never a more pitiful sight have I seen in my life. Medicine Weasel, who we had seen only a year ago, was just a shell of what he had been before, his long hair, stringy and nearly all white now, stuck to the sides of his gaunt face in clumps, and One Shot, who was just as gaunt, looked as if he had aged twenty years.

Medicine Weasel, as he warmed up under the blankets Jessie had thrown over him, finally came around just enough to talk to Jack, switching from Blackfoot to English the best he could with his tongue swollen so bad.

He told Jack that the reservation had become a "death

camp," that the American traders dealt mostly in whiskey. He said after a round of trading, if the braves, drunk on whiskey, didn't freeze to death before they reached their lodges, they would be quarreling or killing one another once they got there. He said it was a bad place and that he and One Shot decided it was time to leave.

"I don't fear death, Jack Wade, as much as I do life now," Medicine Weasel said in his sad, lilting English—then promptly passed out, shocking us all.

"He's burning up with fever," Jack said worriedly as he felt the old man's head and looked over at Jessie. She pulled their covers away for a moment and lifted both of their shirts, revealing a horrible-looking rash.

"Lord, have mercy on us all," Jessie whispered, straightening the blankets back over the men after she had looked both men over. She glanced to Jack, then me and Quinn. "Those fellows got the scarlet fever."

Never in my life have I felt such a cold fear grip me, hearing those words. I saw the fear in everyone's eyes as we quietly went about making our old friends as comfortable as possible, then turned to retreat to our own cabins . . . to our families . . . and wait it out.

Wait? *Wait for what?* my mind wants to shout tonight. For the doctor who will never come? For someone else to stand over them and declare them sick?

Remind me, Lord, who I am. Remind me that you are here with us. And that, like Preacher says, you are shown strong through our weaknesses.

November 11, 1873 . . .

Snow's falling heavy on the roof this morning. I don't like its sound, like a weight settling down over us all, as much as I do the sound of the rain . . .

I almost had a moment's peace while I was rocking Mara Lee, but when I looked down into her face, the question suddenly went through me: *I wonder if she'll get the fever.* Then it was, *I wonder if Rose already has it . . . or Patrick . . . or Quinn . . .* The list rambled on through my mind until I pulled out my Bible and began to pray . . .

Lillie, Jessie, and I waved to each other from a distance this afternoon as we went about our chores. Earlier, we had talked of what to do if one of us starts to show the sickness, and it started sounding insane. We should move little Mara Lee to Jack and Lillie's . . . No, Jack had been in there with Medicine Weasel and One Shot. To Jessie's, then. No, Jessie had been with the sick ones, too. *And so had Quinn and I . . .* So we do what we have no other choice but to do: We wait.

I feel as if I'm back standing on that slope, looking at the immense moon that dwarfs everything else around it . . . only it's not the moon but the words *scarlet fever* that hang over us, and this time I'm not awed. I'm scared.

I can see John-Charles down in front of the bunkhouse this evening. On and off through the slanting sheets of snow, he paces back and forth, reminding me of a wild horse that's been penned up. Only it's his grandfather and One Shot that's been penned . . .

Maybe he feels the same way, judging by the look on his face as he heads back in this direction after Jack and Jessie just sent him on his way. Lillie is waiting for him on the porch, and as she opens the door to their cabin, I can see Mercy is plastered to her side. I know Lillie must be sick with worry, as weak as Mercy's always been, being born early like she was. We're all worried—for the children more than anything. I can see Gale's eyes before me as I write this, and I can't imagine what he must be thinking . . . if he's wondering whether anyone is worried for him.

I need to go in. I just came out for a breath of air, and now my hands feel frozen solid.

Jessie came and talked to me from the porch tonight, shivering in spite of being bundled in Stem's old overcoat, but when I asked her to come in, she was having none of it. "I'm not sure if'n I have it, Callie," she said, her dark eyes kind but worried, "but I don't want t' make that sweet baby sick if'n I do." I handed her a cup of coffee as she told me that Medicine Weasel and One Shot seemed to be holding up but that they weren't out of the woods yet. She told me Jack looked tired, but he's not sick yet and neither was Gale, who seemed to be faring nicely down at her cabin. I asked her then how long it took for the sickness to show.

"Three days, mostly," she said, and by the way she studied my eyes I knew she had guessed that I had started counting down in my mind.

November 12, 1873 . . .

The snow just keeps piling up, forcing Jack and Jessie to use the ropes to drag their way through it down to the bunkhouse to nurse Medicine Weasel and One Shot.

Quinn and Gale go out to scatter hay for the cattle, who are bawling as pitifully as I feel. Rose is helping me bake bread this afternoon, chattering to Mara Lee as she kneads the dough, and I find myself glancing at her from time to time, wondering if her eyes look a little feverish. Patrick, who is always quick to sense how I'm feeling, has done the only thing he can think to do: bring in enough wood to build another cabin.

November 13, 1873 ...

We had just started thinking maybe we were out of the woods ... that maybe none of us would get the fever, when Rose came into the living room after dinner with a look of fear on her little face.

"Mama, I don't feel so good," was all she said, but as soon as the words came out of her mouth, I felt my heart leap up into my throat. Quinn's eyes met mine, his fear mirroring my own; we'd heard about the worst cases—convulsions, blindness ... even death. Of course, all anyone ever remembers about sicknesses is the bad.

"Pa, what's wrong with Rose?" Patrick asked as he looked up from bouncing Mara Lee on his knee. He must have seen the look of fear on Quinn's and my faces, for he stood then.

"Go fetch Jessie, lad," Quinn said quietly, and Patrick handed Mara Lee over to me and was out the door in a flash. Rose didn't show much fear at all until Jessie walked in the door, taking quick to Rose's side to help her up the stairs to the loft.

"I'm sorry, Jessie," Rose whispered pitifully, lying back on her bed. I saw her pick up her Stem doll and clutch it to her chest ... saw her cheeks stained red by the beginnings of fever.

"Sorry about what, little sis?" Jessie asked, looking over her shoulder at me.

"I shoulda listened to you about taking off. But I did it again when I saw Medicine Weasel and One Shot. I didn't make it to 'for the rest of my life' like I said I would."

"None of us ever do, sis," Jessie said, her voice shaky with emotion as she gently tucked the covers up under Rose's chin. "None of us ever do."

Once I got the children down, I went in and lay next to Quinn for a little while, just until he dropped off to sleep. Even without words, we were thinking the same thing as we both searched for each other's hand in the dark . . . as we both sighed once we found it.

November 14, 1873 . . .

It's morning now, and I'm not sure if Rose is any better for my staying up with her or for the willow-bark tea I made her to try to ease the pain in her throat or the salve I rubbed over her little rash-covered body, but I can't *not* do something. Patrick complained of a headache and sore throat when he woke up, but Mara Lee seems fine, thank God; I've heard it's harder on the babies.

I just pulled those little yellow-hearted daisies Quinn gave me out of the pages here. "Tiny but tough," Quinn had said. But I'm not tough . . . I don't *want* to be . . . not without you, Lord.

I think Quinn's been thinking the same thoughts as me today. I found him down in the barn tonight, his broad shoulders hunched over as he sat on the cold, hard dirt floor, picking up Honey's pups out of the pile of blankets with such care, rubbing their coats dry with an old piece of cloth. Like he always has since we first met, he sensed me in the room before turning around.

"Don't know how these little ones got so wet, lass, but they're apt to catch their death if they don't get dry," he said, quiet, not looking up. "They're too little to do for themselves just yet."

"You've always done right by us, Quinn," I said gently, sensing his feelings. "Always fought for us."

"But I can't fight this sickness," he said finally, his voice hoarse, and I realized the mighty oak of a man we all depended on being strong had been hit by a storm he wasn't sure how to fight.

"It's not our fight," I heard myself say, remembering Preacher's words and with the memory, feeling a bit of strength come to me. "It's God's."

Quinn was silent then. But even in the dark of the barn, I saw the wheels turning in his mind, as if, if he thought hard enough, an answer would come. That's when I asked if he remembered Joseph of the Old Testament. I told him he'd always reminded me of Joseph: strong and honorable, never letting go of his beliefs no matter what happened. Then I reminded him how Joseph had stayed faithful—and when he did, God did, too.

"I wish I were really that strong, Callie," Quinn said, soft, then turned his head to look at me. "Do you think it wrong to pray to be that faithful? To pray for that kind of strength?"

I didn't answer but just took his hand in mine and without another word, we knelt together in that dark, hay-filled barn, praying for all we were worth, like two orphans trying to find their way back home . . .

Quinn has finally dozed off, but I can't seem to find sleep. Sitting here writing all of this, I can't help thinking of how Quinn and I *are* orphans in a way, losing our parents as early as we did. I can't help feeling my heart ache with the wish to have Mama here by my side tonight . . . to tell me everything is going to be all right and hear the words of that song whisper through my mind:

> Backward, turn backward, O Time in your flight
> Make me a child again, just for tonight

Mother, come back from the echoless shore.
Take me again to your heart like before.
Kiss from my forehead the furrows of care,
Smooth the few silver threads out of my hair.
Over my shoulder your loving watch keep—
Rock me to sleep, Mother, rock me to sleep . . .

Better yet, let me be *your* child, Lord. Hold me in your embrace
and let me hear that everything is going to be all right.

November 15, 1873 . . .

Still no signs of Mara Lee being sick. Patrick seems to have
recovered without suffering through much of the sickness at all,
but my poor little Rose is worse, still suffering with a fever and
headache. And now her tongue has swollen, making it nearly
impossible for her to talk and tell me what she needs. When she
looked up at me with those pale blue, innocent eyes of hers, I
felt the helplessness of it go through me like a sharp pain. By
the time Jessie came to check on us, it was all I could do not to
throw myself in her large, comforting arms and cry.

Jessie didn't seem to notice my distress at first, busying herself with spooning some more tea into Rose, telling us that it
seemed John-Charles had weathered the fever much like
Patrick, and Mercy didn't have it at all . . . and that Gale, sweet
boy that he is, had been doing Jack's share of the work and his,
too, with Jack helping to nurse Medicine Weasel and One Shot,
then coming back to Jessie's cabin at night to make little carv-
ings for the children. It was only when Jessie and I had sat down
in the kitchen for coffee that I finally gave in to my feelings and
told her I was scared.

"Sometimes it seems no matter how hard I try, I can't shake

my fears," I blurted out. "It's like I almost get there, then something else happens."

Jessie set down her coffee and wrapped her arms around me again, in just the way I imagined.

"*Almost* is human . . . it's jes what we are, honey," she said, pulling back finally to look at me with a kind look in her old, dark eyes. "Ya jes got to let go and let God. When ya *really* let go, that's when ya start seein' *his* work in your life, and there ain't no better beauty than that."

She smiled at me then, and told me to rest a spell. "I got a story to tell ya," she said. "I ain't the fine talker Preacher is, but I reckon I kin help ya see what I'm tryin' t' say." She went on to tell me then that back at the plantation, where she'd lived as a girl, there were weavers. She said once she got old enough, her mama started teaching her how to weave. One of the best lessons her mama told her before she got sold off was about the weaving.

"We'd always leave a flaw in our work; Mama said it was 'out of respect for God'—an' most of the time, we didn't even have to try, neither," she chuckled. "But one day I'd made a fine rug, not a flaw in it, and I wanted it t' stay that way. But I knew my mama was gonna tell me about it, too. So I went to her first and asked why. She said, 'Jessie, reason *why*, is to remind ourselves that no matter how hard we try in this life, only the good Lord is *perfect*—and that anything that even comes close to that in our lives is because his hand be in it.'"

Jessie leaned back against her chair and looked at me with love.

"That feller Preacher spoke of them holes cut in that painting of his'n—that was the same idea. He saw that his work was just that: work—till he let God's light shine through it. That's when it became a . . . what did Preacher call it?"

"A masterpiece?" I said, and she smiled a pleased smile.

"Yes ma'am, that's the word I was looking for: *masterpiece*. I kindly like t' imagine that's what the good Lord be doin' right, now . . . standin' back and waitin' till he can see all his light shinin' through." Jessie leaned forward and patted my hand softly, then she whispered, "Then he kin call *us* his masterpiece."

I told Quinn tonight about what Jessie had said, and he nodded then sat quiet for a while, stoking the fireplace with more wood as I finished nursing Mara Lee. He was so tired . . . I could see it in his eyes: the days of working with Gale and Patrick, trying to keep the cattle from starving or from freezing to death in the snow that never seemed to end. But when he turned back to look at me, I saw the endurance in his eyes, too.

"I think we should pray, lass," he said, and I laid Mara Lee down and joined him, dropping to my knees beside him on the little braided rug in front of the fireplace.

"Father," he began, his deep voice bringing me comfort, "Callie and me, we want to give you *all* of our lives. Not just the parts we can think of to give, but all that we are . . ." He cleared his throat then, and I felt his hand tighten over mine. "We want to give you our trust again . . . our faith . . . to open our hearts to your mercy for us and for our children."

We prayed for everyone then: for Rose, for Jack and John-Charles, for Medicine Weasel and One Shot, for Lillie, who had welcomed the Blackfoot in like they were her family. We prayed for Jessie, who had once again set aside her worries for her own family who hadn't come home yet, so she could help us . . . and for Peach not to be alone anymore. Then we prayed for Willa and Preacher, that they be kept safe and that Willa would be able to trust God, too, for Preacher's safety while he was away. As the prayers were starting to trail off, I felt something in the room had changed, almost like a fresh breath of air had just blown through the house. I know Quinn felt it, too, for he said,

"In Jesus' holy name, we pray these things." Then he turned to look at me with tears in his eyes.

We smiled at each other, then we both said amen together.

November 16, 1873 . . .

It seems the whole world was praying with us last night—or at least a goodly part of Montana—and I can't think of a better day to hear such things than on the Sabbath. Lillie was the first to come to the door this morning to tell me she couldn't handle being away anymore and to say that she had felt led to pray last night and had even prayed for *Mrs. Audrey and her family*! Then Jessie came in with the news that she and Gale had had "church" at her cabin, too. But it was when Preacher and Willa showed up with some news of their own that stunned us the most.

Willa joined us in the kitchen, barely taking a breath before telling us that she had been holed up in town, taking care of Preacher, who had come down with the fever, too. She said she was doctoring Preacher when it hit her that Preacher didn't have to go out of town for something to happen to him. She said it was like a voice came to her heart all of a sudden and said, *You have got to learn to trust me, Willa. You have learned how to survive, but you haven't learned how to live again.*

Willa looked at all of us with great tears in her eyes. "I dropped to my knees right then and started praying. I told God I was sorry. I told him that I didn't know as much as Shawn does as far as the Good Book goes, but I remembered the part where Jesus said he was coming to give us life so that we could live it more abundantly. I said I figured I had insulted him and his Son, living like I didn't know that, and then I asked him for his help."

Willa smiled wryly then. "Shawn opened his eyes right after that and looked at me, kneeling by his bed, and he *grinned* at me. "He said, 'Willa, that was some fine sermonizing you just did. But don't get in your head that you can take my job. You've already taken my heart. Besides, I'm feeling much better now.' "

We all laughed, and when our laughter had died down a bit Lillie happened to ask Willa if she knew anything of the Audreys.

Willa's smile dropped a bit then. "Yes, they're in a bad way with the fever, too, both of them so sick they can't tend to themselves. And their girls are sick, too," she said, shaking her head sadly. "Mrs. Audrey hasn't ever been much of a friend, but I wouldn't wish scarlet fever on my worst enemy."

Lillie got a real thoughtful look on her face then, but before I could ask her what she was thinking, she said she had to go check on Mercy and John-Charles.

It wasn't until later, after I had looked in on Rose again and packed up some food for the men working outside, that I found out what had crossed Lillie's mind. She came back by the cabin to tell me that she was going to take a trip to town . . . that Jack knew about it, and she wanted me and Jessie to watch out after John-Charles and Mercy.

"What in the world are you going to town for?" I asked, shocked, and Lillie looked at first like she didn't want to tell me, but then she did.

"John-Charles isn't sick anymore, Callie," she began. "And Mercy, thank God, she didn't get the fever at all. But I started thinking this afternoon that if she had gotten it, I would have had all the help in the world . . . " She hesitated, then looked at me straight in the eye. "Which is why I've decided to be the one to go to the Audreys, to help with their girls that are sick."

I started to protest, but she held up her hand. "They don't have *anyone*. Willa said Mrs. Pumphrey and Widow Spence are down with it, too." Lillie smiled bravely, and I saw something light in her eyes then, like she realized that all the months of Mrs. Audrey making her feel like she was less than nothing were meaningless when it came to times like these . . . that maybe she had a lot more than she ever thought.

I helped her bundle up, and as we walked out to the wagon, decked out with sled runners that Gale had readied for her, I saw her seem to gather strength inside of herself with each step. We said a quick prayer together, and when it was finished, I saw God's love shining clear in Lillie's eyes.

"It doesn't matter anymore what she said, Callie," she said quietly. "What matters is what I do . . . especially knowing what I know in my heart about Jesus. Because I know if it was me, if it was my babies . . . I know he'd tell someone to come to us. And I hope that there would be enough of him in that person that she would listen, too."

As Gale and I watched her leave, I felt him turn to look at me with a thoughtful look on his face.

"John-Charles was right about his mama, Miss Callie," he said, turning to look back at the wagon fading quick into the distance. "She is kind of a hero, isn't she?"

Willa was as surprised as I was with the news when I came back inside and told her.

"Well, doesn't that beat all, Lillie tending to her tormentor's kids," Willa said, shaking her head with a strange kind of smile on her face. "Who would've ever thought?" She looked out the window then, drying the dishes with a thoughtful look on her face. "'God is a comedian playing to an audience too afraid to laugh,'" she recited softly before turning back to look at me. "I remember reading that once, and I can't help thinking of it now. It's almost funny, but I'm not going to laugh—not just yet, anyhow. I figure I just got in his good grace; I don't want to get out."

We smiled at each other.

"I learned a long time ago that God has a sense of humor," I said. "I figure that's why we do, too, being made in his image like we are. The thing is, you never can tell what he's going to do next . . . or just how he'll work things out."

"Isn't that the truth!" Willa said, sighing. Then she looked up at me with a grin. "I think we ought to sit back and watch the show, don't you?"

"I guess we should," I said chuckling with her in spite of myself.

Later—Rose seems to be on the mend, and I have no one but you to thank for that, Lord. Thank you for everything you've shown me these past couple of days. I was wrong when I said youth was wasted on the young. I'm starting to think the older I get, the better I get at living this life you gave me.

November 17, 1873 . . .

The sun is back out like bright yellow fingers that reach through the gaps in the mountains to peek into the snowy valley. Rose is faring better today and even sat up to take some broth I made her, whispering she loved me in a raspy little voice . . . Patrick is outside again with Quinn, Gale, and the cattle . . . always the cattle. Mara Lee slaps her tin pans to some wordless beat, making Mercy laugh.

It's John-Charles I'm concerned about. Ever since Lillie left for town, he's been trying his best to get into the bunkhouse and see Medicine Weasel and One Shot. Jack told me today that One Shot seemed to be getting better but that he wasn't so sure about Medicine Weasel.

I'm going to go down there tonight and see if I can help in any way.

I just came back in from my visit to the bunkhouse. Medicine Weasel seems a little better, now—so do Jack and John-Charles . . .

I admit when we first walked in I thought for sure Medicine Weasel was already dead. One Shot took one look at us and nodded politely, as if it was the most natural thing in the world for his friend to be lying next to him, dead, then went back to flipping through the pages of a book Gale had left.

Jack gave a worried look John-Charles's way, then walked slow steps over to the side of Medicine Weasel's cot, leaning down to check his breathing. He must have seen something, for the next thing he did was shake Medicine Weasel.

"Don't you think about dyin' on me, old man," Jack said, more his fear talking than anything.

Medicine Weasel finally groaned, slowly opening his eyes to look at Jack.

"I wish you wouldn't have woke me, Jack Wade," the old man said. "I think by the way everything looked, I was almost home."

Jack started to say something back to that, but Medicine Weasel waved his gnarled old hand as if to quiet him, then he rolled his head my way.

"Tell me, what does Grandfather say in his Book about someone who is alive but feels dead?" he asked me. "I feel like I have a lot more dead pieces in me than live ones."

I said a quick prayer to myself and then went on to tell him there was still hope. I said that we all die, little by little, each day because of the craziness in the world.

"But if we ask God to take the dead pieces out of us, he will," I said, thinking of Preacher's and Jessie's stories. "Then he can replace them with new ones of his own."

Medicine Weasel nodded thoughtfully. "This might be a

good thing," he said, then he turned to Jack. "But you know, when I was going home, I don't think I felt those dead pieces."

"Well, you can't go yet," Jack said. "Your grandson needs you."

John-Charles must have felt it was safe for him to step out from the shadows then, for he did and quickly walked over to the side of his grandfather's cot. "Grandfather," was all he said. But I saw Medicine Weasel's eyes light up then, like something had sparked in his spirit, and I sensed the old man hadn't felt needed in a very long time.

Medicine Weasel struggled to sit up then, and as he did, he glanced out the door of the bunkhouse then turned back to John-Charles.

"Do you think you could help me get my lodge set up when I get well?" he asked, and John-Charles promised him he would.

The old man nodded then gave a great sigh, as if he had made his decision.

"I guess I won't die today," he said, smiling softly as he leaned back against his pillow and drifted back to sleep.

Sitting here writing this, I can't honestly say who was more relieved with that old man's decision to live: Jack, John-Charles, or me . . .

November 18, 1873 . . .

Rose's beautiful long hair is coming out by the handfuls now. Jessie says it's because of the high fever, that she's seen it happen before. It just breaks my heart, and I know Rose is hurt, too, but she is trying to put on a brave front for me.

"At least I can talk again, Mama," she said with a tired little smile as I tied a little kerchief around her head for her. But when I got down to the kitchen again to start dinner, I could have sworn I heard her muffled crying from up in the loft.

I think Mercy heard it, too, for she looked at me then scampered up the ladder, and she's been up there for quite a while now as I write this . . .

I am so tired tonight but thought to put down this scripture that I found earlier: *"Hope deferred maketh the heart sick: but when the desire cometh, it is a tree of life"* —PROVERBS 13:12.

I think I know what it means . . . God gives us hope so we don't grow weary in our desire to reach out to him . . . and to find him is to find the tree of life.

Just my thoughts. I'll have to ask Preacher about it sometime.

November 19, 1873 . . .

Another sunny day but still so very cold. Jasper and Honey are on parade as I write this, strutting across the snowy yard, three chubby little pups with snowy faces trotting along behind them. Rose and Mercy have their faces pressed against the window, laughing as they watch. I see Rose reach out and touch Mercy's golden curls with longing, then Mercy throws her arms around Rose's neck, hugging her for all she's worth. Such sweet girls . . . they have grown so close lately with Lillie gone. Jack says she should be back anytime now after getting word that the Audreys made it through . . . I wonder what kind of story Lillie will have to tell . . .

I best close this book for now. Mara Lee is hollering indignantly, sounding much more like a *hawk* than a little bird . . .

November 20, 1873 . . .

Wonders will never cease with this family. But I guess it wouldn't feel like *my* family if something wasn't happening around here. I had just come back from the barn with Jessie and Willa, each of us with a pup in tow to show Rose, when we came into the cabin to find Mercy . . . without any hair.

I remember standing there, holding the puppies in shock, then looking down at Jasper and Honey as if they could shed some light as to what happened. Jasper and Honey looked from Rose to Mercy then to me, their large eyes seeming to wonder if my hair was the next to go. Jessie and Willa took the pups then and quickly made their way to the kitchen . . . I'm thinking, to hide.

"Mercy Wade, what have you done?" I said, finally finding my voice. But Mercy just stared over her shoulder at me with those large green eyes that seemed to see right into my soul.

"I told her not to, Mama," Rose said from the couch. "But she said Jesus told her to."

"What's that supposed to mean?" I asked, looking to Mercy again, but she just shrugged, taking Rose's hand in her own, patting it like a little mother. Finally she said, "He just didn't want Rose to feel sad because I had hair and she didn't. So I cut mine." She looked back at Rose and smiled a sweet smile. "Now we're the same again."

I felt all the aggravation drain out of me then as I looked at Mercy's little head, now covered with nothing but choppy stubble. Then I remembered the first time I saw her, so small and fragile, brought into the world by love, the miracle of mercy allowing her to stay with us . . . And it made me think that maybe the mercy wasn't for her, but for us. And that she had somehow come to earth knowing a lot more about love than most people would in their whole lives.

Mercy turned and looked back over her shoulder at me then cocked her head to one side with a small, curious smile, like she was wondering what I was thinking. I went over and sat with her and Rose on the couch.

"You know, I was just thinking about that night I first held you in my arms, the very first night we met," I said to Mercy, and she smiled. "I remember kissing your cheek and whispering for you to fight for all you were worth. But what I won't ever forget is the look you gave me, like I could hear you speaking to me before you even knew how to talk."

"What did I say?" she asked, all eyes, and Rose leaned forward, too.

"You said, *It's you I'll be teaching how to fight, Aunt Callie*," I said, and Rose grinned at Mercy, who was looking down at her fragile little body like she couldn't imagine it—not realizing yet the giant heart that beat within her and how much it was worth.

"And you know what else?" I said, swallowing past the lump in my throat. "I think God knew just what he was doing when he gave you to us. Because we're a better family for having you with us."

It wasn't until I felt a draft that I turned to see Lillie standing in the door of the cabin. Mercy raced over to her, oblivious to what she had done, and Lillie hugged her to herself, then stood up and inspected her head, which still had patches of hair in some places and nearly bald spots in others.

"Well," she said slowly, "it looks like I'll have to tidy up that work of yours a little, honey. You go on home, now, and I'll be along soon enough . . . "

Mercy gave an excited little wave to Rose, then was out the door. Lillie turned to me, a soft smile on her face.

"You know, sometimes I wonder if her spirit wasn't eavesdropping on my thoughts while I was carrying her; she's everything I hoped and prayed for myself to be . . . "

"Do you remember that ol' preacher's wife I spoke of, the one who got so vexed with me on the trail?" I said then, and Lillie looked at me with a curious smile.

"Della?" she said. "Wasn't that her name?"

I nodded.

"Yes, Della Koch. "'Blood will tell,' is what she was forever saying to me." I looked at Lillie and thought of how brave she'd been to go to the Audreys, of how much of God's love she had in her heart for others, and I smiled. "You know what? I think now is the only time in my life I couldn't agree with her more."

"Yes ma'am, Mercy's blood do tell," Jessie said, coming out of the kitchen with Willa—and thinking nothing of eavesdropping either, now that I think of it.

Lillie smiled then. "You know, the one thing I remember Preacher saying was that once we become Christians, we all become one family. So that would mean we all have the same bloodline now, wouldn't it?"

I will never forget the feeling in that room when our eyes all met and how we looked at each other with such love and gratefulness.

"Well, will you look at Mara Lee," Willa said as she handed her over to me. And just as we all leaned in to look at her, Mara Lee's eyes widened, and she looked past us, up toward the ceiling. Then she laughed like she'd never seen anything so beautiful in her life.

Suddenly it felt like a warm, heavy stillness had settled down over us, and I had the strangest feeling that Jesus had decided to join our little circle of exes—the ex-lady dealer, the ex-slave, the ex-divorcée . . . and, of course, the ex-coward—and I heard those words of Scripture come to me then, the ones that say everyone who loves is born of God and knows God. I think if I could have heard anything else right then, it would have been God's laughter, joining in with Mara Lee's.

November 23, 1873 . . .

Sabbath. But there will be no church—at least not in town, as Preacher is still too weak. But he asked Willa to bring over a Scripture passage he felt sure we were to have. If there was ever any doubt that God walks with our Preacher, well . . . those folks should read the paper he sent to us. Here's what it says:

For ye have not received the spirit of bondage again to fear; but ye have received the Spirit of adoption, whereby we cry, Abba, Father. The Spirit itself beareth witness with our spirit, that we are children of God: And if children, then heirs; heirs of God, and joint heirs with Christ.
—ROMANS 8:15–17

As soon as Jessie finished reading that scripture, she looked up at all of us—but especially at Gale. They both smiled at each other.

"Makes a person think God whispers right into Preacher's ear, don't it?" she asked, but all any of us could do was nod.

As we all stood there, listening to Mercy's sweet little voice begin to rise up in prayer, thanking God for all he had done for us, for all the healings and the laughter, for bringing her mama home safe, I suddenly could have sworn that I heard Mrs. Audrey's words sweep through my mind again: *What a perfect bunch of outcasts*, she had said. But then I noticed something as I looked at Medicine Weasel and One Shot with their heads bowed so humbly . . . at Gale holding on to Rose's hand while Quinn held the other . . . at Patrick holding on to Mara Lee with such love . . . and at Jessie standing in between Jack and Lillie. I looked at those familiar faces and saw such love and thankfulness that suddenly those words didn't matter much anymore. And I noticed something else, too.

Somehow in the rush to join hands to pray, we had made a perfect circle.

PART THREE

Possessing the Land

So the people took what God said was theirs all along, and God was pretty happy they finally did that. But them kings weren't. They tried to take everything away. DON'T WORRY, God said, I WILL MAKE THEM LAY UNDER YOUR FOOT. And he did.
I think God was just sick and tired of them messing with Joshua and the people.

By Rose McGregor
Almost 14
Montana Territory, 1873

There is a wind that blows through here today that is nothing like I've ever experienced before. It's as if everything it touches is made to look up and to try and reach out to grasp hold of it somehow. I see it as I watch the branches of the trees, bare but stretching their arms to the sky, welcoming it into our valley . . . in the way the horses toss their heads side to side, letting it ruffle through their manes. Quinn calls it a *new wind,* and I admit that's what it feels like. Like something new has come calling.

We first felt it when we bundled up and stepped out onto the porch this morning to drink our coffee together before the children stirred. It felt so good for us to be alone together like that, too, watching the sun start to rise up over the mountains . . . not really talking but saying more with our eyes than anything we had said before. It felt like our hearts were saying, *We've come a long way together, but there's still such a wonderful journey ahead of us.* That's when I first felt the stirring of the wind. Quinn felt it, too.

He kind of cocked his head to one side and smiled. "Do ya feel that, lass?" he said, and then he shook his head. "I've never felt such a mild wind this time of year. I wonder if it's what I've heard called a *new wind . . .* "

We watched the cattle trot across the lower end of the valley then, nosing their way through what was left of the hay that had been laid out the night before, and I asked Quinn if he thought they would make it to market.

"Next year we'll take them to market," he said, looking at them, looking at the land. "That'll give them the summer to fatten up on our grasses."

I don't know how to explain it, but there was something in the way he said that—*next year* and *our grasses*—that rang true to me. For the first time in a long time I had no doubt there *would* be a next year . . . or that our grass would return. And I didn't doubt that God had given us this land.

"Next year, then," I said, and as soon as I did, I had the oddest feeling that in the saying of those three words, somewhere out there our names had been stamped upon the land.

"Next year," Quinn echoed. Then he looked over at me and smiled.

I just turned to this scripture when I came in to write this: *"Turn you to the strong hold, ye prisoners of hope: even today do I declare that I will render double unto thee"* —ZECHARIAH 9:12

Prisoners of hope? I can't imagine a better thing to be a prisoner of, than hope . . .

Later—Patrick told us tonight that he has thought it over and figures we are about the best ma and pa he's "ever knowed of."

"I've thought that for a long time, too," Rose said, looking up from playing with Mara Lee. Then she looked over at her brother with a mixture I can only describe as love and endurance. "He just said it before I could."

Quinn and I grinned at each other, and Mara Lee picked that time to let out a yell that would have made Medicine Weasel proud, and we all laughed.

It's funny how in the middle of winter, I can feel in my heart like summer has suddenly come.

November 26, 1873 . . .

It's turned colder yet today, but everyone's spirits are up in spite of it, with Thanksgiving only a day away.

Medicine Weasel and One Shot watch intently from the bunkhouse this morning as Jack teaches John-Charles the finer points of setting up a Blackfoot lodge. Jasper is hopping up and down, that little rabbit hop he does, then he makes a grab for Jack's hat and runs for it. Jack yells, "Patrick!" and everyone laughs, most of all Patrick, who has been teaching Jasper how to snatch hats off men's heads if they forget to take them off when they come in the door . . .

I can hear Lillie laughing, too; she must be watching from somewhere on her porch. She still hasn't said much about her stay at the Audreys', other than that she did what she was meant to do and that Mr. Audrey and the twins were more than thankful. Jessie and I have wondered about that . . . but we've decided not to press her on it. She'll talk if she wants to. In the meantime, I'm just glad she's home.

So is Mercy. The sweet little thing is staying over to help Rose make the nut taffy for tomorrow; they chatter like magpies in the kitchen with their matching kerchiefs snug on their heads, Mercy lining the buttered pans with hickory-nut hearts while Rose pours the boiled maple sugar over them.

"This is hard work, Rose," Mercy says gravely.

"Well, what you can't duck, you best welcome—that's what Mama always says, anyway," I hear Rose say with a great sigh. And I can't help but grin as I write this and wonder if my mama smiled when she first heard me quoting her . . .

I hope so.

November 27, 1873 . . .

Thanksgiving Day and no one up yet but me and the turkey— and if he had a choice, I think the poor thing would up and walk out on me after the abuse I've put him through. Plunged into a pot of scalding water shortly after Quinn shot him out of a tree, then had his feathers plucked off, then rolled in a piece of paper and set on fire to singe off any fuzz, then rinsed. Next I wound up his legs with strips of cloth dipped in lard . . . I laugh as I read Mama's last instruction written on the faded and folded paper. She wrote it when I was just a girl not much older than Rose is now: "And don't forget to cook it, Callie!"

Later—Well, thanks to Mama and a lot of other hard workers, our Thanksgiving has been a wonderful one. The turkey turned out real good, but the company was even better.

Peach was the first to roll in, and it tickled us to see he was all right after the scarlet fever scare. He was grinning ear to ear, holding a pan of green-corn pudding he had made himself that looked so good it shocked me to silence. Peach looked almost as good, like he had taken about ten years off his age, as clean as he was. Jack, being Jack, said, "Why, Peach, I thought you were against takin' a full scrub. Didn't you say you were afraid of going deaf?" to which Peach said, "I guess I decided I'd rather be deaf than lonely. And deaf would be a good thing if I had to stick around you very long!"

We all laughed then and turned to see Jessie marching in with Gale, carrying a fresh pan of johnnycakes—or ash cakes, as she likes to call them—setting them on the table next to Lillie's raspberry shrubs. Then Preacher and Willa arrived with several quart jars of her harvest cider that everyone loves so. Medicine Weasel and One Shot just stood back in a corner of the room and watched the commotion with a kind of dazed expression on their faces. But they were more than eager to take a seat when we told them dinner was ready.

I admit the question went through me then, wondering if they'd had much in the way of food before coming here. I think Preacher was thinking the same thing as he glanced to the two of them then sat down next to Willa. As we all joined hands, he said, "What's that old saying? It's a shame that it takes a poor man to remind you how rich you are." He looked around the table at us then cleared his throat. "Before we say grace, I was thinking maybe each of us should give thanks for all the things God's blessed us with in our lives."

We all agreed that was a fine idea and went around the table then, saying what blessings God had brought to us . . . all but Peach, that is. I think we all would have probably just let it go if it hadn't been for Mercy's persistence.

"Peach, ain't you going to say how God blessed you?" Mercy asked, her green eyes looking even larger as she blinked up at him from under the kerchief that had slipped low on her forehead. I saw Peach was fit to be tied to have to tell her no. "Peach?" she said again, and he took a big sigh then said kind of shaky, "*If'n* yer up there, Lord, I thank ya fer this family and fer makin' me feel like I belong somewheres. Because I reckon I ain't felt like that in a long time . . . if'n ever."

Quinn and I looked up at each other at the same time, touched by the old trapper's honest words—we all were. But it was Gale who appeared to be affected the most by what Peach said. I saw him look over at Peach thoughtfully, like he more than understood, but then he smiled and said amen, just like the rest of us. And like the rest of us, he had to blink several times . . . to get past the tears.

Such a good day . . . I don't think I've ever felt so much love or laughed so hard. Like Preacher says, laughter is cheap medicine—cheap but good—and I'm thinking the children couldn't have agreed with that saying more, the way they were carrying on this evening.

"Patrick, what did you say your blessing was again?" Rose asked for some reason tonight as they all sat in front of the fireplace. I saw Patrick side-glance over at her, as if trying to figure out what she was up to.

If the question was asked in innocence, we'll never know,

because Patrick, so used to Rose setting him up for some sort of fall, finally said, "I said I was blessed for havin' Mama and Pa and you and Bird with me and that if I didn't ever have anything else that was OK because you's was enough." He rushed on before she could speak. "*And* you didn't mean to say that, either. Because I just thought it up and that's *why* I said it first." He smiled, satisfied, then added, "You ol' rag-head, you."

I said, "Patrick!" but all of them had busted into a fit of giggles—including Rose, who looked over at me with a grin after she had composed herself somewhat.

"Oh, Mama," she said, "that *was* funny. So that means it's OK to say." She glanced over at her brother and grinned again. "Ain't nothin' that beats a good laugh." But never to be outdone she added, "You ol' brush-head."

They all burst into another round of laughter at that—even Gale, who kind of shook his head, looking at Rose like she was the most curious but interesting creature he'd ever met.

I can't help but agree—and there *isn't* anything that beats a good laugh. Especially when you hear it ringing out of all those you love . . . like music.

I do thank you, Lord, for the sweet blessings of this day . . . for bringing us all through the sickness and for helping us to look forward again to what lies ahead. Although I do admit I have to fight the urge to glance up and say, "Can you give me a hint?"

November 30, 1873 . . .

The Sabbath bought us another trip to town, with Preacher feeling good enough to hold church now, even though he was still looking a little peaked—and he wasn't the only one. I noticed, glancing around, that there was quite a few folks in the tent that still looked a little pale. But there was a gladness about everyone, too; I saw it in the faces of my own family . . . in Willa's eyes as she looked at Preacher, even in the faces of Mrs. Pumphrey and Widow Spence . . . like stepping out onto your porch after a storm and seeing the sun again and just being so grateful you made it through the storm to see that sun.

When Preacher stepped up to start his sermon, I caught sight of the Audreys, too, and saw that same look on Mr. Audrey and the twin's faces. But Mrs. Audrey had a funny look to her, like she was trying to figure out a way to leave, but then Preacher started talking and I didn't have time to think on it, really, until now . . .

Anyway, the way Preacher looked around at all of us was so funny, almost like he was a little boy pleased to see his playmates had been able to make it over to play. "Well, I can honestly say I'm real glad to see we all made it here today," he said, earning chuckles from all around the tent. He smiled.

"The past few days I've been hearing a lot of stories from folks telling how God saw them through this sickness. One thing I realized was that each story was different, but the *how* of it was the same . . . because every one of you has said that you kept your eyes on the Lord."

Preacher cocked his head to one side and looked at us. "Do any of you remember what happened to Peter when he asked Jesus to call him out of the boat to walk on the water with him?" Preacher grinned. "Well, he walked on the water, of course." Everyone laughed, then Preacher's face grew sober. "But do you remember what happened when Peter took his gaze off of Jesus and looked down at those stormy waves? He started sinking . . .

"*That's* what I want to talk to you about today. I want to tell you that these kinds of trials will come, but if you can just keep your eyes fixed on Jesus, he will see you across those stormy waters. And if you just happen to look, you will see that he's walking through the storm with you."

A few people said amen, then it got quiet again.

"Listen, folks: Jesus walked through storms of life during his whole journey here on earth. He didn't care that he wasn't rich, that no one stood with a crown of jewels to place on his head. He didn't care that he was jeered at and heckled—even though he knew who he was . . . even though *heaven* knew.

"The one thing he *did* care about was people. Think about it: Everything he did was about people. About love and humbleness.

"The *King of kings* humbled himself to wash the dirty feet of men, to talk to a fallen woman who believed she was too far down to be lifted up, to comfort one who grieved for another. He saw us with such bittersweet sadness because we didn't quite understand the truth . . . didn't understand real love. *He* knew that nothing else mattered in this world. Nothing but helping us find our way *home*.

"Yes, heaven is our true home. But never mistake God's understanding for us while we are *here*. Never mistake his ways that even Isaiah said are unsearchable. God knows the true desires of our hearts because he put them there . . . And just as he knew the children of Israel needed a place to rest, a place to lay their heads as they journeyed through life, so he knows we need such a place, too.

"That's why I don't want you to give up. And he doesn't want you to give up, either. God has given us this place to call home; I have no doubt of that." Preacher looked over at Willa and smiled. "That's why I'm willing to press on. And my prayer is that you will, too.

"Listen: The Lord knows these trials will come; he knows all and sees all. And because he sees all, he also knows that joy will come again and so will the rest it brings. Our God, in all his wisdom, knows we couldn't bear the cruelty of the world without those moments, those seasons of joy. King David said he would have despaired had he not believed he would see 'the goodness of the LORD in the land of the living.' What's true of King David, who was called a man after God's own heart, is true of us as well.

"I ask you today not to give up—to have faith, to open your eyes, and to see that Jesus is there, walking right beside you. And if you want to remember any words this day, remember his, not mine. Remember what he promised: 'I will never leave thee, nor forsake thee.'"

"Those were some mighty fine words," Mrs. Pumphrey said behind me as we started to make our way out of the tent. I turned to see her and Widow Spence smiling kindly at me.

"Too bad there are those who don't seem to want to listen," Widow Spence said sadly, and they both glanced Mrs. Audrey's way for some reason.

The crowd surged forward, and all I could do was wave as I was led along with the rest heading in a hurry to their buggies and wagons. With it being as cold as it is, there would be no picnics after church until spring. Which is why we were all a bit surprised to find Peach slicked up again and standing just outside the tent.

He said hello to everyone, but it was clear he was nervous about something. Then I realized what it was as he chanced a glance over at Widow Spence, who was heading away to her buggy. Lillie looked to Willa, then over at me and winked.

Jessie saw it, too.

"Well, Peach, did *you* hear anything good?" she said over her shoulder as she and Rose climbed into her old wagon.

"Mebbe a thing or two," Peach said offhandedly as he shuffled his feet and glanced toward Widow Spence again.

Jessie handed the reins to Rose, who after her bout of sickness was back in good graces, and Rose grinned like she knew it. Jessie shook her head, smiling, and turned back to Peach. "Yer off to a good start, Peach," she said then, "but yer goin' have t' do better than that if ya want t' land yerself a fine Christian lady."

We all chuckled, and as I climbed up in our own wagon, I caught Mrs. Pumphrey watching us all with a pleased smile on her face, and I knew she had heard. I knew, too, that before the hour was out, Widow Spence would be hearing all about it, and I wondered how Peach would handle that.

I recall glancing down at Mara Lee then, bundled so good that all I could see was her blue-gray eyes and her mouth as she blinked up at me once then grinned like she thought Peach would do just fine.

Later—Preacher and Willa made a special trip out here after church to tell us that Willa's decided to start a Sunday school, and I never saw a more excited little bunch—even Gale, who is usually so serious. Rose was the only one who took the news with casual indifference.

"Oh, I remember goin' to Sunday school in Californy," Rose said, like she was old hat at it as she spun the top they were play-ing with.

"Did you like it?" Mercy asked, all eyes.

"Well," Rose said slowly, "all I remember about it was I couldn't read yet, and they wouldn't let me talk *at all*."

"That must have been bad for you," Mercy said in all seri-ousness, and we all couldn't help but laugh.

But it wasn't until we got the children all down for bed and the men had gone to the barn to look at the horses that we heard the real shocking news from Willa.

"I know I probably shouldn't talk, but I just don't under-stand it," she started, taking a glance over at Lillie, who was fill-ing her coffee cup.

"It's about Mrs. Audrey," she said, and Lillie looked over with a kind of worried look on her face. "Percy came to Shawn after church and told him Mrs. Audrey's decided to leave town—and I mean, *leave*: Percy, the girls, everything. He said that ever since she came out of the fever she's been acting real restless, saying she needed to get away. Then today after church she says to him, 'It took me nearly dying to realize I want to have a life—and living here is not what I call life.'"

Willa went on. "So Shawn goes with Percy to try to talk to her, but she already has her buggy loaded and is heading out without so much as a good-bye to Percy or the girls." Willa shook her head. "Shawn said when he looked into her eyes, it was like there was nothing there but darkness. Then she says to Shawn, 'Preacher, if God sees everything, why hasn't he seen me?' Then he said she laughed real mean and left not long after that."

We all watched Lillie sit down at the table with a heavy sigh. "She was acting that way when I was there, too," Lillie said sadly. "Last day I was there, I was in her room, trying to tidy it up, you know, and she just started saying the most hateful things. She said, 'So, you're not just a dealer but a nurse now, too? Well, you might think you know everything, Lillie Wade, but you don't know me.' Then she laughed real hard and said it again: 'You don't know me.'"

Lillie looked at all of us with tears in her eyes. "I didn't say anything because I thought I should maybe just pray for her first. I was just so sure that God wanted me there . . . "

We gathered around her then, like we always did with each other, patting her on the back and trying to comfort her. But we were so shocked about all we'd heard, I can't even remember if we said anything. It was Jessie who seemed to break the spell, brushing her old, callused hand over Lillie's long curls.

"You did right, chil'," she said. "You did jes what the good Lord tolt ya to do, and that's more than a lot of folks." Jessie looked at me and Willa, and I saw almost that same look come over her sweet face that I'd seen on Lillie's face the day she went to take care of the Audreys.

"Best thing we kin do right now is pray for them Audreys," Jessie said. "The good Lord will do the rest. He always does."

And because we knew the truth of that, all four of us got down on our knees in my tiny little kitchen and joined hands. And we prayed.

December 1, 1873 . . .

I had the oddest dream last night. I dreamt I was standing in the road in the middle of town, and suddenly I saw Preacher, standing at his pulpit. But the pulpit was in the middle of the road, too, and Preacher was dressed in what looked to be a judge's robes. Then I turned and saw that Jessie was standing next to me. She didn't turn to look at me but just kept looking up to the sky and then she said, "Pray, and the good Lord will do the rest. He always does."

Then Preacher raised this huge judge's gavel he had in his hands, and he struck it down against the pulpit.

And that's when I woke up to find Mara Lee banging on her crib for all she was worth . . .

Rose and Patrick finished their lessons and their chores and were leaving to meet the others down at the barn for a round with the pups just as Jessie came in this afternoon. She took the cup of coffee I offered her and said in a distracted kind of way, "Do you remember when they said they'd be back?"

"Before Christmas," I said, knowing she meant her children.

Jessie just nodded and said, "Well, I don't know why, but

they have been on my mind so strong today, I feel jes like I kin reach out and touch them."

She stayed for a while, talking small talk with me as I bathed Mara Lee, but she left not long after that. I watched her from the porch as she made her way to her own cabin, still distracted and every once in a while, glancing to the road that leads into the ranch.

This has been a strange day, to say the least . . . and I didn't even get the chance to tell Jessie about my dream.

December 3, 1873 . . .

Well, Jessie's mothering instincts have not faded in spite of her children being full grown. They all showed up at the ranch early this morning full of good news about their search for land.

Jessie was beside herself with happiness, and we all grinned at each other as we watched her hug each one like there was no tomorrow. "I jes knew you all was nearin' me," Jessie said, laughing. "I *felt* it in these ol' bones of mine."

"Not so old, Mama," Jessie's oldest boy, Jonah, said with tears in his eyes as she hugged him. "Not so old."

We finally got them all ushered into our cabin, being that it was the closest out of the cold, and Medicine Weasel and One Shot followed the rest of the group right in, too, their eyes filled with curiosity over the happy little group. Jack says it's because they haven't seen many black people. Medicine Weasel was quick to sit down at the table with them to get a good view, just as Jessie's daughter Sara told us all how they had got caught in a snowstorm just northeast of us. She said they ended up taking shelter in a tiny cabin with an old trapper-fellow named . . . *Peach.*

We all started laughing, and Jessie shook her head, grinning. "The good Lord surely has a sense of humor," she said. "And that ol' coot didn't say a thing when we saw him, either."

Sara looked around at all of us and shook her regal head in a way that reminded me so much of Jessie I couldn't help wondering if she was what Jessie looked like young.

"Well, whoever he is, Mama, he sold us the land for our town," Sara said with a triumphant grin as she looked at our shocked faces. Medicine Weasel was the only one that looked merely thoughtful.

"You all look about as shocked as we did when he made the offer," Jonah said, his eyes crinkling with a smile. "We had just about given up—but I say *just*—because none of us wanted to come home to Mama without our land."

"It was all Mama's doin'," Rachel, Jessie's youngest, agreed. "She gave us a talkin' to that would have lit a fire under a snail."

Jessie chuckled, wiping the tears from her eyes. "Oh, now, I jes told ya to remember them daughters of Zelophehad that Preacher spoke of before," she said, her dark eyes widening innocently.

"Uh-huh. What you *said* was, 'Maybe you all ought to start thinkin' like them girls did instead of like some orphans without a pa,'" Sara supplied. "You said them girls knew their *real* Pa—and knew they was good enough to step up to Moses and claim the right to their land. You said we'd be fools not to do the same—'cause we ain't orphans. The good Lord knows our names sure *enough*."

Jonah and Rachel chuckled with their sister.

"Why, Jessie, I never knew you could sermonize like that," I said, grinning.

"I think she could give Preacher a run for his money," Quinn added, and Jessie sniffed, folding her arms across her ample bosom in a perfect imitation of Rose.

"Might be I could do jes *that*," she said with a haughty air that made us laugh again. Not too much longer after that, we saw Gale walk in. He skirted around the tumble of children in the living room then stopped in the entry way to the kitchen, looking slightly amazed at all the new people in the room.

"Come on in, Gale Norton," Jessie said with a grin a mile wide. "You got some more family to meet."

I read to everyone the story of the daughters of Zelophehad tonight as Jessie and her family crowded in around the fireplace in our front room, read how these daughters who had lost their whole family in the wilderness had enough courage to go before Moses himself to claim their right to their father's and brother's inheritance. Then I read how Moses brought their case before the Lord:

"'And the LORD spake to Moses, saying: "The daughters of Zelophehad speak right,"'" I read to them. "'Thou shalt surely give them a possession of an inheritance among their father's brethren; and thou shalt cause the inheritance of their father to pass unto them.'"

"God did that cause they were risktakers, didn't he, Pa?" John-Charles said then, surprising us all, and Jack smiled at his son with pride.

"Why, yes, I believe so, son," he said.

"And because the Lord ain't no *suspector* of persons," Jessie added. "A very good friend of mine told me that awhile back, and I've found it to be true."

"I know who that friend was! That friend was *me*, wasn't it, Jessie," Rose said sleepily, looking up from where her head had been resting on Jessie's lap. Jessie chuckled softly and patted Rose's little turbaned head.

"Yes, little sis," she said, "that friend was you."

Rachel stood then and took out a worn scrap of paper and

read to us all what they planned to put in the newspaper to invite others to come to their town. I copied it down here so I could always have it to remember:

TO THE COLORED CITIZENS
OF THE UNITED STATES:

We, the company of the Town of Justice, are now in possession of our lands and the Town Site of Justice, which is located just east of Livingston, Montana Territory, and are happy to say it is the finest country we ever did see. The soil is rich, black, sandy loam, and the valley is eye pleasing, too.

We have secured the service of Mr. Coy Harper, a man of energy and ability, to survey and locate our colony. Now is the time to come secure your home in the Town of Justice, Montana Territory.

Not quite 90 days ago we secured our charter to locate the town site of Justice, and it has been by the grace of our God that come spring we will begin to permanently settle on our land.

Join us. Don't delay.

As soon as Rachel finished reading the announcement, we all clapped, and she grinned, glancing over to Jessie with tears of such love in her eyes.

"Why did you pick the name Justice?" Gale asked, and it was Quinn who told him about Stem and how he had given his life for Rose and the others . . . how Stem had been the one to help Jessie find her children again, even after his death.

"Never did know why everyone called him Stem," Jessie said softly. "But his mama, she named him Justice, and I recall Preacher tellin' him once that was a fine name and that his mama surely knew what she was doin' namin' him like that."

I walked with Jessie and her children down to her own cabin, and it was as we were walking that it suddenly hit me that soon enough Jessie would be leaving . . . that she wouldn't be with us on the ranch anymore . . . that, worst of all, I wouldn't have her anymore.

"Oh, I don't think I'm going to be able to bear it when you leave here, Jessie," I said, a part of me knowing it was selfish to say, but I couldn't help it. "It would be like losing a part of my heart, and I don't think I have much more I can afford to lose."

Jessie chuckled her dry, comforting kind of chuckle and hugged me close to her. "Well now, honey, that's the thing about hearts," she said as she patted my back. "They tend to mend in spite o' our doubts, and Lord, we been given some doubts, ain't we? But they do mend, mebbe not the same as before. But I kindly like t' imagine them little mendin' scars bein' like new roads for us t' follow . . .

"And who's to say you can't come callin' down that new road of mine, huh?" she added with a sweet smile on her old face.

When she finally pulled away, I had the strangest feeling . . . almost like that day when Quinn and I had stood on the porch of our cabin and felt that new wind blow into our lives . . . And I knew then that it had blown into Jessie's life as well.

December 5, 1873 . . .

The snow has started to fall again this morning: big flakes that blow and swirl past the windows, already piling on top of what was left before. I think the mighty hand of Providence held it back just until Jessie's family made it safe to the ranch. And being that he did, Quinn and Jack now have all the help they could ask for.

Medicine Weasel and One Shot are teasing John-Charles in Blackfoot somewhere outside. I can hear them all laughing as I hold Mara Lee and try to write this at the same time. But I feel led to write this . . . to say it seems as if the pieces to the puzzle of all of are lives are coming together now more than ever before.

Medicine Weasel made a rare appearance at the cabin this evening while the men were down at the barn, checking on one of the horses that was getting ready to foal. Rose and Patrick had taken off earlier with Gale to Jack and Lillie's for a game of Drop the Handkerchief with Jessie's grandchildren, so I was left alone with Mara Lee when I heard the knock at the door. I had to call out, "Come on in!" twice before I saw the door finally open and Medicine Weasel cautiously step inside.

I could tell he had tried to make an effort with his appearance, dressing in some of the clothes Jack had given him and braiding his long white hair, but he still looked too thin. I tried to steel myself against the memory of the proud medicine man who had saved Jack's life all those years ago.

Medicine Weasel smiled at me then sat down on the floor in front of the fireplace with a slight groan. Then he looked at me for what seemed like an eternity before he talked.

"Jessie's people, with hair like the buffalo, do they fare as well as the whites?" he asked, and when I told him no, he merely nodded, as if he suspected as much. He pulled out a piece of jerky and chewed off a tiny bit and stared into the fire.

"So, getting land of their own, this has been a difficult thing?" he asked finally.

"Yes," I said. "There are some whites that don't want them to have any land. But they didn't put their faith in those people; they put their faith in God."

"And it has turned out well for them. This is good news," he said, rising to leave. Then he stopped at the door as if a thought had suddenly occurred to him. "You were right," he said. "Grandfather does bring you hope to fill where those dead pieces used to be."

December 6, 1873 . . .

Another day of snow; falling like big feathers through the gray sky, hitting the earth with a hush that seems almost impossible. I can just barely make out Medicine Weasel's lodge from the window, but I do see the spirals of smoke trailing upward before they're swept back down with the snow. The valley and beyond looks like it's been covered by a huge white blanket, and I feel like going back to bed for some reason.

I think Mara Lee feels the same; I can hear the soft baby chatter she does when she's drifting off to sleep. She said her first word today, which sounded to me like, "Nodunt," and it wasn't until I had her repeat it in front of Quinn that Rose and Patrick looked at each other and burst into a round of laughter.

"Bird's saying, 'No, don't,' Mama," Patrick said, and Quinn and I laughed as he picked up Mara Lee and brushed over her thick, black curls. I should have known. "No, don't" has become the most-said words around this cabin since she's started crawling and reaching for things.

Well, I best lay this pen down and get to work while our little Bird takes a nap—in spite of me wanting to join her.

Later—I have an idea now why I had such a yearning to take a nap earlier.

I'd just finished another round of mending and then washing and stringing clothes all over the cabin until they started taking on the appearance of oversized Christmas ornaments, draped on everything as they were, when Rose and Patrick came in with a fresh load of wood to tell me they had invited everyone over for a Bible story.

I was almost tempted to run to Medicine Weasel and One Shot's lodge and stay there, but there was such a happy look to their eyes that I didn't have the heart to really run . . . or to say no.

Quinn knew it, too, for there was a sympathetic smile on his tired face as he quickly set the children into action helping him straighten up the cabin before our company arrived. And truth is, I'm so glad I didn't say no . . .

We watched them from the porch as they came from all directions, trudging through the snow, hanging on to the ropes that connected us all to each other. And as I stood there, I thought how blessed we were to have such a family that would go through a bitterly cold night to get together . . . and to hear God's Word.

Jessie, her two girls, and Lillie quickly herded the little ones in and got them settled, then set to fixing some coffee to go with the rice puffs Lillie had made special. Medicine Weasel and One Shot surprised us by coming in, too. And after they had convinced us they were more comfortable sitting on the floor with the children, choosing which story to read was the next order of business. Everyone finally settled on Moses and the burning bush.

And that's when the questions began: "Well, how come people always have to take their shoes off when an angel comes? Are their shoes real dirty?" said one. "I'll bet the angels just don't like shoes. They don't need them anyways, 'cause they fly," said another. "No, that was the angel of the Lord—that means God," said another, followed by a great sigh. "But he's God. He don't need shoes, either," said one. "I wish we didn't," whispered yet another.

It was all I could do not to laugh, so I tried my best to keep my eyes off of Jessie, Lillie, and the others, who I knew were having a time of it by the way they were excusing themselves to disappear into the kitchen every so often. I went on, telling how Moses asked God if he could see him face to face, and that's when Jessie's grandbaby Noel leaned forward, his dark eyes wide with the thought of it.

"Miss Callie, is God black?" he blurted out suddenly, and I felt every small head in the room look up to study my face. Even Medicine Weasel appeared to be extremely interested in my answer as he leaned forward, too, waiting.

"I don't think God is a *color* at all," Gale said, suddenly speaking up before I could. "He can't be. Because the Bible says he's perfect love, and there isn't a color to *love*."

Noel sat back, satisfied, and Medicine Weasel did, too, as if the weight of the world were suddenly lifted off their shoulders. Gale turned and looked at me then, his eyes searching my face.

"Am I right?" he asked finally.

"Yes, you surely are," I said, smiling. And this time, I did look up to Jessie and Lillie and the others, and when our eyes met, it was with the feeling of wonder over this young boy who seemed to have wisdom far beyond his years. When I glanced over at Rose, I could see she was looking at him in a different light as well.

"You're pretty smart when you want to be, Gale," she admitted, and Gale grinned, looking suddenly like he'd won a prize.

I do thank you, Lord, for this night. For showing me that some great blessings can come in the smallest of packages . . . and for giving me the chance to learn that those packages can be delivered at any time.

But especially when we least expect them.

December 10, 1873 . . .

Where have the days gone?

It's been snowing here the past few days like it has no plans to stop, and we have all had to pitch in, trying in any way we can to keep ahead of the snow, riding through thick drifts to spread out as much hay as we can for the cattle. Jessie, Lillie, all of us are pitching in—even Medicine Weasel and One Shot, although neither of them has much use for cattle. *Buffalo*, now, they know enough to dig through to the grass, One Shot explained.

It's been like this: up before sunrise, cook, clean, kiss the baby and hand her to Rose, then ride out as fast as I can, praying that somehow I don't run into a deep ravine or an outcropping of rock that has been hidden by the snow and also praying that I don't lose the bundle of hay, that I'll find enough cattle to give the hay to . . . that no one comes up lost or frostbit . . .

Yet every time we ride back in at the end of the day, I see the strong spirit of endurance among us that wasn't there before. I see our family pulling together for all they're worth because now it's not just another day. Somewhere along the way, God has sealed it in our hearts that it is our *future* we're working toward . . . our land.

Quinn said as much tonight when we finally made it into the cabin, so tired and dirty.

"Did you see everyone out there today? Did you ever think it would feel so good to feel so tired?" he said, smiling down at me like we had just come in from a dance, not a blizzard, as I took off my bonnet.

I looked up at him then, and I knew by the look in his eyes that my hair was sticking up every which way to Sunday.

"No, I didn't," I said, trying to keep my face straight, and then we couldn't keep ourselves from laughing. Once our laughter had died down, Quinn took me in his strong arms and hugged me to him. "The joy of the Lord *is* our strength, isn't it, lass?" he said, his voice thick with emotion and thankfulness . . . and I couldn't help but agree.

It has finally stopped snowing. I can almost hear the valley sigh along with my loved ones who are sleeping now . . . and I have just spotted a huge bull elk looking through the window at me, so close his nose blows circles of steam against the glass. Five years ago such a sight would have scared me to pieces. Five years ago a lot of things would have scared me to pieces.

I wonder if he will leave if I stand up. I have the oddest urge to go and put my hands against the glass where those circles of steam are . . .

December 11, 1873 . . .

It's so bitterly cold out there that everyone stays inside today, feeding the fireplace wood like you might feed a starving friend. Rose is working on her sampler, much to my surprise, and Patrick is carving away at something, but neither one is talking much.

Between Mercy's birthday and Christmas coming up, everyone has become so secretive around here, you can't get a simple answer to a question.

I just asked Quinn if my old washtub might be down at the barn, and he looked up from putting more wood on the fire, startled. "And why would you be lookin' down there, lass?" he said. Rose and Patrick looked at each other and grinned.

Mara Lee, not wanting to be left out, yelled, "Nodunt!" from her crib, causing us all to laugh.

December 14, 1873 . . .

So much work to do today and still so bitter cold out . . .

I wonder what *is* down in that barn.

December 15, 1873 . . .

It's Mercy's *fourth* birthday today. Sometimes it seems like only yesterday that I was holding her in my arms for the very first time. Then there are times when I look at her and imagine her being so much older than the little body that holds all she is.

Today she was just a little girl, though, smiling shyly as everyone gathered at Jack and Lillie's to celebrate. Preacher and Willa were the first to show up after all of us, braving the winding, snow-choked trail to get to Mercy, and Peach wasn't far behind them in coming. Even Medicine Weasel and One Shot seemed determined to witness Mercy's big day. Looking around at all of their faces, it wasn't hard to figure out why. Mercy, as was her way, had awed them by her heart . . . awed all of us, even as young as she was.

But it was Jack who seemed almost moved to tears as he watched his little girl opening her gifts, patting her small head that had been bound with the bright new kerchief Lillie had made special for her birthday.

"Pa said it was an angel that came the day she was born," John-Charles said, seeming to sense Jack's feelings. "He said it was because God wanted the world to have Mercy in it."

We all fell silent for a moment, his words meaning more than he really knew to this ragtag group of settlers who have prayed for mercy too many times to count in our lives. It was Preacher who finally broke the silence, his face telling of his own struggles.

"Well, your pa couldn't have been more right," Preacher said, looking at all of us.

"I *know* it was an angel unaware, Uncle Jack," Patrick said with a conviction that hadn't left him after all this time. "I didn't get to see that one. But I'm always on the lookout now, just in case."

Mercy, who had been gingerly picking up each gift that had been made for her, looked up, then chanced a quick glance over Peach's way. "But angels have their own teeth, right?" she said, and delighted laughter broke out all over the room as the little ones surrounded her, oohing and ahhing over her presents.

"Looks like you're going to go down in history 'bout them teeth, Peach," Jessie said with a teasing look in her eyes as we moved toward the kitchen and let the little ones play. Peach, who had been looking quite sentimental himself, turned and winked at Jessie's children.

"Ya never know, old woman," he said with a kindly look to his eyes. "I might jes surprise ya and do somethin' real rash."

"Well, if selling land to colored folk ain't rash, I don't know what is," Jessie said, enjoying their banter, and it was easy to see Peach did, too. He chuckled but looked real pleased with himself.

"Maybe what he means by *rash* is proposing to Widow Spence," Lillie said, grinning, and Peach blushed so hard it made us all laugh again.

"Speakin' of weddings," Quinn said, glancing Preacher and Willa's way. "It keeps snowin' like this, Preacher, and we're going to have a time of it gettin' the lumber in to start raisin' your church."

"What say ya?" Peach said then, his attention suddenly piqued. We explained to him about the plans for the church—and how Preacher and Willa would marry as soon as it was finished, all of us talking more excitedly as we went on. To have a real church in town instead of a tent seemed to make it feel more permanent. But especially to Willa.

"Once it's finished, we'll marry," Willa added with a curve to her lips that was the starting of a smile.

"Oh, we'll have our church built by spring, Willa," Preacher said with a determined look. "Count on it." Then he grinned. "It's easier getting a fishhook in than it is taking it out—but you should know that after all these years."

We all had a good laugh then—even Willa, who tried her best to appear mortified, but we could tell she was secretly pleased, too . . .

It *would* be wonderful to have a real church. The more roots a tree can put down, the better chance it has to stand against a storm when it blows in, my pa always used to say. I have a feeling that's what we've all been doing lately, without maybe even realizing it. Putting down roots.

I told Mercy tonight as we were leaving that many birthdays from now she would be walking down the aisle of our church with her husband and she would remember this night when she was four and our church was just a dream.

Mercy nodded somberly and looked up at me with those huge green eyes of hers, clutching the new rag doll Jessie had made for her in her arms. She crooked her finger for me to bend down. "I'll remember, Aunt Callie," she whispered, and cocked her head to look me in the eyes for a long moment. Then she smiled, and the words she whispered next, I don't think I'm likely to forget.

"You're not scared anymore, are you . . . "

It is snowing *again*.

December 21, 1873 . . .

Sabbath. The last few days of snow made it impossible for us to get to town to hear Preacher today. But maybe it was just God's way of getting us to slow down, to be still and once again draw closer to him after these last days of battling once again to keep our cattle fed . . . his way of encouraging us that no matter where we are, he is with us.

As Quinn slowly opened our Bible to the Book of Isaiah, I realized that God didn't just whisper in Preacher's ear, but in my husband's ear, too, and when he began to read, I saw Jessie and her children all begin to smile and nod, saw the look of tiredness on Jack's face begin to ease: " 'Remember ye not the former things, neither consider the things of old. Behold, I will do a new thing; now it shall spring forth; shall ye not know it? I will even make a way in the wilderness, and rivers in the desert.' "

It was Gale who seemed to speak for all of us, though, as he suddenly glanced up, a sweet smile on his face as if something had just occurred to him. "He *is* doing a new thing in us all, isn't he?" He looked around the room at us. "Because none of our lives are really the same as before, are they?"

I thought of Willa then, and how God had changed in an instant the way she thought all those years . . . I thought of Lillie and how he had taken her heart beyond what she would've ever thought to reach out to someone who had caused her nothing but pain . . . and of Jessie and her children, how he had proved faithful in giving them their land . . . and of Peach, dear Peach . . . and Gale, who he had led away from such sadness and given him a real place to call home . . . and Medicine Weasel, how he had given him new hope. And then I thought of how he had given me a new hope, too.

I pondered how he *had* blown this new wind into all of our lives . . . and when I finally glanced over at Quinn, smiling down at Rose and Patrick with such love, I realized it didn't even have to be Christmas to know that we had all been given a gift better than what we could ever imagine . . .

December 22, 1873 . . .

Christmas is in the air around here. Everyone is tiptoeing around, casting furtive little glances each other's way, then smiling like the cat that ate the canary . . .

I was just down at the barn, looking for that little washtub so we could fill it with a spiced ginger drink I want to make for Christmas Day, when Jasper and Honey—even their pups—kept watching after me as if I was on the verge of breaking a commandment. They made me feel so guilty I finally came back in here to get warm again. I honestly haven't been snooping.

And I never found my washtub, either.

Quinn brought in a fine tree tonight, and we had such a good time of it, trimming it with strings of popcorn and red berries and walnuts wrapped in little bits of tinfoil. We just couldn't spare the candles to add to the trimmings, but the children don't seem to mind.

Rose and Patrick are sitting by the fireplace now, as I write this, looking at the tree with pleased little looks on their faces. But Mara Lee, who can't bear being that far from the "pretty," crawls over to the tree and lies just beneath the bottom branches, looking up with those eyes of hers, wide as saucers. She knows she isn't to touch, so she holds her chubby fingers out, just a whisper away from the branches. *So close,* her expression says, *so close, but so far . . .*

December 23, 1873 . . .

Overcast, windy day today and so cold that even the logs of this cabin creak and groan their protest.

It's a good day to finish up my own little surprises for everyone, little journal. I have just a few more stitches to make on the shirt I made for Quinn. Patrick's new trousers and Rose's dress are ready, as well as the sweet little burlap dolls I made for Rose, Mercy, and Mara Lee. Quinn showed me the three little wooden "treasure boxes" he made for Patrick, John-Charles, Gale, and Jessie's grandbaby, Noel, and I only hope Rose doesn't feel left out, thinking of herself as one of the boys like she does . . .

Mara Lee is leaning out of her crib for all she is worth, trying to reach the tree—I best close for now before our little Bird falls out on her head . . .

Early Christmas Eve morning, and not a mouse stirs . . . but a little Bird does, and as I look down at her sleeping in my arms, I want to thank you, Lord, for all you have given me . . . and for sending your Son to bring light into this sometimes dark, lonely world. I can't imagine any mother or father not understanding what a great sacrifice that was . . .

December 25, 1873 . . .

Christmas Day. And what a beautiful day it has been. I am going to try my best to put everything down just as it happened, for I never want to forget this day. I recall Mama saying that life isn't measured by the breaths we take . . . but by the times that take our breath away. And this day, little journal, was one of those breathtaking times.

Jack and Lillie were the first to arrive, then Gale, looking a bit shy but expectant, too, like he was hoping to see something he had only dreamed of before. Jessie and her children and grandchildren were next, with Peach, Medicine Weasel, and One Shot following close behind. But it was Preacher and Willa's entrance that gave us such a surprise, for they had brought Mr. Audrey and the twins with them!

"I hope you don't mind, Callie," Willa said, taking me off to one side as we watched our men greeting a slightly dazed-looking Mr. Audrey. "But when we went by to check on them, Percy broke down to Shawn, saying Leah seems to have gone for good, and all I could think of was that poor man and those girls being alone on Christmas."

We watched Rose and Mercy take the twins' hands and lead them up to the loft, chattering happily . . . but I couldn't help noticing how thin and drawn the girls looked, their pretty blonde hair usually so well kept like their mama's. Today they looked frowzied, like they had just woke up.

"Mind?" I said, smiling grimly. "Shame on me for not think-ing of it myself." Lillie and Jessie had joined us by then, and they looked about the same as I felt. So we did the only thing we knew to do, and that was to try and make it as good a Christmas for them as we could.

As soon as the men headed for the barn to look after the horses, Jessie's girls, who are as tender-hearted as their mama, joined us as we moved the table in front of the fireplace, taking extra special care to set it quick with extra plates so they would feel they had been expected all along. I got out my best table-cloth, and Jessie and her girls went and fetched some pine snip-pings that Willa thought might look "festive" placed around the bowls and platters of food we had made. Then Lillie ran to her cabin and brought back two real pretty silver candleholders that, she told us with a chuckle, she'd won in a card game in Virginia City years ago.

"I always wondered why I carried them with me. Wondered what I would do with them out here," she said, shaking her pretty head. "Now I know they were meant for this day—to cheer Mr. Audrey and his girls."

Rose came down not long after that and took me to one side

to tell me she thought it would be a good thing if I gave her presents to the Audrey twins. "I don't mean to hurt your feelings, Mama," she said, solemn as a judge. "But I just figured they might get cheered up if they thought someone remembered them today . . . with their mama forgettin' and all." Mercy, who was standing behind her, nodded her agreement, then smiled.

I hugged my sweet little girl then and looked over at Willa and the rest of the women and saw we were all trying to blink back our tears.

Gale was next, bringing out a beautiful wooden cross carved with vines and flowers from behind his back. "Miss Callie, I carved this for you," he said, suddenly looking torn as to how to say what he needed to say. "I thought if you didn't mind, I would give it to Mr. Audrey. I remember you saying to keep our eyes fixed on the cross when we're troubled, and I thought maybe it might help him to have something to look at."

Patrick and John-Charles were so desperate by then to think of something to give they were offering their presents as well, but we told them the dolls were enough.

"I never seen a family like this in all my life," Willa said. "Too bad we're out in the middle of nowhere; the world could use a good dose of you all."

By the time the men hit the porch, stomping the snow from their shoes, we had the presents set out, the table ready, the candles lit . . . and a baby wild from trying to get out of her crib to reach all the "pretties."

"Mine!" Mara Lee yelled, clear as a bell, shocking us all before we burst out laughing. "That's our Bird," Patrick said, real proud, as he rubbed his hand over her curls.

But it was Mr. Audrey's astonished face that said it all as he looked in wonder at the spread before him. We had him and the girls open their gifts then, and I saw great tears come to his eyes as he pulled the brown paper off the cross Gale had so lovingly carved. The girls smiled sweet smiles, showing him the burlap dolls, then thanked us in such a grateful way, you would have thought they had been given a china doll like the ones in their mercantile. Rose and Mercy looked at each other, pleased as anything.

After Mr. Audrey hugged his girls, he turned and faced us again.

"First I thought we would be alone today," he started, then cleared his throat. "Then when Preacher and Miss Willa came by, I told myself that it would be good for the girls. But it's been real good for me, too, and I thank God for all of you today, for making us feel like part of your family."

"Be careful, Percy. They're real sneaky like that," Willa said then, trying to make him smile. "Look at me; I was happy living alone and being an independent divorcée who didn't believe in God. I start coming around this bunch, and the next thing you know I'm engaged—to a preacher!" We all laughed at that—even Percy.

Preacher just shook his head as we were seated and said wryly, "I can't imagine a better time to begin a prayer."

Such a good prayer it was, too. I don't think I'll ever forget the laughter around our table or the love. Or the way Percy and his girls looked as they finally waved their good-byes to us. Medicine Weasel explained it best as he stood next to me and Quinn on the porch and watched them go.

"Grandfather is giving him new pieces now, to replace the ones he lost," he said, then he turned from us and, without another word, shuffled slowly back to his little lodge in the snow.

Rose and Patrick were so excited from the day that we could hardly get them to sleep tonight. Rose had to tell me how glad she was that Mercy liked the sampler she had done for her—the one that made all of us laugh so hard, our stomachs hurt: "Better love hath no woman," it read, "than to cut off her hair for a friend." Patrick opened and shut his treasure box so many times, I thought the lid would come off. Then he said something that nearly brought both Quinn and me to tears.

We were tucking him in, and just as I got the blanket under his chin, he looked up at me, his eyes wide in the dark. "Mama," he said, "did Mary kiss baby Jesus when he was born?" and when I told him yes, he nodded and then seemed to think of something else.

"I wonder if she knew she was kissing God when she did that," he said, his voice trailing off sleepily, and Quinn and I just looked at each other in wonder.

"Just when I think I know their minds . . . ," Quinn said, grinning.

Once we were downstairs again, Quinn gave me the surprise he had been hiding away all this time. Well, actually it was from him *and* Jessie. Quinn had made a beautiful frame, carved with vines and curlicues, to hold a sweet memory quilt Jessie had made me, much like the ones she and Lillie had made for themselves, each scrap taken from a piece of my life. Jessie had sewn the memories together, I thought, looking at the tiny, intricate stitches, like a quilt of words.

I gave Quinn the shirt I'd made him, and he went on and on about it, like it was the best he ever had. Then we grinned at each other and hugged, sitting in front of the fireplace with our heads together like two little kids.

"I wish Mr. Audrey had what we do, Quinn," I said after a while, for some reason the memory of Percy's sweet face coming before me. Quinn turned and looked at me then, and I saw he had been thinking of Percy, too.

"I do, too, lass," he said. "I wish it for him *and* for his girls."

As I sit here writing this, I can't help wondering what could ever possess a mother to leave her children like that. Quinn says that's why she could leave, because she *wasn't* a mother, but I have this niggling suspicion there's more to it than that . . .

Funny, those words of Jessie's from that dream I had keep coming back to me as I write this: "Pray, and the good Lord will do the rest. He always does . . . "

I do pray for that poor family . . . and for Leah Audrey, too. I wonder where she is on a night when being with family seems to matter so much.

December 29, 1873 . . .

Willa came tonight to deliver some news, and my mind just refuses to believe it. She said Mrs. Audrey is on her way to Missouri . . . to be put in *jail*. Willa said Percy came to ask her if she would watch the girls while he went to see what happened, and she told him she would. It seems he got the news from a man that had come into the mercantile saying he'd been to Virginia City and had seen an old woman pointing out Mrs. Audrey on the street. The man said she had been standing just a hair's distance from him. He said he saw the marshal's men come right for her and waste no time in apprehending her—and that she had begged him to tell her husband what had happened and that they were taking her back to Missouri. The man didn't know much more than that . . .

Even if there was more, I don't think I could write it. Now that Willa is gone, the only thing I can think to do is pray for them all while I wait for Quinn to come back from checking on the cattle.

I feel like that strange dream I had has come true . . . Only it's not a dream. It's a nightmare . . . especially for poor Percy and his girls.

And Mrs. Audrey . . . Is she scared? Is she looking out at the cold night sky tonight, thinking of her husband, of her little girls?

I can't help but wonder.

December 30, 1873 . . .

The sky is such a vivid blue this morning, the mountains rising up so sharp and clear in the distance, that I feel like we've woke up in another place. But the pitiful bawling of the cattle tells me we haven't.

Quinn just left to go check on them with Patrick and Gale trailing behind him while Jack and John-Charles tend the horses. Rose will be in soon from milking Tulip, and I plan to put her straight to work helping me get the bread started—and anything else I can think of to keep her busy.

"Our Rose finds out about Mrs. Audrey, and there will be no end to it," Quinn said just before he left, the look on his face somewhere between a grin and a grimace, and I know he is right.

He was also right when he said we all need to stand in prayer for *all* the Audreys. Good or bad, he said, we're a community now, a church family, and we have to stick by each other in times of trouble.

We gathered at our cabin tonight to pray for the Audreys, Quinn being the one to go round up the troops after the work was finished. As I watched them all file into our cabin behind Quinn, I couldn't help feeling so blessed to have a husband like him, so willing to do what he felt the Lord expected of him.

Before we started praying, though, he sat Rose down with the other children and explained to them what had happened.

And just as he predicted, no sooner was the sad story out of his mouth than a spark of "I told you so" lit up Rose's eyes.

"Now, Rosie," Quinn said in a gentle but firm voice, "we don't know the full reason of it yet, and what we are here to do tonight is pray for *all* of them. Do you understand?"

Rose nodded silently, her love for her pa outweighing her urge to crow. Quinn recognized the urge, though, and I saw him steel himself against smiling. Then he turned to the rest of the children, who were watching him and Rose with wide, serious eyes. Jessie, Lillie, and I looked at each other and smiled.

"I want you all to listen to the Lord's Word I'm about to read. And maybe you'll understand better what God says we are supposed to do," he said. Then he sat down next to me, bowing his large frame over the Bible in his work-worn hands as he slowly turned the pages.

"I came across this scripture this morning in First Corinthians, and I thought it fitting," Quinn said, looking up from the Bible to all of us in the room. Everyone nodded quietly, and he began to read: "'And those members of the body, which we think to be less honourable, upon these we bestow more abundant honour; and our uncomely parts have more abundant comeliness. For our comely parts have no need,'" Quinn read softly. "'But God hath tempered the body together, having given more abundant honour to that part which lacked. That there may be no schism in the body; but that the members should have the same care one for another.'" Quinn looked up, and I saw Jessie's eyes meet with his. She smiled, finishing the scripture for him:

"'And whether one member suffer, all the members suffer with it,'" Jessie recited, tears in her eyes but her face aglow with the soft smile of a woman who had lived by those very words. Then she looked at her children. "'Or one member be honoured, all the members rejoice with it.'"

Jessie's daughters, Sara and Rachel, were dabbing their eyes with their handkerchiefs. Even their husbands were blinking hard, but Jessie's son, Jonah, allowed his tears to run free down his face as he smiled at us all.

"And that's why they call him, 'the First and the Last,' 'cause there ain't *never* gonna be another talk such as that," Jonah said with deep sincerity.

Jack cleared his throat, and I saw him glance over to John-Charles, then to Medicine Weasel, and he said, "And there ain't no one better than him that listens, either."

We joined hands then, and as we did, I felt as if we were knitted together by more than just our hands but by our spirits, too; each of us *had* been where the Audreys were now, maybe not in the same way . . . but we all knew what it was like to suffer. And we all knew how good it felt to know God was holding our hand through that suffering in the form of another person who believed.

Quinn began the prayer, each of us adding to it as we felt led, when suddenly I heard Rose's small voice saying, "And, dear Lord, forgive me for my mean thoughts. I don't know if Mrs. Audrey really is the fearless Banditti of the Plains, but whatever she's done mean, well, I've done mean, too. So I'm asking you to help her like you've helped me and just about everyone else here, too."

Quinn and I smiled at each other, and we all said amen. When I looked up I saw Gale was smiling at Rose, too, like he couldn't believe she could surprise him again. Patrick saw the look and nodded like he understood.

"She's pretty smart, Gale," he said with all of the well-earned wisdom of a brother who has endured. Then he added, " . . . when she wants to be."

December 31, 1873 . . .

Another cold but sunny day. Could it be God's way of telling us we are on the verge of a bright New Year? I would like to think so.

It seems so much has happened since I started this little journal, and it hasn't yet been a full year. When I think on it, we've come so far in such a short time—more than I could have imagined, and I have a pretty healthy imagi-nation. We *have* seen some bad times, but we've also seen so much good. Most of all, we've learned more about holding on to our faith and about seeing with our own eyes the promise of God's hand move because of it.

This afternoon, while I was watching Mara Lee sleeping, I started thinking about all the times when I was just a young girl imagining what it would be like to be a mother and a wife. It got me to thinking so much that I went and pulled out my old jour-nal—the first one I ever kept. And as I was thumbing through the pages, I came to an entry I had wrote just before we had left our farm in Missouri to set out on that wagon train for Califor-nia. "With age comes wisdom and virtue," I read. And I admit I had to chuckle.

What eighteen-year-old girl knows of such things? I guess back then I thought I already had life figured out . . .

You know what I think now, little journal?

What a blessing it was that I didn't . . .

January 1, 1874 . . .

I woke up this morning to my husband and children standing over the bed with the biggest grins on their faces.

"Say it, Bird," Patrick said suddenly, looking over at Mara Lee, who was planted happily in Quinn's arms. She looked from Patrick to Rose to Quinn, then finally she looked at me and grinned, too.

"Mah-mah!" she said just as plain as if she had been saying it forever. We all laughed as I struggled to sit up in the bed. Then it hit me that it was still much too early for them all to be up—either that, or I had overslept for the first time in my life. I started to throw the covers back then, but Quinn stopped me.

"Mara Lee was just the beginning of your surprise. We didn't even plan that part," he said happily, looking to Rose and Patrick.

"We already made you breakfast, Mama," Rose blurted out, unable to contain herself. "And then you get to do any old thing you feel like. And not chores, either. Pa says this is *your* day to play."

"You can even use my treasure box if you want to, Mama," Patrick offered in a gesture of extreme sacrifice.

"We just wanted to say we love you, Callie," Quinn said, and Mara Lee clapped and said, "Mah-mah!" again.

What I did next, I think any normal mother of three children, living on a ranch out in the middle of nowhere, would do. I took one long look at my sweet, loving family and promptly burst into tears.

I have just come back in and have so much to tell. But first I want to say how grateful I am to have such a family as mine. I will never forget the looks on their faces as they sent me off for a visit to Willa's today, so happy over what they had done that you would have thought it was for them, not me.

Quinn secured the runners onto the wagon and hitched the team as Gale, happy to be a part of it, packed the front seat with hot, flat rocks covered with straw, then Rose and Patrick topped me off with a goodly amount of blankets to make sure I stayed warm, and off I went.

Never had the cold felt so good as I watched the beauty of the snowy landscape go by me: the immense trees bowing low with ice and snow that sparkled in the sun . . . the way the valley rolled and swelled white all the way up to the mountains, no other sound but the steady drum of the horses' hooves as we wound around the long trail that led out of the valley. And the more I rode along, the more I got to thinking I needed to go see Peach instead of Willa.

To say God was with me is an understatement, for I only had a vague idea of where his cabin was from listening to Jessie's children talking of it. Even now, I can't really explain it, but I just knew that was where I wanted to go.

Finally, after what seemed like hours, I came to a short clearing and spotted a small cabin a little farther up the slope in the woods with smoke trailing from the chimney. I turned the team in that direction and had only climbed halfway up the slope when I saw Peach come out on the porch with his rifle at his side.

"Are ya friend or foe?" he hollered, squinting at me.

I said, "I'm Callie!" then laughed, and I heard him chuckle, too.

"Well, that makes all the diff'rence in the world," Peach said. "Light from yer wagon and come set a spell." And so, as soon as he had turned my horses into his barn, that's just what I did. I'll say, too, I was pleasantly surprised to see that the inside of Peach's cabin wasn't what I expected it to be. First of all, it was cleaner than I ever saw a single man's cabin to be. Whether it had come from Peach's new turn of heart or had always been that way didn't seem to matter as I sat on the chair Peach pulled next to the fire for me. I glanced around the cabin and noticed that Peach's little bed was covered with the whitest sheet I'd ever seen. On the other side of the room was a sturdy rough-hewn wooden table with a single chair, but what really got my attention was the little cracked jar filled with what looked to be nearly a dozen faded paper roses.

While I rested with a cup of coffee in front of the fire, Peach set about fixing us some "vittles," and while he did, we talked small talk. Or I should say Peach talked. He told me how he'd left his home in "Virginny" after the war and had come west to look for gold, but after nearly starving to death he'd decided it was easier to find game than gold. He said that all the years of trapping ended up bringing him more money than he would ever need.

"Thing is, money don't make fer good company," he said, shaking his head. There was something about the painful look to his eyes that told me then that he had suffered more than his fair share of loneliness, and that's when I knew I had been right to follow my feelings and come.

"No, it doesn't," I said. "But friends do, if you let them."

Peach looked at me with a hopeful expression on his face. Then, after a pause long enough to take a breath, he asked me if I had heard about the Audreys. I told him yes, and he went on to tell me he'd heard about it when he went into town and "jes happened upon Widow Spence," who had heard it from Mrs. Pumphrey, who had been told by Percy himself, according to Peach.

As Peach handed me a steaming plate of his green-corn pudding and bachelor biscuits, I caught him studying me for a long moment. Then he went over to the little makeshift cupboard in the room and took what looked to be an old, faded piece of advertisement from one of the drawers.

"Now, I ain't showed a livin' soul this-here piece until you, Miss Callie," he said gravely. "But I figger it's time someone knowed of it." He handed me the paper, and when I looked at it, I saw Mrs. Audrey's face staring back up at me underneath the large black lettering that said she was "wanted." The paper said she had done "heinous" crimes not fitting to a person of her gender and was wanted for further questioning as to the whereabouts of a gentleman who was last seen in her company. After I got over my shock, I asked him where he had got it, and he told me he had come across it by way of an old half-crazy woman who sold paper roses on the streets of Virginia City. He said he always tried to buy a rose from her when he went to town but that the last time she had sold him his rose, she told him she wanted to show him a picture of her "daughter." She had opened up the piece of paper I now held and laughed a crazy laugh. "She ain't really my daughter," she'd said. "But she could've been." He said he had to buy nearly her whole lot of paper roses to get the wanted poster from her. Then he worried after he got home that she might have had other copies of it anyway.

"Leah Audrey was mostly mean as a snake, as fer as I kin recall," he said then. "But I figgered that man of hers was good and them little ones shouldn't have to pay for what she'd done. I never knowed my own ma, her dyin' right after I was born . . . but I always kindly imagined that I would've liked t' have knowed her . . . "

He had such a wistful look about his craggy face that I wanted to rush over and hug him. But knowing Peach, I resisted . . . for another moment or so. Then, unable to bear it, I did rush over and hug him. He looked startled at first, then he looked pleased as anything, a bright grin spreading across his face to show his fine, white teeth.

"Why, Miss Callie, I believe that's about the best thing that's happened t' me in a long time," he said. "That feller of your'n said I didn't know what I was missin', but now I think I do."

We both laughed again, but soon afterward we noticed the sun on its way down, and I was forced to leave the warmth of the little cabin to make my way back home. Peach hitched the team for me then said he would escort me most of the way back, being that I "was a lady and all." We rode in silence almost the entire way home, until we reached the head of the trail that led into our valley. Then I saw Peach pull back on his horse and look back at me as he waited for me to catch up.

"Ya know what's funny?" he said, when I finally reached him. "I was jes wishing earlier t'day that I could have me some comp'ny. And here you showed up at my door . . . How's that for a wish comin' true?"

"Did you ever think God might have heard you wishing?" I said, suddenly realizing my urge to go to Peach had been just that. "Sometimes a wish can sound just like a prayer if Someone's listening just right."

Peach looked at me real thoughtful-like, then he smiled, and I couldn't help but smile back.

"No, I never did consider such a thing," he said finally as he turned his horse away to leave. "But I might jes have t' think on that tonight, Miss Callie. I might jes have t' think on it."

I watched him ride away until he was long out of sight, and as I did, I couldn't help thinking how looking at Peach, you would never know the heart that lay inside him. How a man that most wouldn't give the time of day to had took it upon himself to try to protect a wanted woman for the sake of her husband and two little girls . . . Then I looked down at the faded poster Peach had given me, and I realized something.

I realized what the Good Book meant about being as wise as a serpent but as gentle as a dove, because people can fool you. And sometimes that's a good thing, to find out you were wrong. But there were times, too, that it was bad.

Percy Audrey was on my mind through the rest of the evening, but I waited until after the children's bedtime to show the rest of the family the wanted poster Peach had given me. The first thing Quinn said was, "Next time you decide to go on a spur-of-the-moment adventure, can you at least let me know where you're off to?"

"Well now, Quinn, how would that be spur of the moment

then?" Jack said, winking at me. Then he motioned to the loft above where Rose and Patrick were sleeping. "Apple never does fall too far from the tree, does it, sis?" and everyone had a good laugh at that.

But then, as the paper got passed from hand to hand and I began to tell them all that Peach had said, the room got quiet, and I sensed everyone was wondering what would become of Percy and the twins.

"Why, Jack, you know who Peach was talking about?" Lillie said, looking up after a while. "It was Alder Rose. I used to watch her from the window of my room as she walked the streets. I haven't thought of that poor woman in such a long time." Lillie shook her head, then she turned to look at me. "How strange is it that Mrs. Audrey would end up being caught by the words of a crazy woman no one ever paid much attention to?"

"Well, the Bible says the Lord will use the foolish things to confound the wise," Jessie said slowly. "An' I've lived long enough to quit tryin' to figure out his ways of things because they's always turned out better'n mine in the end."

Medicine Weasel, who had been quiet up to that point, spoke up, surprising us all. All but Jack, that is.

"What was it you told me about falling on your back, Jack Wade?" he asked with a thoughtful look to his face, and I saw a light come into Jack's eyes as he smiled at his old friend.

"I said that sometimes when you're knocked flat on your back, you don't have no other choice than to look up," Jack said, looking around the room. "Maybe that's what God's doing with Leah Audrey. Maybe he's lettin' this happen now so she'll look up again."

"It's not a bad view," Medicine Weasel replied casually, then he glanced my way with a smile. "Once you decide to open your eyes to look."

We prayed again for the Audreys not long after that, all of

us agreeing it was the right thing to do, no matter what Mrs. Audrey had been accused of. Then we talked until long into the night about our own lives and how it amazed us all, looking back, to see God's hand at work in us all along the way. And now that I'm sitting here, pen in hand, I can't help wonder at the way this day turned out . . . All from me getting the simple urge to go see Peach instead of Willa.

Only something tells me now, that urge wasn't so simple.

January 2, 1874 . . .

We had a warm Chinook wind blow in overnight, but like Jack likes to say, she's a fickle lady, and she proved him right, changing her mind on me shortly after I hung the clothes out to dry. I had only been back in the cabin maybe an hour when a north wind suddenly came sweeping down the valley with no warning, freezing my laundry solid as rocks.

Willa showed up not long after I had come in with the clothes. She took one look at the shirts and trousers standing on their own by the fireplace and grinned.

"I never heard of a clothes graveyard," she said, "but I have the eeriest feeling I'm looking at one now."

"'Tis enough to spook a man, is what it is," Quinn said, grinning as he finished stoking the fire for me. Then he turned to the Audrey twins and told them the other children were down at the barn, looking over the new colt, and they scampered out. Quinn waved a quick wave to us and headed out the door, too.

"Cattle?" she said.

"Cattle," I answered, and we both laughed and sat at the kitchen table for coffee while Mara Lee napped.

I admit I didn't waste much time before I pulled out the paper with Mrs. Audrey's picture on it and showed it to her. Willa looked shocked, then grim.

"I had a feeling it was bad," she said, then sighed. "What is

Percy going to *do*? How's he going to explain this to the girls?" No sooner had those words come out of Willa's mouth than we felt a cold breeze of air come through the room and turned to see Rose, Mercy, Zora, and Nora standing a short distance away, their smiles wavering as they tried to figure out what was going on. I noticed both Zora and Nora's eyes go to the paper in Willa's hands.

"My father has one of those," Zora said then. "He said it was a joke."

I saw Nora glance uncertainly at her sister then back to us. "Our mother is in trouble, isn't she?" she said, then promptly burst into tears.

Willa left with the girls not long after that, trying to comfort them as best as she could. Then I tended to our own girls. As soon as Quinn came in, we all prayed together as a family— a prayer as much for us as it was for them—and as we did, every one of us felt a peace come over us like a balm to soothe our troubled minds.

"'Tis the peace that passeth all understanding," Quinn called it before he went off to bed. And he is right, because there is so much I don't understand right now.

Like how Percy Audrey could have known that his wife was *wanted*. I just can't imagine it . . .

Lord, I won't pretend to understand what is happening because I don't. But I do know that you are with us more than ever after feeling your peace come over me tonight . . . come over us all. I just wish I could know your thoughts . . . My mama used to say there was reasons for everything, and I sense there is a reason for all this to be happening, too. I pray that you show us what to do to truly be of help . . . that your will be done. I always have made such a mess of things doing it my way, so I'm asking you to take my will and replace it with your own.

Because that's the only way I can see anything good coming out of this.

January 3, 1874 . . .

I just woke up from a dream . . . I can't recall the dream now, but there was a line of Scripture I was whispering as I opened my eyes: "The steps of a good man are ordered by the LORD: and he delighteth in his way. Though he fall, he should not be utterly cast down. . . . "

I'm not sure what it means, but I do have the feeling right now to stand in the gap for Percy and pray. So, Lord, hear my prayer this morning and send your Holy Spirit to minister to that sweet man . . . to strengthen him. And if he falls, give him a hand back up in the way that only you know how to do . . .

January 7, 1874 . . .

It's storming this morning. The oddest weather I've ever seen—not that I haven't ever seen a storm. But this one is different somehow. Despite the cold there's a feeling of heat in the air. Lightning is flashing in wide swipes across the sky, hovering low over the mountains as its bony fingers reach into the valley here. You can see the clouds lighting up from time to time, and it makes you crane your neck to look. It's like there's something mysterious going on just beyond what you can see.

Medicine Weasel and One Shot are watching it, standing just outside their lodge . . . I see Gale, too, standing in the doorway of the bunkhouse, looking up in awe.

It reminds me of something I heard one time, that whenever we see a storm flashing in the sky, that is when the angels are doing battle for us.

January 25, 1874 . . .

Our Sabbath, and if ever there was a group in need of hearing God speak to us and uplift our weary spirits today, it was us.

Preacher knew it, too, for he had seen the way the last couple of weeks of never-ending rain had sapped all our strength. Just before his sermon, I told him what I had thought that first day, when the lightning had come like it did, and he looked at me for a long moment then said, "Remember, Callie: Sometimes the battle is short, and sometimes it's long—or longer than what we'd like it to be. But the one thing I've noticed is, the longer the battle, the more of God's amazing work is revealed when we come out on the other side."

I thought about that, too, as I took my seat with the others and watched as Preacher made his walk to the front of the tent. Once he was situated, he looked up and smiled at us, then he leaned forward on his podium and clasped his hands together (lions' paws, Stem always called them), making us feel like he was getting ready to share some secret we had never heard before.

"I'm just wondering," he said slowly as he looked around the room. "Is there anyone else here but me who would like to see a little sunshine in their lives?"

"Did Noah?" an old miner yelled from the back, and everyone chuckled at that, even Preacher.

"Why, yes, he did. And now that you mention it, Noah had to wait fourteen days after the flood had receded before he got some good news," Preacher said as a wide grin began to spread across his face. "And here I've only made you wait until Sunday."

Everyone chuckled again, and I felt the mood starting to lift amongst us as Preacher's face grew serious with what he was setting forth to say.

"Scripture says, 'He maketh his sun to rise on the evil and on the good, and sendeth rain on the just and on the unjust.' Have you ever thought about what that means? For a long time, every time I would read that scripture I would just concentrate on the *rain* part of it, thinking it meant that God sends his *rain* down on us all." Preacher smiled. "But I was wrong.

"Because if you look at what it's really saying, it's that God

142

is a nurturer. The world's farmer, you might say. And because he has yet to separate those who walk with him from those who don't, he won't withhold those things . . . because he wants *his* crops—his people and those who are to be his—to grow."

People were nodding all over the tent by then, and Preacher stepped away from the podium to get closer to us.

"Listen: It's going to take some sun and some rain, too, for any seed planted to struggle free from the earth. And then it's going to take a little more to keep it growing strong. It's the same with us.

"Except our sun and rain are our faith.

"That mustard seed of faith you have in your heart right now, who do you think planted it? And how do you think it's going to grow?" Preacher looked around again, studying the faces of the crowd.

"It's Jesus that is our light, our pure water. Jesus said it himself: 'If anyone is thirsty, let him come to me and drink.' The more we accept him into our lives, little by little, the more that seed is going to grow, going to take root . . .

"That mustard seed of faith," Preacher said again, a soft smile coming to his face, "is the least of all seeds; but when it is grown it is greater than the herbs and becomes a tree.

"Have any of you seen a mustard seed? The funny thing is, if you ever have, you'd never imagine the huge tree it grows into. You couldn't imagine it.

"But God could . . . God *did*.

"Folks, there is so much he has planted in you, so much he wants to see take root and grow. But there is going to be a struggle. There are going to be times when you think you'll never be able to reach hard enough or high enough to feel the warm touch of his light."

Preacher paused then, his eyes moving over our heads to the back of the tent. "But you *will* feel his light," he said finally, a look of compassion spreading across his handsome face. "And when you do, you will bloom into that tree you were always meant to be."

More than a few of us turned around then, and that's when we saw Percy Audrey standing at the back of the tent, looking like he was trying his best not to cry.

We all stayed behind in the tent after everyone else had left, knowing without really talking amongst ourselves that Percy needed our support.

As I watched Zora and Nora run to him, for a brief instant I could have sworn I saw Peach trailing out of the tent with the others, too. But the crowd started pressing forward to leave, and my attention was soon turned back to Percy, who had joined us in the front.

Percy tried his best to put on a good face. He said Leah had to stay behind in Missouri for a while to "clear up some matters." Then he tried his best to smile, but we could all see it was a great effort for him to do so. "A case of mistaken identity, I'm sure," he added, avoiding our eyes.

"They saw the paper with Mother's picture on it," Nora blurted out to him, unable to bear the war she saw going on in her pa, and that's when the mask he had tried so hard to keep on began to crack. His smile began wavering until, without warning, he broke down, crying, in front of us all. When he was finally able to be led to a chair, he sat down shakily and began to really talk.

He said he had known she was wanted before they even married, that he'd found the poster with her picture on it in Helena. "I thought if she just had a chance at a different life . . . I thought she just needed a chance," he said, looking around with a lost look on his face. "I've been so alone with this."

"You're not alone any longer, Mr. Audrey. We've been praying for you for a *long* time," Mercy said, sidling up next to him as the twins fairly clung to him on the other side. Then she took his hand in her own and patted it, and I saw Percy look down at her and smile sadly.

"I prayed, too," Percy said. "But it seemed the more I prayed, the meaner she got." He shook his head sadly.

"God hardened her heart, Mr. Audrey," Rose suddenly piped up. "Remember, he hardened Pharaoh's heart so he'd get in trouble and have to listen. I bet that's what he's done with Mrs. Audrey; he's hardened her heart, and now she's gonna have to listen."

"Rose!" I said, looking over at Quinn, who was just as shocked as I was. Patrick, Gale, and John-Charles started to edge away, sensing trouble was coming, but Preacher held his hand up.

"Now, she might have a point," he said gently. He looked at Rose, who was fairly beaming at her rescuer, and smiled before he went on. "Sometimes it takes things like this for people to come back to God—if they do at all." Preacher looked over at Percy then. "And sometimes it takes things like this for people to understand who God is—and who they are to him."

We all left for home not long after that, bundling up and climbing into our wagons for the long ride, and I can honestly say I don't think any of us said much to each other on that ride home. I think we were all thinking of what Preacher had said in his sermon about growing and about questioning whether this was part of the struggle. But most of all, I think we were thinking about what Preacher had said at the end, that sometimes it takes things like this for people to come back to God—if they do at all. And maybe we were wondering what would become of Percy and the twins when all was said and done.

I know *I* was wondering about all of it.

January 26, 1874 . . .

What a good day Rose and I have had together, one I will remember for a long time—and I hope she does, too.

It all started as we were doing yet another load of wash this morning, mainly Rose's pinafores and cambric drawers—the latter had been white only once. And that was before the first time she had put them on. Day after day of planting herself astride the top rail of the corral had permanently stained them with pine pitch, and we were having a time of it, trying to get them clean. I had said something to the effect of wondering why in the world a girl her age would spend hours perched on a rail like that, when she stopped scrubbing for a moment and gave me a thoughtful look.

"You ought to try it sometime, Mama," she said, smiling. "It's the best seat to see things in all the ranch." I don't know if it was her smile or the twinkle in her eye or remembering the sadness of Percy and his girls, but suddenly I heard myself saying, "Let's rinse these and go then. Just you and me."

"It'll be our secret?" she asked, and when I said yes, she fairly beamed. Soon we were on our way, dropping a happy Mara Lee into Jessie's arms then turning to walk arm in arm the rest of the way down to the corrals.

We took our seats, arranged our coats around us, and for a good long while we watched life go by. We laughed together over the antics of the new foal. We watched Jack and John-Charles work on a green-broke horse. Then we witnessed Quinn, Patrick, and Gale coming down a steep slope, the immense mountains framing their silhouettes as they brought a sickly cow in, puffs of snow flying up from the horses' hooves as the sound of their voices mingled in the air, and I felt like I was seeing my family for the very first time.

"You were right, Rose," I said, hugging her to me. "This *is* the best seat to see things in all of the ranch."

I feel nearly froze solid now that we're back inside. But to see the look of happiness such a simple thing like today has put into my little girl's eyes has made it well worth it.

Mara Lee is finally asleep after nearly terrorizing us at dinner tonight. Every time one of us would try to talk, she would launch into what Patrick calls her "Bird chatter," trying to outtalk us in jabbering—not to mention volume. Gale thought it was just the funniest thing. But then, Gale seems to find anything our family does fascinating. I think he's been so very alone in this world until he came here . . .

Patrick is reading the book Gale passed on to him after dinner, *Around the World in Eighty Days*, written by someone called Jules Verne. Rose is writing in her own little journal tonight, scribbling away. I just asked her how she liked Sunday school yesterday.

"Fine, Mama," she said in her cheerful little voice then went back to scribbling.

Then Quinn asked her, "What is it you're writing about, fair Rose?" and she looked up at him, great serious eyes much like his own. "I'm writin' about what's been happenin'," she said. Then she cocked her head to one side, looking between us. Finally she looked directly at me and smiled. "Every once in a while things can get real interestin' around here."

"I'm glad we can oblige you, lass," Quinn said earnestly, but after Rose nodded and went back to her writing, his eyes met mine, and I could see the laughter in them . . . and the love . . .

My cup runneth over, Lord.

January 29, 1874 . . .

Back to work again today. I've swept, dusted, and made breakfast, and now it's nearly time for lunch. Just stirred the stew. The cornbread is ready. Rose churns, singsonging to Mara Lee, "Come butter, come. Peter standing at the gate, waiting for a butter cake."

Mara Lee claps, looking so comical in the little coverall I sewed together from sugar sacks for her. She was having such a time of it with splinters constantly tormenting her knees from crawling like mad to see where everyone is going all the time that I had to do something. It seems to be working, saving both her knees and her clothes . . .

Patrick just came in with the men, took one look at Mara Lee, and laughed. "I can't wait till she gets older so I can tell her she wore gunny sacks for clothes," he said, and everyone laughed.

Everyone but Mara Lee, that is. She took one look at all of the laughing faces in the room and did something I'd never seen her do before. She puckered out her bottom lip and folded her chubby arms across her chest, refusing to look at them anymore.

Quinn says I may have saved her knees, but I've "wreaked havoc on her vanity."

The ladies of the ranch have been invited to Willa's for a little sewing get-together tomorrow. I, for one, am looking forward to it—I know the others are, too. It seems like it's been forever since we've gotten together with "just us girls" and had some normal conversation. With all that's went on lately, that will be a treat in itself.

January 31, 1874 . . .

Well, I've just come back from Willa's, and we did have a fine time of it—even if our conversation didn't end up being as normal as I had expected.

It was starting to snow a little when we were getting ready to head out, but Quinn and Jack thought quick and ran down to the river and cut some willow poles, fashioning a sort of covered wagon for us. Jessie's son, Jonah, filled the back of the wagon with some bluegrass hay, blankets, and a buffalo robe from Medicine Weasel. Then Gale volunteered to drive, so we all clambered into the back: me, Lillie, Jessie, and her two daughters, and off we went. I have to say, after we got going, I was glad for the snow, for it gave us a chance to laugh and talk the whole way over. It also gave us more of a chance to get to know Rachel and Sara better. Listening to them banter, it wasn't hard to see that the two sisters are just as sweet and funny as their mama.

By the time we reached Willa's place, we *all* felt like old friends. Willa, as always, was tickled to see company and ushered us in real quick, taking our thick shawls and scarves as she directed us to the table where the coffee and cake was waiting. Then she grinned at Gale, who was looking like a fish out of water, and told him there were books to be found on the table in her front room.

"Poor thing," Willa said, grinning. "He doesn't know it, but he's in for a long day." No sooner had she said that than there was another knock at the door, and in came Mrs. Pumphrey and Widow Spence. There was another round of greetings for Rachel and Sara, and I couldn't help thinking as we stood there, chatting to each other, that something had been mended between us all. Mrs. Pumphrey and Widow Spence, living in town as they did, had always been caught between Mrs. Audrey and the rest of us, and I saw the stress of that conflict was gone from their faces. I think Mrs. Pumphrey sensed it, too.

"It's good just to be in each other's company today, isn't it?" she said, smiling at us as she sat down with a huge sigh, and that seemed to be the sign for us all to pull our sewing from our bags.

"I guess Percy is in for a rough go of it," Mrs. Pumphrey said, as always getting right to the point. "It's almost unnatural to think of a man raising little ones on his own."

"Maybe he won't have to. Maybe those folks in Missouri will take pity on her being a mother and all," Widow Spence said shyly. She must have seen the doubt on our faces, for she ducked her head again to sew. "I just like happy endings, is all," she added softly.

Lillie and I smiled at each other, and I know it was because of the silent thought of Peach running through our minds.

"Well, the Lord works in mysterious ways, that's for sure," Jessie said, glancing to her daughters, who smiled back at her. "I never thought I'd see my babies again in my lifetime. And right here they are . . . all because of a letter . . . "

"Well, I'll be the first to say I can't imagine what will come of this mystery," Willa said. "But then, I couldn't have imagined Leah Audrey as a criminal, either. Mean maybe—but a *criminal?*" Willa shook her head.

"I never did understand why she was forever going on about that high-society family she came from," Mrs. Pumphrey said, shaking her head sadly. "I always said there were two things you didn't have to talk up: your blue blood or your faith. Because if you had a speck of either, it would show in you anyway."

"Maybe she was thinking those lies in her head was better than the truth," Lillie said then, looking around at us all with a thoughtful look on her face. "Maybe she thought if she said them enough, she would believe them as much as we did."

"I remember Jack saying once that you can run, but you just can't ever get far enough to get away from yourself," I said, and Jessie's daughter Rachel turned toward me with a considering look.

"Could be that this was the only way God could stop her running," she said, and her sister, Sara, nodded.

"And maybe that jail she's in will be the mirror she finally can't turn away from," Sara said, and I remember looking up, startled, when she said it, recalling months back feeling that God had been the mirror to my own fears . . .

"Percy told Shawn they think she poisoned the man she was married to before him—and Percy thinks she might have done it, too," Willa said hesitantly, like she was trying to decide how much to say. Finally she set her sewing in her lap with a sigh. "He said he had caught her about a year back sprinkling something over his food, and it hadn't set right with him. He said he started making his own meals after that, and that's when she got meaner."

"It's no wonder he was always acting like he was scared to death of her," Lillie said softly, her big, round eyes reminding me of Mercy's.

We all fell silent then, lost in the shock of what Willa had told us, trying to imagine what could ever cause a person to go so bad. Jessie was the one who finally broke the silence, sensing the thoughts on everyone's minds. "Don't matter how she got that way. What matters is the Lord has stopped her now," she said firmly. "And maybe because of that, Percy and them girls will have a chance."

"It's like what Preacher said, Mama," Sara said then. "Sometimes it takes things like this for people to understand who God is—and who *they* are to him."

Everyone nodded and picked up their sewing again, as if Sara's words had settled at least that much in our troubled minds. Soon enough, our talk turned to the building of the church, and a hopeful light came into Willa's eyes at the mention of it. It was the first time I could recall that she had asked for something so humbly as she did when she asked us then to pray for mild weather so Preacher could have the cut lumber delivered.

On the way home, as I thought of the hope Willa had for a new life with Preacher, I also thought of Percy Audrey and the life he was leaving behind. My mind turned back over the years of our knowing him as the kind, gentle soul that he was, but how we never had the chance to know much more than that. Then the idea struck me that, as bad as it looked, maybe this was a new wind blowing into Percy's life now, too. Maybe, I thought, we all might just get a chance to see the man God intended for him to be all along . . .

The mustard seed is the *least* of all seeds, Preacher had said, and I guess if people were to look at any one of us, that might be what they'd see, too: the least of all. But I remember what the Word says happens to that tiny seed: "When it is sown, it groweth up, and becometh greater than all herbs." It becomes a *tree*, Preacher said.

Quinn told me tonight he's had to put two more weak heifers in the calf corral to be fed, making it four now. "But I think our hay just might last until the snow goes off," he said with a note of relief. "Funny thing is, I thought this would be our worst winter for losses." He shook his head in wonder. "But so far it has turned out to be our best winter. Who would have ever thought?"

"Well, *God* would have," I said simply, and he looked at me for a long moment, then we started smiling at each other at the same moment.

February 4, 1874 . . .

Clear, cold day today . . . but calm, too. There's a stillness in the air that has everyone—including me—looking up to the sky from time to time as we work. It's like we all feel something is brewing.

I just pray it isn't more snow.

February 5, 1874 . . .

No snow has come—but we were surprised by both Willa and Peach showing up at the ranch today. I think we're even more surprised what's come out of the visit, though.

I'd heard the wagons and went to glance out the window to see who had come when I spotted Gale unhitching their teams for them. Then I saw them both turn and shuffle through the snow together toward our cabin, and I fairly ran to the kitchen to make sure I had some coffee and johnnycake to offer them. When I finally opened the door, they were both grinning.

"It looks like we both had the same idea," Willa said. "I was just telling Peach here that fine minds think alike."

"Well, I don't know 'bout that," Peach said, ducking his head, embarrassed, but it wasn't hard to see he was pleased, too. "I was just thinkin' mebbe we both had a hankerin' for comp'ny, is all."

Willa looked at Peach for a moment as we sat down at the table, then she said he was probably right about that, with Preacher still being gone and all. That's how the whole conversation about the church got started.

"Well, I bet he gits tired o' bein' away, too, Miss Willa," Peach said kindly, already reaching for his second piece of cake.

"Well, he doesn't complain," Willa said with a small smile. "But then, we're at the mercy of this weather, and how can you fight that?" She sighed. "It's like trying to wrestle the wind."

"Well, I don't know 'bout that, neither," Peach said, narrowing his eyes as he glanced at her sideways. Willa's philosophical side always made him uneasy. "But my grandpappy used t' say when there's a will there's a way, and he was 'bout the smartest feller I knew of. They don't give jes anyone *gradgiation* papers from the third grade, you know."

"Well, he sounds smart to me, Peach," I said, and Peach fairly beamed at me.

"He sounds smart to me, too," Willa said, grinning. "As far as *will*, we have that. It's just trying to figure out a *way* now . . ." Willa's voice trailed off, and no sooner than it did, Quinn and the children came tromping in for the noon meal. Pretty soon Jack and Lillie were there, too, after spotting Willa and Peach's rigs. Then Medicine Weasel and One Shot and Jessie and her family came, too—"To see what the ruckus was about."

By the time we had the meal prepared, the cabin was nearly bursting at the seams: children playing, men talking by the fire, Jasper on the lookout for anyone who hadn't taken his hat off while Honey lay curled up in the corner with her pups. It would be hard for anyone to imagine a clear thought coming out of the pandemonium at that moment—harder still to imagine the answer to the raising of our church coming from a confirmed "heathern" such as Peach—but it did.

In no time at all we had agreed on his plan to pitch in and start building—weather permitting or not. And I don't think any of us could be more excited about it. Except for maybe Willa, that is.

"Lunatics," she declared, sniffing to try to keep back the tears as she rocked Mara Lee. "But what would I ever do without you all?"

"Nodunt!" Mara Lee declared then, looking up at Willa with a grin, and we all laughed. Especially Willa.

"I guess that settles it then," she said wryly.

Quinn just told me that Gale has gone on to help Peach get started clearing the spot for the church and that he, Patrick, Jack, and John-Charles would meet them first thing in the morning to start felling the logs.

"What about me, Pa?" Rose said, looking crestfallen, and I heard Quinn go on to tell her that it was men's work and he was sure that once everything got started, there would be plenty of work for us to do, too. I saw right off that his explanation didn't set well with Rose, and I admit, it didn't set well with me, either.

"Oh, we're going, too, Quinn McGregor," I said, setting my pen down. "I didn't practically *walk* from Missouri to California, survive deaths, desert, and a mudslide for you to tell me I'm too *delicate* to help." Rose looked at me in awe then fairly beamed, and I saw Quinn grin, too, as he glanced over to Patrick.

"I guess she told me, didn't she, son?" he said, and Patrick nodded somberly as he fed more wood into the fire.

"You can't look them in the eyes, Pa," he said sympathetically. "I learnt that from Rose. If I don't let her see my eyes, then she can't guess how to get at me." He shook his head as he stood up and dusted his hands on his trousers. Then he added gravely, "If you don't learn that quick, you're done for."

We all laughed then—even Patrick—but only after he took a quick glance my way and smiled his best charming little smile at me . . .

Quinn came up and hugged me from behind as I was writing this, saying he should have known better than to expect me to stay home. Then he whispered into my ear, "Our little lad has a lot to learn still, as well," he said. "Because I knew I was *done for* the first time I laid eyes on you, lass. And I've never regretted it."

"I haven't, either," I said, pretending to busy myself with writing again. "Not much, that is," I added and managed to keep a straight face until I glanced over my shoulder at Quinn, and we both started to laugh.

February 6, 1874 . . .

"When God answers our prayers, he sure does it up right, doesn't he?" Jack said, grinning as we all packed for town this morning, and all of us couldn't agree more. We had all said we'd pray for good weather before bed last night, but the beauty before us was more than we could've hoped for: a warm, mild wind had came from out of the blue, blanketing the valley with a calm we hadn't felt in months as we watched the sun shoot through the gaps of the mountains, lighting up the sky with pinks and golds. Even Medicine Weasel and One Shot seemed to perk up as they trotted by on their horses to keep watch on the cattle while we were gone.

By the time we reached town, we were all in good spirits—especially Jack, who soon spotted Peach and Gale as we pulled our teams in just past the mercantile. It appeared Peach was having a time of it, getting his mules to listen. He was so engrossed in arguing with them that he didn't hear us clamber in behind him.

"Why, Peach, what are you doing in the middle of the road with a wagon full of brush?" Jack yelled, grinning, and we saw Peach startle, then he and Gale both looked over their shoulders at us.

"Well, I'm fixin' to git this church spot of your'n cleared if'n ya don't give me a heart failure first," Peach said grimly, and we all laughed, hopping down from the wagons to lend him a hand. Not long after we got Peach's wagon back on its way to dump the brush, I turned to see Percy watching us through the window of the mercantile.

Percy waved at us. Then, as if he'd made a sudden decision, he turned and disappeared from the window. The next thing I knew, he was crossing the street to meet us, Zora and Nora fairly running behind him to keep up.

"Peach told me what you all plan to do," he said, looking at each of us one by one. Then he cleared his throat. "The minute he said it, I got it in my mind that I need to donate any nails or tools or whatever other supplies you might need from the mercantile to get our church going. I suppose Preacher has made more of a difference in my life than he'll ever know, so me doing this is a small thing, compared to that."

"Mother is going to be livid if she finds out," Zora said suddenly as she came up from behind him, her pale brows creasing in a worried little frown. Percy turned to his daughter with a frown of his own.

"I think I know what I can donate and what I can't, Zora

Audrey," Percy said in a firm voice that none of us had ever heard before. "I ran this mercantile fine before your mother, and I will run it again."

I don't know exactly how to describe it, but when he said those words, I felt as if something had suddenly changed . . . as if Percy's life had taken a sudden new turn. I saw his girl Nora step forward then as if she sensed it, too, looking at her pa with a kind of newfound appreciation.

"Do you want me to help you load those things up, Father?" she said, and when he smiled and nodded yes, I saw Zora go over to help her sister, looking back over her shoulder at her pa with a thoughtful look.

"You're a good man, Percy Audrey," I said, turning back to him. "I just wish Leah would have seen that sooner."

"Oh, I haven't given up on her yet, Mrs. McGregor. I pray for her every day, just like I pray for me and my girls," he said. Then he crooked his finger for me to come closer, dropping his voice to a whisper. "I even mailed her one of them new Bibles we have in the mercantile . . . I guess it's up to her now, if she decides to read it."

There was such a hopeful look on his face after all that he had been through that I wanted more than anything for it to stay.

"That's the best reason I can think of for us to keep praying for her, don't you think?" I said, and Percy smiled a grateful smile at me.

"Yes ma'am, Mrs. McGregor," he said. Then Peach was there, arms folded across his skinny chest like a small general as he looked between the two of us.

"What are you two jawin' about while there's work to be done?" he asked with a spark of mischief in his eyes. I saw everyone turn back to look then as Lillie, Jessie, and her girls all exchanged amused looks.

"We were talking about praying," I said, crossing my own arms, and Peach couldn't help himself from grinning.

"You know, you and that family of your'n is about the pray-in'est bunch I ever did see," he said, shaking his head. Then he peeked up at the sky. "But it seems to be workin', and I ain't one to mess with success." He walked off, and the children scampered behind him, all talking a mile a minute, Mercy bringing up the rear, struggling to keep up as she pushed Mara Lee in her carriage.

"Percy, I just have one thing to say to you, now that we've endured a dressing down from Peach together," I said as we watched them go.

"What's that, Mrs. McGregor?" he said, glancing over at me with a sudden bit of anxiety on his face.

"Stop calling me Mrs. McGregor," I said in my best somber tone, and I saw Percy start to smile again. I smiled, too. Then we headed together up the small hill where Preacher's "tent of many colors" stood and joined hands with everyone to pray before we set to helping clear the spot nearby where our new church would stand.

Willa arrived not long after we had finished the clearing and was quick to pitch right in as we began set-ting down the stone foundation. Then suddenly Mrs. Pumphrey and Widow Spence were there, too, working right alongside of us, and as dirty and hard as the work was, none of us seemed to notice; we laughed and talked and sweated—and sometimes even groaned—while the men shook their heads, grinning as they stripped and notched the logs. But we placed that foundation together, stone by stone . . . and I couldn't help thinking as I looked around at all the tired, dirty faces—the faces of all of our children, of Jessie's children and grandchildren, too—that we had laid more than just the foundation for our church. Rose said it best when she scrambled into the back of the wagon at the end of the day with Patrick and Gale, her new honey-red hair peeking out beneath the handkerchief under her bonnet, her face streaked with dirt and grime.

"It's just like we're one big family now," she said happily, and I saw Gale look over at her and smile.

I am so tired tonight—we all are—but I couldn't help putting this to paper. We will be back to town again come morning for another day of work. But today . . . Today was the beginning, and I don't ever want to forget it.

February 7, 1874 . . .

Dawn is peeking up over the mountains, and we will be leaving soon. There is a chill in the air that wasn't there yesterday, but it hasn't dampened anyone's spirits, judging from the talk and laughter going on just outside as the men get the wagons ready. And now Mara Lee is up.

I pray you prosper us in our work this day, Lord, and that you lead us in all that we do . . .

We have just come home, and I guess the only way I can describe this day is to say it went from good to bad to good again . . .

We had just half of the shell of the church stacked, pleased that the logs were fitting so snug in place while the children ran about with shiny new buckets from the mercantile, gathering up sticks and woodchips that would fill the gaps before the chinking, when a freak storm blew in out of nowhere. First cold rain, then sleet, then finally snow, all in a matter of minutes as we tried to pack our wagons. Then Percy was yelling in the midst of it all for us to take cover in the mercantile, and so we did, dripping wet and shivering as we filed into the store. It was no time at all before Percy got the stove going full strength, and we all helped each other peel the layers of clothes from the children first then tended to ourselves in a kind of disappointed silence.

"I had been hoping Shawn would see it finished when he got back," Willa said finally, breaking the silence with what we had all been thinking ourselves as we sipped the hot cider Percy made for us.

I saw the children gather at the large window of the mercantile then, staring out into the storm, and I saw Patrick look over at Willa before he glanced down at Jessie's grandbaby Noel, who was holding his sister Clary's hand tight as he stared wide-eyed out the window.

"That sure is a beautiful church," Patrick said softly. "I like the way that chinking stands so white in the sun against the dark logs, the way the windows look so clean and sparkly . . . and look at that steeple with the cross on the top. I think Preacher's gonna love it, too."

"Can you see it?" he said, kneeling down next to Noel, who looked again and then nodded happily. I saw Gale and John-Charles move in closer to stand next to them then as they gazed out the window, too.

"I see it, Patrick. I think I've always seen it that way," Gale said, and they smiled at each other. John-Charles glanced from them back to the shell of the church and stared for a long moment. He was known for his honesty, so I knew he wouldn't say anything unless he was sure. Finally a look of relief crossed his face, and he nodded. "I see it," he said.

"I see it, too," Mercy said, bobbing her little head, her short blonde curls sticking out every which way from under her handkerchief. Then Rose, not to be left out, blurted out in her impulsive way, "Oh, I see it, too." But I saw her turn back when she thought no one was watching, squinting her eyes *just to be sure*, and we all smiled at each other. All except Willa, who was looking out the window with such a wistful look that I couldn't help thinking Patrick had helped her see the vision, too.

"Here it is," Quinn said then, causing us to turn, and I saw him sitting on a little stool, his large frame hunched over one of the new Bibles Percy had told me about. "I was just sitting here and for some reason, that story of Nehemiah came to mind." Quinn looked up at all of us for a moment. "I kept thinking how a lowly slave had such a heart to rebuild Jerusalem's gates that God gave him favor . . . so much that the king himself even gave him letters to get the timber he needed. And how he started to build in spite of everyone's doubts." Quinn smiled, wry-like. "And I remembered what happened next, how everyone and everything started coming against him. But most of all, I remembered what he said when that happened." Quinn ducked his head to read again: " 'The God of heaven, he will prosper us; therefore we his servants *will arise and build.*' "

Jessie and her children looked at each other with small smiles, nodding to themselves.

Then Patrick said, "What happened next, Pa?" and all the children (adults, too) moved closer to where Quinn sat. "Listen to this," he said, and he started reading again.

" 'So built we the wall; and all the wall was joined together unto the *half thereof*: for the people had a mind to work.' " Quinn looked up at the shocked faces of the adults and the puzzled faces of the kids and smiled again.

"What's that mean, Pa?" Patrick asked.

"It means they had the wall halfway built," Quinn said patiently, "about like our church is right now."

"And then what happened?" Patrick asked, knowing something good was coming.

"Then they were attacked again," Quinn said, "just as the gaps in the wall were beginning to be closed. But Nehemiah knew what to do . . . he prayed."

Then Quinn looked over at Patrick. "Because of his faith in

God, I imagine Nehemiah could see the wall finished before it really was—just like you're seein' our church."

Patrick smiled a shy smile, then we all joined hands—even Peach, who looked slightly dazed as Widow Spence took his hand in hers. Quinn began the prayer, and we each added to it as we felt led, even the little ones, and before long, we felt a new strength fill us . . . a kind of peace that told us we were going to finish our church.

I saw Jack and Lillie smiling at each other, and even Willa, who seemed so discouraged, perked up considerably after that, walking down the aisles and looking at goods as the storm raged around us outside.

"Why, Percy Audrey, you've been doing quite a bit of changing, from the looks of these cheap prices," Willa said at one point, dropping a tag from the bolt of goods she had been casually looking at. I saw, too, that Percy had been strengthened then, the way he didn't shy away from her words.

"Sometimes change is a good thing, Willa Cain. You of all people should know that," Percy said, drawing himself up to his full height. We all looked at Willa, whose brows were arched high like she couldn't quite believe what she'd heard.

"Well, it's about time," she said, then added, "You beat all, Percy." And when she started to laugh, we did, too. But it was the look on Peach's face I'll never forget, so thoughtful, as he glanced shyly Widow Spence's way before he turned to leave . . .

The storm blew over not long after that, and we all took our leave, waving to Percy and the girls, to Mrs. Pumphrey, and to Widow Spence as we headed out of town. It was a cold ride home, but the children were snug under the straw and blankets. And truthfully, I can't really remember much of the cold myself as I sat next to Quinn. But I do remember us talking nearly the whole way home about all that had happened and how faithful God was to put the story of Nehemiah on Quinn's heart to read.

"Do you know what's funny, Callie?" Quinn said. "From the time I started reading that scripture, I felt it lifting my spirits the same as the others."

"That's how God works," I told him, snuggling in closer to him as we finally made our way down the snaking road that led into our valley. And as I watched the light of the moon glancing off the snow-covered hillsides, I realized that something had changed in me, too. I realized it didn't matter anymore about the snow or the scorched earth beneath it. What mattered was I felt good coming home again.

I told Quinn that, and he wrapped an arm around me, hawing the team on toward the ranch, and even by the pale light of the moon I could see the quiet joy on his face. "That's how God works," he said finally.

February 8, 1874 . . .

Sabbath. The sky is dark gray, choked with snow clouds hanging down so low that you might think if you reached your hand up, you could touch them. But we are all determined not to concentrate on the clouds or the thought of more snow. Instead we try to keep our minds focused on the scripture Jack read to us from the Bible this morning, and such a beautiful scripture it is:

Let thy work appear unto thy servants,
and thy glory unto their children.
And let the beauty of the Lord our God be upon us: and establish
thou the work of our hands upon us;
yea, the work of our hands establish thou.
— PSALM 90:16–17

I'll never forget how Jack had looked up after reading that, how his eyes met Quinn's and they both smiled at each other—

or the look on Jonah's face, his eyes closed and such a sweet smile coming to his lips as he listened to the words.

Or Mercy as she tugged on Jack's shirt saying, "It said *children*, Pa. That means us, doesn't it?" . . . how the rest of the children beamed when he said yes, that meant them . . .

Thank you, Lord, for this day, for reminding us again that you are in charge over all that is yours. I *know* this church is yours . . . and I know we are, too.

February 9, 1874 . . .

Another day working on the church. Mother Nature's threat of snow came through just as we rolled into town, but so did our prayers. Peach said he'd never seen a more determined group than us, the way we all ignored the cold and snow and set to finishing the top part of the shell. "Even yer little ones," he said, shaking his head as he watched the kids work like anything to fill the gaps in between the logs with their buckets of sticks and wood shavings.

"We're in the Bible, too, Peach," Mercy announced with grave importance. "It says 'their children,' and that's who we are. You can even ask my Pa."

"Oh, I reckon I see the truth of it in your eyes, Mercy," Peach said, gently touching a weathered old hand to her head. When he looked up I saw his eyes catch with Widow Spence's, and I saw, too, the thoughtful smile on her face as they did . . .

We took our noon break not long after that; a picnic of sorts in the mercantile, with hot biscuits from Mrs. Pumphrey and venison stew Peach had made outside in a covered iron pot over a fire, adding to it the bacon we'd brought. Then Percy broke out some canned fruit, and we poured that over the johnnycakes Jessie had brought for a fine dessert. We had such a good time, praying and talking together, that it didn't even seem to matter about the snow as we all tromped back out in it together to work again. I don't know how to explain it, but the snow and cold we had to deal with seemed to only draw us closer together . . .

I saw it in the way Quinn walked back up that hill with Gale after the noon meal, and heard it in their laugh and talk. Then I heard Quinn ask Gale about his parents, and I saw the boy duck his head for a moment, looking off across the town before he spoke.

"They left awhile back, Mr. McGregor," Gale said finally, and I heard Quinn ask him what he meant by "left."

"I went to check on them when the scarlet fever came, and they had already gone," Gale said. "Cleaned about everything out of the cabin, too."

There was only a brief silence, then I heard Quinn say, "Well, I guess you're ours for good now."

Gale smiled over at him then, the biggest smile I'd ever seen. And it was then that I recalled Rose's words: "It's just like we're one big family now," she'd said, and I thought then that truer words had never been spoken as I watched Quinn put his hand against Gale's back, just like a father might do a son.

I witnessed so much of that spirit all day long: the way Jessie, Rachel, and Sara worked side by side with me, Willa, and Lillie as we mixed the chinking in the mercantile so it wouldn't freeze and took turns tending Mara Lee then running outside with our buckets to shove it into the gaps before it could freeze . . . and how Jack and Widow Spence both lunged for John-Charles at the same time when he was nearly struck by one of the logs . . . and Percy, swallowing his fear of heights to help Quinn and the boys with the shingles . . . even Jonah help-ing Mrs. Pumphrey up when she slipped in the snow, telling her she was as light as a feather when she tried to shy away, saying she was too heavy for him to lift.

It comes to me as I'm writing this that the good Lord isn't

just helping us build a church, but a real family of people who truly care for each other . . .

But most of all, of people who care for him.

It appears we weren't the only ones determined to see our church finished.

Jessie just left after waking us up by banging on our door so hard she nearly scared us all to death. She had Medicine Weasel with her, and the poor old fellow looked a sight. Seems that sometime after midnight he realized one of the sick heifers we were keeping in the barn had escaped, and he took it on himself to go fetch her. One Shot had found him an hour or so later, nearly froze solid, and by the time they brought him to us, he wasn't much better. His face looked mottled, and his ear was so red and swollen it stuck out at a frightening angle, cracked right at the seam where it joined his head. I set to dropping some warm glycerin in it with a turkey feather, but he kept pushing me away.

I finally asked him what was the matter, and he said, "Promise me you won't tell Jack Wade about this." I asked him why, and he looked at me with those rheumy old eyes of his and said, "Just promise me."

He finally let me and Jessie doctor him after I promised not to tell, although I can only pray we did some sort of good, as bad as that ear looked. Jessie and I stood on the porch after that to make sure he and One Shot got safely down to their lodge, and that's when she turned to me suddenly with a funny look to her face as if a thought had struck her.

"You know what I think, Callie?" she said, smiling softly. "I think Medicine Weasel didn't want Jack to know because he knew Jack would stay here at the ranch to make sure he was all right." She turned to peer back down at the lodge. "I think that old Indian wants to see that church finished as much as we do."

The Other Side of Jordan

It has been a long, bitter-cold day but worth every moment we've spent putting the finishing touches on the outside of the church. The chinking has been laid in, and oilcloth covers the windows for now until we can get the glass shipped in. Quinn, Jack, and Jonah are down in the barn with the boys finishing up on the steeple we'll bring to town with us tomorrow—made, by the way, just as Patrick described it that day . . .

Lillie, Jessie, and her girls are here, sewing for all they're worth so we can get the wagon sheets put together for a floor covering. We're all feeling the race against time now as Willa has told us she thinks Preacher will be home by the thirteenth.

I am bone tired. Rose is calling, "Come on, Mama!" as she sews on her part of the cover, and Mara Lee hollers from her crib, "Here, Mama!" and everyone laughs.

I suppose I could pray for patience, but the thing is, it's always been the one prayer of mine that gets answered *so quick*.

February 12, 1874 . . .

I have missed a day of writing in all the rush, but we have gotten so much done, little journal, I think you will forgive me. I can spare only a moment now, as we are fixing to leave again.

Yesterday was spent cleaning and scrubbing the inside of the church so we could lay down the new floor. And now that it is down, we are ready for the furnishings.

Quinn, Jack, and Jonah have just finished the benches, and our boys—will wonders never cease—have made Preacher a new pulpit out of white pine, sanded so smooth it feels like silk.

For the front of the pulpit Gale has carved a beautiful cross that would make the angels sing. And the smile he just gave me for saying so could as well . . .

Later—I think we are all going to see a very surprised Preacher, come tomorrow—if we don't all drop from exhaustion before we *can* see him.

And before I do drop for the night, I want to say thank you, Lord. Thank you for the blessings of bringing this unlikely group of people together and making us a family, for guiding us through all the tough times and for giving us a preacher who has such a heart for you, a preacher who has taught us that you *can* see those tiny mustard seeds within us and that, more than anything, you want to watch them grow . . .

February 13, 1874 . . .

I don't think any of us have ever witnessed Preacher go speechless, but we did today . . .

We were all hiding inside the church, watching as he pulled up with Willa in the wagon. He looked to have been saying something when he glanced up, and that's when we saw Preacher go completely still as he looked in shock from his tent to the little log church that stood next to it and then to the steeple above. He quickly climbed down from the wagon, and in a few long strides, he had opened the door to see us all standing inside. His handsome face looked tired from the days of traveling but dazed, too, as if he couldn't believe what he was seeing.

Then, without a word to us, he stepped inside, and we parted to let him pass, watching with grins on our faces as he stepped forward and gazed in wonder around the fresh-scrubbed room, his eyes traveling from the floor to his old stove we'd shined up and built a crackling fire inside. Then he moved on to the new benches and the pulpit that stood at the head of the room. He walked over to it and ran his hands over the cross Gale had carved, lingering over the tiny vine of thorns that wrapped around the cross and the single rose that lay at its foot. Then he turned to us and smiled a shaky kind of smile.

"It's like you said, Shawn," Willa said with her own shaky smile as her eyes filled with tears. "It's easier to get the hook in than it is to take it out. We just didn't want to do without you anymore . . ."

Preacher looked at Willa, then his eyes went to each and every one of our faces. He seemed about to say something, but it was as if he couldn't form the words.

Then that six-foot-tall Preacher, built like a lumberjack, sat down hard on one of the benches in his new church . . . and he cried.

I will say this: A man crying makes other men more uncomfortable than I've ever seen. Jack and Quinn suddenly found their feet very interesting, and Jonah looked over at Jessie as if trying to find something other than Preacher to fix his eyes on. Percy tried to be sympathetic as he had broke down before, too, but even he didn't know where to look. Peach just looked ill. It was Medicine Weasel who surprised us all by slowly shuffling over to Preacher in a pair of ancient boots he refused to toss even though they pinched his toes horribly. (Boots, by the way, that Jack swears the old Indian took off him all those years ago when he found Jack lost and half-dead in the Montana wilderness.) Medicine Weasel touched Preacher's shoulder gently, and when Preacher looked up at the old medicine man, his face suddenly lit up.

"Why, Medicine Weasel, I thought you said you would never set foot in a church," Preacher said, smiling.

"That is because this is not a church," Medicine Weasel said

simply with a soft smile coming to his old face. "It is a home—
Grandfather's home—and I like to visit the homes of those that
mean much to me."

"That's exactly how I felt when I walked in here," Preacher
said, looking up at Medicine Weasel in wonder. "That this was
his *home*."

We all started to smile again then, glancing at each other
with tears in our eyes, for it did look like a home. All that time
we had secretly worried about our little log church not being
like the "real" churches in other towns, the kind we imagined
Preacher would prefer—built smooth with hewn lumber and
painted white. All that worry had been for nothing. The smile
on Preacher's face was proof of that. But more than that was the
truly peaceful feeling that we were in God's home . . . that he
was right there with us, too.

Preacher came around and hugged each of us then, and
when he got to the children, their happy grins and laughter,
mixed with ours, made me feel as if we were having more of a
family reunion than a church opening.

What a reunion it was, Lord. I don't ever want to forget this
day, the way my loved ones laughed in it or the feeling that you
were there, surrounding us with your love as Preacher said grace
over the meal we had all prepared. I don't ever want to forget
the looks on our little ones' faces as they realized they had been
a part of something greater than they could have imagined.

"For the Lord thy God blesseth thee," your Word says.

And I believe you did.

Quinn and I have been watching Patrick as he sleeps
tonight . . . wondering if he thinks we have forgotten his birthday is tomorrow with all the rush to finish the church. It doesn't
surprise me that he hasn't said anything. He is so much like his

father at times . . . such a good, honorable little spirit dwells inside that stocky little body that it amazes me at times that he is mine . . . that God has given me such a gift.

I wonder what this new year will bring him. Whatever it is, Lord, I pray your face continues to shine upon him and that you bless him as much as he has blessed me.

Bless all of us, for that matter.

Because that would be a better gift than anything I could ever think of . . .

February 14, 1874 . . .

It's so hard to imagine Patrick being nine today—but then, I admit, sometimes I forget he is *only* nine, too. For example, there's what he said this morning when we all woke him up, singing "Happy Birthday" and filling his lap with the little gifts we had made for him once he got settled on the settee.

"I had so much fun yesterday, I thought that was kind of my birthday, too," he said, looking at all of us with a shy kind of grin. But as he opened his first gift, a new hunting knife from Quinn, we saw the little-boy light come to his eyes as he grinned and lifted it up to show Gale and John-Charles.

"Just wait till we go fishing, come spring," he said. Then he went on to open the rest: a buckskin jacket from Jack, a horse blanket from Jessie, and an elk-tooth necklace from Medicine Weasel. Gale made him a beautiful carving of a trout, and Rose had fashioned him one of her horsehair whips she's so good at braiding.

But Rose, being Rose, could not bear to let her brother's birthday go by without some form of teasing. She waited until she felt the time was just right. It just happened to be when he pulled the new trousers I'd made him out of the brown wrapper. He had been begging me to "fox" him some trousers like Quinn and Jack wear. They're really just britches with a heart-shaped piece of buckskin sewn into the seat and down the inside seam of the legs to save wear from riding. But it was clear Patrick was tickled to death over them.

"What kind of pants are those?" Rose said suddenly with a mischievous look to her eyes, and Patrick frowned, sizing her up before he went on to speak.

"The same kind of pants Pa and Uncle Jack wear," he said warily.

"Well, you're gonna look strange wearing them," Rose announced cheerfully.

"I like 'em," Patrick said, frowning again.

"Well, you're *gonna* look strange," Rose repeated, then she smiled, and the cat was out of the bag. Patrick grinned, too.

"Well, I *like* them," he said again, refusing to let her have the last word. So, just to throw him off *and* because it was his birthday, Rose let him.

"I'm sure glad *we* don't act like that," John-Charles said, looking down at Mercy.

"Me, too," she said, but we saw her unconsciously cover her bear's mouth as she slid a glance toward Peach. We all couldn't help but laugh.

We have been so blessed the past couple of days . . . but I am so very tired, too. Now that the little ones are bathed and asleep, it's all I can do to write this.

I *have* to get some sleep. Sabbath is tomorrow—in our new little church—and I am looking forward to it more than I can say.

February 15, 1874 . . .

Sabbath, and what a moving message it was that Preacher spoke to us today. I have never felt such a gladness in my heart as I did today, listening to his words. I don't think any of us will forget them . . .

"A beautiful day, wouldn't you say?" Preacher said, smiling broadly as he stood behind his new pulpit. We all smiled, too, nodding amongst ourselves as we looked around in wonder at how many people had braved the bitter cold to be there. "With this warm fire in our stove and so many friends and family here, I can't imagine it being a better day to share a story," Preacher said, and suddenly all the rustling and shifting in the seats stopped as everyone leaned forward to listen.

"It's the story about another son who was given his father's inheritance," Preacher said. Then he held up his hand. "Remember, I said *another* son—I think we all know the story of the prodigal son well enough. No, this is a very different story, one I hope you will remember for a very long time."

Preacher looked around, his eyes falling on Peach for a moment, then he went on.

"Shortly after this son is given his inheritance, he is sent on a long journey to a faraway land. He's been told by his father not to let on to too many people about his wealth because there are some who would try to steal it from him . . . and though this son was the sharing type, his father also told him there would be some people who didn't deserve for him to share it with them. This son knew how wise his father was, so he listened. 'You'll know the ones who are our kind of people and the ones who aren't,' the father assured him. 'In particular, watch out for the men that go around acting holy, waving to everyone they see on the street, but behind closed doors steal widows' lands for their own.'"

"I knowed some rough characters like that once," Peach blurted out suddenly, unable to contain himself, and everyone chuckled, including Preacher. Then he went on: "Now, I have to say, even knowing this, the journey for this young man wasn't an easy one. It seemed every time he was doing something good, someone had it in for him."

A few of us caught Peach nodding vigorously and looking

like he was itching to say something, but then Widow Spence put a hand on his shoulder. Peach turned to her and smiled, shy, then seemed to calm down after that.

"But a funny thing happened," Preacher went on, a glint to his eyes as though he'd seen Peach. "The more trouble that came his way, the more he saw that money wasn't the answer. See, this son decided he would use the part of his inheritance he best knew how to handle—the riches he'd never really had to deal with because his father had always handled that when he lived at home. Instead, he remembered the *words* his father had taught him . . . words of wisdom that had been sown so deep in him that no one could ever uproot them . . . "

Preacher paused for a moment then and looked around at us.

"If he came across people who were being greedy, he would try to persuade them of a better way, saying, 'It is better to give than to receive.' If he found people judging others, he tried to warn them so they wouldn't have to face a hurtful end: 'Judge not, that ye be not judged.' And when people brought their children to him so that he might just touch them, only to have his disciples try to send them away, he held his hand up and looked upon the little ones with love, saying, 'Suffer the little children to come unto me, and forbid them not: for of such is the kingdom of God.'

"You see, my friends, that Son, *Jesus*, knew that the child-like faith our children have, the complete love and trust, is what Jesus had for his Father. He knew that the greatest part of his inheritance God had given him to use on this earth was love.

"He knew that his wealth was his love.

"God has given us our homes and land as part of our inheritance, but the other part of our inheritance—the most important part—is our love for others. I can't imagine a finer showing of love than that shown by the folks who worked so hard to build this church—or better, 'God's home,' as a very wise man so aptly named it."

We all looked over at Medicine Weasel, who had suddenly straightened his back and had what might pass as a pleased smile on his face.

Preacher stepped away from his pulpit then and walked closer to us. "Can't you feel it?" he said, looking around at us with such a beautiful look on his face. And suddenly I did feel something settle over us in the room. Preacher smiled. "God has granted us our inheritance; he has given us our land. And he has also given us his Word." Preacher held up his Bible for all to see. "*This* is how we learn to tend our land. *This* is how our seeds of faith will grow . . . how they will stay sown so deep that no one or nothing will ever uproot them.

"These words are what will remain when everything else passes away, for the greatest of all of these is love. That's what he has given us here. And that is what he asks us to give as well, to share our inheritance with others just as his Son shared it with us."

We all fell silent, feeling the truth of Preacher's words come over us like a balm to our hearts. Then, instead of Preacher walking to the door of the church like he usually did, he sat down next to Willa, and we were surprised to see Percy walk slowly to stand in front of the pulpit.

"That was some fine words you spoke, Preacher," Percy said, his voice a bit shaky, and Preacher smiled at him and nodded. Percy turned back to us then, and that's when I noticed that he was holding a paper in his hands.

"I asked Preacher if I could read this after the sermon, and I have to say now, it seems more fitting than ever. This paper I'm holding is a letter from Leah—and it was written as much to all of you as it was to me." Percy looked at all of us and took a deep breath, then he began to read.

First Leah asked about the girls, then she told Percy she was thankful for the Bible he had sent her. She went on to say that she realized she had to get caught to be found again. She said she had been living a lie for so long that she had forgot who she was before she started the lie.

Then Percy read in a shaky voice that she had been really reading the Bible in earnest—that she really wanted to know who God was and not just hear of him from others . . .

What he read next surprised us all.

She told him to ask two things of us. The first was if we could forgive her . . . and the second was if we could mention her in our prayers.

No one seemed to be able to say anything for the longest time. Then I felt Quinn stand up next to me. "Preacher, I was thinking this might be a good time to pray for her, with everyone here now, don't you think?"

Preacher said he did and asked us all to stand and join hands, and as we did, Percy's eyes met mine, and I saw an endurance and a kind of peace that I had never seen before. And that's when I realized what that feeling was I had felt earlier.

It was a new wind from God, coming into Percy's life . . .

February 17, 1874 . . .

The sound of water is everywhere, running off the rooftops and trees; rain is falling down through purple skies, running here and there like warm fingers tugging back the shroud of snow to bring to life again what's beneath it. It came in with the Chinook that roared up the valley from the south last night. The cattle felt it first, and thinking it gave them the go-ahead to roam, they're now spread out everywhere, huddled wet in pockets throughout the valley, their legs bogged down in old snow and new mud.

The men have been out in it since before dawn, moving like molasses through the sludge-covered hills and coulees. I am so grateful for Gale and Jonah to be here to help—Peach, too. He showed up out of the blue this morning, saying he just "happened to be passing by." He really is such a dear friend to us . . . Quinn thinks God's hand is what nudged him our way nearly five years ago.

"Think of it," he told me last night. "Who else *but* God could convince a 'confirmed heathern' to push us into getting our church built?" We grinned at each other and shook our heads; I don't think either of us will ever get over the wonder of seeing God's handiwork in our lives—or the lives of others . . .

I best close for now; they will be in for the noon meal soon, and already I can picture their muddy footwork on my clean floor . . . I think Rose can see them as well; she looks from the window with a grim look to the floor then back to Mara Lee, who has just pulled herself up to stand next to my chair. Mara Lee claps then looks startled as she wobbles, grabbing ahold of the chair again. Steady again, she looks over at Rose with a grin.

"You just wait, Bird," Rose declares gravely. "It might be all fun, now. But the older you get, the harder the work gets."

It is taking everything in me not to laugh . . .

Muddy footprints notwithstanding, the men have succeeded in getting our cattle back down closer to the lower valley. I don't think I've seen a more tired or happy crew than them as they finally called it quits for the night, sliding their chairs back from the dinner table, sharing looks of kinship and gratitude. Seeing them like that, I couldn't help thinking how God's hand has nudged all of us together in a way that I never would have imagined.

But it's what Peach said to me just before he left that I don't think I'll forget.

I had a pretty good idea he was wanting to say something, the way he kept glancing over at me through dinner, and it didn't take long to find out I was right. He lingered around until everyone had filed back out to the barn to take a look at one of the calves, then he announced almost offhandedly that he thought he'd go—but didn't budge.

I asked him if he would like to walk out on the porch with me then, and he looked almost grateful for the suggestion.

"It don't matter how long I live out here. It's always a shock when warm weather shows back up," Peach said, looking up to the sky. Then his voice got quiet. "But there's a lot of things that kin shock a person . . . " Peach glanced at me sideways for a long moment then went on, as if a decision in his head had been made. "Like I surely never thought I'd set foot in a church," he said. Then he cocked his head to one side. "The strange of it is that even when we was gettin' it built, I didn't think of doin' sech a thing. It was jes like I was walkin' through them doors a'fore I even knowed what I was doing. But ya know what, Miss Callie? I'm glad I did. I ain't ever been one for flowery sayin's, but the way your Preacher spoke of thet Jesus got me thinkin'. Because Jesus sounded like the kind of feller I wished I had knowed . . . "

"He's not gone, Peach," I said, feeling my eyes well up with tears in spite of my trying not to. Peach saw the tears, but for the first time didn't seem uneasy about my show of emotion. I saw his face soften as he nodded, then he looked back over the dark valley.

"Widow Spence said much the same. Gave me one of them Bibles from the mercantile, too, and tolt me to read it fer myself," he said. Then his voice dropped almost to a whisper as he looked up at the sky again. "An' from what I've read so far, I reckon if'n anyone had the right to beat ol' death, Jesus sure did." Peach turned back to me as if a thought had suddenly occurred to him.

"Does it tell in the Good Book how he beat it?" Peach asked. And when I grinned and told him yes, it did, his head bobbed up and down, and I saw an almost childlike excitement come over him.

"I was hopin' it did," he said, smiling.

He left not long after that, and as I watched him ride away I couldn't help remembering how amazed his face had looked, trying to figure out just how he had walked through those church doors without really thinking on it first.

But you know what, little journal? I'm not so amazed.

February 20, 1874 . . .

It seems that early spring, like everyone else that has blown into our lives in a day, has decided to stay for a while. I have been so busy trying to keep up with the endless rounds of meals and mud that I haven't had much of a chance to write, but Peach has been awful strong on my mind since we talked. I found a scripture in John this morning after praying for him, and I think it's fitting:

And the sheep hear his voice: and he calleth his own sheep by name, and leadeth them out. And when he putteth forth his own sheep, he goeth before them, and the sheep follow him: for they know his voice.
— 1 JOHN 10:3–4

There is another scripture I remember reading, about how God knows us before we are even in our mother's womb, and I can't help thinking *that* is why we know the sound of his voice so well when he calls . . .

I wish I would have thought of it to tell Peach when he was here! I'll have to remember it when he comes again . . .

Well, good-bye for now, little journal. Mara Lee is hollering to be let down from her crib. Quinn caught her trying to shimmy out of it herself last night and laughed, saying she'll be walking in no time, as determined as she is to catch up with the others.

Seeing her grinning little face looking over at me as I write this, I don't doubt it.

February 21, 1874 . . .

I can hear the last of the huge cakes of ice sliding off the roofs of the cabin, the bunkhouse, and the barns, hitting the ground with such thuds that Jasper and Honey run to bark at the intruder. I've never thought of spring coming as an intruder, though—more of a friend, I think. The kind of friend that makes you want to do *something* . . . Already everyone is thinking ahead to those somethings, talking of fishing and swimming, of planting gardens . . . of getting married—the latter being the talk of the evening—well, *that* and Rose.

Willa has finally set the date for April and has asked us all to help make her dress, and of course we agreed, which led to us discussing it after dinner . . .

"I'd make ten weddin' dresses to finally get that girl up the aisle," Jessie sniffed as we all sat at the table, talking, and everyone smiled.

"Well, if Peach has his way, you might just be asked to make another dress," Lillie said then, and Jessie nodded sagely.

"There's another one that needs to quit dawdlin' 'fore it's too late."

"Is there anyone around here that you *don't* have to keep after, Mama?" Rachel said, laughing as she looked over at Sara.

Jessie grinned. "Not that I kin think of offhand," she said, and we chuckled.

"She's always kept after me, ever since I was born," Rose said suddenly, and we all looked at each other in stunned silence as none of us had even seen her in the room. Then Jessie lifted up the tablecloth, and by the wide smile on her face, we knew she had found Rose.

"Now, what you doin' under there easedroppin' on folks, Rose McGregor?" she asked, trying to sound firm.

There was a brief silence again, then: "Oh, I don't know anything about *ease*dropping, Jessie, but I do know this is the best place to sit and listen for news to put in my journal."

"Ever think I might have a good reason to keep after you, little sis?" Jessie asked, and we just couldn't hold our laughter in any longer.

Rose scrambled out not long after that, her short honey-red hair curling up every which way as she sat down next to me with a charming little grin on her face. "So, is Peach really gonna marry Widow Spence?" she asked, all eyes.

As I hugged her to my side, I couldn't help wondering what I would ever do when that funny, impulsive child who had breezed into my life one day . . . what I would ever do when she decided to breeze out of it.

I can only pray that Willa and Preacher are as blessed with such a family as Quinn and I have been given. And dear old Peach—I pray that he and Widow Spence do somehow find their way to each other . . . I don't think God ever intended for any of us to be alone; otherwise it wouldn't hurt so much when we are . . .

Makes me think of something Jack said in a letter to me so many years ago, but I have never forgotten it, for how it made me laugh—and made me think, too. He said, "As fickle a bunch as we humans can be at times, we can't seem to live without each other either, can we?"

If he asked me that today I would tell him no, we can't live without each other. And then I would tell him that if any of us could learn one thing from Preacher and never forget it, it would be that our wealth *is* our love.

March 3, 1874 . . .

We witnessed the most beautiful thing tonight. It was after dinner, and we were standing on the porch, reveling in the nice weather and talking, when I heard Gale say, "Look up there." And we looked up to where he was pointing and saw a huge swash of what looked to be blue-white fire arcing through the night sky, as if God himself had took his finger and decided to suddenly move some stars. Then, just as we were watching, a lone star appeared to separate itself, and it came shooting across the sky, lighting up the valley below for a moment.

I heard everyone let out the breath they had been holding in then, and as Quinn put his arms around my waist I looked over to where the children were standing in front of Medicine Weasel's lodge and saw their awe-filled little faces. Then I saw Jessie, Jonah, and his sisters holding hands and Jack and Lillie smiling up into the night sky. But it was Peach's face I don't think I'll ever forget as he stood next to Gale, so filled with wonder. Then he turned to look at all of us, his smile saying he was glad to be sharing the moment with someone.

"It's kindly like he was puttin' on a show jes fer us, weren't it?" he said with such childlike earnestness, none of us had to ask who *he* was . . .

March 6, 1874 . . .

All day today as I have done the wash outside, scrubbing the clothes and hanging them on the line, I have seen tiny bits of green life poking up, trying to push free from the mud, and for some reason those words of Preacher's keep running through my mind about the tiny mustard seed in us, struggling to break free from the earth so it can reach up to touch his light . . .

The Other Side of Jordan

Peach surprised me this morning by showing up at the door and asking if I would like to take a ride out through the valley with him, and I'm so glad I did.

We rode in silence most of the way until we got to the high meadows, then as if something about where we were suddenly made his decision for him, Peach dismounted and came over to help me down off my horse.

"Looks like spring is really here now, Peach," I said, smiling as we looked out over the valley together. He nodded, a pleased look coming to his old face.

"Yes, and it looks like that new grass has taken root, too," he said, sweeping his hands through the air in such a poignant but grand gesture I felt as if he were introducing me to the greatest performance I would ever see . . . and in a way, that's just what he did.

I turned and looked across the valley to where he had pointed and saw the new grass that had begun to take over the scorched places of earth. There was still some curvy patches of bare earth here and there, almost like little trails, but as I looked at those little trails, I couldn't help thinking of what Jessie had said about the mending scars being new roads for us to follow. And for some reason, I just knew that the grass would grow stronger than before along those scars of earth . . .

"Most folks kindly like to think an old feller like me wouldn't like change—but I think I would, now," Peach said, cocking his head sideways to look at me thoughtfully. "Havin' hope agin, it helps you look forward to something new, don't it, Miss Callie?"

"Yes, it does," I said, and he nodded.

"Well, you helped give me that hope, and that's why I wanted to bring you out here, to give you some hope, too," he said, and I had the oddest feeling come over me when our eyes met. It felt like everything else had faded away—Peach's old, shabby clothes that had seen better times, the scruffy mane of hair he could never seem to tame. So many differences stood between us, yet they were suddenly gone, and all I could feel was Peach's spirit and mine, recognizing each other, like long-lost family members feeling each other's love. It was like we were suddenly brother and sister.

I hugged Peach then, startling him at first, but then I felt his old, weathered hand rest on my shoulder, felt him pat my back in a way that I hadn't felt since my pa died.

For some reason, the memory of a story I'd read came to my mind then, the story of a man who said he'd had a sparrow land on his shoulder for a moment while he was hoeing his garden . . . and how that moment had made him feel more important than if someone had clipped a priceless jewel to his shirt. Right then I felt I knew what that man had meant as I stood there hugging Peach while a warm spring wind whipped around us.

Only my jewel wasn't a sparrow but a grizzled old man everyone called Peach—who was better than any jewel I could ever imagine.

So, this is what you planned for us to be, Lord, my heart whispered as we finally rode back down to the valley together. *This is how we would've all been if we hadn't believed that first lie . . .*

I can't help thinking even as I write this now what a tragedy it is that the devil took that kind of love from us—but what a sheer blessing it is that Jesus brought it back . . .

Because that love, after all, is as much our inheritance as this land.

PART FOUR

Bountiful
Harvest

Then Joshua divided the INHERITANCE among the people and God Shined His Face on them and the people were glad because God has a nice Face. And he gave them a lot of good stuff, too.

By Rose McGregor
Almost 14

If I could imagine such a thing as paradise, I would imagine it a bit like our valley in the spring—only better, I'm sure . . . But still, there is something about the sharp, clear blue skies and the hills rolling with new green and the immense mountains that rise up with such grandeur in the distance that makes you almost believe it's never been touched by the world. That somehow God cupped his hand over it and let what we call progress walk on by, unseeing . . .

Quinn and I were standing out on the porch, drinking coffee together this morning, when I told him how I felt, told him that it made me realize just how blessed we are to be trusted with such a gift.

"Did you ever think that's why he gave us this land, Callie?" Quinn said. "That he knew our love for him allowed us to see that it *is* a gift?" He took Mara Lee from my arms and kissed her cheek, and when she laughed at him, he looked over at me and smiled. It was then that I noticed how deep the lines at the corners of his pale blue eyes had become—little trails of weather and worry, Mama used to call them . . . But it was in those lines that I saw so much of our lives, too. Saw the young man he'd been when we first met, so alone in the world . . . but so willing to love and never giving up on me in spite of my fears. Then I saw the husband that bore our hardships as well as others' with such compassion. But most of all, I saw the man that God had made him into along the way.

"Nothing compares to what he gives us, does it?" Quinn said softly, his voice filled with such emotion that all I could do at first was nod.

Then I looked across the land again, to the hills starting to dot with the white faces of cows and calves trotting down to dip their muzzles in the river, and as strange as it sounds, as I watched them, I felt like I, too, was drinking in that crisp, clean water—like the newness of it was running through my blood, and I looked over at Quinn and smiled.

"Do you remember what I asked you that time we danced in the middle of that prairie we found along the trail?" I said, and he hesitated for only a moment then smiled, too. The memories of our journey west on that wagon train were still as strong in him as they were in me.

"You said, 'Where have you been all my life?'" he said, and when I asked him if he remembered what he had answered, he said easily, "Looking for you." I saw a softness come to his face as he said it, and in my heart I felt the effect just the same as the first time he said it.

"I'm glad you found me, Quinn," I said, blinking back my tears. He pulled me to him and kissed me, Mara Lee laughing delightedly between us.

The door of the cabin flew open then, with Rose peeking out first. "They're doing it again," she announced gravely, and we saw Gale, then Patrick, add their faces to the opening in the doorway. Gale looked at both of us then grinned happily. "You kind of get used to it," Patrick said, shaking his head as he grinned. "They've been doing that as long as I can remember, and I don't think they're going to stop."

Quinn and I started laughing, and this time, I didn't think of it as the poetry of the moment dying. I couldn't help thinking it only became more beautiful with the laughter of all our children surrounding us, joining in with ours.

Quinn was right: *Nothing* compares to the gifts God gives us.

Well, our muddy little troupe cleaned up nicely after helping drive the cattle today—and after my promising to read another Bible story. Such an eager look to their little faces as they gathered around my rocking chair in the crowded cabin this evening . . . Medicine Weasel and One Shot looking almost comical, their heads rising high above the others as they, too, sat cross-legged on the floor, waiting for the story to begin. But it was how the gathering ended that made it such a night . . .

"John the Baptizer," as Patrick calls it, was the story they finally agreed on, and I noticed when I got to the part where John said, "I indeed baptize you with water, . . . but he that cometh after me is mightier than I . . . : he shall baptize you with the Holy Ghost, and with fire," that a sudden spark came to Medicine Weasel's eyes. He glanced over to One Shot, who nodded and said something in Blackfoot, and they both leaned forward. I started up again, reading how Jesus, in order to teach the people humility, came to the Jordan to be baptized by John . . . how when he was standing in the water, praying, the heavens opened up and a dove came and rested on his head and how the people heard a voice saying, "This is my beloved Son, in whom I am well pleased." And as soon as those words were out of my mouth, Medicine Weasel and One Shot turned to Jack, talking excitedly in Blackfoot, and we all stopped to listen.

Jack said something back. Then he turned to me and smiled, but it was John-Charles who spoke up first as he leaned forward from in-between Patrick and Gale.

"They want to be baptized, Aunt Callie!" he said, glancing back at Medicine Weasel. His grandfather nodded at him to go on. "They said they had been feeling like God was waiting for them to do something more before he could bring the Holy Ghost for a visit."

None of us said anything for a moment, and in the silence I couldn't help thinking how easily the two Indians had accepted the gospel . . . with such childlike acceptance that I couldn't help wishing everyone looked at God and his Word that way.

"One Shot, too?" I asked when I finally found my voice, and John-Charles nodded then smiled, seeing the surprise on my face.

"Oh, One Shot's been listening all along, too. He and Grandfather pray together all the time now," John-Charles said easily. "He just doesn't like to speak our language. He said God hears him just as good in Blackfoot."

"Well, now, I bet he does, too," Jessie said then, looking over at her children then back to me, her dark, old face filled with a kind of soft understanding. I saw Gale glance around to us all with a thoughtful look to his face. Then the rest of the children looked back up at me, ready for me to keep reading as if what had happened was the most natural thing in the world . . .

"You can go on reading, Mama," Rose announced, the pleased smile on her face echoing everyone else's in the room.

But no one looked more pleased than Medicine Weasel and One Shot as I opened that Book again and began to read . . .

As I write this tonight, I can't shake the feeling that the Lord is once again at work with his plan in our lives . . . in my mind's eye I can imagine a great hand gently patting the earth over the seeds that it has sown. I can imagine the water, much like what I felt running over me today, falling upon that earth so clear and pure . . . and I can imagine the most beautiful, expectant smile waiting for those seeds to sprout up and grow. What was it that Solomon wrote? Something to the effect of the generous soul will be made rich, and "he that watereth shall be watered also himself."

March 15, 1874 . . .

Our Sabbath morning woke us up to a warm, sunny dawn— warmer than usual this time of year—making our trip to town so pleasurable after all the chill and snow that we almost didn't make it to church on time. But we weren't the only ones; Preacher came rushing in a little after us with Willa on his heels, looking flushed but pretty as she took a seat next to us, grinning sheepishly while Preacher explained he and Willa had taken a walk through the garden this morning before church.

"Ah, the things we do when we are in love," he said with a teasing look in his eyes. Willa blushed hard then, and when we all burst out laughing, Preacher did, too. But after a moment, his smile softened.

"But you know what?" he said, looking around the room. "When I was out there gardening, it came to me what I needed to say to everyone today. It happened just as I had raised up from planting a new row, and when I looked out across the yard, for some reason I was struck by the way the trees in some areas looked almost like they were grouped together like families. And that got me started thinking about how that came to be. How once a tree grows to maturity, it begins to drop seeds of its own . . . How those seeds will be planted right into the earth . . . and begin to take root during that first winter of their lives. And when they are ready, they will spring up and grow tall and healthy to stand next to that tree . . . " Preacher paused then and looked around at us, as if a thought had just occurred to him.

"But what if that tree didn't drop its seeds?" he asked. All of us kind of glanced to each other with puzzled looks on our faces. Preacher just nodded and opened his Bible as if he expected as much.

"Well, it talks about that very thing in the Gospel of Matthew," he said. "Does anyone remember the story Jesus told of the man who went on a journey and left his servants to handle his wealth for him?

"Well," Preacher went on, "the first servant took the portion he was trusted with, and he doubled his master's wealth. The second servant did the same. But the third servant, thinking he was wise, buried his master's wealth so that no one else could touch it. Now, when their master returned and found what the first two had done, he was pleased as anything. 'Well done, thou good and faithful servant,' he told them. 'Thou hast been faithful over a few things, I will make thee ruler over many things: enter thou into the joy of thy lord.'"

Preacher looked about the room then, his face turning serious.

"But that last servant? The one who buried his master's wealth? Scripture says the master cast the unprofitable servant into the 'outer darkness.'"

Preacher held his hand up and stepped away from the pulpit so he could stand in front of us. I caught sight of Peach sitting next to Widow Spence with Medicine Weasel and One Shot on the other side of him. The three men leaned forward together just then. Behind them, Widow Spence's eyes met mine, and we smiled.

"I can tell you right now that God, our Father, does not want that to happen to any of us," Preacher said, and we saw the three relax a bit. "But, you see, he had a Son who so loved the world that he invested *all* his inheritance in us . . . including *his own life*. So, how much is he really asking of us to share what we have of him?" Preacher shook his head sadly.

"Not much, I think . . . "

"I don't think it's too much to ask, either, Preacher," Peach said suddenly, unable to contain himself any longer. Then he looked toward Medicine Weasel and One Shot, who nodded their agreement, and we all smiled—Preacher included.

"That's a good thing, that you can see it that way, Peach," Preacher said. "Because I can tell you what he hopes to see happen for each of us. Jesus said it best, so I will read you his words . . . " Preacher ducked his head and began to read: "'When the Son of man shall come in his glory, and all the holy angels with him, then shall he sit upon the throne of his glory.'" Preacher closed his eyes for a moment, and the soft look on his face made me think he was imagining that very thing. Then he opened his eyes and looked at all of us and smiled, reciting the last words by heart: " 'Then shall the King say unto them on his right hand, Come, ye blessed of my Father, inherit the kingdom prepared for you from the foundation of the world: for I was hungered, and ye gave me meat: I was thirsty, and ye gave me drink: I was a stranger and ye took me in: naked, and ye clothed me: I was sick, and ye visited me: I was in prison, and ye came unto me. . . . ' "

Preacher glanced over at Percy and smiled, and I saw the tears in Percy's eyes as he smiled back. Then Preacher turned and looked at the rest of us.

"Jesus has given us a portion of his wealth, our inheritance as children of God . . . But what I want you to ask yourself is, What are you planning to do with yours?

"I know what I want to do," Preacher said, his voice going soft as he sat down on a chair next to his pulpit, looking down at his hands. "I want to love like Jesus loves. I want to see every seed around me take root and grow tall to stand beside me . . . I want to be the hand someone reaches for in the dark of their lives. And I want to know the Lord will send such a hand to me in the dark of my life, too . . .

"I want people to know how close God really is—Jesus is— and I want them to feel his love like I do." Preacher smiled a small smile and gave a little shrug as he looked to us again.

"But that's just me . . . "

"No, Preacher. 'Tis all of our hope," Quinn said then, the passion in his voice matching the Preacher's. I saw the whole room glance our way, and I knew some of the new folks were sizing up Quinn in much the same way they did Preacher, thinking it couldn't be weakness that led such a strong ox of a man to speak like he did. Jack turned to Quinn then, and the two smiled at each other like they were blood kin.

"Amen, brother," Jack said, and I felt a catch in my throat. When I glanced over at Lillie and the rest of our family, we all echoed an amen to his . . .

It wasn't until after everyone else had filed out that we learned why Peach, Medicine Weasel, and One Shot had been in such a state; they had decided amongst themselves before the service that they ought to be baptized *today*. And as soon as Gale heard of their plan, he decided he wanted to be baptized, too. So, with our eager Preacher in tow, we all headed for a stretch of river near the picnic grounds, laughing and talking as the children scrambled in all directions. Percy offered to carry Mara Lee for me while we walked, which gave me the chance to ask him how he was faring.

"Well, Leah hasn't sent the Bible back, so I'm looking on that as good news," he said with a look of good-hearted endurance. I saw that his girls looked better as well; their faces had filled out some, and their hair was neatly braided, though Willa was right about their needing a woman's touch with the way their dress hems hung lopsided from Percy's attempt at sewing. Those hems were noticed by every woman in the group as we exchanged looks of silent understanding before we turned to watch the baptisms begin.

Despite the warmer than usual sunshine, the air was still brisk, and the water was icy cold. So the baptizing was a slightly rushed affair. Peach was first to go into the water with Preacher, then Gale, followed by Medicine Weasel and One Shot. Preacher quickly baptized each one in the name of the Father, the Son, and the Holy Spirit. And I don't think there was a dry eye to be found along that river as we watched their beaming, steamy faces come out of the water. It was all over in about a minute, and when Preacher finished with One Shot, Jessie turned to me and smiled.

"Looks like you have quite a little forest growing around you now, honey," she said, and when I realized what she meant, I smiled back.

"Not just me, Jessie," I told her. "That little forest was

planted by all of us." We turned and looked at everyone lined along the banks, adults and children, and I couldn't help thinking how we did look like a grouping of trees, both old and young. I saw Mrs. Pumphrey say something to Willa and heard her and Lillie laugh as the newly baptized Christians—the old trapper, the solemn Indians, and young Gale—quickly hopped out of the water and shakily reached for the blankets and buffalo robes we all rushed to wrap them in. Then I saw Widow Spence hand Peach her picnic cloth to wipe his face, and that's when I realized that none of them had a dry change of clothes.

It was Percy, bless his sweet soul, who got the idea to bring the "boys" back to the mercantile and gift them all with new trousers and shirts. So we all headed for the store, teasing our "baptizees" as they trotted behind Percy to the back of the store, dripping and grinning with happiness.

"Now you will be 'putting on the new man' in more ways than one," Preacher chuckled, and we did, too, as the men slowly emerged from the mercantile one by one wearing their new outfits. Peach chanced a shy smile Widow Spence's way, and Gale looked like it was all beyond what he could have imagined. But Medicine Weasel and One Shot both appeared to be in some sort of pain.

"Does Grandfather's Word say anything about having to wear such clothes if we are to remain baptized?" Medicine Weasel asked me with a concerned look to his old face.

"Oh, no," I told him, trying to keep a straight face. Then I couldn't help but smile and add, "As soon as your things are dried out, you'd better get 'em on. Otherwise he might not recognize you!" Medicine Weasel's eyes widened one quick second then crinkled into a smile as he nodded, relieved. One Shot did, too.

"I was hoping you would answer this way. Because these clothes are scratching me to pieces," One Shot announced suddenly *in English*—the only English he had ever spoke. It startled us all so much it was a long moment of shocked silence before we all began to laugh.

Even the children laughed—although I'm not sure they realized what it was they were laughing about. Except for John-Charles.

I'll never forget his wry grin, so much like Jack's, as he shook his head at One Shot . . . or the way he glanced toward his grandfather after that with such a look of love . . . or how his eyes met Jack's and they both smiled wide smiles, as if at the exact same moment they had both found what they were looking for . . .

The only word I can think of to describe it is *home*.

March 16, 1874 . . .

Back to work again today, and what a long day of it. But the weather has held, along with everyone's spirits. Especially for Peach, who decided to stay over and help us get our cattle to the high meadows where the grass is already growing tall from the warm spell.

"If you folks don't have the Almighty's ear turned to ya, I don't know who does," Peach said as we finally reined in at the mouth of the meadows, watching the cattle trot forward with purpose as they spotted the lush grasses.

Even Jessie, who had been clinging to her mount for dear life only moments before, was captured by the abundant beauty of it all, and I saw her nod then, a satisfied look to her old face as she glanced around.

"He ain't never early, ain't never late . . . " she began.

"He is always on time," we all said together with her. Then we laughed as Jasper and Honey bounded through the grass like rabbits past us as their puppies tried their best to keep up.

We had almost finished with lunch when I happened to spot

"Callie," the cow Jack so kindly named, as she headed back down the slopes in the opposite direction of the other cattle. I told Quinn I would go turn her around. Peach looked up from eating, and I saw him frown.

"You best let one o' the fellers do that," he said casually, and Quinn and Jack looked over at him and grinned just as I felt my hands go to my hips.

"Is there any reason why you think I can't handle it, Peach?" I said, and as everyone started to chuckle, I saw a dawning come to Peach's face, then a mischievous grin. He turned to Quinn.

"Guess you might at least try t' convince her t' listen to good advice now and then, young feller," he said to Quinn. "As fer as I've seen, them stringy little ones live a long time."

"Stringy!" I started in, but Quinn was laughing too hard for me to go on. Instead, I turned and marched over to my horse, determined to show Peach just what I *could* do.

And as it turned out, "Callie" had the same thing in mind herself. She trotted resolutely down the hillside as if she meant to show me what *she* could do. And for a while I wondered if she might win. She took me up one side of the slope and down the other and twice around a clump of thorny brush before I think she just got tired of the chase and let me drive her back to the herd.

It didn't take me long to figure out that it had been quite a show, judging by the grins on everyone's face when I finally got back to where they stood.

"Well, I did what I set out to do, didn't I?" I said.

Peach looked over at Quinn. "She don't give in easy, does she?" he said, trying to keep a straight face.

Quinn followed suit, shaking his head sadly. "I guess I'm in for the long haul, Peach," he said with a sigh.

"Well, yes, I kin see that. But it's a mystery to me why you look so *happy* 'bout it," Peach said, shaking his old head, and everyone couldn't help but laugh. Then they laughed harder as Peach tried to help me down from my mount.

"Gimme that little hand of your'n, an' I'll help ya down," he said, and the peace offering of his hand must've put a look on my face, for he and everyone else continued to laugh.

"Aw now, Miss Callie, I was jes joshin' ya about bein' stringy. Why, you have a goodly 'mount of meat on ya." He looked at me hard, narrowing his eyes. "I kin see it if'n I squint my eyes jes right," he added with a twinkle in his eyes. I tried my best fierce look on him as I slapped his outstretched hand away, but Patrick ruined my act.

"Don't worry, Peach," he announced cheerfully—and loudly enough for all to hear. "Mama's smiling under that old bonnet. I just saw her teeth."

A quiet night for writing tonight, Lord, as everyone has fallen into an exhausted sleep. Everyone except me that is, writing again . . . I remember reading in one of the books Willa loaned me, I think it was Byron, that if he didn't write to empty his mind he would go mad. I don't see my writing that way, I guess. I see it more like a song I write of my life, of all our lives—a song that sings through the trials as well as the triumphs . . .

March 18, 1874 . . .

Mara Lee took her first steps on her own today, and Jack was convinced it was in honor of his birthday.

"Look, she's coming right for me, sis," he said, grinning, as Mara Lee crossed the room on wobbly legs, a determined look on her little face. But instead of Jack, she went for the table, reaching and stretching her chubby arms toward the half-eaten birthday cake.

"Mine!" she declared, and Jack laughed, picking her up. Then Jack, being Jack, leaned her forward and let her plunk her hands right into the cake, laughing again as she quickly stuffed them into her mouth.

The rest of us groaned, but Jack just sat back with his little niece, a pleased look on his face as she offered him some, too. When his eyes met mine, I saw so much of Pa in him . . . so much of the easygoing kind of love we had grown up around that I couldn't help but smile.

Jack smiled, too, the corners of his green eyes turning down like little half-moons like they always did when he was touched by something. Medicine Weasel said something in Blackfoot then, and Jack nodded and said something back before turning to me.

"He was trying to figure out our word for beauty because he wanted to say we have a lot of beauty in our family."

"Well, what *is* our word for beauty, then?" I asked, and Jack smiled.

"Closest I could ever figure what the Blackfoot meant by beauty was *love*. But they don't have a word for love. Medicine Weasel told me a long time ago, they didn't need the *word* to love."

"Beauty almost sounds better, doesn't it?" Lillie said, smiling softly, and everyone couldn't help but agree—especially Mara Lee, who picked that moment to put her sticky hands on each side of Jack's face and kiss him on the cheek, making all the children laugh.

Patrick turned to Gale with a shrug. "See? Bird's already doin' like Mama," he said. "I think it's kind of in the girl's blood."

"You boys just wait. One day it's going to be in your blood, too," Jack said, grinning, and they all groaned. All but Gale, who just looked happy to be included in another family tradition.

My tears have went and blurred some of this page, but I can't seem to help myself . . . Jack just came by the cabin to give me a poem that he'd written on the trail right after our sister Rose had died. He said he found it in Mama's old Bible and thought I might like to have it. Then he shuffled his feet a little, looking at the floor as he handed it to me.

"Remember when I was alone with John-Charles in that cabin after his mother, Raven, died? That's when I found it in Mama's Bible. I was glad I did, too; it always reminded me of you whenever I read it," he said, softly. "But now that we're here together, I thought you might like to have it . . . "

Here's what it says:

CALLIE, REMEMBER WHEN?

Remember when
The sunrises captured our youth, and marigolds
　　along with your smile played joyfully
　　in the sun?

Remember when
We swam in dirty water with broken grass clippings
　　in our hair?

Remember when
We walked and joked and laughed about our lives to
come
　　with Rose by our side?

Remember when
You were saving up for that dress, but bought
　　me a new pair of boots instead?

Remember when

We thought heartache could never
   touch us?

Remember when?

I showed the poem to Quinn tonight after Jack left and said, "Can you believe Jack wrote this?"

He just smiled and hugged me to him. "I can believe that Jack loves his sister more than anyone could imagine," he said. "Except for me, that is. I could imagine it."

March 19, 1874 . . .

From the porch I watched Jack breaking in a green horse this morning just as the sun was rising up over the mountains, and I wish I could put to paper the beauty of what I saw . . . Maybe *beauty* isn't the right word. Maybe it's *awe*. Or maybe it's just a gratefulness to have witnessed the moment, to have seen the look on Jack's face as the horse sunfished, the dust coming up to meet the golden rays of light hovering above the corral . . . Watching, I couldn't help thinking about all the nights I worried over my wild, reckless brother. Worried that I would never see him again . . . and ached for a world that might never know the true heart that lay underneath all the wildness.

But God knew . . .

He knew all along. I realized that truth this morning as I watched Jack. Because even now, the wildness isn't gone. God has just shown him how to claim it. All the days and nights that we had lived through the fever, through the trials of this past year, they're gone now, and Jack's way of celebrating was what I saw before my eyes.

As strange as it sounds, the words "a man after God's own heart" kept whispering through my mind as I watched Jack finally rein the horse's head toward the corral gate and nudge it into a dead run across the valley. I saw the joy break over his face as he rode across the land, drinking it in like he was seeing it again for the first time, and I thought of that story in the Bible telling how King David danced through the city to praise God. I knew then that that was what Jack was doing.

Dancing.

When I turned to go back inside, I caught site of Medicine Weasel standing outside his lodge watching Jack, too. I saw him clapping his old weathered hands together as he watched, as if he knew the beat of Jack's dance by heart.

March 23, 1874 . . .

Medicine Weasel surprised me tonight by pulling a pair of tiny moccasins out of his buckskin jacket just before he left for his lodge, telling me they were for Mara Lee. "So she won't slip and fall on the grass anymore," he said, adding that "it is a bad thing for one so young to get discouraged trying to walk.

"I can make another pair for her, once the buffalo come," he said, smiling at me with his rheumy old eyes. I must have looked like I had never heard the word *buffalo*, for Medicine Weasel ducked down and put his hands to his head, two fingers up, mimicking the shaggy beasts. Then he looked up at me, crooking his finger for me to bend close.

"You wait and see; they are coming," he whispered. "I know these things."

March 24, 1874 . . .

I have been washing and hanging clothes all day, back and forth, back and forth: Fetch more water, boil another panful, find someplace that isn't already draped with wet clothes, blankets, or linens . . . all the while watching Medicine Weasel and

One Shot come out of their lodge to stare off toward the distance like they are waiting for someone.

And now they have me doing it, too.

March 27, 1874 . . .

Medicine Weasel was right. The buffalo *did* come . . . I just wish I could shake the low feeling I've had ever since seeing them. Even Medicine Weasel tried to cheer me up.

"Do not look sad. We've seen a great thing today," Medicine Weasel told me with a smile tonight after dinner. I had the oddest feeling, too, seeing him walk over and hug first John-Charles, then Jack . . .

But as he shuffled his way down to his lodge, his old shoulders stooped over by age, I had to wonder at the weight those shoulders have had to carry . . . thinking of all he has had to endure since we whites have come west . . .

I admit, the feeling that swept over me earlier today wasn't one of "greatness."

When we gazed out over what Jack says will be the last of the great buffalo herds, I couldn't help feeling plain sick, for lack of better words. Over and over in my head tumbled pictures of the monstrous stack of bleached bones I saw last year when we rode through Miles City.

Today when I looked over at Jack, I could almost feel the emotion passing between us—thankful to see the herd but ashamed, too, knowing our own people had been pushing the slaughter. Are still pushing it.

Without really thinking, my eyes fell on John-Charles then, wondering where he would fit in it all. I waved to him to come to me, but he sat, mute, on his pony between Jack and Medicine Weasel, his long hair whipping in the wind, his tawny face turned up to the sky, his mind as far away as the clouds he peered up at. I leaned over and tugged at the reins of Rose's pony and called to Patrick and Gale, then I pointed out over the vast valley of raising and lowering humps of black.

"*This* is Montana," I told them with a tremor in my voice, praying they would understand what they were witnessing . . . and wondering if they would remember this day after the crowds came and buildings rose to meet the sky like cheap imitations of the mountains I'd fallen in love with. This was the Montana we'd all fallen in love with . . .

Suddenly John-Charles was there beside me. He looked at me for a long moment; those green eyes so much like Jack's stared and stared, and I saw the wisdom in them, saw the Solomon to Jack's King David. John-Charles tilted his head to one side with a slow, easy kind of half-grin, and I knew he understood my feelings—but had seen past them, too.

"*We* are Montana, Aunt Callie," he said simply, and I watched him ride off to join Jack, Medicine Weasel, and the other men. Then I heard their laughter as they rode over the slope toward the herd.

And now that I'm writing this, I think I understand that feeling I had when I saw Medicine Weasel with John-Charles and Jack. Medicine Weasel had realized it before I had: His old life has been replaced by a new one now . . . and so has Jack's . . . and John-Charles is the thread that wove them together.

I can't help thinking how beautiful life is, how my brother, who had searched for peace nearly his whole life, had been blessed with a son who would give it . . .

March 30, 1874 . . .

We have all been working on Willa's dress every spare moment we've had over the past few days. Even looking on it as a labor of love didn't help us tonight, as tired as we all were . . .

"My body's went and got old on me without askin' me anything about it," Jessie declared, shifting in her chair with a groan as we sat around the fireplace, sewing. We all chuckled our agreement. But then I saw Rose suddenly look up with a frown.

"You're not old, Jessie," she said in all of her thirteen-year-old wisdom. "You still have lots of time left."

"Don't have much time left in the valley, little sis. Soon enough we be headin' for our new land," she said, glancing over at Sara and Rachel. "And as far as bein' old—you best tell my grandbaby Noel different. He rubbed my face the other day and says, 'Grandma, did God make you?' Yes, I say. Then he rubs his own cheek. 'Did God make me, too?' he says, and I say yes again. And you know what that boy says, then? He says, 'God's getting better at it, ain't he?' "

We all laughed, but I knew by the look on Rose's face that she hadn't heard anything past Jessie's saying she was leaving. I knew it by the pang of sadness that had come to my heart, and I saw it in Lillie's eyes as well.

Rose didn't utter another word but set down her part of the sewing and quietly excused herself, shutting the door to the porch behind her. Later Jessie and I found her still out there, curled up under several blankets in one of the rockers.

"I ain't helpin' to finish that dress—not if Jessie's going to leave after the wedding," she said defiantly as we both knelt down next to her. Then she looked up at us, and we could see the tears. "'Sides, if Jessie goes, I go, too. And don't say I can't go 'cause I ain't black. Even Jonah says if he closes his eyes, I sound just like Sara and Rachel, the way I carry on, and that's just as good as being black."

I glanced over at Jessie, who, like me, appeared to be caught between laughing and crying. She shook her head.

"Now, honey, *this* is your home," Jessie said. "But that don't mean you can't visit me."

"It ain't the same," Rose said, jumping up and running past

Mercy and Gale, who had just stepped outside. I saw a worried look come to Gale's face.

"She isn't really leaving?" he asked me, and I shook my head as I put my arm around Jessie's shoulders. After they went back inside the cabin, Jessie turned to me, and I saw a bittersweet look to her face.

"Even when the good comes, that don't mean it's always easy, does it Callie?" she said. I said no, it doesn't mean it's always easy. Then, because neither of us knew what else to say, we hugged each other, standing on the porch in the dark until Lillie came out to join us, too.

"I'm sure gonna miss this valley, miss all of you," Jessie said after a while. Then she took a deep breath. "But I'm ready for me and my family to start our new lives . . . to walk the land the Lord has given us . . . "

We smiled at each other, and that's when I felt a soft wind come across the valley. The looks on Jessie's and Lillie's faces told me they felt it, too. And though none of us said a word, it was as if we knew what that wind meant . . .

March 31, 1874 . . .

Rose is still smarting over Jessie's leaving. The proof of it showed in how cranky she was with poor Gale today. Quinn and I were sitting on the porch after dinner, watching Mara Lee toddle after Jasper and Honey's pups in her new moccasins, when we overheard them on the way down to the river to go fishing.

"Well, maybe you should just go with Jessie when she leaves, then," Gale was saying, the frustration clear on his face even from where we sat.

"Maybe I should," Rose said, picking up her pole and marching off toward their fishing hole.

Gale marched the other way then stopped after a few paces and looked back. I saw him frown, watching Rose continue on, nose in the air—saw him frown harder when he realized she wasn't going to look back.

"Aw, what's the use!" he said, picking up his own pole again and heading after her. That's when I heard Quinn start laughing.

"I feel the lad's pain," he said, winking at me when I turned to him with my eyebrows raised. "But Rose is young yet. She still has time to work through the legacy of that red hair." He put his arms around me, and I couldn't help but laugh with him. "She reminds me so much of you, you know," Quinn added, and that's when I pulled back to look at him.

"She's not exactly like me, Quinn. *I* would've looked back . . . eventually," I said with a sniff, and we both laughed again.

Still, in spite of our laughter, I can't help thinking of Jessie's words as I write this. *Even when the good comes, that don't mean it's always easy . . .*

We have been so very blessed—more than I could have ever imagined a family to be. But I do feel led to pray for Rose and her ways, Lord. There is something so restless in her that it gives me pause at times. And I worry that, like Jack in his youth, the dreamer in Rose can make the good great and the bad . . . sometimes even better.

"Trust in the Lord with all thine heart; and lean not unto thine own understanding" . . .

And I do trust you, Lord.

April 10, 1874 . . .

It's been another little stretch since I've written in here, but with all the rush and hurry for us to have Willa's wedding dress finished . . . and all the decorating we've done, I just haven't had the time. But it was time well spent; their wedding today was proof of that. And if ever there was two people who deserved to be happy after all they've been through, it is Preacher and Willa.

Willa looked just like the pictures of those ladies in *Harper's Weekly*, her raven hair swept up in a loose bun with soft strands of curls hanging down, her dress of white embroidered mull fitting her slender figure better than we could have imagined as me, Jessie, Lillie, and the rest of the women beamed at each other with gladness. And Preacher, I don't think I've ever seen him look so handsome—or so happy—as he stood tall and strong next to Willa while the new missionary who will be taking over for Preacher performed the ceremony.

By the time they said "I do" we were all sniffing back our tears. Mrs. Pumphrey was the first to pull out her handkerchief and wipe the tears that streamed down her wide face, though, and when she caught Mercy looking at her, I saw her wink and straighten her new hat that she wore special for the occasion, saw Mercy smile and straighten her little bonnet in return.

Even Peach wiped away a tear or two then pretended to dust a speck off his new clothes, looking so much shinier than usual that Jack couldn't help but comment on it as we began to trail out to the yard for the party. "Why, Peach, I didn't think you could get any better lookin', but you proved me wrong again," Jack teased, but Peach just glanced sideways at Widow Spence. "That ain't so hard to do. Guess I'll be provin' a lot of folks wrong before long," he said, causing a ripple of chuckles to go through the crowd. But there was a poignancy to the way he looked, too: shy, but determined, like he'd finally caught on to what was important after all these years. I looked around the crowd of us then and saw that we were all catching on, really. But it was Willa who said it best as she hugged all of us.

"Do you ever think God looks down and says, 'Well, now, you're finally getting the hang of what I've been trying to tell you all along?' she said, grinning, and we all couldn't help but laugh. And we laughed again as Mara Lee tried to make a wild dive for the cake on the table, Medicine Weasel catching her up in his arms just in time.

Then we were sniffing again as Quinn surprised even me. I saw him signal to Jack, and together they lifted a huge piece of stone from the back of our own wagon and settled it into the cut in the earth made right by the steps of the church.

"I can't think of a better day to give you this, Preacher and Willa," he said, "to give to *all* of you." We all huddled around then to read the inscription my husband had carved with such care: "Blessed be the Lord, that hath given rest unto his people Israel, according to all that he promised; there hath not failed one word of all his good promise."

"And he *hasn't* failed us," Quinn said, looking to Preacher and Willa. Then he glanced to each of us, his eyes finally resting on Percy, who, we'd heard just before the wedding started, had found out Leah had been sentenced to only five years, for lack of more evidence. Percy cleared his throat and looked to his daughters. "He hasn't failed us," he echoed softly, and then Quinn opened up his Bible and began to read:

"'And Joshua wrote these words in the book of the law of God, and took a great stone, and set it up there under an oak, that was by the sanctuary of the LORD. And Joshua said unto all the people, Behold, this stone shall be a witness unto us; for it hath heard all the words of the Lord which he spake unto us.'"

Preacher looked around at all of us then as he stood with his arm around Willa's waist, and I saw the tears in his eyes, too.

"I don't think I could have imagined a finer group of friends if I had handpicked them from heaven myself," he said. "But I didn't have to, because God did that for me."

And you could tell by the look on everyone's face, we were glad he did, too.

I think the *dilemma* of marriage was fixed on the boys' minds long after we had reached home tonight—especially after them hearing of Peach's proposing to Widow Spence. But it was what they said that got Quinn and me so tickled . . .

"Well, I ain't *ever* gettin' married," Patrick said first as they sat around the fireplace together. Quinn looked over at me and grinned.

"Well, how come them men in the Bible married so many women?" John-Charles asked.

"I don't rightly know," Patrick said slowly. "Maybe they were goin' by the rules—you know, four better, four worse, four rich, four poor . . ." Patrick shook his head then. "I think ol' Solomon had a better idea. Rose said he had a pack of porcupines instead of wives. I think I'd rather have porcupines anytime than some ol' girl."

"I never heard Solomon had porcupines," John-Charles said, frowning.

"Well, all I know is, if he did, he must have been good at handling them," Gale said, adding to the discussion. "Because Rose can be *sharper* than a porcupine sometimes, and I don't think I could handle more than one of her."

"That's right," Rose hollered down from up in the loft where she was supposed to have been reading. "And don't you forget it."

It was then that Quinn and I chose to go out on the porch for a breath of fresh air . . . something that comes in handy when you're having a hard time breathing for laughing so hard.

April 11, 1874 . . .

I've said it before, and I'll say it again: I believe the gifts from God sometimes come in the smallest of packages—and at the most unlikely times. And that is just what happened today as Quinn and I were out at the corral with the horses.

I spotted Rose running toward us and thought she might be hurt by the look on her face, but instead of coming for me, she headed straight for Quinn. And it wasn't until she got closer that I noticed she was cupping something in the palm of her hand.

"He was still in his cocoon when I found him, Pa," she said, her voice shaky as she opened her cupped hands to reveal a tiny, fragile-looking butterfly. "I helped him out, but now he's acting like he's hurt."

"Well, lass, you shouldn't have helped him," Quinn said gently as he knelt down next to her, and I saw Rose look up at her pa with a stricken look.

"But why?" Rose said, near tears.

"Because, lass, the reason God lets the butterfly push and struggle its way out of its cocoon is because while it's struggling, it's also getting stronger. Every time it pushes its little legs, every time it stretches against the cocoon holding it in, it's gaining the strength it will need to fly."

Rose started crying in earnest then, and Quinn smiled and cupped her face with such love that it brought tears to my eyes. "It's just God's way," he said finally, and Rose threw her arms around his neck and hugged him as she cried her sorries into his shirt. "There, there," he whispered. "You didn't know any better, but you do now. It's just God's way."

I stood there for a long time, just watching them and thinking on what Quinn had said. Thinking on it even tonight as I put this to paper . . .

How many times over the years have I questioned in my heart why God hadn't come to our rescue I can't say, but I did. I imagine I've just been too much of a coward to write it until now . . . As if you didn't know already, Lord.

I guess it doesn't seem to matter how old I get, sometimes I still think like such a child, think that you don't know the thoughts of my heart unless I say them out loud . . . unless I write them here. But you knew all along, didn't you, Lord?

You knew, and in your amazing way, you waited for just the right time to give me my answer. Because I'll never forget this day . . . never forget listening to the comforting words of a father explaining to his daughter that having to learn to fight your way through something makes you stronger, that if someone were to step in, you wouldn't earn the strength you need to have for yourself—the strength you were always meant to have . . . the strength it takes to know you *can* stretch your wings and fly . . .

Seems fitting that these will be the last words I'll be able to fit in this journal now. I am a bit curious what the new pages of our lives will bring . . . but hopefully I'm wise enough to know now that there is no figuring it out beforehand. And maybe that's why God tells us to take our lives day by day . . . because he knows us well enough to know that part of the fun on our journey is to look to him and wonder what *is* next . . .

Acknowledgments

The saying "Art imitates life" has come to me again and again as I've thought of my own journey while writing *The Other Side of Jordan*. There have been many moments of intense struggle, as if I were treading water with only my nose above the waves, but there have also been wonderful moments in which I've witnessed God's own hand sweep down upon my life with such beauty and love. I truly believe our wealth is our love—the agape love we give to others as well as the love we receive. So, to all of those who gave me their time, their prayers, and their love, I say thank you for all you have given me. You have made me wealthy beyond measure . . .

To my Lord Jesus Christ: I will always thank you first and foremost for changing my life, for giving me a hope and a future in you . . . and for inspiring me to write for others, to touch this beautiful but troubled world with the message of your love. My deepest desire is to show others how much you truly do care— and how very close you are if they only take the chance to reach out to you.

To my family . . .
My *son, Mitch:* Thank you for your love, your prayers, for being *you* . . .

My *parents, Diana and Joe McClure:* For your love, prayers, and all the help and inspiration you have given me.

My *brother, Dan Becker,* who, by the way, actually wrote *me* the poem I use in the book from Jack to Callie. I love you, bro'!

Acknowledgments

To my nieces, Raelyn and Kaitlyn Becker; my nephew, Shawn-Michael Becker; and my grandparents, Doug and Dorothy Vance: I am so grateful to God for each of you, and I love you all more than you will ever know.

To my friends . . .

Billy Allen, a man after God's own heart. Your awesome songs and music have inspired so many—including me! Thank you so much for your phone calls and prayers and for being such a godly friend. I pray that you and your wife, Rhonda, are blessed and prospered as you continue forward in your ministry.

Kris Bearss, Integrity Publishers: Thank you so much, Kris, for all your prayers, encouragement, and hard work as I was putting the finishing touches to this book. It is a blessing to be a part of such a godly group of people as Integrity.

Shelly Guy: Thank you for being such a great friend, Shell, for all your help and prayers . . . and for making me laugh when I needed it the most.

Chad Gundersen: Thank you for your friendship, your prayers and phone calls, and for all your suggestions that have helped me grow as a writer. They have really meant a lot to me. A special thanks to you and your family for inspiring the names in this volume: Mara Lee (Bird) and Gale; they helped bring those characters to life! I truly pray God prospers and lifts you up in your desire to be a strong voice for Him in the movie industry.

Sue Ann Jones, a great editor and friend. Thank you so much, Sue Ann, for being so willing to take the journey with Callie and her family again . . . for all of your wonderful words of encouragement, for your hard work, friendship, and for all your prayers. Working with you again has been a wonderful experience.

Laurie White: It seems like we have been friends *forever.* It amazes me we can still come up with new material to make each other laugh—and always at just the right times! Thank you, thank you for your true gift of friendship, for your phone calls, and your advice . . . for always caring. I am so grateful to God for you, Lou.

To my pastors, Jeff and Patsy Perry: Thank you once again for being such an important part of what has inspired me to lift Jesus up in the written word. And thank you for believing in me and for your wisdom, encouragement, and love.

And to all the staff and members of Family Church: Thank you, thank you for all your help and kindnesses, and most of all, for your prayers as I was completing this new book. You all are a true gift from God.